# UTOPIA PROJECT

## THE ARROW OF TIME

# BILLY DERING

Printed in the United States of America

First Printing, 2022

Trade Paperback ISBN: 978-1-7354929-7-1
Electronic Book ISBN: 978-1-7354929-6-4

Published by: Pinewald Press, Toms River, New Jersey

Website URL: www.utopiaproject.com
E-Mail: billydering@aol.com

Book cover design: Hampton Lamoureux
Interior book formatting: David Provolo
Editing: Jack M. Germain

*As always, I would be remiss if I didn't thank my family and give a big shout out to my extraordinary Utopia Project series team of Hampton Lamoureux (cover), David Provolo (interior formatting), Jack M. Germain (editing, third book), Frank Bianchetti (website) and Design 446 (social media).*
*Thank you all for your diligent efforts and your professionalism throughout this journey. You have all enlightened and inspired me in your own ways, and this trilogy is better because of you.*

*This book is dedicated to the many advance readers and everyone who has stuck with me on this long and winding road. There are so many people I need to thank (too many to list, and I am always worried I will inadvertently miss someone!), and I will be sure to thank you all individually. I am forever grateful.*

*Finally, and with great appreciation, this book is dedicated to you — the reader.*

# PROLOGUE

December 24, 2044
Saturday, 11:30 PM Central European Time (CET)
Island of Capri, Italy
**Two days before the cataclysmic event
that would change the world**

As she sat alone on the hillside of the island, Dr. Adele Carmelo stared at the equally restless Gulf of Naples. By the faint light of the moon, she could see the water churning and spitting. The breeze was constant, and the chill seemed to bite harder with every passing minute. The cold never bothered her when she was younger, but now that she was one year north of 50 years old, Adele could only endure it for so long. She was braving the elements for the sake of a decent mobile device connection, hoping she would finally receive the email she had been waiting for.

She was about to give up and make her way down to her raft at the waterline when her device finally chirped. Adele entered a series of passwords and accessed her email, which was a separate account not tied to her real identity in any way. While she waited for her messages to load, she could see her bright green eyes reflecting back from the screen of her device. She was glad she could not see the rest of her face because she looked old and ugly. Two large, hairy fake moles were stuck to her cheek, two of her teeth were blacked out and her wig of white hair was like a rat's nest. But even late at night she could not let her guard down, so she wore the humiliating, but effective, disguise.

Her heart jumped when her spam folder refreshed. She had received a solicitation from JC Lifestyles with a subject line indicating, "This one is the real deal!" Although she typically loathed email solicitations, this one was special so she hurried to open it. JC Lifestyles was a real company, but the advertisement would contain a coded message from General Eric Hyland that only she could decipher.

While she impatiently waited for the advertisement to appear on her screen, Adele thought of Eric. She had not heard from him in several days, and given the tension currently gripping the world, she was worried sick. But it was not just worry she felt, it was guilt. Her confidential memo about the Utopia Project had ignited an international crisis, and her stomach tightened more at the thought. The document she authored was now headline news every day, triggering protests in the United States and other countries linked to the top secret project off the coast of Greenland. The public outcry was only growing, and with Eric still on the ships, so was Adele's discomfort.

She really wished he had left the project with her a few weeks ago. She had pleaded with him. When it came to his duty, he was rigid in his stance, almost maddeningly so. The last time she was with him in person, Friday, December 9, 2044, she gave him a subtle but urgent signal to request privacy so she could confide in him regarding her plans. After he turned off the two-way monitor in his room on Utopia Project Ship Number One, she whispered, "Eric, I'm done. I'm leaving the project. Resigning. Today will be my last day." Although it was taboo on the ships, she was no longer concerned about using the long vowel, 'I.'

His eyes opened wide. "What? Why would you leave now?"

Although still whispering, she exploded. "I am ashamed that I ever allowed myself to be a part of what has been created here. I've been trying to get them to back off the excessive levels of conditioning for years now. How can the leadership continue to insist that the level of conditioning is optimal? That has never been the conclusion at all. Such extreme levels would be harmful to any society, and that has been outlined in reports and confirmed by studies time and again. After begging them to hear me out, I was finally allowed to meet with the full Board of Elders yesterday. It was a disaster."

"How so?" he asked.

"They would only allocate a couple of minutes of the agenda for me, so I presented a two-page summary of what we have done and the harm we are doing to our participants. It was my last ditch effort to make them see this clearly and see how inhumane our project has become. As soon as I was done, I was summarily dismissed from the meeting. Me! Their lead psychologist. They wouldn't even look at what I presented or give it a second's consideration. Eric, I've been raising these issues for how many years now?"

He pondered a moment. "Seven? Eight?"

Adele shook her head. "Ten. I first raised this nearly ten years ago. You know, when I took the position of lead psychologist fifteen years ago and became Elder-62, I really thought the project leaders were well-intended and that I could make a difference. And the big paycheck and perks mattered at that stage of my life. But I see it all differently, clearly, now. Things like money don't mean the same to me as they once did. I just know this is wrong and after *years* of trying, I can't get them to see the light. I can't live with what we are creating, and the monsters we are creating, so I'm done."

She also shared her grave suspicions that the project leaders would stop at nothing to ensure the survival of the project. Gently grabbing his arm, she begged him to leave with her.

Despite seeming conflicted, he would not step away from the project. He told her that as General Eric Hyland, and as Elder-41, he had to stand by his duty and serve his country and the project. He also said Adele should keep trying to convince the Board of Elders to change the conditioning regimen. She had tried too many times to believe that was a viable option. He asked her to stick it out, but she had made up her mind and was as rigid in her stance as he was.

He then put his hand on her arm. "But where will you go?" She could still feel his touch.

"Into hiding," she answered. "I know they will not just let me walk away from my contract as Elder-62. They will try to compel me to return to the project."

"Will you go back to your real house, since it is already off the grid?"

Eric was one of the select few people who knew the location of her true residence. She had set up a fake front many years ago when a patient from her private psychologist practice became obsessed and started stalking her. Unfortunately, he was also obsessed with firearms and was prone to fits of rage, so she fled her hometown of Naples, Italy. She purchased a small condominium in the town of Capri on the island bearing the same name and staged it so it appeared she was living there, just in case she was tracked down. Concurrently, using an assumed name, she had purchased her true residence- a large, secure house and hideaway on the water in Anacapri, the other town comprising the island.

"No, I can't go to the house in Anacapri. They will eventually find me even there. I mean *really* go into hiding," she clarified. "Remember when we did that boat tour of my island several years ago, and I told you about the hidden rooms under Anacapri? The ones only a few of the locals know about? That is where I will go for a few months until the smoke clears."

"Are you sure? That seems extreme."

"The leaders of this project are extreme, so I'm not taking any chances. They will discover my resignation Monday morning, but by then I will already be living under the island."

Since Eric could not talk her out of it, he said he would do everything in his power to keep them off of her trail. If the Utopia Project leadership was closing in he would warn her, but he needed a surreptitious means of making contact. It was then that he devised a clever communication methodology. Eric explained that he would hack into the database of JC Lifestyles, his provider of all-natural vitamins, and use their advertisements to send her coded messages using a cipher coding system. She just needed to set up an anonymous email account using a fake name. Then, she could communicate with him by replying to the ad. Her response email would not come to him, but would be dumped into a cyber trash bin that he could access. For the next hour, they developed their own cipher key to translate their communications. It bothered her that she would not be able to actually speak to him and hear his voice, but it was better than having no communication at all.

Before departing that last day, as a last ditch effort, Adele left Eric a hand-written note with an open-ended offer to join her. She was waiting for a coded message indicating he had finally accepted, and was on his way to be with her.

*Maybe this message will be the one.*

As she pulled a notepad from her deep pocket, she thought of the message he sent the prior weekend, which concluded with, 'Adele, just know I love you.' Despite her disappointment that he had not yet decided to leave the project, his words had still warmed her heart.

She looked down at her phone and started reading the new JC Lifestyles advertisement now populating her screen, the one claiming to be the 'real deal!' As she decoded the message, that subject line reverberated in her mind, seeming more and more sinister with every word revealed.

<br>

December 24, 2044
Saturday, 5:00 PM Eastern Standard Time (EST)
Wrightstown, New Jersey
**Two days before the event**

<br>

In a small coffee shop in Wrightstown, New Jersey, General Eric Hyland ended the phone call with his mother in Vermont, and wiped the bead of sweat running down his cheek. He had successfully given her a coded warning, and knew his father would decipher it in a second. He was relieved to get off the line before his mother picked up on his apprehension, which was only further elevated upon learning that she was almost out of the medication she needed to take every day to live. Eric had not given that enough consideration, and just assumed she always had an adequate supply of Levonesex 212 on hand- at least enough for a few months. This was an unexpected problem, and one that would have to be quickly rectified after the destruction.

He took a sip of his tepid mocha coffee and opened his laptop. The second and final person he needed to communicate with was Adele Carmelo. Without looking at the screen, and using only his recollection of the keystrokes, he pulled up his template of an advertisement for JC Lifestyles. Fortunately he had set up the phony advertisement over a week ago, before the tracker was inserted in his neck on Utopia Project Ship Number One. He had used the ad to communicate with Adele once already, and knew it was successful because she had replied right away and understood his message. Looking at the screen, he now just needed to edit the text within the promotion to create a new coded message.

His work was hurried, and he did not have time to fully and properly massage the wording. Many of his sentences were grammatically incorrect or contained random, out-of-place words. He even invented a new vitamin name. The actual ad would not make sense to anybody but Adele since she alone had the cipher key. He hit send and closed his laptop. He was confident she would get the email quickly as she checked her account multiple times per day. All he could do now was hope that she would properly translate his message and be under the Island of Capri in two nights hence; and that the relentless operatives would not find her first.

He could only shake his head when reflecting on how she had gone from simply quitting her job to becoming public enemy number one in the eyes of the Utopia Project leadership. When Adele, Elder-62, left her position as the lead psychologist, the Utopia Project leadership predictably tried to find her to convince her to come back. But she had disappeared and was nowhere to be found. Less than 10 days later, her confidential memo winds up in the hands of that bloodhound of a reporter, Lily Black, and the story just…explodes. The Utopia Project leadership was quick to reach the conclusion that Elder-62 released the memo herself and that was why she was in hiding. Eric could not buy that Adele released the memo, she would never, but he had to admit it did not look good. The Utopia Project immediately engaged operatives to hunt for her around the clock. In no time they had traced the memo's mailing to a post office in Sicily, to an old woman, and to the ferry terminal in Palermo. Knowing Adele was hiding under the Island of Capri, and wanting to keep the operatives from focusing on that part of Italy, he doctored some information and created phony intelligence to show that the old woman had gone to Africa after leaving on a ferry from Palermo. But just yesterday he heard that the relentless operatives had finally captured the woman they were tracking in Algiers, only to discover she was not who they were looking for. With another week they may have found the real Dr. Adele Carmelo, but the timer marking the destruction of the world was ticking down. She just needed to avoid capture for two more days.

He put down his coffee cup, picked up his laptop and headed for the door, passing a smattering of patrons along the way. Most were alone, reading or checking their mobile devices, but two were huddled in a dark corner whispering conspiratorially like young lovers. He paused and looked back one last time. Within a few days, these people would all be dead, and not a one had the slightest clue it was coming.

December 24, 2044
Saturday, 11:45 PM (CET)
Island of Capri, Italy
**Two days before the event**

Extracting the letters from the JC Lifestyles advertisement using the cipher coding system, Adele worked to assemble the message. After reading the words she struggled to take a breath and rolled onto her side. Her head was resting on the cold ground as her mobile device slipped out of her hand.

"Please, no. It can't be," she whispered as tears streamed down her cheeks.

Eric's words affected her heart again, but quite differently than the prior weekend. Rather than being warmed, her heart was chilled, completely.

Seeing her device on the ground, she reached for it with trembling fingers. The JC Lifestyles advertisement was still on the screen so she confirmed that she had deciphered the message correctly.

The translation was the same.

'Round up people you can 100 percent trust and secure rations before eve of 12-26. Then remain under island until I come for you. Hurry. Cataclysmic event- imminent.'

# I:
# ERADICATION

# CHAPTER 1

January 10, 2045
Tuesday, Morning (EST)
New Jersey coast, Utopia Project Ship Number One
*Fifteen days after the cataclysmic event
that changed the world*

At last, Elder-3 was the ruler of the Utopia Project, and the entirety of the new world. The two obstacles to his ascension, Elder-1 and Elder-2, were among the dead and missing, so he was next in line to be the lead elder. Although he should have been the leader from the outset, this new empowerment was not lost on him and would not be wasted. As a former *Shang Jiang* in the People's Liberation Army in China, he could now run the Utopia Project the right way.

The three Utopia Project ships were anchored off of Long Beach Island on the New Jersey coast, and Elder-3 was focused on the establishment of the new base camp in Surf City. He had already dispatched a couple of the elders with a background in engineering to harness and re-route the power from large solar farms on the mainland, just over the Route 72 bridge. The proximity of these fields, with row after row of panels, had been one of many contributing factors in choosing Long Beach Island for the site of their base camp. The engineers would be working around the clock to create a power grid large enough to sustain their encampment.

Besides expediting the setup of the base camp, Elder-3 had other orders of business and other obstacles that needed to be addressed. He summoned Elder-12 to the deck.

Leaning against the rail of Utopia Project Ship Number One and peering at the choppy waters of the ocean below, Elder-3 did not even turn as his fellow elder approached and stood beside him.

"Elder-12, you were in charge of offspring production, and because the results were inadequate, it prompted Elder-1 to allow the survival of production age females. And because of that, a small group of survivors made fools out of us and caused the death of multiple elders and members."

The older American huffed dismissively, "That is not th…" but his words cut off.

Elder-3 turned and felt great satisfaction as he removed his Medusa firearm from Elder-12's side. One of the things he loved about the Medusa weapon was that its shot contained a pinhead sized dose of a powerful neurological agent that instantly froze all of the muscles in the body, including the diaphragm, resulting in rapid death. Elder-3 had taken the shot mid-sentence, and he relished the look of stark realization that was frozen on his fellow elder's face. "Our project will no longer suffer because of your incompetence," he snarled and pushed the rigid body over the deck rail.

After bobbing back up to the surface, Elder-12 was on his back and his eyes were unable to close. With no ability to move, his open mouth started taking in ocean water.

From the deck above, Elder-3 grinned and maintained eye contact while the elder's head slipped under the water. *You had it coming.*

Someone yelled, "Man overboard!"

"Leave him! That is an order!" Elder-3 barked and went inside.

Moments later, Elder-10, originally from Germany, walked into the Communications Center with a piece of paper in his hand. "This will be of interest."

"What is it?" Elder-3 asked.

Holding out the document, Elder-10 said, "We discovered this among Elder-41's belongings. While reviewing all of his files we discovered a hidden note."

"Elder-41? General Hyland," Elder-3 muttered as he turned his eyes down and read the note aloud. "Eric, if you also leave, we can legitimize our relationship once and for all. After finally telling your daughter, we could then work toward the marriage we talked about, and I continue to dream about. Please reconsider. You know how to reach me. All my love, Adele." He stared at the piece of paper and repeated, "Adele?"

"Yes. And since we only had one person with that name, it can only be Adele Carmelo, Elder-62. But for years it had been rumored that she was secretly carrying on an intimate relationship with Elder-41. This note finally confirms it."

"First her desertion, then her release of a scathing, confidential memorandum, and now we confirm she was having a romantic relationship with that traitor Hyland? How did we not know, or see, that she had such a tendency to be disloyal?" Elder-3 asked angrily, and he nearly slipped and cursed in Mandarin Chines, his native tongue.

"Sir, we have a hunch," Elder-10 said and turned to a computer terminal. After a few quick keystrokes, he turned the monitor toward Elder-3.

The left side of the screen contained a large picture of the green-eyed psychologist, and the right side provided Elder-62's background and history. Over the next several minutes, Elder-10 highlighted information in the database regarding the background of Dr. Adele Carmelo. She grew up in Naples, Italy, went to college in America and for a time served as a psychologist for the Army. She inevitably came back to Italy and her last known residence there was a small one-bedroom condominium on the Island of Capri. She never married, had no children and could maintain confidentiality, which led to her invitation to join the Utopia Project. At the time she joined 15 years ago, her credentials and background had been thoroughly vetted, and her loyalty and trustworthiness, fully tested.

"While we appreciate the background, what is this hunch?" Elder-3 demanded as he stared at the green-eyed traitor on the screen.

"It has to do with the last 'malfunction area,'" Elder-10 said and then called the lead elder in the Data Center. He hung up the phone and a knowing smirk came to his face. "That confirms it. It seems that when Hyland hand-picked a few areas of the world that would survive, his third 'malfunction area' just so happened to capture portions of the Island of Capri, Italy, where Adele Carmelo lived. That cannot be a coincidence."

"No, it cannot," Elder-3 agreed and stepped away from the computer terminal. He stopped and turned around. "We want a list of elders who are pilots and can fly an American M3. We must accelerate our plan to search the area left unscathed in Italy!"

While continuing to hunt down General's Hyland group of survivors in North America, Elder-3 now wanted to wipe out any survivors in Italy without delay. All individuals from the old world were a threat to their members, but Dr. Carmelo, even more so. She had been the lead psychologist for 15 years and nobody knew the member conditioning regimen better than her. In addition to paying for her betrayal, she had to be eliminated to alleviate the threat to the new society.

A half hour later, Elder-3 met with Elder-85 and Elder-98, who were trained pilots. He found it odd that neither of them were from the United States, yet both were sure they could fly an American M3. They both claimed to have flown comparable aircraft in their own home countries of Britain and Japan. Elder-3 wished there were additional pilots in their midst as Elder-85 was known to have a blood lust and a short temper. But without much choice at the moment, he laid out the mission for the two elders. They were to leave at dawn the next morning for nearby McGuire Air Force Base within the Joint Base, along with 15 regular members. There they would secure M-3 transports, load some food rations aboard and move expeditiously to carry out the mission to eradicate all survivors in Italy.

Heidi Leer walked slowly up the hall of ship number one. Her thoughts were on her pregnancy. Although unconfirmed, she was sure she was carrying Kid's child. She passed the Communications Center and stopped when she sensed a commotion as elders scurried about. She walked in and approached Elder-3. He turned to her with a scowl that distorted his Asian facial features. Her steps slowed as she tried to turn around, but it was too late.

"What is it?" he barked at her.

"We noticed the activity in here and were curious as to what is going on."

"A team is being sent to Italy to scour the third missed area and eradicate any survivors there." Elder -3 sounded more impatient than usual.

"Understood. We…" She gasped aloud as she spotted a picture of a woman with mesmerizing green eyes on the monitor.

"What is it?" Elder-3 asked.

As she stared, she whispered, "Those green eyes." She had seen the woman before. Snapping out of it, Heidi said, "Sorry, Sir. The woman on the screen, who is she?"

"Why? We can't imagine she is familiar to you?"

"Yes, she is. We have seen her before."

"She departed the ships before your time here," Elder-3 responded and turned away.

"No, it wasn't here. We recall in vivid detail a picture of her," she pointed at the screen. "The picture was taken in Italy."

Elder-3 stopped what he was doing and turned to Heidi. His interest seemed to be mildly piqued. "She lived in Italy."

"But who is she?"

"That is Elder-62, Dr. Adele Carmelo. She was the lead psychologist for the project for 15 years and deserted her post a few weeks before the world's rebirth. What picture are you referring to?"

"The picture we saw belonged to Sara, the daughter of Elder-41, General Hyland." Peering closer at the screen, Heidi's wheel were turning. "She meant something to them," she muttered in a low voice.

"So it seems," Elder-3 agreed. "We now have confirmation that she and General Hyland were a couple. It cannot be a coincidence that her small condominium in Italy just so happened to be in the third area he saved from the destruction."

"Small condominium?" Heidi scoffed. "Yeah right."

"What do you mean by that?" he snapped.

"Sorry, Sir. But at least as of last summer, she lived in a big fancy house with a patio overlooking the water. Even the back of the picture said, 'Adele's incredible *house* in Anacapri, Italy. Summer 2044'," replied Heidi.

"And her residence was supposedly in Capri, not Anacapri,' he muttered. Turning abruptly, the head elder demanded, "Where is this picture?"

Wanting to join the team and destroy this woman, or anyone that meant something to the Hylands, Heidi was not about to reveal that the picture was stuck in a mirror frame in Sara Hyland's house. Heidi would be left behind and they would simply secure the picture themselves.

"We have no idea. It was in a pile of pictures that Hyland's daughter, Sara, showed us when we were in Vermont," she lied. Then she saw Elder-3 tighten his hand into a fist. He was about to snap. She had to offer a solution and quick.

"But we can locate her house. Besides remembering the statues and columns she had on her patio, we remember the exact vantage point of the Sorrento Peninsula. It was unmistakable. We have it all right here." She pointed to her head.

Elder-3 followed her finger and stared at her blond hair. He seemed frustrated that he would have to rely on her.

Trying to control her own sudden surge of anger, Heidi added, "And we would love nothing more than to assist in destroying Hyland's grand plans and him as well."

She wanted to scream *because that fucking manipulator is responsi-*

*ble for the real Sara Hyland's survival…*

Finally, he relented. "You will accompany Elder-85 and Elder-98 for the Italy mission at dawn tomorrow morning. The shuttle to the mainland will be leaving within moments. Go now."

"With pleasure," she hissed and turned toward the door.

As she started running, she heard Elder-3 say to Elder-10, "Call Elder-76 and have her meet me in the elder dining room immediately." His words sounded quite ominous.

# CHAPTER 2

January 10, 2045
Tuesday, Morning (EST)
New Jersey coast, Utopia Project Ship Number One
**Fifteen days after the event**

Elder-3 sat down at a table in the elder dining room and pulled a vial out of his pocket. *What is it with these troublesome psychologists?* Between Elder-62, Adele Carmelo, and Elder-76, his trust in the masters of that profession was quite low. Such incompetence and counter-productivity should not be tolerated for a second. Even now, were it not for the need for experts and services in the conditioning process, he would have executed every psychologist they had. Maybe in due time he would further evaluate them all, but for the moment, his focus was on Elder-76 alone.

The woman had been a liability to the project since the day she was chosen by her home country of India to be their representative. Maybe it was her background in psychology, but she always seemed to be manipulating people and situations. That had served her well in her home country as she was credited with single handedly fostering a successful collaboration of the major political leaders in India. Back then she was not only cunning, but desirable. In her heyday she was quite attractive, which gave her another weapon in her manipulation arsenal. It certainly worked on Elder-1. Rumor had it that they were intimate partners on occasion, which only furthered her stranglehold on the former lead elder. That is why, upon Elder-62's departure, Elder-1 promoted Elder-76 to be the lead psychologist, despite the objections of several members of the Board of Elders. Elder-3 had objected, strongly, and in the end, justifiably so.

A few moments later, Elder-76 came in. She stood at attention, her long white hair swaying gently. Her dark face was tight as she chirped, "Sir!"

A cup of tea was already prepared and waiting, so Elder-3 motioned with his hand. "Sit. We have some things to discuss."

Elder-76 seemed nervous and only played with the handle of her cup.

"We have much to get done, and we want you to know that your background will be very much critical to those efforts," Elder-3 continued as he casually sipped his tea and willed his fellow elder to do the same. "We are also considering reversing your demotion and reinstating you as the lead psychologist."

The conversation made the elder from India ease up. She seemed surprised by the direction it was going, so she lifted her tea cup. "Thank you, Sir," she said, but did not move the cup to her mouth.

Elder-3 added, "We must figure out a way to strengthen our conditioning since we are now moving to the mainland and exposing the members to an entirely new environment."

"We have been working on a new conditioning module, or strand to address that," she said and sipped her tea.

Smiling, Elder-3 thought, *finally.* "Yes. We must." He waited until she took another good slurp of her beverage, and then he pounced. "On second thought Elder 76, we are not sure you should lead, or even participate, in anything we are doing. First, you failed to recognize the flight risk, volatility, and fearlessness of the captives a few days ago. That oversight on your part led to the death of multiple elders and members. Not to mention the delays and problems that have ensued."

Putting down her cup, Elder-76 stared at her trembling hand and started sweating.

"And, do you remember that time when we wanted to terminate the services of Elder-62, Dr. Adele Carmelo? That was just a week before she deserted the project. You went around convincing a number of the members of our board, starting with Elder-1, who had a terrible soft-spot for you, to allow Elder-62 to put together her findings about our conditioning and present them to the board?"

Elder-76 loosened her collar. "It is not that black and white, Sir. We just thought…" She started coughing.

"Thought what? That it would be acceptable to generate a scathing memorandum about our conditioning and the treatment of our members? The very same memorandum that went to the press in America and inevitably destroyed our project plans and the world?" he yelled and whipped his tea cup against the wall, shattering it.

The other elder started coughing more, and sweating profusely. She tried to loosen her collar further.

*Good*, Elder-3 thought.

"You fool. Had Elder-62 been fired when we wanted to do it, she never would have brought down our project and put us in this position. So you too…" he reached across and grabbed Elder-76's uniform under her chin, "…must go down!"

Now gasping for breath, Elder-76 reached for her throat. She started wheezing more desperately and sounded like a pig in a pen. "Sir! Please!"

Elder-3 merely sat back and sipped his tea as Elder-76 tried to stand and fell on the ground. "We've never heard your voice so rough. We like it. Your manipulations cannot save you this time, nor can Elder-1," he said as he watched the distressed elder hold her throat and roll around, white hair flailing, until the poison finished the job.

Walking into the dining room, Elder-10 ran over as soon as he saw Elder-76 on the floor. "Sir," he said as he checked for vitals. "She is dead!"

"Yes, she is."

"But Elder-3, her knowledge of our conditioning program…"

"Enough!" Elder-3 snapped. "She was another liability to the project."

Appearing to understand the risk of saying another word, Elder-10 merely nodded and hustled out the door.

January 10, 2045
Tuesday, Early Morning
Bayville, New Jersey
**_Fifteen days after the event_**

Karen Stone dragged her feet as she walked with Maria Stefano and Romeo (formerly Utopia Project member number 801). Despite the early hour, she already felt fatigued as they made their way across the roof of the eighty-story hideaway they called, 'RPH,' an acronym for its original name -- 'Royal Pines Hotel.' Although it was most recently used as a health and rehabilitation center, Karen thought the building still had the feel of the 1920's gangster-era luxury hotel she was told it once was. From the decorative inlaid floor in the foyer to the heavy wood beams and old hanging chandeliers in the dining room, the structure had never lost its original aura from when it was built over one hundred years ago. Jess said the locals were steadfast in their belief that the notorious gangster Al Capone had frequented the hotel in its day.

The top of the sturdy, Gothic-looking brick building, built with walls inside walls, provided them with a panoramic view of the entire area. Leaning over a cut in the battlements, Karen had to turn her eyes down and away from the brilliant sun that had just risen. Her eyes passed over the frozen lake and settled on the boathouse, which was just on other side of the entrance road from RPH.

"I am trying to visualize what Kid was talking about with the tunnels down there," she said to Maria.

The prior night, Kid Carlson had told them the history of the building and the wild speculations surrounding it, but she was still having a hard time getting a lay of this unfamiliar land.

"Do you know Maria?"

Out of nowhere Karen felt a wave of nausea, as she had too many times since the destruction. She had learned that if she closed her eyes and took deep, slow breaths, the wave would pass.

"Not really," Maria answered. "With how long I have lived around here, you would think I would know the crazy history of this building. Then again, I'm only nineteen-years-old, so there is much I don't know," she added as her boyfriend opened the door to the roof and joined them.

Jess Kellen stopped to stretch his lean but muscular five-foot-eleven inch frame and reach for the sky. Lowering his hands, he vigorously tousled his dirty-blond hair and quipped, "I forgot, you're still a teenager. I'm a cradle robber."

Maria rolled her eyes. "You're less than six months older than I am. And if you're the cradle robber, then why am I always coddling you?"

As the wave of nausea passed, Karen smirked at the banter and then pointed down.

"Doc McDermott said he used an underground tunnel to get from the basement of this building to that boathouse right there. And from what Kid told us, a tunnel used to run from that boathouse out under the lake behind it. But Doc said he didn't see any other tunnel entrances when he was under the boathouse."

"It's was probably sealed up a long time ago," Jess responded. "Actually, they said multiple tunnels ran under that lake and met in a room under there, like a central hub."

"Tunnels from where?"

Jess pointed east, "One tunnel supposedly came from that way, where there used to be a community center building on Central Boulevard and a pavilion on the bay," he turned and pointed south, "and another came from that way, from a mansion with Spanish-style roof tiles."

"Whose mansion?" Despite still feeling queasy, Karen was intrigued.

"I don't know. I think it was a front. Around the time of prohibition, they built it on the bank of Cedar Creek just up the road. Actually, if you go into the woods, there's still a section of a wall standing. The rumor is that they made bootleg liquor on the creek and took it from the Spanish mansion to the hotel through an underground tunnel."

"Do you believe that all of these tunnels exist?" Karen asked.

"I don't know." Jess pondered for a second. "I probably wouldn't, but we know for a fact that there is a tunnel between the building and boathouse, so they obviously knew how to make underground tunnels and had the equipment to do it…get down!" he suddenly screamed. "Everyone down, now!"

All of them lay and covered their heads. Karen did not know why Jess sounded an alarm until two planes zoomed overhead, speeding east toward the ocean.

After they passed, Jess jumped to his feet and stared at the sky. "Who the hell was that?"

Maria hastily put on the ultraviolet-blocking sun glasses, crouched down and aimed the telescope at the sky. Sweeping her black hair from the olive colored skin of her face, she bent down and peered through the lens. "Where did those planes go?" she mumbled.

Karen got up slowly. "We need to go tell Kid and General Hyland about this." She turned to leave.

"They must have come from McGuire," Jess concluded. "But if they now have access to planes, we are in big trouble." He looked over and screamed, "Maria! No!"

Karen crouched again.

Maria flinched and smacked the telescope with her hand, knocking the tube to the left. She reflexively reached for it and swung it back around.

Jess sprinted full speed and shoved the end of the tube toward the ground.

"What are you doing? See the sun?" he pointed east. "We can't have the sun glaring off of the mirror inside the scope, especially if you have it aimed in the direction of the ships. That's why we said we can't use this to look in that direction until midafternoon when the sun is behind you."

Maria's voice was meek as she said, "Sorry. I forgot about that little rule."

"Little?" he snapped. "It won't seem little if we give our hideout away."

A sense of foreboding washed through Karen, as if her heart was now pumping chilled water rather than blood, upon hearing Jess's next words.

"I just hope we didn't already."

January 10, 2045
Tuesday, Early Morning (EST)
New Jersey coast, Utopia Project Ship Number One
**Fifteen days after**

Elder-3 headed to the bridge of Utopia Project Ship Number One as soon as the call came in. The elder watchman reported seeing a strange, unnatural point of light and said he had pinpointed its location.

Holding binoculars to his eyes, Elder-3 noted, "There is a structure way out there. Its tip can be seen through the trees, but that is all we can see." He put down the binoculars. "Are we sure the light was not random?"

"No, Sir. It was tiny, just a pinpoint of light, but it was fixed for several seconds and then moved as if jiggled by a human hand. It was not a blip," the watchman replied.

"It must be them. We need a team to make for the origin of that point of light." He thought for a moment. "We have a dozen elders already staying on the mainland with a couple hundred members, and they are well-armed." Turning to the watchman, he said, "We need the coordinates and specific location of that building out there, and fast."

A few minutes later, Elder-3 picked up his walkie-talkie and contacted Elder-78 on the mainland. He provided him with the coordinates and even the specific address of the structure where the survivors appeared to be hiding. He concluded by saying, "Take a team of 25, no, make it 40 of the best trained soldiers we have on the mainland, and mobilize now, right now! We want them all dead before midday."

*We have them,* Elder-3 thought with certainty. *It will be a slaughter and we will finally be rid of them!*

# CHAPTER 3

January 10, 2045
Tuesday, Late Morning
Bayville, New Jersey
**Fifteen days after the event**

Thoughts swirled around Kid Carlson's mind as he sat on the edge of a plush chair. Jess was seated next to him in the lounge on the second floor of the RPH building and looked as uneasy as Kid felt, maybe even more so. General Eric Hyland paced with his head down, revealing meandering rivers of gray hair flowing through his military buzz-cut.

Jess asked, "Should we go relieve them up on the roof? They've been back up there for a couple of hours." After reporting the aircraft flying overhead, Karen and Romeo had gone back up on the roof to keep watch.

"I guess we should," Kid answered. "I just wish we knew where those planes were going. No need to determine if they were friend or foe, given that all of our friends are accounted for."

The general stopped in his tracks as if he just had a realization. "No, they're not," the general muttered.

"What?" Kid asked.

"It should have been the first thing to hit me when you said the planes were heading east!"

Kid and Jess waited expectantly, so the general continued. "They had the coordinates for the third area left unscathed, and if they now have transports, I fear they have launched a search and destroy mission." The general started pacing again. "Any survivors in Italy are in grave danger."

"So how can we save them?" Kid asked.

"Are you feeling up to saving anything?" Jess asked.

"I'm not 100 percent, but I feel a hell of a lot better than yesterday." Kid was without a heartbeat for over four minutes just two days earlier after being shot by a bolt on Mallard Island. In truth, he still felt very sore, but after resting and rehabilitating himself for the entire previous day, he felt strong enough to act if he needed to. Dr. McDermott had examined him that morning and had marveled at the bounce-back capability of the young, noting that someone 20 years older would have been knocked off of their feet for a week.

"We need to get to McGuire Air Force Base right away, secure an M3 if any are left, and get to Italy," the general answered.

"If there is an M3, who would fly it?"

"Melanie, although she…"

Karen burst into the room, helped by Romeo. She looked pale and could hardly breathe. "They're coming!" she huffed. "A bunch of vehicles are heading this way!"

General Hyland and Kid ran over to the window and stood shoulder to shoulder.

Spinning around, the general stated, "They're already here!"

"I am so sorry," Karen sputtered. "I would have seen them sooner, but I was on my knees about to throw up. I think Romeo was watching me instead of the roads."

Kid fought the immediate shock and anxiety as he watched a parade of vehicles coming toward the long entrance road. There were several vans and trucks. The soldiers were coming in force and they were already close. Too close.

"We need to assemble right away in the dining room. Now! Kid, get Clarence," the general ordered and ran up the hallway to alert the others. Everyone knew the drill and put on their coats while securing weapons.

Kid ran downstairs to the first floor where Clarence Moore was guarding the front door. "Clarence, make sure the doors are locked and come back to the dining room! Hurry!"

After getting everyone assembled Kid checked his pockets to ensure he had extra bullets for his 38-caliber pistol. He heard a loud rattling sound so he pushed open one of the two swinging dining room doors. He could see a group of soldiers trying to break through the glass front doors, while others ran past them. It seemed the soldiers were encircling the building.

"Can't we slip outside and escape?" Jess had an urgency in his voice.

"It's too late. They're surrounding the building!" Kid answered.

"We need to hide and establish a defensive position," General Hyland concluded.

"But where?" his daughter Sara asked. Her hazel-colored eyes were sharp and focused.

Kid thought for a second and then turned to Dr. McDermott. "Wait, how did you access the basement? From where?"

The doctor pointed to a door around the corner and up the passageway.

"Would we be trapping ourselves down there?" General Hyland asked. "Remember what I've said about always having a second exit?"

"I think there may be a walk-out down there, but I can't say for sure," Dr. McDermott said.

Kid felt the enemy closing in and knew they had to move. "We're already trapped. They are covering the exits and the windows. Heading down to the basement might buy us a few minutes to set up a defensive position, but only if we move fast."

General Hyland nodded in agreement.

Kid handed over a battery powered lantern to Dr. McDermott. "Doc, you've been down there. You should lead the way."

The group stood behind Dr. McDermott as he opened a door

and paused. Looking past him, Kid saw a stairwell disappearing into the pitch black below. The doctor held the lantern in front of him and started down. Reaching the bottom, he opened another door and turned left.

Kid and Jess were right behind him and cased out the basement. Many areas were being used for storage. The only area not covered in a thick layer of settled dust was one that had tools, hardware, and supplies, which Kid assumed were used for building maintenance and repairs.

"Hold up!" Jess yelled. He moved a sledgehammer and grabbed some wood planks. "Kid, do they have nails over there?"

"A ton of them."

"Grab a handful of the longest ones they have."

With everyone down, they closed the door at the bottom of the basement stairwell and hurriedly nailed wood planks across it.

Dr. McDermott held out the lantern and led them across the room. Walking past large boilers, he continued through a long, narrow tunnel that ended in a storage room under the boathouse. The group followed him through the musty, dank tunnel bored under the entrance road that ran between the boathouse and the main building.

Approaching a door, Dr. McDermott said to Kid, "We never tried to open this, but I assume there are steps that go up to ground level." He grabbed the door handle and it turned, but the door would not budge. Holding the handle and yanking, they could hear something heavy jiggling on the other side.

Kid put his ear to the door. "It's padlocked, on the outside."

"Dammit!" the doctor muttered. "Sorry, I was hoping…"

The general turned. "Dad, let's set up a defensive position facing the door down to the basement. This room can be our fallback position."

Retired army general Chris Hyland nodded and followed his son back through the tunnel to the basement space under the building.

At a loss, Kid was about to also run back when something in the room caught his eye. He focused his flashlight on an oval section of wall where the concrete was a different color than the surrounding areas. An idea, born out of the desperation and speculation, came to him. He knew it was a long shot but while General Eric Hyland and his father were setting up a defensive position he would give it a quick try.

He ran back through the tunnel to get Jess, and some necessary tools. When they returned to the storage room under the boathouse, Kid went over to the concrete wall. He had a sledgehammer in one hand and a hammer and chisel in the other. He turned his head as sounds reached the room through the tunnel.

Taking a few steps back and straining to hear, Jess blurted out, "They're beating on the door to the basement. They must know we're down here! We're trapped!"

Pointing to the oval section of concrete, Kid said, "Unless this is covering an entrance to somewhere, we need to bust through and find out."

He wielded the sledgehammer and began slamming the wall with all of his might. Jess helped with a hammer and chisel, knocking off chunks of concrete from around the perimeter of the concrete oval.

A loud crack resonated up the narrow tunnel. The soldiers must have smashed one of the boards nailed across the door to the basement.

"Kid! Jess! We need you!" Sara called into the tunnel. "They're almost through!"

Time was running out so Kid took a vicious swing. As the head of the sledgehammer hit home, a large chunk of concrete thigh-high dropped to the floor. Peering closely, he took his fist and rapped on the smooth surface which was now exposed. A metallic thud reverberated.

"It's a door!"

Jess chiseled away at the concrete and exposed a hand wheel in the center. "A watertight door." He chipped away the concrete around the wheel and tried to turn it, but it was stuck. "Give me the sledge-hammer!" Taking the tool, Jess slipped the wood handle through the spokes and pulled up hard. The wheel freed, so he started turning it with his hands.

Kid said, "Keep working to get it open. I am going back to get them!"

Reaching the others in the basement under the building, Kid called out and pointed, "Everyone, come on! We found a door in that storage room back there!"

General Hyland had his weapon aimed at the boarded-up door. "Leading to where?"

"I don't know. I think it is the opening to the underground tunnel system."

The general looked over and seemed concerned about the prospect. Kid answered the unspoken question.

"It may be our only way out."

Both braced as another board covering the door splintered.

Kid grabbed a piece of lumber and nailed it to the door frame in between the violent slamming from the other side. He then added more 10-penny nails to reinforce the ones that were cracking. He could hear an elder on the other side of the door barking orders to the members. Kid tapped in a nail and was about to drive it home when the door shuddered and popped out, skittering across the basement floor like it was shot out of dart gun.

"Get to the storage room!" Kid yelled. "I'll be right behind you."

"This way everyone, and bring the lanterns!" General Hyland called out as he headed for the tunnel.

Thoughts were coming to Kid's mind in rapid fire fashion. He grabbed two shovels and a roll of duct tape that were sitting on a work bench. He found a drop cloth used for painting and headed through the tunnel to join the others in the boathouse storage room. When he walked in, he saw the lower half of the oval of concrete had been broken away and the metal door behind had been pushed open. The opening was only waist-high, requiring a person to enter only by crawling. Crouching down and aiming his flashlight into the opening, he shuddered as he contemplated where the tunnels went and what condition they were in after all of these years.

"Come on, we are all in," Jess said from inside the opening.

"Hold these. We may need them." Kid handed the sledgehammer, shovels, hammer, and chisel in to Jess and Romeo.

Kid then used the duct tape to secure the painting blanket over the opening in the wall. It was not a neat job, but it would have to do. After crawling in, he ensured the painting blanket was draped completely over the opening to conceal it. Rising to his feet, he switched on his flashlight. He went to close the door and froze upon hearing the crack of another board echoing up the tunnel, but also... voices? Kid knew that time was running out, so he reluctantly pushed the door closed and cringed as a dull thud echoed in the ominous tunnel. He spun the hand wheel until the door clicked making a seal.

"I need that sledgehammer," Kid said as he grabbed it from Jess. Hesitating, he knew that he was about to cut off their only certain means of escape from the tunnels, but there was no choice in his mind. He used the head of the sledgehammer to pound the hand wheel until it was bent. A couple of people gasped when they saw what he was doing, including Sara's grandmother, Evelyn Hyland. Kid grabbed the mangled wheel. It no longer turned.

"We need to make it hard for them to follow us," he justified. Holding up the sledgehammer, he added, "We can break it open later if we need to."

He turned toward the others, and his nostrils flared. The air in the tunnel was heavy and smelled musty, as if it had not moved for decades. The walls of the tunnel appeared damp, even slimy. Kid could have sworn he heard the sound of dripping water echoing in the tunnel, but he was unsure if his imagination was playing tricks on him. A cold chill ran down his spine, generating a spasmodic shiver. The others were silent as they stood in a line waiting for him. A couple of people held lanterns so that the group was not in complete darkness. With each person appearing shorter and shorter, he realized that the tunnel had a gradual decline before leveling off.

Holding his hand above his head he was just able to stand upright. The oval-shaped tunnel was just a bit over six feet high and only about four feet across. As Kid squeezed his way toward the front of the group, he stopped to check on Evelyn, who appeared winded already.

"Did you take your medication this morning?" he asked her.

"Yes, and don't worry. I always keep a two week supply on me now." She patted her coat pocket.

"Thank God." He recalled all they went through to secure the medication necessary to sustain her life. "We can come back for the rest of it later." He made eye contact with Chris Hyland, who gave an assured nod.

Evelyn patted Kid's arm and waved him forward.

After passing the McDermott family and the Moores, Kid pinched the cheeks of the frightened Spatz girls. In front of them was Wendy Levy, who had hobbled the whole way on a dislocated ankle. If that wasn't hard enough, she raised her bandaged, sprained wrist as Kid squeezed by. "Help Wendy if she needs it," he said to Romeo and continued until he reached Jess and General Hyland at the front.

"I'm not so sure about these tunnels." Jess shined a light on the walls. "There are cracks everywhere."

"What do you expect? They're over 100 years old." Kid stopped for a moment to gather his courage and resolve. He stalled by patting down the partially unstuck bandage covering the deep scrape on the back of his hand, a souvenir from his fall when he was shot at Mallard Island. "I'll go first. Follow me." He walked forward, flashlight in one hand and a sledgehammer in the other.

Kid's beam of light was devoured by the seemingly eternal darkness ahead. He just hoped that no unpleasant surprises were lurking. "If this goes to where they said it goes, there should be other tunnels that connect ahead."

"Let's keep our bearings," Jess noted. "We are behind the building and heading east."

"Behind the building heading east?" General Hyland asked. "Isn't that the direction of the lake?"

"Yes," Kid answered.

"So how are we getting around it?"

"We're not going around it."

The general stopped walking. The look on his face made it clear that he already knew the answer.

Kid glanced back. "We are going under it."

# CHAPTER 4

January 10, 2045
Tuesday, Midday
Bayville, New Jersey
**Fifteen days after the event**

Taking slow, deliberate steps forward, Kid said, "Under the lake is where all of the tunnels supposedly connected."

Sounding dour, Maria uttered, "Great! We're going through a cold, wet, creepy tunnel based on a 'supposedly'?"

"Did we have another choice?" Jess asked, in front of her in line.

"Yes, stay and fight."

"Fight?" Jess snapped, his voice echoing in the darkness.

"Now is probably not a good time for bickering," General Hyland interjected as he continued walking. "Kid, what is our plan? Where are you trying to take us?"

"I was hoping to find a tunnel with an exit far enough away from the building that we could escape without them spotting us. These have to lead somewhere." Kid moved further along and then stopped. "Hold up for a second." Fearing they were being pursued, he listened closely but heard nothing.

Taking a cue from Kid's pause, Jess said, "I'll stay back and guard the rear. If I start flashing my light, that means there's trouble behind us."

Kid nodded and continued forward, feeling like he was on a pathway into the bowels of Hades. The dark tunnel continued, and he instinctively turned his eyes up when he realized that they were now below the frozen lake. He could feel the heaviness of the solid layer of ice pressing down on the brown water over them. He could smell the cedar. Looking down, the floor now had a small layer of standing water. His shoes began to make squishing sounds as he plodded forward.

He touched the gritty and damp cement walls to his side, but he pulled his fingers away when a small chunk of concrete fell to the ground. Kid slowed his pace and shined his light. Sections of the wall resembled cracked glass, where it seemed that one touch could cause the concrete to shatter into a million pieces. It was obvious that the tunnels were very old, and he feared a collapse was imminent. It was also obvious that his group was the first to disturb the confined space in many, many decades and maybe even the last century. He hoped that their presence alone would not be the straw that breaks the camel's back. *The tunnel will hold. They just don't build things like they used to,* he told himself as he tried to take his anxiety down a notch.

Kid had been counting his steps, and after walking for nearly 400 feet by his tally, the tunnel finally ended in a small square room. Kid shined his flashlight and noticed two heavy-looking doors, which he assumed were also watertight as they were equipped with hand wheels.

Sara came up next to him. Her voice echoed up the tunnel, cutting through the stale air.

"Where do you think they go?" As he turned to answer her, she ran her fingers through her dark hair. In the subdued light her lips, with their naturally bright red color, seemed to be glowing.

Kid recalled that when the Pinewald area was being developed in the 1920s and 1930s, there was a community center building due east on Central Boulevard and a pavilion even further east at Barnegat Bay. He wondered if the tunnel straight ahead originally went to either or both of those locations.

"I don't know, but if we keep heading east toward the bay, I would assume that the odds increase that the tunnel will be flooded," Kid said.

"Makes sense. Then again this tunnel is under the lake, and it is still intact," Sara noted.

He almost uttered, 'barely,' but he knew his sarcasm would only elevate their already-high level of anxiety. Instead he said, "True, but the lake is not corrosive salt water."

The door on Kid's right faced south. "This one probably headed to the old Spanish mansion that once stood along Cedar Creek, and it's mostly still woods out that way."

General Hyland stepped in between Kid and Sara and shined his light around the square room. "More watertight doors. When they built these tunnels, they definitely considered the risk of flooding," he noted.

Kid did not want to express the thought that chilled him inside. One of the tunnels, if not both, had to be collapsed on the other side of those doors. The inch of water they were standing in was likely seeping in from under one or both of the originally watertight doors.

"Which one do we pick?" The general shined his light on both doors. "Do we have an educated guess?"

"That's what I'm trying to reason through." Kid closely examined the doors. "If we open one, and the tunnel behind it is filled with water, we will never be able to close it. The tunnel will flood, and there is no way we would get out in time."

"And where would we go anyway, back into the building where the enemy is waiting for us?" Sara asked.

"I'd rather die fighting than drowning in a tunnel. I can't think of a worse way to die," Maria responded.

General Hyland and Kid finally agreed that the best shot was to open the door to the south since the other tunnel continued east toward the corrosive salt water of the bay. Kid convinced the general to move the group back toward the RPH building so that if water came rushing in, they would at least have a fighting chance of making it back to the building before drowning. Even then, they would have to be quick in smashing the mangled doorknob to get the door open.

As the group started making their way back up the tunnel, Kid froze as he saw a rapidly flashing light in the distance behind them. Jess was signaling, which meant there was trouble. The group turned back and ran toward him.

Kid scrambled to turn the hand wheel to open the heavy door facing south, but it would not budge. When Sara reached him, he yelled, "Grab the top of the wheel and pull! It's stuck in place."

While Sara strained and yanked, Kid slid the handle of the sledge-hammer through the spokes of the hand wheel for leverage like he had seen Jess do. He lifted up. Keeping tight pressure, it felt like the handle could snap at any second. Finally, the mechanism emitted a loud creak and began to turn.

"Hurry! They got through the tunnel opening and are coming this way!" Jess called out as he reached the group.

Despite the hand wheel unfreezing, it did not get any easier to turn. Kid and Sara both worked feverishly until a loud click sounded. Kid froze and waited for water to squeeze in around the edges of the door. With nothing coming in, he pushed the door, fearing he would encounter the resistance of a waiting wall of water, or worse, would jar the door enough to break the seal and start a deadly flood. Instead, the door swung open with relative ease. Only a small trickle of water escaped at the bottom of the door's threshold so he swung it open. The groan of the door hinges echoed up the tunnel.

Shining his flashlight, the tunnel seemed even more dark and dreary than the one they had just traversed. He assumed that was because they were getting deeper and deeper into the tunnel system. Kid led the way, not sure if he was taking them all to a dead end and to their demise. Once everyone was in the new tunnel, Jess pulled the door closed. The sound of it sealing echoed down the passageway.

Kid stepped forward with trepidation. "Watch your step, broken glass." He imagined that the glass was once a bottle containing boot-leg liquor during prohibition, which meant that someone had made a costly mistake. A little further along, Kid spotted a piece of paper.

He picked it up and put his light on it. It was a faded brochure for the Royal Pines Golf Course, which was part of the original project. On the back of the brochure was a hand-written order with a list of liquors and quantities. Kid tossed the brochure and walked faster.

Several paces ahead, Kid spotted another item on the tunnel floor. He did not have time to investigate every trinket along the way, but for this one he had to pause. Moving his light closer, he knew what he was looking at -- a hand. There were no other body parts, such as a radius or ulna, just a lone hand. Despite the decomposition, the bones almost seemed held together by some invisible thread. All five fingers were fanned out on the concrete floor. Having never been disturbed, the hand remained exactly as it lay when it was severed. It probably belonged to the klutz who broke the glass bottle a ways back. His punishment must have been immediate and harsh. Kid did not want the Spatz girls to see such a gruesome sight so he scattered the bones with his foot and kept walking.

Kid turned back to check on the group. Evelyn's breaths were labored as she inhaled air that was stale, in limited supply, and was not being replenished. Everyone else looked haggard and afraid but ready to proceed. Jess checked the magazine in his Glock 9mm pistol.

"I'll watch our back again, but I only have 17 shots."

The group moved ahead at a quicker pace, deeper into the more than century-old passageway, which seemed to go on forever. Unlike the first tunnel, this one did not run straight and had subtle bends. Kid knew this because when he looked back, he could not spot Jess's flashlight. As Jess neared, the light came back into view. Kid noted that the condition of this tunnel was even worse than the first. Cracks ran in every direction with many of them crisscrossing. Mold or moss seemed to be growing in, or through, some of the deeper crevasses.

Kid continued counting his steps to keep a good gauge of the distance they were traveling. The first tunnel was 400-feet long, and they had already walked an additional 2,200 feet in this second one with no end in sight. To keep his mind occupied and his anxiety at bay, he tried to do a calculation. He knew there were 5,280 feet in a mile and with his steps approximately 3 feet apart, they were coming upon the half-mile mark in total tunnel distance traveled. No wonder his leg muscles were burning. He was about to stop for a quick break when his light shone on something in the tunnel ahead.

"Stop. Everyone, stay where you are."

Taking a few steps forward, he huffed and struggled for air, given the lack of it in the confined space. "No," he muttered. "Dammit, no!"

Turning around, he said, "Listen. The tunnel is collapsed ahead and we are blocked by a wall of dirt. Jess, grab a shovel and come up here!"

While they evaluated the situation, Jess tapped the tip of the shovel head against the top of the passageway. In an instant, the roof started to collapse. Dirt and concrete rained down. Kid and Jess jumped back hurriedly.

"Everyone back! And fast!" Kid yelled and started running.

The cave-in did not remain isolated to where Jess had touched the roof. It chased them as a chain-reaction ensued, with the collapse following the group as they ran.

"Keep going! Go! Go!" he yelled.

To his dismay, debris continued to fall on Kid's head and back, with some clumps large enough to almost knock him to the ground. If the tunnel continued its rolling collapse, they would be buried alive. As the group scrambled to retreat, they bunched up since some in the group could not move as quickly. Kid begged for the collapse to stop.

Finally, just as he thought they would never outrun it, the collapse ceased as quickly as it had started. After running a little further, Kid barked, "Hold up! It stopped. Just don't touch a thing." He then doubled over with heaving breaths and shook the dirt from his hair.

"Let me check our rear." Jess ran past the group and disappeared beyond a subtle bend in the tunnel. Suddenly, his voice cut through the dusty air. The group could not see Jess, but his words were clear and conveyed an urgency.

"I see a light behind us! Get out your weapons!" Kid commanded. Jess came around the bend and stopped. "What is that sound?" "What sound?" Kid asked.

Raising his flashlight, Jess turned and yelled as a half-wall of water hit him thigh-high. A soldier caught in the current slammed into his legs. Jess raised his weapon and shot the enemy who was thrashing like a shark in the water. "Look out!" Jess yelled, but his words were too late. Half of the group was knocked over by the rushing wave.

Kid stayed on his feet and held Sara steady. He realized that the other tunnel connecting to the square room under the lake must have been compromised, and the enemy must have opened the door and released the pent up water. He turned and watched as the wave slammed into the wall of earth blocking the tunnel ahead. The surge ate away some of the dirt, but it stopped, and the water level began to rise. A dread swelled within him when he realized that they would drown long before they could make it back through the tunnels.

Jess fired and took out a couple more soldiers who had been swept their way.

Both of the Spatz children began to scream, verbalizing the panic that was coursing through the entire group. Melanie bent down and hugged both Katy and Karly. She lifted them into her arms and out of the water. She struggled to hold both, so Wendy took Karly and held her in her good arm.

Glancing up, Kid said, "Jess, keep watch for other soldiers being swept our way. Sara, grab the shovels, quick!" Kid used the handle of the sledgehammer to clear away some of the dirt mound of front of him. He carved out a ledge and then climbed up while crouching.

"It'll take too long to clear the tunnel," the general stated assuredly as Sara brought the shovels forward.

"I wasn't thinking of going forward." Kid pointed up.

Using the tip of a shovel, Kid carefully chipped away large chunks of earth from above his head. Dirt fell on him and into the ever rising water in the tunnel. He was careful to keep away from any concrete, lest he trigger another collapse. Making quick progress, Kid was soon standing on another ledge made from the earth he had loosed. With his upper body inside the opening he was carving, he continued to spear and scrape away at the dirt layer above his head. He would then scoop the dirt at his feet into a mound, pack it and flatten it with the shovel and step up. It was as if he was creating a set of earthen steps up to the surface.

General Hyland was trying to keep the group calm, but Kid could sense that the panic was rising with the level of the water. He felt it even in himself.

"Sara, try to keep the dirt packed under my feet. I keep slipping," Kid said.

"The water keeps eating it away," she noted.

"Hurry Kid!" Jess called out in a quivering voice. "The water is above my waist."

Kid dug faster toward the surface as the others below urged him on. *How many feet down is this damn tunnel?* Kid asked as his arm and shoulder muscles ached.

Thrusting the shovel upward it almost left his hand as he broke the surface of the ground above. "I'm through!" he screamed. All hope was not lost. After grabbing a thick tree root next to the hole, he pulled himself out to find he was in the middle of the woods. He widened the opening in the ground and pulled Sara up. Crouching down, Kid dropped the head of the shovel through the hole and held the handle tight.

"Grab this, and we'll pull you out!"

Melanie held up young Katy Spatz, who was crying and shaking. "You got it honey. I won't let you fall," she assured her as Katy grabbed the shovel head with both hands and climbed the dirt mound. When she reached the surface, Sara grabbed her hand and pulled her up while Kid dropped the shovel for the next person. Karly Spatz was next, and Kid knew she would try to outdo her sister. He was not surprised that she climbed out quickly.

Looking closer into the hole, Kid could see that the steps he had created were now submerged in the rising water. Most of group, including Melanie, the Moores, the McDermotts, and the Hylands all had to be pushed up from behind one at a time, while Kid and Jess used the shovel head to pull them out.

Soon only Romeo and Wendy Levy remained in the collapsed and flooding tunnel, but the water was up to their necks. Wendy yelled in pain as she tried to climb the muddy mound while holding the head of the shovel. Her wrist, which Kid knew had been sprained on a ski slope in Vermont, had obviously not yet healed enough. "Romeo, hurry, lift her up!" Kid yelled.

Reaching under the water, Romeo wrapped his arms around her knees and lifted. As Wendy neared the surface, Kid grabbed her good arm and pulled her out.

Kid lay back down on his stomach and looked into the hole. He could see the water had almost completely filled the tunnel and was up to Romeo's chin. To Kid's horror, the water level rose in a matter of seconds to the top of the tunnel, leaving only Romeo's outstretched hands visible. "Hold my ankles! We're losing him!" he yelled.

General Hyland grabbed one of Kid's ankles, and Jess grabbed the other. They lowered Kid head first into the hole. To Kid's dismay, Romeo's hands disappeared. "Lower! Before he drowns!" Kid yelled.

Romeo's hands reappeared and clawed at the mud and dirt mound in vain. Kid tried to grab either of the hands, but they slipped below the water. The next time, and possibly the last time, the fingers of a hand pierced the surface of the water, Kid plunged. Under the surface, he snagged a wrist with of his both hands and held on with all of his might. "Pull me out, now!"

As Kid was yanked up, Romeo's head rose out of the water, gasping, spitting, and gulping for air. The general and Jess dragged them both out and away from the hole. Laying on the ground and panting, Kid and Romeo had to get up and move further back as the tunnel water reached the top of the opening and spilled into the woods, creating a fast moving stream.

Kid sat for several minutes trying to catch his breath. Rising unsteadily, he glanced around. Through the trees he could see Western Boulevard, and he knew where he was. The RPH building was just up the road. Since the soldiers had opened the door to a connecting flooded tunnel, it was likely that they all drowned. He then stopped breathing as he heard the sound of a motor.

"Don't move!" Kid called out as a white van passed by on Western Boulevard. He could only make out that an elder appeared to be driving with one of the Utopia Project members in the passenger seat. He assumed they were survivors from the flooded tunnels who were heading back to the base camp on Long Beach Island. Kid's group remained motionless, hidden by the trees and underbrush.

After the van passed, General Hyland was quick to refocus on the issue that was on the table before they were attacked at RPH. "I need to get over to McGuire, grab an M3, and get to Italy before it is too late for the survivors there. Come on. We can find a new hideout on the way."

# CHAPTER 5

Elder-78 drove the white van away from the tunnel fiasco at the tall building with feet that were cold, and not just from being wet. He would have to call in and provide a status update to Elder-3 some time. The lead elder was going to be downright hostile. Maybe perishing in the decrepit tunnels would have been merciful. But no, Elder-78 and three members survived, although just barely. After they had pried open the half-exposed door to the tunnel system under the boathouse, his claustrophobia kept him from going in too far, which likely saved his life when the raging flood came. The three other members had only survived because they were assigned to stay back and assist him.

Raising his walkie-talkie to his lips, Elder-78 exhaled and depressed the call button.

On Utopia Project Ship Number One, a walkie-talkie came to life. "Elder-3 here. Go ahead."

"Sir, Elder-78 here. We fear that most of our members, as well as Elder-119, perished in an underground tunnel that collapsed and flooded behind their hideout."

"What?" Elder-3 asked, sounding enraged.

Elder-78 needed to get to the next part quickly. "But the enemy appears to have perished as well."

After an agonizing pause, Elder-3 asked, "How so?" His anger seemed to have come down a notch.

"The enemy was deeper into the tunnels than we were when the flood started. They would have had to turn back and pass us to escape, and they did not. Our members were not as far in as they were, and our members still could not make it out in time. Only we survived, as well as three of the members."

Another agonizing pause followed.

"We are not pleased to have lost more members, but with Hyland and the survivors now dead, and with the anticipated success of the cleanup mission in Italy, we will finally be able to focus all of our energy and resources in setting up our base camp and the new world." Elder-3's voice then turned bitter. "We have had enough distractions."

• • •

Jess and Dylan McDermott sprinted away to find transportation in a nearby residential subdivision, so Kid sat on the ground and took a minute to catch his breath. Besides the physical challenges he had already endured that day, he realized that he was still not 100 percent after having been shot on Mallard Island. Moments later, he was making sure his pistol wasn't waterlogged when two sport utility vehicles pulled up.

"It seems like there are SUV's at every house in New Jersey," Dylan quipped as he got out.

"Just be happy there are, and that they have heat," Kid noted as the group loaded into the two vehicles. Without any third row seating, both vehicles were packed tightly with soaked people sitting on laps and laying in rear cargo compartments.

While Jess drove with the heat on full blast, Kid and General Hyland discussed the game plan. Since they needed to get to McGuire Air Force Base and find an M3 transport to take to Italy, they contemplated possible hideouts near the military base.

"We need a place that has a better second exit than RPH did," Jess said.

"The one good thing is that I doubt they will keep looking for us," the general noted. "I'm sure they think we drowned in those tunnels."

"That's true, but we still need a place that is really secure."

"We've talked about hideouts near the military base, but what about within the base?" Kid asked.

The general nodded, "We could. We just need to figure out where."

Without hesitation, Jess recommended Hangar One in Lakehurst, referring to it as the 'Hindenburg Hangar.' He explained that he knew the layout, since his vocational school class had worked on a project there in high school. The original underground control rooms for the dirigibles had been converted into classrooms and offices. He said there were many areas where the group could take refuge in the hangar, so Kid and the general went with Jess's suggestion.

While they drove, General Hyland mentioned that despite the Hindenburg being Hangar One's most famous airship, a lesser known dirigible housed there called the U.S.S. Akron had crashed with an even greater loss of life. Despite living in the area his whole life, Kid was completely unaware of this other airship disaster, and he wondered why it was not famous like the Hindenburg crash. Maybe because the latter's dramatic, fiery demise was captured on film.

After breaking into the hangar and getting everyone inside, General Hyland and Kid were preparing to leave for McGuire Air Force Base. Although it was also part of the Joint Base, McGuire was still a good distance from Hangar One. With Kid going, Sara was as well after having made it clear she was not leaving his side. Melanie claimed to be fully recovered after getting knocked in the head with a heavy glass vase a few days before, so she was chosen to pilot the M3 if they were lucky enough to find one.

General Hyland, Kid, Sara, and Melanie jumped into an SUV. Running his hands up and down his pant legs, the general said, "I have pretty much dried out. How about the rest of you? Does anyone need to change?"

Sara and Mel both declined the offer. Kid felt his pants and coat. "Maybe a little damp, but I don't need to change either."

"Don't worry, I'll jam the heat for the ride. That should finish drying everyone out," the general said as he turned on the vehicle. "Weapons? I dried mine out, but does everyone have a working handgun, one that isn't waterlogged from the tunnel?"

"Sara's and my 38's never really got wet," Kid answered. "I already checked them. I'll check Mel's on the way."

The general nodded, put the vehicle in gear, and headed for McGuire.

Kid glanced over as Melanie, who was still wearing a headband to hold a bandage over the cut on her head, turned to look out the back window. He did the same and spotted Karly and Katy Spatz, both waving without excitement.

Melanie opened the vehicle window, leaned out and blew kisses to her girls. "Son of a gun, they both look like their asshole father when they have sad faces," she muttered as she gave a final wave and rolled up the window. "I pray that my two angels stay safe, and that I make it back."

Sara, sitting in the back seat next to her, took her hand. "You will Melanie. Mark my words. You will."

"Thanks. Please, call me Mel. That's what my family and friends call, or should I say, called, me." Putting her hand on Kid's shoulder, she added, "That goes for you guys up here too."

Kid nodded and patted her hand as he watched out the window. He was relieved that General Hyland knew the various routes and shortcuts through the Joint Base. It would have been easy to get lost or drive in circles. As they came upon the intersection of two roads, the general pulled over and got out.

When Kid walked over, the general noted, "These are fresh." He pointed to tire tracks in the snow. "And there are two sets. They came in force which means that there might not be any more M3's left to take."

"Only one way to find out." Kid hopped back in the vehicle. He could tell the general was concerned that they would have no way to get to Italy. And the unspoken message was that if they could not get over there to help and fast, the Italy survivors were as good as dead.

General Hyland continued speeding and within moments they turned up an access road and headed toward a small gate near the back of McGuire Air Force Base. After parking, the general led the group through the gate to the air field. He followed the sidewall of a building and then sternly raised his hand. They all stopped.

Kid crept up next to him and whispered, "Where are we?"

"The main terminal." Peering around the corner, the general snapped, "And there's an M3 left! If we could get to it, I could get it started. I memorized the startup procedures and controls."

"Then why did you even need me?" Mel chimed in as she joined them.

He put his hand on her shoulder. "Because someone needs to actually get it off the ground and fly it."

"Great," she muttered.

Kid peeked around the corner. The air field seemed relatively small, and the runway layout was not discernible given the snow covering. He spotted the aircraft, which was about the size of a large Cessna plane but military green with huge swivel thrusters on each side. Craning his neck a little more, he followed the vehicle tire tracks, which led to two vans parked in front of the main terminal. "Do you think they all went to Italy, or would they leave some back?"

"Not sure," the general answered. "They may have left some members to guard the last M3."

Sara came forward and brushed against Kid's chest as she tried to take a look. Even in the tense circumstances, he was warmed as he put an arm around her waist to steady her. Trying to decipher the layout of the airfield, Sara asked, "Where are the runways?"

"There are only a few runways, but they are buried under snow out that way." The general pointed. "From high above, the air field resembles a triangle with two runways and one taxi lane making up the sides. The control tower over there is inside the triangle. The M3 is parked in the taxi lane in front of the terminal, but it can ascend vertically so runways are irrelevant."

Kid nodded. "That explains why none of the runways are cleared."

"Do we need those movable stairs to get into the plane?" Sara pointed. It appeared that the movable stairs in the taxi lane were used to load the other M3's that were taken.

"It would help, but it is not necessary," the general concluded. "I was studying these transports for just such a moment. Under the door hatch is a pull-down ladder. I know where the releases are. But listen, we need to make a break for that last M3."

"I'll get the vehicle and drive us so we can get to it faster and keep some element of surprise, in case they did leave anyone to guard it," Kid suggested.

"Good idea. And we can use the vehicle for cover if need be," the general added.

Kid took off, and as soon as he brought the vehicle through the gate, the general, Sara, and Mel jumped in.

The general turned to the group. "You all keep guard while I get the M3's ladder down and open the door. Got it?" After everyone acknowledged, he said, "Weapons out. Hit it, Kid."

Speeding through the snow, they headed straight toward the M3. They were not even half way there when two male soldiers and one female soldier came charging out of the terminal building and started firing. Kid brought the SUV to a sliding halt behind the M3, and General Hyland jumped out.

A bolt hit Kid's window as he went to open the door, so he scooted across the seat. "Everyone out! Use the passenger side!"

When Kid exited, he saw the general free the M3's emergency ladder, drop it to the ground and start climbing.

Joining the girls on the passenger side of the vehicle, Kid leaned across the hood and took aim. Before he could fire a shot, he had to duck as a bolt skimmed off of the hood. "Damn, another sharpshooter." He was reminded of the soldier at the Hammond Covered Bridge up in Vermont, who was also an incredible marksman and nearly took him and Chris Hyland out.

"Dad, hurry!" Sara called out.

Lying down, Kid peered under the vehicle. He could see the soldiers' feet as they ran full speed in the snow. He aimed and fired. A bullet shattered a soldier's shin. When he fell to the ground, Kid's next bullet struck him in the neck.

The female soldier tripped over a pipe hidden under the snow, fell flat on the ground, but quickly got up and resumed her advance. Sara stepped out from behind the vehicle and shot her in the chest. Then she dove back for cover.

The sharpshooting soldier kept swiftly charging. Despite having to aim at a moving target from under the vehicle, one of Kid's bullets hit the streaking soldier in the foot. The adversary stumbled but continued his bull-rush with a limp.

"Watch behind us! Two more are coming!" Mel called out.

Turning his head, Kid was stunned to see two more soldiers running at them from the direction of the control tower, where they must have been stationed. His group was now trapped and caught in the middle.

Swiveling his head back around, Kid saw that the soldier he had shot in the foot was down, having apparently stumbled. But from the ground, the soldier was firing under the vehicle. A bolt zipped right past Kid, so he jumped behind the only cover he could find, which was the front tire. The girls were huddled close together behind the back passenger tire. But then the two soldiers coming from the control tower also started blasting away, with their bolts pelting the side of the vehicle.

Mel screamed.

"Lay flat!" Kid yelled. With fire now coming from the front and from behind, there was nowhere to take cover. The situation seemed hopeless. But then Kid jumped upon hearing a loud burst of gunfire. He turned to see General Hyland manning the machine gun mounted to the side of the M3. The barrel swept around and cut the soldiers from the control tower nearly in half from close range.

"Saved our asses," Kid muttered as he turned and focused on the lone remaining soldier from the terminal building. Peering cautiously under the vehicle, Kid gasped. The soldier was no longer there. He listened intently and heard the slow scrape of a foot dragging on the ground in front of the hood of the truck coming their way.

Knowing it would be nearly impossible to out-duel a sharp-shooter, Kid retreated toward the back tire and pulled Sara and Mel behind him. He waved for them all to fire when the enemy came around the corner. Kid fully expected to fall right there, but he hoped that his body would protect the girls long enough for them to take the soldier out. Kid maintained his focus on the front of the vehicle as he knelt on the ground. Sara had one arm around his waist and had her pistol aimed over his shoulder with her other hand. Her breaths were rapid and trembling, but her hand was steady. Kid's heart was beating so hard that his pistol seemed to be jumping with every thump of his chest cavity.

As the tension reached an apex and the soldier stepped around the corner, General Hyland opened the door of the M3 and yelled, "*Ion!*"

The conditioned word put the soldier into a zombie-like trance, and he collapsed on the ground in front of Kid, Sara, and Mel. The enemy's arm was outstretched, and the barrel of his weapon was aimed at the group. Instinctively, Kid jumped up and kicked the weapon from the combatant's hand.

"Come on. Everyone in," the general instructed. After the group boarded, he pulled up the ladder and directed Mel to the pilot seat.

She turned on the ignition and familiarized herself with controls. "Definitely buckle up," she called out.

General Hyland sat in the passenger seat, buckled up, and checked the gauges. "We are almost full with fuel. Barring any unforeseen problems, we should have more than enough for the round trip."

"Can't we just add fuel over in Italy before we fly back?" Mel asked.

"This craft has its own special fuel, and mixture, so we can't just look for jet fuel to fill it. I, unfortunately, do not know how to make it. There is a fuel pump here at McGuire," he hesitated as if considering it, and then waved his hand, "We should have more than enough. Let's get in the air."

Kid looked out the window toward the back of the craft and watched as Mel rotated the thruster on his side. It stopped at a 45-degree angle, but the dazed soldier was supine on the ground right behind it. "Ah, Mel…" he started as she pushed the throttle and fired up the engines. The soldier was torched and skin melted away. Kid cringed and turned around. "Never mind."

Mel rotated the thrusters to their perpendicular position, pushed down on the throttle, and the M3 lifted off the ground. She tried unsuccessfully to keep the craft level and steady. The equalization technology disguised the jerky movements as she overcompensated with the sensitive controls. Kid stared out the window and started to feel dizzy. Mel pulled up and banked to the left, almost hitting the control tower, before finally leveling off and ascending.

Kid exhaled loudly and leaned forward. "You got this?"

"Trying," Mel answered.

Sara stopped whispering prayers and opened her eyes. She looked out the window and said, "Good job, Mel. That was as smooth as can be. I couldn't even tell we had taken off. You are an ace at this already!"

Mel turned around and went to speak, but as soon as she met Kid's eyes, they both burst out laughing.

Sara looked at Kid quizzically. He grabbed her hand and said, "Let's just say it is a good thing you had your eyes closed. Next time, I may do the same."

"Hey!" Mel blurted out, sounding mildly insulted. With the craft now moving steadily, she said, "Anyway, when it comes to aviation, the hardest part is taking off and landing."

"The learning curve there needs to be accelerated," the general stated. "It could make a difference between life and…" He paused and seemed annoyed at himself for opening his mouth.

# CHAPTER 6

January 10, 2045
Tuesday, Late Afternoon (EST)
Over the Atlantic Ocean
**Fifteen days after the event**

Flying east in the M3, General Hyland had a realization and said, "Don't gun it yet, Mel." In his haste, he had almost forgotten to call in to the group at Hangar One. He pulled out his walkie-talkie. "Dad! Come in, over."

"Here, son," Christopher Hyland answered. "Did you secure an M3?"

"Yes. We wound up in a battle, but we had no casualties or injuries on our side. Listen, our 20-mile radio window is going to close quickly, so we are signing off. We are heading to Italy."

"Got it Eric. Good luck and get back soon. Out."

General Hyland put down his walkie-talkie and turned to Mel. "Hit it."

She worked the controls and started to accelerate over the Atlantic Ocean. "Wait!" She pulled back the throttle and pointed at the ocean below. "What is that?"

"It's a cruise ship," Kid said from the back.

The general looked out at the vessel floating on the ocean.

"And one of the popular ones," his daughter added. "I recognize the three tall water slides above the deck from the advertisements. Together they form the shape of a trident."

"For a second I thought it was supposed to be a pitchfork," Kid commented.

Staring out the window, the general said, "That 'pitchfork' is now a grave marker for a large floating tomb." He could only imagine how gruesome it would be to step inside the vessel.

"It is not very far offshore," Mel noted.

"Maybe at some point we can take a closer look, but we need to get to Italy. Full speed ahead."

At that, Mel pushed the throttle to its stops.

The general noticed the wry smile on her face. It was the first time her love of flying had shown. She appeared downright exhilarated as the clouds, with undersides painted pink by the impending dusk, came and went in the blink of an eye.

January 10, 2045
Tuesday, Late Afternoon (EST)
Hangar One, Lakehurst, New Jersey
**Fifteen days after the event**

At Hangar One Jess was creating bedrooms by reorganizing two classrooms which were originally control rooms in the days of the dirigibles. Hearing footsteps, he walked out into the main corridor and met up with Chris.

"Any word?" Jess asked as they walked up the hall.

"Just heard from Eric. They are all fine," he said as they turned into a large, empty room. The group intended to use this larger room as a dining hall and meeting space. Dr. McDermott's family was setting up folding tables while Evelyn and Karen cleaned them. "Eric said they have an M3 and are on their way to Italy," Chris added.

"That's a relief," Jess responded. "But I have to say, it's hard to stay back when the action is out there."

"You're lucky Mom isn't here!" Katy yelled out as the Spatz sisters sat next to each other in folding chairs.

"*You're lucky Mom isn't here*," Karly repeated in a high-pitched voice, mocking her older sister.

Standing behind the girls, Wendy Levy cleared her throat.

Turning quickly, Katy said, "Miss Wendy, did you hear her? She is repeating every word I say!"

"No I am not." Karly put a hand over her mouth. "*She is repeating every word I say.*"

Chris turned to Jess and commented, "Obviously not all of the action is out there." They both laughed.

Rubbing the bandage wrapped around her wrist, Wendy separated the girls and made them sit further apart from each other. She then hobbled on her injured ankle and went to a closet in the next room which Jess knew was still half full with school supplies. She came back with notebooks, pencils, and markers for the girls.

Chris put his hand on Jess's shoulder. "We do have to go back to that RPH place. We left too many important items, including Evelyn's medication. She always keeps a bottle on her, but the rest is in the room we were using on the second floor over there."

"Maria's diabetes medication are still there too. I'll take a ride over there first thing tomorrow and get everything."

"Alright. We just need to be careful in case any more of them survived the tunnel flood. And we need to make sure that they are not staking out the place," Chris advised.

"Got it."

"Oh, we should grab Eric's computer. It must have some important information because he kept it by his side all the time."

"And Jess, not to pile on," Marissa Moore chimed in, "but we could definitely use those heaters we had over there. Poor Clarence has a case of the shivers."

Sitting on a folding chair, Clarence was wrapped in what appeared to be a painting drop cloth. His wife, and the group's resident nurse, Marissa, pulled the cloth as tightly as she could and hugged him.

"And for some reason…it won't stop," Clarence huffed out through chattering teeth.

"Then we need to do something about that now. Let me see if I can find anything to help warm him up," Jess said. Moments later, he came back with a stack of grungy and tattered shop towels he had found in the hangar. He handed a few to Clarence.

Wendy took off the girls' shoes and socks, which were still damp from the tunnels under RPH, and they were each given a towel.

Karly held up her towel. "Hey, this is dirty!"

"*Hey, this is dirty!*" Jess repeated in a high-pitched voice.

After Karly gave him a pouty face, Jess added, "It is stained, but it's clean and dry!" He tousled her hair vigorously until she started laughing and slapped at his hand.

"Jackpot!" Maria declared as Romeo and she entered the room with stacks of brand new sweatshirts, sweatpants, and socks. "We found the company store. Everything but underwear. We even came across a lost and found with a bunch of coats! We couldn't carry it all, but we can go back for more."

Within moments, everyone had changed out of their damp clothes and were wearing new, matching 'Joint Base' attire.

"You can copy my clothes," Katy said to Karly as she pointed at her baggy Joint Base sweatshirt.

"I am not copying you. My shirt is different."

"No it's not."

"Yes, it is!"

As Jess went to walk out the door, he smiled at Wendy and said, "Good luck keeping the girls amused." He noticed that she was rubbing her wrist. "How is the healing process coming along?"

"One day at a time. It's tough. I really miss him." She was referring to her late husband James, to whom she had been married just one month before he perished in the missile attack at Mallard Island.

Jess realized his faux pas and put his hand on her shoulder. "It will take time."

Wendy turned her eyes down and while massaging her wrist, she seemed to have a realization. Her face turned red, highlighting the strawberry blond color of her hair. "Oh, Jess. I'm sorry. You were asking about my wrist. It just gets a little sore when I use it too much."

"It is alright Wendy. Healing takes time, no matter what the wound is."

He was surprised by his response. It was unusual for him to utter words so deep, if not in his opinion, downright poetic.

January 10, 2045
Tuesday, Late Evening, Central European Time (CET)
Sorrento Peninsula, Italy
**Fifteen days after the event**

With their two M3's now parked in a small field on the Island of Capri, Heidi stared at the plume of smoke, visible in the light of the nearly half-moon.

Elder-85 turned to her and said, "We depart at daybreak to search the rest of this island. Today we spent most of the limited daylight searching for Elder-62's house."

"But we did find it," Heidi said, pointing at herself, "and laid ruin to it, as planned."

"Yes, but we wasted too much fuel searching for it. We hope in the end we have enough to get back across the ocean."

Heidi chose not to respond and simply laid her head back. She wanted to get a few hours of sleep. As she started to drift off, she smiled at the vision of the house exploding in a huge ball of flames, hoping Adele Carmelo was inside.

While flying across the Atlantic Ocean in the M3, Sara could not get the vision out of her head. "That cruise ship, especially at dusk, looked like a floating ghost vessel."

"It was definitely…eerie," Kid agreed. "And you were right about the slides resembling a pitchfork."

Mel muttered, barely audible, "Reminds me of the Southern Guard."

"What is that?" Kid leaned up between the front seats.

"Whenever you mention a pitchfork, the first thing I think of is a picture in our local newspaper from a couple of November's ago. I kept a copy of it on my coffee table because it had a picture of Karly on the bottom of the front page picking pumpkins. But at the top of the page was a story about a clash in Bridgewater between bikers and farmers, and the picture was of an angry rider from the Southern Guard holding up a pitchfork."

"A biker group called the *Southern* Guard, in Vermont?" Kid asked.

"Yeah. Kind of ironic, right?"

Sara was interested in the conversation and leaned forward. "Why were they fighting? Do you remember?"

"The farmers were complaining about the packs of motorcyclists speeding all the time, and scaring the livestock by gunning their loud engines. So one day the farmers put out an obstacle course of hay bales on the road, and they stood along the path with signs in their hands telling the bikers to 'slow down, or leave town.' The next day, the hay bales were still there so the entire biker gang stopped in the middle of the road in Bridgewater. Some of the biker gang supposedly had pitchforks strapped to their backs, and they started forking the hay out of the road. The picture was of the face-off between a Southern

Guard biker with his pitchfork and a local farmer, but I didn't keep the newspaper copy to be reminded of that fiasco. I kept it because my baby's picture was on the front page."

"Sounds like a lot of unnecessary commotion," the general commented.

"Tell me about it," Mel blurted out. "It caused a traffic jam on Route 4, and we were stuck in it for over an hour. We got home from pumpkin picking so late that the girls were asleep in the car."

Sara crawled up between the front seats. "Did you say that was in Bridgewater a couple of November's ago? As in 2043?"

"Yes. It was Karly's fourth birthday, and she wanted to go pumpkin picking."

"When is Karly's birthday?" Sara grabbed Kid's arm firmly, almost desperately.

Looking back, Mel said, "November 7."

Sara knew her mouth was agape as she uttered, "Dad…"

"I know," he started and turned to her. "That is the day you picked me up in Boston after I first met with Professor Cofflin. The beginning of the end."

"Professor Cofflin?" Mel asked.

"The inventor of the neutron beam weapon system. The one just used to annihilate the world."

"Oh, God…"

"But remember I was late getting to Boston because of traffic?" Sara said. "I never knew why until now."

Kid appeared confused, so she clarified. "The day you and I first met in Vermont, remember I left you a note on the bench because I had to run down to Boston to pick up my dad? I was way ahead of schedule, but I got stuck in traffic on Route 4 in Bridgewater for almost an hour. I'm just finding out now that the road was blocked because of a battle between farmers and bikers. And talk about small world, Mel was sitting in the same traffic jam that night."

"And I wasn't happy about it," Mel added. "Not happy at all."

The general stared absently out the window for a moment, as if in a trance.

Sara sensed her father's dismay. "What's wrong, Dad?"

He shook his head. "A few months ago, the day before Professor Cofflin took his life, he shared something with me that I will never forget. But it means so much more now than it did at the time. He saw our loving father-daughter interaction when you finally got to Boston to pick me up, and he said that if he had seen that before he handed over his neutron beam design plans, he would have destroyed the plans, and the weapon never would have been created."

"And the world would not have been destroyed," Sara whispered. "If only I wasn't late."

"It was not your fault, Sara." Her father's voice was firm. "Don't *ever* blame yourself."

"If anyone is to blame, it is the Southern Guard, for holding you up," Mel interjected.

"The Southern Guard," the general repeated as he made eye contact with Sara. "It almost seems like infernal powers were at work that night, ensuring you didn't make it to Boston in time."

For a few minutes nobody said a word. The general checked his watch.

"By eastern standard time, it is now 6:00 P.M. Italy is six hours ahead of us, so it is midnight there," he said.

"How long does this flight take?" Mel asked.

"It is a fairly short trip with how fast we are flying. What's our speed?"

"2,700 miles per hour!" she blurted out in surprise as she checked her gauges. "It just doesn't feel like we are traveling that fast."

Sara agreed. It did not even feel like they were moving.

"It will probably take an hour and 45 minutes or so in total," the general said.

"Then we should get there in less than an hour from now."

"Yes." The general unfastened his seat belt. "Kid, Sara, we need to familiarize ourselves with the weapons we have at our disposal before we get there."

Within moments, Kid and Sara had acclimated themselves with the limited armaments within the M3. The weapons included only four missiles and two side mounted Browning .50 caliber machine guns. The general had used the machine gun back at McGuire, so he demonstrated how to operate it.

"This is all the weapons we have?" Kid asked as he stared at a computer screen with the targeting system for the missiles.

"Yes. The M3 was designed to be a transport, not a fighter plane."

Sara leaned forward. "Dad, what are we supposed to do when we get there, since it will be the middle of the night in Italy? How are we supposed to find anyone?"

"I've been thinking about that. If we come in and there are any active battles, we engage. If all is quiet, we may just park somewhere and pick it up at first light."

"That makes sense," Sara said. "How much further?"

The general checked a screen and said, "We passed Spain not that long ago, but we are already passing over Sardinia."

Sara knew Sardinia was an Italian island in the middle of the Mediterranean Sea and was not that far from the Island of Capri. "Then we are almost there," she noted.

"Yes. Time to switch to lights-out mode for our approach," the general said and flicked a few switches, plunging them into total darkness.

"Whoa," Sara uttered. It seemed like someone had instantly brightened every star in the sky. For several minutes she absorbed the unbelievable view until she dropped her eyes. Sitting forward, she looked closer. "Ah, Dad, look up ahead. Is that…smoke?"

# CHAPTER 7

January 11, 2045
Wednesday, 1:00 AM (CET)
Sorrento Peninsula, Italy
**Sixteen days after the event**

A t 1:00 A.M. Heidi awoke with a start in the passenger seat of the M3. The craft was aimed in so they could watch the beautiful plume of smoke rising from the smoldering wreckage of Adele Carmelo's home not far away on the island. Heidi was in a half-dream state and sat upright upon something registering in her field of vision. She looked closer. She would not wake up Elder-85 unless she was sure there was something out there. Again! She saw it a second time. Something in the air by the plume of smoke had reflected the moonlight for a split second. "Sir, please wake up!" she said close to Elder-85's ear.

He jumped up and said irritably, "What now?"

"Sir, we think we saw something in the air over by the island. It may be another aircraft."

Huffing, he flipped on the computer screen between the seats. "We see nothing, but let us check by infrared." A second later, Elder-85 sat bolt upright. "There is another aircraft. Although its lights are out, the heat signature shows it to be another M3 like this one!"

He pulled out his walkie-talkie and radioed Elder-98 in the M3 parked next to him. "We have an incoming aircraft and must consider it hostile. Please confirm, you still have three missiles left?"

"Confirmed, Sir."

"We only have two as we used two to ensure Elder-62's house was fully obliterated. Be prepared to fire upon my command. Turn on infrared."

"Yes, Sir. Should we stay in lights-out mode?" Elder-98 asked.

After thinking for a second, Elder-85 said, "Yes. The incoming craft is an M3 and also has infrared, but lights-out mode may buy us a few seconds. Now get in the air and let's take this bastard down!"

As soon as the words left Elder-85's lips, he lifted his M3 into the sky.

•  •  •

General Hyland studied the plume of smoke ahead, which looked more like a wide, dark funnel against an even darker background. He uttered in disbelief, "I think that was Adele's house."

Sara gasped.

"Hold on, she wasn't supposed to be there. She was living in a place under the island."

Looking only partially relieved, Sara said, "Unless she decided to go back home."

"I don't think she would. I told her stay under the island until I came for her." The general pondered for a moment and asked a question directed at nobody in the craft. "How did they find her house?"

Kid said, "Mr. Hyland?

He heard a voice, but it seemed far away as he continued, "The deed wasn't even in her name. She…"

"Mr. Hyland!" Kid said louder. "We must've been spotted! Look at the infrared! Two aircraft!"

The general snapped out of it and looked at the screen. He saw them, two M3's coming their way. "Damn, go Mel!" he snapped.

"Go? Where?"

"It doesn't matter, just go!"

Mel buried the throttles and turned. A short time later, she called out, "I can't see anything!"

The general turned on a bright spotlight and aimed it forward. "Rome. I guess you turned to the northwest," he muttered. At such a low height the landmarks were unmistakable. St. Peters Basilica, one of the largest churches in the world, stood prominently in the distance. "Watch yourself. Don't get too low."

While General Hyland operated the spotlight and navigated for Mel, Kid crawled up between the seats and took control of the missile targeting system. "They're still behind us. We need a game plan," he said.

"We have four missiles aboard. Can you figure out how to fire them?" the general asked. As crazy as the thought was, the general knew that Kid's proficiency with video games would benefit him with using the M3's missile system.

"Let me try," Kid said. A moment later, he blurted out, "I got it! One missile is armed. I just need to lock onto a target. Wait, now what is that?"

The general turned and looked at the screen. It showed the infra-red images of the two pursuing aircraft, but then Kid pointed to a third image- a small, red dot behind them, moving quicker than the enemy M3's.

"Incoming missile! Evasive maneuver!" the general barked.

"What? How?" Mel yelled.

"See that church?" He aimed the spotlight at St. Peters Basilica. "Get behind it and fast! The missiles are not heat-seekers."

Mel, clearly not yet acclimated to the speed of the M3, drastically overshot the basilica. She held on tight and yelled, "I went too far! We're in the open!" She continued turning and was heading back to the southeast. The missile was closing in and the general knew that they had lost their opportunity to use a structure to cut it off.

"Locked. Missile away!" Kid called out and tapped the red button on top of the joystick. A missile launched from the M3 and made for its target. It found its mark as it slammed into the incoming missile and both exploded in a mid-air ball of flames.

The concussive blast of the missiles kicked the back of the M3 and spun it around 180-degrees.

The general looked out the side window and recoiled upon seeing a tall obelisk right next to them. They were dangerously close to it.

Mel steadied the craft, but they were now facing the oncoming M3's.

"Hold for just a second Mel," Kid said.

She gripped the throttle as she hovered.

"Hold…"

"We have to move, and watch out for…" the general started.

"Locked, and missile away! Punch it Mel. Go!" Kid's second missile burst forth and headed for the closest M3.

Mel banked up and to the west, but as the general turned the spotlight, the world outside turned a cold, hard gray.

"Watch out for the obelisk!" the general called out. With the M3 just feet away from the structure, he braced for impact.

"It's going to be close!" She pulled into a nearly vertical ascension. "Come on," she urged and then exhaled as the craft cleared the tall structure.

The general watched out the window as the obelisk disappeared beneath them.

"The maneuverability of this thing is incredible," she muttered.

The enemy M3 tried an evasive maneuver to shake the missile Kid had launched, but they were too late. As the nose of their craft turned toward the sky, the missile hit them in the tail. The general watched with relief as an explosion followed and what remained of the M3 fell to the earth in burning chunks.

Continuing south, Mel nearly ran into the other enemy craft as it also ascended.

The enemy M3 quickly banked to the north and disappeared.

The general pointed. "Maintain a course to the southeast. Although it may be dissipating, head back to the island with the plume of smoke." He turned around and said, "Sara, Kid, keep a close watch. Their M3 scattered, but make sure they don't sneak up behind us."

"Got it," Sara answered and turned to Kid. "You take that window and I'll take this one."

"That was some impressive shooting Kid. Lucky for us you got the hang of the missile system," the general commented.

"I guess that is what you call battlefield training," Kid said as he peered out the window.

Turning to Mel, the general said, "Speaking of that, nice maneuvering for someone who has never flown an M3 before."

"Thanks. But I obviously still have a lot to learn. I almost hit that obelisk."

"I am glad we didn't. That monument is pretty sacred," the general noted.

"What is it?"

"It's called the Lateran Obelisk, and is the largest standing ancient Egyptian obelisk in the world."

"Egyptian? How did it get to Italy?" she asked.

Sara chimed in and clarified, "Via river and sea on specially built boats."

"Correct." The general was impressed, but not surprised that she knew this. He leaned forward in his seat. "There's the island. Slow down now before we overshoot it."

"Already slowing. We're learning," Mel said. "Where are we aiming for?"

"See the rock face to the right, on the northwestern side? Right above the rock face is a restaurant. We can land in the parking lot. Shut it down and get the M3 covered before they can locate us."

She turned her head. "A large parking lot?"

"Not really, but I am sure you'll do fine."

A nervous laugh escaped Mel's lips. "Mr. Hyland, I have never landed one of these before, and now I am going to land in a tight space in the dark?"

"When you are about to land, we can turn on the landing lights for just a minute," General Hyland said as he directed her where to go. She slowed down and hovered over the small parking lot.

"See anyone trailing, Sara? Kid?" the general asked.

"No," they both called back, almost in unison.

Turning on the landing lights, he said, "Let's hurry and land this thing."

With the thrusters perpendicular to the ground, the craft descended rapidly. The parking lot would have been a perfect landing spot were it not for two cars that were occupying spaces. Mel tried to delicately work the controls, but the craft continued to bob and weave as she neared the ground.

"Steady," the general said quietly. He tried to sound calm, but he had a tight grip on the seat belt fastened across his lap.

She got a handle on the roll as they landed without the wing tips on either side touching the asphalt, but the yaw spun the M3 in a circle.

The General turned off the landing lights and patted Mel's knee. "I told you we would be fine," he yelled over the screech of metal on metal as the wing scraped across the top of a parked car. "Shut it down 100 percent. We'll find something to cover the craft." He opened the door and they all climbed down the emergency ladder.

Within moments, Kid and the general returned with a large gray tarp from a nearby construction site. They stacked a few paver blocks on each corner to hold it down.

Climbing under the tarp and back into the quiet craft, they all took a minute to catch their breath, regroup, and get their bearings.

"So what now?" Mel asked.

General Hyland had his fist against his chin and was deep in thought. "Well, they already took out Adele's house, although I still don't know how they found it. And we've eliminated one of their M3's. I had us park here because Adele's hiding spot under the island is close by. But we need a boat to access it, which I wouldn't even try in the dark. So let's stay put until daybreak, which should only be," he checked his watch, "around four hours from now. Try to get some rest, or even some sleep."

The general turned around and saw that Kid and Sara were holding each other in the backseat. He couldn't tell if they were dozing off.

"I can't sleep," Mel muttered. "After a dogfight and then a white-knuckle landing, my heart is still racing too much."

"I don't know if I can sleep either," the general said as he laid back and closed his eyes. But within moments, he was kneeling in front of his wife's tombstone in Georgia, and didn't know if it was a twilight recollection or a full-on dream.

General Hyland and the others all woke at the same time. Although the M3 was covered with a tarp, enough light filtered through to make it obvious that the sun had risen. "Wait here. I am going to check things out," the general said. He climbed down the ladder and stepped out from under the tarp. Looking around in every direction, he saw no sign of the enemy.

"Eric?" a voice called out from the direction of the Tyrrhenian Sea. He froze for a second, but it was a voice he knew. "Eric, it's me."

Stepping out from behind a stone wall, was Adele Carmelo. Her dark hair was tied back in a ponytail, but her eyes shone an unmistakable bright green. A wave of immense relief washed over him. He ran to her, and they embraced for a long minute. When they separated, he glanced over his shoulder to ensure that nobody had yet departed the M3, including Sara.

"How did you know we were here?" he asked.

"I didn't. I came up here because I saw a plume of smoke and I was going to check it out. But then I saw some craft covered by a tarp that wasn't in this parking lot yesterday. I was staying out of sight until I knew who was here. I almost fell off the steps when I saw you come out from under the tarp." She hugged him again. "When did you get here?"

"Late last night. And we wound up in a battle with the two M3's that were sent to take out any remaining survivors over here. We shot down one, but one is still out there."

Adele looked at the sky. "M3's? Sent over by whom?"

He hesitated. "The Utopia Project."

The air seemed to leave her lungs as life drained from her face. "I was afraid you were going to say that. So they survived all of the destruction?"

"Survived? They were the ones behind the destruction," he clarified.

She seemed stunned for a second, "But, how? With melted bodies everywhere someone would need access to..." She paused.

He nodded. "The lead elders were able to take control of the United States neutron beam weapon system long enough to unleash all of this upon the world."

He could see she was struggling to comprehend his words, and the implications, so he changed his focus. "And as far as the smoke, don't even bother making the trek. Let's just say that I'm glad you were hiding somewhere else because they leveled your house with missiles."

Adele put her hand on her forehead. "That's what I feared. And we almost went back to live there. The attack happened over two weeks ago, and I had started to doubt that you, or anyone, was ever going to come for us."

"Sorry it took so long, but it took me some time to get off of the ships, and then a lot happened after that," the general said. "I assume you were under the island when the destruction came?"

"Yes, it hit us in the wee hours of the morning. We didn't even see it happen."

"If you did, you would have been flash blind. How many people were you able to take with you?"

"Ten of us are hiding under the island."

"Ten?" He knew he sounded disappointed. "Is that everyone?"

"No, five more people, one family actually, are staying at the

Minerva Tower at Punta Campanella Point on the Sorrento Peninsula. They keep fires going all night on the roof over there. They think that someone will eventually spot it and save them. I have asked them a couple of times to join us under the island, but they won't leave the tower."

"And that is everyone?" the general asked. "That's a pretty small group."

"I know, but you said to only bring people I could 100 percent trust. Some people whom I *did* trust refused to believe it and wouldn't come."

"We need to gather the people you do have and head back to the United States. The other survivors are there, and we need to stick together. Since you don't have a large number of people, I think we can cram them all in our M3," he said as he pointed to the craft.

They turned to start walking. "There is nothing but death everywhere, so how did we survive under Anacapri?" she asked.

"I was able to save three small areas, including here…"

She stopped in her tracks. "Three small areas? How far did this destruction go, Eric?"

"Besides the Utopia Project members who survived?"

"Forget them."

He exhaled. "Not counting your people, we have a small group of survivors from an area in New Jersey and another group from an area in Vermont. Less than 20 of us in all."

"What?" She looked aghast and raised a hand to cover her mouth. Lowering her palm enough to speak, her words came out as a choked whisper. "Are you saying the rest of world was destroyed?"

His voice was equally somber. "Annihilated. Completely."

Adele burst into tears.

# CHAPTER 8

January 11, 2045
Wednesday, Early Morning (CET)
Island of Capri, Italy
**Sixteen days after the event**


A dele had never felt such despair and needed to get a hold of herself before she hyperventilated. She wiped at her eyes and for a minute took slow, measured breaths. "It was my project memo that escalated everything. Look at the destruction it caused," she muttered solemnly. "How?"

"Nothing, no document or piece of paper, should have ever pushed things to that point," General Hyland said, putting his arm around her. "I'm sorry, Adele. I'm sure you never expected your memo to cause that kind of upheaval."

"Not in a million years," she agreed. Given that it resulted in the destruction of the world, she resolved right then that she would never discuss the God-forsaken confidential memo ever again. But Eric would not leave it alone.

"Do you know how your memo was smuggled off the ships and got to that press reporter, Lily Black?" he asked.

"No, I really don't have any idea," Adele said firmly, trying to shut down the conversation. She regretted the next words as soon as they left her mouth, but after a hesitation she added, "…how it got to the press."

December 10, 2044
Saturday, Morning (CET)
Palermo, Italy
**_Sixteen days before the event_**

As the old-looking woman approached a post office in Palermo, the capital of the Italian island of Sicily, she paused and leaned on her wooden cane. Her fear had to be kept buried deep inside. She exhaled and forced herself to relax a notch as she adjusted her worn and mismatched clothes. Her calf muscles were aching and starting to tighten. Although she had only walked a short distance from the ferry terminal at the port, she was exhausted from lack of sleep and the non-stop scrambling over the past 24-hours. She had hoped to snooze on the 11-hour, overnight ferry ride from Naples, but her mind would not stop racing.

Facing the door of the post office, she stared at her own reflection in the glass. Adjusting a satchel as it hung on her shoulder, she pulled her hood tightly over her head to fend off the cool December breeze. She did not recognize herself as she peered at the brown contact lenses hiding her bright green eyes. A couple of her teeth were blacked out, and her cheek had two dark, prominent moles. She looked no less than 75 years old and found it a bit disconcerting that it took such minimal effort to make her 51-year-old body appear so much older. But Dr. Adele Carmelo, now _former_ lead psychologist for the Utopia Project, was satisfied that she was unrecognizable and that her plan was still on track.

She reached for the door handle and again paused, feeling uneasy, and even unsure. But the Utopia Project had to be exposed before its dark evolution became irreversible. The members of the governing body of the project were no longer focused on aiding society with reasonable controls effectuated through social conditioning. Now, they were intent on controlling the entire world by stripping people of everything that made them human. They had developed a fleet of automatons on the ships that were 100 percent under their control, and they planned to replicate such influence in many large countries around the world. The entire human race would be next. The damage to society would be irreparable and needed to be stopped now.

She made sure the hood was secure over her head and then adjusted her multiple layers of clothes. Leaning on her cane and resuming her old-woman persona, she pulled an envelope out of her satchel. Inside it was her incriminating, confidential memo to the Utopia Project Board of Elders. The document provided information regarding the extreme conditioning regimen on the ships in Greenland. It detailed the harm being done to the involuntary participants, who she characterized as tortured and abused prisoners.

After being exposed, she did not know how the Utopia Project leadership would respond. The aggregate power of the leadership was formidable and still growing, as military and civilian leaders from many countries continued to be added. What started as a cooperative multi-national project had become an entity all its own, independent of the countries supporting it. They were a serious force to be confronted. That is why the memo needed to be mailed from a place far enough from her official address in Capri, Italy, and why it needed to be mailed by someone who could not be identified as Elder-62, Dr. Adele Carmelo. Although it was her memo, its release could never be traced back to her.

Exhaling, she finally pulled open the door and hobbled up to the counter. She conversed in Italian with the young female clerk, trying to distract the woman and keep her from noticing who the envelope was addressed to. The clerk readily took the bait and hardly turned her eyes down after the old-looking woman inquired about the plethora of young, handsome men in the area. When the letter was dropped in a nearly-full bin, Adele stood taller to peek and was thankful that the envelope was upside down, hiding the addressee.

As the old-looking woman paid and tried to leave, the young clerk asked her why she had such an interest in young men and all but accused her of being perverted. Adele laughed and said she wished she was young and energetic enough for such a romp, but that it was her granddaughter who needed a suitor. The clerk did not seem to believe her.

A dark-skinned man, who appeared to be the clerk's supervisor, started sifting through the outgoing mail and held up Adele's letter. His lips were hidden by a thick, black mustache as he snapped, "Look!"

Adele froze.

The supervisor, 'Antonio,' according to his name tag, turned toward the counter. His eyes passed slowly over the old-looking woman and stopped on a young man at the next counter station. Antonio pointed to the top of the envelope, showing how much space needed to be left to affix postage for mail going to the United States.

The young man nodded and hurried away. The supervisor turned to the young clerk and pointed to a word on Adele's envelope. He smiled while saying, "Like my new sister-in-law."

The clerk started laughing. "Come on now, Antonio. Just because she has pale skin."

"Pale? She's as *white* as a ghost," he said as he threw the envelope in the bin and walked away.

The old-looking woman waved to the clerk and hobbled out the door. *Phew…* The deed was done.

As she slowly strolled up the street, she secured her hood over her wig. She felt as old and tired as she must have looked. The ferry did not return to Naples for several hours so she walked until she found a quiet bench in a park. She curled up and tried to sleep, but unfortunately her mind was still racing as it replayed the events of the prior 24-hours.

Her entire plan had hinged on her being able to smuggle a copy of her memo off of Utopia Project Ship Number One. That would be no small feat. The search procedures when departing the ships were thorough and screeners had the capability to find something as small as a pinhead stashed on a person. The search of electronic devices, including computers and mobile phones, was even more precise, and they could sniff out unauthorized data that was hidden in a block of storage one-one thousandth the size of a pinhead. She knew by reviewing the schedule that Elder-152, a United States Navy officer, would be manning the security checkpoint all day Friday, December 9, 2044. She also knew, and it was critical to her plan, that Elder-152 did not have a strong stomach.

After arriving yesterday morning for what she knew would be her last day of work ever in the Utopia Project, she was properly flagged by the screener for having a tampon inside of her. As per protocol, she was taken to the search area and required to pull the tampon out for inspection. Elder-152 seemed to be enjoying the show at first, but he cringed when she grabbed the string, pulled the tampon out and laid it on the table. Even though the tube was not blood-soaked, he seemed reluctant to touch it. He finally put on rubber gloves and used two pens to poke and prod. With a grimace on his face, the elder advised her she was clear and quickly threw the two pens in the garbage.

"We have more tampons in our room. We will insert a new one when we get there. This one can be discarded," Adele said and started walking out.

He stopped her. "Do not leave that there. Put it in the garbage."

She showed no reaction but was inwardly pleased at his squeamishness.

His voice then conveyed his disgust. "Have you no sense of decency?"

She almost responded but bit her tongue. The gall of this jerk to say anything about *decency* when women had to suffer through the humiliation of removing their tampons for inspection? If she was not working on a plan, she would have surely lashed out, but instead she grabbed the string and threw the used tube in the garbage.

As she knew would be the case, Elder-152 was still working the same security checkpoint at the end of the day. He again required her to show her tampon, but when she pulled the string, she uttered, "Oh, God…" as a bright red tip emerged. A few drops of blood dripped on the floor. With his face turning white, and appearing even more aghast than he did that morning, he said, "Stop! That's far enough. You are clear." As he turned away and left the room, he called back, "Clean up your mess!"

Pushing the tampon fully back in, Adele was relieved that he did not make her remove it for closer inspection since this one contained a tube with a tightly folded and rolled copy of her memo. Despite the bloodied tip, she was not bleeding, at least not down there. She had pricked her finger and used the blood to soak the end of the tube before gently inserting it. When she pulled it out for Elder-152, a quick squeeze of the engorged end was all it took for the blood to start dripping.

Having successfully smuggled out a copy of her memo, she wasted no time in carefully ironing the paper to eliminate the creases. She then made a good copy, put it in an envelope, and neatly addressed it with her left hand. After putting on her old-woman disguise, she had made it to the terminal in Naples in time to catch last night's ferry to Palermo.

Giving up on the nap idea, Adele sat upright on the bench and checked her watch. The time was barely moving. She wanted to sleep, and *needed* to sleep, but she was too worried that she would miss the 8:00 P.M. ferry back to Naples. If she missed the Saturday evening ferry, she would have to wait until Sunday night, which would be too late given the trip took eleven hours. She needed to be in hiding under the Island of Capri before early Monday morning when her resignation letter would be discovered on her desk on the ship.

She did not know how long she would have to stay in hiding under the island, but she was prepared to stick it out as long as she needed to.

January 11, 2045
Wednesday, Early Morning (CET)
Island of Capri, Italy
**Sixteen days after the event**

The pause in Adele's words caught General Hyland's attention. *No, I really don't have any idea…how it got to the press.* He realized that she covered the second part of his question, but not the first: how her memo was smuggled off of the ships. He was about to inquire when Sara's voice cut in.

"Aunt Adele?"

General Hyland turned to see Sara, Kid, and Mel peeking out from under the tarp covering the M3.

Adele seemed relieved. The general did not know if it was because she saw Sara, or because she was happy to end the current conversation.

"Sara? Come here!" After sharing an embrace, Adele eased back. "Look at you! You are…a woman."

"And you are…a psychologist, who worked for the Utopia Project?"

After a slight hesitation Adele answered, "Yes, the lead psychologist actually. But I left the project several weeks ago."

Sara smiled and then turned to her father. "How is it I never knew any of this?" Her tone conveyed surprise, with an undertone of displeasure.

The general knew there would have to be an explanation at some point, but now was not the time. "Listen, we'll go over all of that later." He waved Kid and Mel over and introduced them to Adele.

"Now that we've found the group of survivors over here, can we get them in and get back to America?" Mel asked.

"That is the idea, but with an enemy M3 still out there, we need to figure out the best way to do that," the general said. "They have to gather their necessary belongings, and we have to get them up here unseen…"

"Everyone stay where you are!" Adele snapped. "Don't move a muscle!"

# CHAPTER 9

The group stood motionless as the remaining enemy M3 passed slowly overhead. Despite the tarp being held down by paver blocks, Kid watched as one side came loose and was blown in the air by the thrusters of the low flying craft. *You should have used more weight to hold it down!* he reprimanded himself.

"Did they see us?" Sara asked.

As if hearing her question, the enemy M3 stopped over the blue water and made a 180 degree turn.

Kid felt a spike of fear. The tarp had blown almost completely off their craft.

"They're coming back!" the general snapped.

"Follow me down to the water. Quickly. Be careful going down the steps." Adele stepped through an opening and disappeared behind a stone wall.

Rather than follow, Mel ran to the now-exposed M3.

"Come on Mel! Leave the plane!" Kid yelled as he stopped.

"We can't! Go!" Mel started climbing into the craft.

The general came back and waved her down. "Mel!"

"Sorry Mr. Hyland, but this aircraft is our ride back, and my ride back to my girls. If they take it or destroy it, we're screwed!"

"Alright, alright, but listen to me." He seemed resigned to the fact that she was not leaving the craft. "Take off and lose them, then hide somewhere to save fuel. Rendezvous with us right at this exact spot at 10:00 P.M. Italy time."

"Got it. Until then, be safe," she said and closed the door to the craft.

"Come on Kid, hurry," the general said as he went around the corner of the stone wall.

Kid stopped at the top of steps, which appeared to descend all the way down to the Tyrrhenian Sea. He turned as Mel engaged the M3's thrusters. From the cockpit's side window she waved Kid away. He was torn. He did not want to leave her alone, but the enemy M3 had stopped and was now eerily still as it hovered in front of Mel. A cold shiver went down his spine when he realized why. He waved at Mel, who must have come to the same conclusion because she lifted off in a hurry. To Kid's dismay, his fear was confirmed as the enemy craft fired a missile.

"Kid!" Sara screamed from the stairwell.

He took a small step back, but watched as Mel, in a mad rush to lift off, smacked the tip of her wing against the ground. She punched the thrusters and was heading straight for the restaurant. The craft gained some altitude, but not enough as the underside of the wing bounced off the roof of the building. The craft was bobbling, and she seemed to overcompensate. Kid gasped as the M3 rolled on its back, plummeted over the side of the island, and disappeared from view. The missile narrowly missed her craft and slammed into the roof of the restaurant.

Kid's senses issued a stern warning. *Duck!* He scrambled behind the stone wall and down a few steps. Sara was right there, so he pulled her down and covered her head.

The fireball that erupted over the restaurant was far enough away that Kid was not injured, but a wave of heat rolled over him and his ears were ringing. It was as if he had A-note tuning forks inside of his ear canals and someone had given them a firm tap. As the ringing subsided, he heard the general's voice calling up to them.

Kid looked up, deathly afraid of seeing a second fireball from Mel's diving craft. Instead, he spotted a fast-moving object gliding along the surface of the Tyrrhenian Sea. He could not believe his eyes. It was Mel, flying with the cockpit only a few feet above the water, but the M3 was upside down! One false move with the controls and she would dive into the sea. He was relieved to see her gradually gaining altitude before righting the craft and turning east toward the mainland.

Sara put her hand over her heart. "That was close. Too close."

Taking Sara's face in his hands, Kid asked, "Are you alright?"

"My ears are ringing, but I am fine. Come on," she said as she took his hand and headed down the stone steps. General Hyland and Adele were waiting in an inflatable raft and started paddling as soon as Kid and Sara jumped aboard.

Kid looked to the sky to see if they were in danger. All was clear, so he figured the M3 must have gone after Mel.

Adele steered them toward a rock wall.

"Where are we going?" Kid asked.

"We're here," she answered.

"Alright, but where is here?"

"See the nook?" She pointed to an inverted v-shaped opening. "That is the entrance to the sea cave."

"How are we supposed to fit through that?" Sara blurted out. Kid was thinking the same thing.

"It will be tight. When the tide is too high or choppy, you can't get through the opening unless you swim under water. Given the temperature, getting in the water is not a viable option. Duck," Adele said as she grabbed a guide chain affixed to the rock wall and pulled. Halfway through, the raft became wedged against both sides of the opening. They were stuck fast.

Kid could see that the tide was already too elevated for the raft to fit through the crevasse.

"The only way to do this is to swim, or if we all push against the roof of the opening and get the raft lower in the water, we might scrape through," Adele said. "Kid, lay back and pull the chain with all you've got!"

Adele and General Hyland pushed against the rocks above their head until the sides of the raft were only a couple of inches above the waterline, Kid grabbed the chain and pulled. He was able to drag them further through the opening, but they were more tightly wedged and the rolling tide was cresting over the back of the raft, dumping buckets of water inside.

The general grabbed the front of the guide chain and heaved with Kid. As the raft inched and scraped its way through, Kid and Sara had to lay flat in the rising pool of water.

"Push down against the arch over your head. We need just a little more clearance!" the general called out.

Kid extended his arms and exerted until the raft was lower in the water, but they were within an inch of being swamped. He glanced back and froze. "M3 behind us!" The aircraft was descending, and he could see multiple people. "And it's not Mel!"

For a split second Kid saw someone waving hands, and although he could not see the face, it appeared to be a hostile woman. With the craft perfectly aimed his way, he could see that all four missile tubes were empty. Spent. But a panic surged through him when he remembered the M3's dual machine guns.

"Mr. Hyland, pull!"

• • •

From the window of the hovering M3, Heidi spotted Sara in the back of the raft. "There she is!" She turned to the gunner. "See the girl in the back? Blast her! But do not aim for the guy next to her. We need him alive!"

The elder in the front seat turned as if to question her.

"Elder-3's orders!" she snapped and then yelled to the gunner, "Fire!"

She was lying, but the elder paused long enough for the machine gun to come to life.

• • •

Bullets strafed the rock face and the back of the raft, so Kid pushed as hard as he could against the rough, rocky arch above his head. Like a tidal surge breaching the top of a dam, water began pouring in over the submerged rear and sides of the raft as the general heaved and pulled them through the tight opening. Kid draped himself over Sara to protect her.

Now through the crevasse in the rock wall, Adele guided the raft to the side and out of harm's way. The machine gun fire ceased.

General Hyland turned quickly. "Are either of you hit?" The cave applied reverb to his voice, even at low volume.

"I'm fine, but Kid's arm was hit!" Sara called out.

Kid looked down to see that his upper coat sleeve was torn and the gray fabric was dark red. He never even felt a shot hit him.

"How bad?"

"Not bad," Kid responded. "I think it was just grazed."

Adele and the general started bailing out water with their hands, so Kid and Sara followed suit. Finally, Adele said, "That's enough. We're stable."

Kid sat and leaned back for a moment to catch his breath. The grotto was silent, save for the occasional echo of dripping water and the tide lapping at the walls of the cave.

"We got in here just in time. And we are lucky the tide is rising so they can't follow us in," Adele stated. "And by the time they can, we will have disappeared."

The general said, "We just need to stay safe until 10:00 P.M. tonight, when Mel comes back for us."

"Assuming they haven't shot her down," Adele noted.

"They better not," Sara said as she helped Kid take his coat off so she could check his wound.

A small chunk of meat, less than an inch long, had been blasted from his shoulder. As Adele also took a look, she said, "That is heavy ammo they were firing, but fortunately you were barely nicked. It is superficial. We have medical supplies where we are going so we can dress that." Pulling a handkerchief from her pocket, she balled it up and said, "Don't worry, this is clean. The bleeding is already slowing, but use this and keep pressure on it."

"Thanks," Kid said. "Not that I'm in any position to be picky."

Adele stood up and the floor of the raft was soft and spongy. "We're losing air. They must've hit the raft too. Eric, we have to get to the back of the cave."

Without hesitation, the general and Adele began rowing in earnest.

Now more than halfway across the underwater pool, Sara exclaimed, "Wow. Look at that."

Kid glanced up and saw that her eyes were fixed on the water. When he turned his head, he understood why. "What is this place?" His voice was barely a whisper.

With the morning sun, the color of the water inside the cave was mesmerizing. It was as if a huge neon blue sign was lit at the bottom of the pool.

"The Blue Grotto," Adele stated as she paddled. "You should see it in the afternoon. That is when the blue is at its most brilliant."

Sara stared and seemed spellbound. "How is the water so blue? It almost looks artificial."

"It has to do with the way the light comes through an underwater cavity and the small opening where we came in," Adele answered.

Checking out the cave, Kid saw a couple of nooks, but otherwise, there appeared to be no way out. "Can I ask where are we going? It seems like we're trapped."

"It does appear that way, but we're not. Only a handful of locals know of the rooms under here. See the dark back corner that looks like a dead end?" Adele responded.

Kid nodded. It sure seemed to be a dead end.

"Some ingenious Roman engineers and stone workers created a hidden door in the wall, Adele continued. "It's made of stone and perfectly blends into the surroundings. There is a multi-step lever system that allows the door to open. It still works 2,000 years later."

They approached the turn into the dark corner as she kept explaining. "Without knowing the secret way to unlock it, forget trying to move the stone door by hand, or even with machinery. A bulldozer couldn't move it."

As the raft began to turn the corner, Kid glanced down and could see that within moments water would begin to spill into the deflating raft. "We are barely treading water," he said as they made the turn and headed into the darkest corner of the cave.

"Almost there." Adele switched on a flashlight and scanned the wall head high. She climbed onto a narrow rock outcropping and ran her fingers over a cluster of jagged protrusions, stopping when she touched the right one. Turning the jagged, baseball-sized knob counterclockwise, a muffled but audible click sounded. "One down." She jumped back into the deflating raft.

Rowing the raft backwards and away from the dark corner, they pulled up against the wall. "Hold the raft in place," Adele said. As Eric reached over and grabbed onto a rock formation, she stood and put her hand into the blackness of a crevasse in the wall. Her arm was swallowed almost to her shoulder. A second click could be heard, and she jumped back in the raft.

They rowed again toward the dark dead end. Adele climbed onto another rock outcropping. Finding a particular flat rock, she placed her foot on it and pushed down hard as she extended her arms and leaned into the stone wall. There were cracks in many places on the wall, but Kid could not discern any obvious seams. He was stunned to see an irregularly shaped section of stone, four-foot high and four-foot wide, push into the wall like a door swinging on a hinge.

Adele pointed. "It's only a couple foot gap, but that's as far as it goes."

"How did you know about those hidden latches, and this entrance in the cave wall?" Sara asked as she climbed onto the rock ledge.

"It is a secret known only by a small, and I mean small, group of people. The knowledge has been passed from generation to generation."

As Kid went to stand, water started pouring in, further swamping the raft. When he stepped with his drenched shoes onto the rock ledge, Adele reached down and opened an air-release valve on the side of the raft. She waited a minute and pulled it out of the water, squeezing out the air all the while. "Luckily, we have two more of these down here."

The general turned to her. "Why didn't you just use a small boat instead of rafts?"

"Remember, I was here before all of the destruction. I couldn't leave a boat in the corner of the grotto out in the open. We needed to cover our tracks every time we came in here," she said as she carried the rolled up raft through the entrance in the wall. "Follow me, and watch your heads."

They all had to crouch as they followed Adele through the opening in the wall. She pushed the door closed behind them and turned on her flashlight. The light revealed heavy metal hinges attached to the back of the rock door. "Just need to reset the locking mechanisms," she said as she forcefully pushed three levers. Each one made a loud metallic click when reset. She then picked up the raft and walked forward. General Hyland followed her.

Kid went to take a step and stopped. "Great. Another tunnel." He fought the distress rising within him after nearly being buried alive and then almost drowning behind RPH in New Jersey. He sniffed his sleeve and turned to Sara behind him. "I can still smell the cedar water from the last one."

"Let's just hope this one holds up better than that one," Sara said.

He looked at her. Neither one of them cracked a smile.

# CHAPTER 10

After walking for several feet Kid was relieved to be able to stand upright as the tunnel became progressively taller and wider. They walked for several minutes until they were deep under the island. Wall sconces were placed along the way, and he assumed they once held candles.

Adele stopped and called out, "It's just Adele, with friendly company!" She turned and said, "Wait here just a second." She threw the raft to the side, pulled out a lighter, and went ahead. Walking around a room, she lit four candles, each shoulder-high in ornate wall sconces.

In the somber glow, Kid could see Adele was standing in a large circular room. He turned off his flashlight and let his eyes adjust to the dim light. Behind her were two wall alcoves with bronze statues. "Look at those," he muttered as he pointed.

Adele turned around. "Oh, meet Neptune and Triton."

Casing out the rest of the space, Kid counted four adjoining rooms off of the main circular room. Two of the dark rooms came to life as battery-powered lanterns were turned on. He stepped closer and saw that in those two rooms Adele's group had cots and sleeping bags laid out in every direction. As introductions were made, Kid realized that besides Adele there were only four women, two men, two male children, and one female child. Of the four women, two of them were over 60 years old. That would not bode well for the reproduction efforts of their small group.

A white-haired older woman, who Kid had pegged to be in her mid-sixties, put down a broom and offered her hand. "I'm Estelle Severino. It is so great to see you. All of you. I knew the Lord would answer our prayers."

Kid almost slipped and told her that if he was all the Lord could give her, she would have to consider her prayer request mostly still on back order. Not knowing this woman, and not wanting to offend, he shook her hand and said, "It is great to meet you as well."

"These are my sons, Tony and Emilio," she added. Kid shook hands with the two men. Both appeared to be in their thirties.

Adele walked up and said, "Estelle's family tree extends back a long time on this island and the Sorrento Peninsula. I have known the Severino family my entire life."

"Yes, you have," Estelle acknowledged. "You are family to us."

"It was Estelle who told me several years ago about the secret chambers down here," Adele added.

"My family has been helping maintain this secret entrance for centuries." Glancing at Kid's upper arm, Estelle put her hand over her mouth. "You're bleeding."

"It's just a scratch," Kid said.

"I have medical supplies to take care of that. Please, take your coat off."

Kid nodded and carefully removed his damp, blood-soaked coat. Looking up, he noticed that the main room had four tubes in the ceiling that he assumed connected to the outside to provide fresh air. Adele saw him peering up and noted that only two of the four were still functioning, and just barely. The other two were clogged, blocked or broken somewhere along the line.

After Estelle bandaged the wound near Kid's shoulder, he thanked her and walked around the circular room. Finally he asked, "What is in the two rooms you aren't using?"

"Roman time-capsules," Adele said. "Go see for yourself."

Walking to the doorway of the first room, Kid turned on his flashlight and was stunned. The room contained an ornate metal bed frame with no mattress. Gold chalices, only slightly discolored, stood prominently on a fancy metal table next to the bed.

Adele answered his unspoken question. "All original, a couple of thousand years old. Tarnished, but still intact."

"Amazing. This room really is like a time-capsule," Kid uttered, wondering how the Romans were able to get the furniture down here. He suspected it was brought down in pieces, and then assembled in place. In the next room was a large, decorative rectangular table, which was also made of metal but had a thick glass top. Food items secured by Adele's group were stacked at the far end, and the table was surrounded by eight chairs. The back of the over-sized armchair at the head of the table contained a dramatic and stunning design that had Kid spellbound, until he was interrupted by his bladder.

Kid turned to Adele. "I hate to ask, but where do you go to the bathroom?"

She let out a quick chuckle. "You realize pretty quick how much you rely on modern conveniences when you're living down here. Back in the tunnel where we came in, where it starts to get wider, there is an alcove down low. Under a large, flat stone, there is a deep hole which is the latrine."

Clearing his throat, Kid said, "I should…check it out."

"I'm surprised it took this long," Sara jabbed.

Kid, having finished his business, walked back up the tunnel as the general asked, "This is an unbelievable hiding place, but is there an exit other than going back through the Blue Grotto?"

"Over here." Approaching the statue of Neptune, which sat snugly in an alcove, Adele lifted the statue's bronze trident. The thick shaft ground coarsely through the grip of the statue's fingers until it had been raised six inches. "They loved their little secret latches," she said.

She then pushed the torso of Neptune. The statue and the rounded wall of the alcove slid back into a compartment, opening a seam a couple of feet wide. Adele pointed into the space. "We haven't fully explored this corridor yet and haven't really needed to, but I assume it was an escape route that led to some point on the surface."

Kid used a flashlight to inspect the dark space. "Even if it was, any escape routes that old may be collapsed by now." He was thinking of the compromised tunnel behind RPH in New Jersey. That tunnel was in its infancy compared to anything down here. Taking slow and deliberate steps into the opening, Kid shined his light in every direction. A metal plate stuck out of the floor. "What is that for?" He bent down and brushed the dirt and dust from the surface.

Adele peeked her head in. "When the statue is back in place, hitting that foot lever raises the trident and allows a person to pull open the alcove wall section from the back, assuming it is not locked."

"How do you lock it?"

"If you twist the trident a half turn, it can no longer be raised when the foot lever is pressed."

"They really thought these things through," Kid added as he started walking. "I'll be right back. Let me case it out and see how far I can get."

"Be careful Kid. No telling what is back there," Sara said.

He nodded and continued into a narrow passageway with cobwebs galore. He felt like he was in a classic Indiana Jones movie. It was much more unnerving being in a dingy, untouched tunnel than seeing one on a screen from the often touched couch in his house. Ahead of him, a set of stone steps ascended sharply. "Adele, can you ask Ms. Severino if I can borrow her broom?"

Handing it in, Adele said, "Don't lose it. She would be lost without it."

Using the broom to clear the webs in front of him, Kid started climbing the stairs. The tunnel was almost six-feet high but narrow enough that if he stood square, both shoulders would have touched the walls on either side of him. He focused on breathing slow and easy. The space was suffocating and not just for the claustrophobic but for anyone requiring oxygen to breathe. Tight spaces had never bothered Kid before, but at the moment his heart was uncomfortably racing. *Is it the confined space or the fear of not knowing what is ahead?* Probably some of both.

After climbing for several minutes, he reached a landing, which had steps going in two different directions. His best guess, based on the cardinal direction he thought he was heading in, was that if he took the stairwell to the left he would be heading toward the Gulf of Naples on the northern side of the island. It probably led to an exit at the water in case the escape was by sea. That would probably not be of any help at the moment, so he decided to try the other stairwell.

As he turned right and started up, he stepped through dried mud, a tell-tale sign that an exit ahead had been compromised. Some kind of vermin, possibly a rat, scurried up ahead. *Follow him*, he thought. *He will lead you out of here.* He slowed as he shined the light in front of his feet. The tunnel was noticeably wetter, and the steps were getting slippery. Crouching further, he spotted a mass blocking the path in front of him. For a second, the shape looked like a hibernating bear. That would be a big problem. He talked himself down when he realized that it was unlikely that there were bears on this island. Nearing the blockage, he could see it was just a massive collage of spider webs and vegetation. As he poked at it with the broom handle, he jumped back as a horde of rats burst out and ran in every direction. He willed himself to stand still while several ran over and past his feet. Others headed upward. He knew he had to be close to the surface.

He swiped at the spider webs, which were not vacant like the ones he had encountered upon first entering the tunnel behind the alcove. Clearing a thicker web, he saw that there were spiders everywhere. Large ones and small ones, all with beady eyes. Many dozens of legs started churning at once, spooked by the first human disruption they had probably ever experienced. Arachnids scurried and unlike the rats, if one reached his foot he stepped on it. He didn't know if they were poisonous. A couple of spiders took divergent paths to where he could not follow both with the light. Instinctively, he shined the light over his head, fearing that a huge spider would be dangling there, waiting to drop on him.

Pushing the webs and vegetation against the side of the tunnel and squeezing past, he identified a small rectangle opening overhead. One corner had eroded enough that he could see a small hole, which the rats and spiders were using as an exit. Squeezing the flashlight between his legs, he held the wood broom handle with both hands and tried to push up the rectangular cover. It barely moved. The cover was made of stone and was heavy, but he feared it was stuck. There was no telling what had grown or been built over the exit in the last 2,000 years.

"Kid?" he heard faintly, as if in a dream. It sounded like General Hyland. He ran down the steps with the scurrying spiders. Following the stairwell, he turned the corner and stopped on the landing. "Mr. Hyland!" he yelled. He saw a light shining up in his direction, but it was far away. He didn't realize how high he had climbed. "Up here. This way."

"I came to check on you." The general came up the steps and spotted the fleeing spiders. "Seems you already have company. I hope you don't suffer from Arachnophobia."

Kid led him past the wad of webs and vegetation and pointed up at the small rectangle opening.

The general stopped. "It sure looks like an exit." He shined a light while Kid tried to move the cover.

While pushing with the broom handle, Kid said, "Something is keeping the cover from lifting, and it is more than just its own weight."

"Try each corner," the general recommended.

The advice proved helpful as one corner lifted up. "I'm going to try and push it to the side. Keep your head up in case it slips down into the opening, or breaks and falls on us."

Kid struggled with the stone cover until he was able to move it a couple of feet to the side. A rush of air sucked through the hole. The opening was tight, but he wormed through. He found himself in the middle of a dense patch of mature trees with the sun peeking through where it could. Kid breathed in the fresh air, unaware of how badly he needed it. He noticed that the area was covered in stones, large and small, allowing the lid to blend in with the natural surroundings. Kid bent down and wrestled the stone cover from under a tree root. It left an opening large enough for one person to climb through without much difficulty.

The general climbed out and glanced around. "I have my bearings. We just need to get back to the restaurant by 10:00 P.M. so Mel can pick us up. It is over that way," he pointed, "but I can't tell how far. I can't see beyond these trees."

Kid and the general climbed back down through the opening and left the cover off. They hoped the fresh air might make its way down below. They retraced their steps and finally made it back to the chambers where the group was waiting.

Adele held her arms up and took a deep breath. "Fresh air! I guess you guys reached the outside world."

Squeezing past the statue, Kid could feel a breeze coming into the room with him. The two functioning air pipes in the chamber were drawing it in and spitting it out somewhere on the surface, creating circulation.

"It's getting cold, but let's leave the opening alone for a few minutes," Adele said as she took another deep breath.

For the next ten minutes, Kid and the general summarized their tunnel exploration findings. Finally, Adele pulled the statue back into place and rotated the head of the trident so that the secret entrance was locked.

Kid grabbed a can of beans and took a seat next to Sara on the ground in the circular main room. As soon as his rear end hit the ground, he groaned from exhaustion. Across from him against the opposing wall sat Adele and General Hyland. Kid stuck a spoon into the can. "So Adele, who would go to these lengths to create such a secure hideaway?"

Sara cut in, "Since she mentioned Roman engineers who were on this island a couple thousand years ago, my guess would be a Roman emperor named…Tiberious?"

Adele nodded. "Despite looking drained, you do remember your history. Tiberious wasn't too thrilled with the political scene in Rome, and he was paranoid that he would be assassinated like Julius Caesar, so he took residence on this island and ruled the Roman Empire from here. The Blue Grotto out there was his personal swimming hole, fully decorated with statutes of Neptune and Triton like these." She pointed to the two statues in the alcoves. "And do you think a Roman Emperor, paranoid enough to exile himself to an island, would have a personal swimming area with only one way in or out?"

The general, while eating a cold can of soup, peered over and raised his eyebrows. Kid could only nod, recalling the general's life-saving advice back on Mallard Island in New Jersey about never holing up in a place with only one exit.

"Was his residence here as grandiose as his pool?" Kid asked. At that moment he realized just how green Adele's eyes were. They almost glowed.

"He had a palace, if that answers your question," Adele said. "Villa Jovis, on the northeastern side of the island. Most of it is gone now, but the place overlooked a 1,000-foot sheer rock wall, off of which many a poor soul, young and old, were tossed to their gruesome deaths from around 27 A.D until Tiberious's death in 37 A.D."

"Wait a minute, given that time frame …" Kid started, but nearly choked when he made the connection. "Tiberious was Emperor of the Roman Empire while Jesus of Nazareth was being crucified outside of Jerusalem!"

"You know your history too," Adele commented.

Kid offered a smug smile to Sara. He was playing it up, knowing full-well that she was much more versed in history than he was. But from his church days he knew that Jesus was said to be in his early thirties when he was crucified, so he knew the dates coincided. Sara smirked and patted his knee.

"For all we know Tiberious may have been frolicking right here in the Blue Grotto, or even in this very room, while Jesus was being nailed to the cross," Adele affirmed.

The room fell silent as everyone contemplated the heaviness of her words.

Several moments later, Adele turned to the general. "Some dots just connected in my mind. Do you know what I just realized?"

"What's that?"

"Who does Tiberious remind you of, in terms of behavior?" The general looked down, clearly pondering, but Adele couldn't wait. "You know them and saw them almost every day for the last twenty years."

"The elders," General Hyland answered.

"Yes! I don't mean every one, but many of the top ones exhibited the same egotistical, selfish, depraved, and narcissistic traits as Tiberious." offered Adele.

"And even the same paranoia," the general added.

"Exactly. They too were compromised by being too empowered and acting like people were nothing more than disposable pawns that existed only to serve them and their master plans," said Adele.

The general nodded in agreement. "They, like Tiberious, wanted to rule the entire world."

"And they all routinely abused people, even young people, for their own pleasures and purposes. They only difference being that Tiberious threw them over a cliff when he was done, whereas the elders just threw them back into the project, to be used again," Adele continued.

"I guess there is just something about human nature when someone feels empowered, and believes they have God-like status," Sara chimed in. "And that is why history repeats itself, over and over again."

Adele opened her mouth to respond and paused. She gave an appreciative nod. "I could not have said it better myself."

General Hyland added, "Me neither. Well said, Sara."

Finally, the group finished eating and after gathering only essential belongings like medications, prescription glasses, and warm clothes, the group resolved to get some rest before leaving to meet Mel. Kid and Sara held each other while lying on a blanket, which did little to soften the hard ground. After sharing a quick kiss, they both tried to nap. Although it was barely 4:00 in the afternoon Central European Time, the last 24 hours had been harrowing to say the least. Kid knew they needed some rest because the hours ahead offered all the potential for more of the same.

# CHAPTER 11

January 11, 2045
Wednesday, Evening (CET)
Island of Capri, Italy
**Sixteen days after the event**

At 9:30 that evening, the entire group followed Kid into the tunnel behind the statue of Neptune. He made his way up the multiple stairwells until he reached the exit to the outside. After climbing out, he was pummeled by a breeze that was constant and cold, but not frigid like Kid was used to. Crouching down, he assisted everyone out one by one until the entire group was huddling next to a dense cluster of trees.

"Follow me." Adele led the way through the woods and the brush.

Nearing the restaurant above the Blue Grotto, they came upon the stone wall and the steps down to the waterline. The general whispered to the group, "Maintain silence and stay right here."

Turning to Kid, he said, "Come with me." The general unholstered his weapon and added, "Do not fire unless completely necessary. My weapon hardly makes a sound, so let me fire."

"At whom?" inquired Kid.

General Hyland pointed down at the water and raised his finger to his mouth to request silence. They crept down the stairs, maintaining a stealthy approach. From the dock at the water, they could see a boat guarding the sea cave exit. Two Utopia Project members, including one elder, sat in the bobbing craft.

The general slipped into a small rowboat and motioned for a quiet launch toward the cave. Kid pushed the rowboat as hard as he could without making a splashing sound. Lying low, the general drifted in the direction of the inverted v-shaped cave entrance. The tide got hold of the craft, and in the faint light of the moon Kid could see it was drifting in the wrong direction. The general must have also realized it and opened fire. Bright bolts soared just above the waterline.

The first Utopia Project member was hit and frozen in place. The elder stood and pulled out his weapon. Before he could locate a target, he was also hit. Kid could see the silhouette of the standing elder and as soon as a wave rocked the small boat, the elder's body tipped and went overboard. The elder was likely still alive when he hit the water and was now faced with the horror of his lungs filling with water and not being able to even close his mouth. Kid looked up upon hearing the splash of paddles as the general started rowing back to the dock.

At 9:45 P.M. Kid and the entire group were waiting by the restaurant, which was still smoldering from the missile strike earlier. They were hidden behind a row of bushes. As 10:00 P.M. came, Kid started to worry. Maybe Mel could not escape the enemy M3. A muted hum with ever-increasing pitch made him glance first to the sky and then down to the water. An M3, which had been hovering just above the surface of the water, rose ominously and came into view. Were he not 100 percent focused and alert, and were it not for the moonlight, he never would have spotted the craft as it was flying in lights-out mode. The craft started creeping toward the parking lot. If it was Mel, she now seemed to have much better control of the M3 than earlier in the day. A lump came to Kid's throat as he contemplated what to do if it was not Mel.

The M3 landed in the parking lot, and all pulled out their weapons. Kid shined a flashlight on the windshield. Mel waved and then frantically motioned for him to kill the light. She opened the side door as General Hyland came over and released the step-ladder.

"Hurry! Get in," Mel said with urgency.

"I can't tell you how happy we are to see you." Sara gently touched Mel's arm. "Where did you go?"

"Greece! Took a nice long nap. Let's get everyone in and quickly." She saw a swarm of people approach. "If we can fit them all!"

Mel turned to Kid, who was crouched between her and General Hyland in the front seats. "You seemed like an ace with that missile system, so get ready. If they didn't spot me, we have a small window where we might be able to take out that other M3."

"How so?" the general cut in.

"I was flying low. In the moonlight I spotted their M3 parked on the peninsula across the water."

"Where were they on the peninsula?" Adele asked as she boarded.

"I don't know the area, but it was parked next to a square block structure at the tip of the land mass where it meets the sea. The structure looked ancient."

"Oh, no. That's the tower."

"Tower?" Kid asked as he turned on the missile system screen.

While helping Estelle into the back of the M3, Adele clarified, "It's called the Minerva Tower, over at the ruins of the temple to Athena and then Minerva. It sits at one of the points where in Greek mythology a siren sang a mesmerizing song to try and lure Ulysses into the rocks." With Estelle now seated, Adele turned. "But listen, a family of five was staying there."

"If the Utopia Project members are at the tower, then the family over there is dead," the general said bluntly. "Mel, what is your plan?"

"I thought we could catch them off guard. I was going to speed there so Kid could take out the M3 with a missile before they even realize what is going on."

"We need to hurry if we are going to give it shot," he concluded. "You were able to spot them, so presumably, they could have spotted you."

With the screen on and the joystick controller in his hand, Kid said, "System is live and ready. Is everyone in?"

"Yes," Sara answered. "We almost needed a shoehorn, but we got the door to close."

• • •

Elder-85 asked Heidi a question and pointed. She froze and tried not to throw up.

She was distraught beyond words and needed to be alone. Luckily, the family that had been staying in the tower went to the trouble of bringing an extended ladder to get on the roof, so they could light signal-fires that nobody would ever see. She walked across the stone tower's large open room and started climbing the tall ladder. Emerging through the opening in the roof, she dropped her feet onto the hard, uneven stone.

She panted as she took a few steps, avoiding a fire pit full of half-burned logs. She walked around a large puddle and stopped to stare up at the open sky. The half-moon seemed to be mocking her by providing enough light that when she looked down, she could clearly see the blood stain on her pant leg that the elder had just pointed out. Was it her blood, or someone else's? Tears welled and burned her eyes as she unzipped her uniform, pulled her arms out and pushed the garment down below her knees. The frigid air highlighted a wetness below, so she stretched the waist band of her underwear away from her body. She needed to look, but hesitated. *I need to see white. Please, nothing but white.* Finally turning her eyes down, she saw fresh, dark blood. Clenching her teeth and starting to scream, she twisted the underwear in her hands. Her tender vagina was aflame, but she didn't care. She let out a bellow and ripped with all of her might. Her underwear tore and pulled free. Blood splattered her body, including her face. Whipping the foul undergarments, she dropped to her knees and bawled uncontrollably. Tears and blood burst from her body with every convulsive heave.

It was over. Her last hope that she was carrying her and Kid's child bled out of her and dripped on the hard, stone roof. Despite her trying to will her period away, it had arrived and was gushing like never before.

With her greatest fears now realized, she had nothing left to live for. She could never be Kid's. She could never be the Eve of the new world. Her life was ruined, and she should just end it now. Gazing straight ahead, she could dive headfirst off of the tower. The edge of the roof beckoned to her. But her death would bring them all joy and satisfaction. No, it could not end that way. Her anger swelled, and she felt an uncontrollable thirst for vengeance. It was a sudden desperate need that could only be sated with the suffering and pain of others. But not just anyone. Two people in particular.

Heidi rose to her feet, grabbed her dirty uniform, and put it back on. She turned her eyes to the sky and sneered at the half-moon. She was not consciously doing it but caught herself humming long, melodic notes.

Yes, two people in particular.

Sara and Kid.

• • •

A chill went down Kid's spine, and he rubbed his hands together. "Let's get over there and do this."

"Ready for takeoff." Mel engaged the thrusters. "And don't worry about how low I will be flying. I didn't mean to, but when I was escaping I got a lot of practice."

"How is the fuel level?" the general asked.

"Between a quarter and a half. Is that enough?"

"Usually it would be, but…" he glanced back at the passengers crammed into the craft, "…we are fully loaded, so I am not sure. It will be close. We can't waste any time."

Mel lifted off the ground. Although the craft wobbled a bit, she quickly leveled off. She swooped low to the water, took a wide turn, and rocketed toward the Minerva Tower. "Straight ahead Kid," she called out.

"I can't see it on the screen yet. It's still too dark and nothing shows on the infrared." He felt helpless as he saw only different shades of darkness on the monitor. It was a collage of black and blacker smudges.

"Get it locked. They will be able to hear us coming any second!" General Hyland warned.

"I still can't see anything on the screen. Do we have a spotlight?"

Mel and the general looked at each other. They seemed uncomfortable giving away the element of surprise.

The general relented. "If we turn on the lights, you have to fire quickly Kid and hit the mark. Otherwise, they will be in the air in seconds."

"Go for it. I'm ready." Kid's eyes were fixed on the screen.

General Hyland took control of the spotlight. "Here we go. Kid, are you ready?"

"Ready."

"Now!"

A beam of light shot out from the front of the craft. Mel turned toward the peninsula as the general adjusted the beam. The second the enemy M3 was in the light, Kid yelled, "Locked!"

"Don't fire yet! Hold!" the general barked and held up a hand. "Hold…"

Kid could see the Utopia Project members scrambling from the tower structure and piling into their M3.

Mel said, "We're going to lose them!"

"Hold!" the general repeated loudly and paused for what felt like an eternity. "Now! Hit it!"

Depressing the red button on the joystick, Kid yelled, "Missile away!"

Mel banked up and to the west. She then turned the craft so that they could see the outcome. The missile found its mark, and the enemy M3 exploded. The Utopia Project members in and around the craft were obliterated, but the tower withstood the blast.

The Italian occupants sitting behind Kid all gasped. Estelle let out a high-pitched shriek and screamed, "Oh Lord!" as a ball of flames rolled skyward.

Out the window, Kid watched as the flames illuminated someone standing on the roof of the tower with hands outstretched, like the ghost the evil siren who tried to lure Ulysses.

Sara was sitting next to him with her head turned away from the blast. She uttered, "No."

The sound of her word was guttural, as if carried by a breath emanating from somewhere deep in her soul. It was like she knew someone was out there, but she had not even looked out the window. Only then did Sara lean over him to get a view. She sharply inhaled and put her hand over her mouth.

As his eyes adjusted and the scene came into focus, Kid's heart sank. By the light of the flaming wreckage of the M3, he could see the person standing on the tower. He turned to Sara. "How did you…" But the words got stuck in his throat.

"I don't know," she answered, seeming perplexed and uneasy. "Somehow, I just…felt her."

Standing on the roof of the Minerva Tower, awash in the unnatural orange glow, was Heidi Leer.

The last time Kid had seen Heidi, he was jumping in front of a weapon shot that nearly ended his life; a shot that was meant to end his soul-mate's life. Anger swelled in an instant. It was then that he realized that it wasn't the last time he had seen her. She must've been the hostile woman in the enemy M3 that tried to gun him and Sara down when they were stuck in the entrance to the Blue Grotto. At that moment, it became crystal clear. Heidi would not rest until she had exacted her revenge on Sara and him. Kid couldn't live that way. They had to beat her to the punch, and he realized that now was their chance. Such an opportunity might never come again.

Making eye contact with Sara, Kid could feel the rage flowing through her. She whispered, "Evil incarnate," as she touched the arrowhead locket hanging around her neck.

"That was a perfect strike," the general said. "Let's get out of here and head back to America and hope we have enough fuel to get there."

"Wait! Don't leave," Kid called out as he turned to Mel and the general. He pointed to the roof of the tower. "We need to take them all out! See the person on the roof?"

"We are fortunate to have taken out their M3 before they took us out. The ambush did the job. With the fuel situation there is no time," General Hyland said.

"Uh-oh. Speaking of," Mel started, and sounded concerned. "The fuel level looks like it dropped just in the last few minutes."

"We need to go," the general said definitively.

Driven by deep anger and fear, Kid lunged for a side mounted machine gun. "Sorry, but the job is not done! Not with Heidi Leer still alive."Holding the handles and aiming for the roof of the tower, he snapped, "Get closer, Mel!"

"I can't."

"Closer!"

"I can't!" she screamed back. "Do you want us to crash into the rocks?"

Kid pulled the trigger and launched a hail of .50 caliber bullets. His aim was high, but he adjusted before his target could move. The roof of the tower was raked with bullets, and Heidi's body jerked violently. She fell hard on her side and rolled. Kid tried to adjust his line of fire, but the gun fell silent. The ammunition clip was spent.

He turned to see the occupants of the M3, who were packed in like sardines, all staring at him. Estelle had her hands over her ears.

"She's hit!" Sara stated while pointing out the window.

The general appeared agitated, but aimed the light beam at the roof. Heidi lay motionless in large puddle of blood.

Mel cringed. "Do you see that? She's done."

"We need to land and make sure," Kid said.

"Definitely," Sara agreed. "We need to confirm."

General Hyland interjected, "The threat is over." Turning around he went to speak, and hesitated upon seeing his daughter's expression. Her jaw appeared clenched, and her fingers were balled into tight fists. Her eyes were ablaze with an angry, defiant determination. She appeared ready to explode at the next words out of his mouth.

He was saved by Mel. "It looks like she has already bled out on the roof down there, and she's not moving."

The general nodded. "She's dead. And we are going to run out of fuel if we don't move, now. Right now."

Kid turned to the monitor. "Wait, we still have one missile left!"

Placing a firm hand in the air, the general said, "Kid, don't waste it. A missile might inflict some damage, but it will not destroy a heavy, stone structure like that. Not this particular kind of missile."

Sara exhaled a trembling breath as she hung her head.

"Not to mention, we may need it. Who knows what awaits us over in America," the general added.

Exasperated, Kid dropped to his knees. He couldn't dispute the general's reasoning.

Turning his head, Kid stared at the roof of the Minerva Tower one last time. There should have been some satisfaction or sense of triumph with their successful rescue of Adele and her group while overcoming soldiers and enemy M3's, yet all he felt was a disquiet in his soul. A part of him needed to feel the stillness of Heidi's heart. It was a closure he needed. Making eye contact with Sara, he could tell she felt the same.

With one last obvious attempt at reassurance, General Hyland glanced back. "With all of that blood, I would say Heidi died as soon as you hit her."

Met by silence, the general turned to Mel. His expression and tone were subdued, but stern. "Full throttle and head due west to McGuire."

"Not Hangar One?" Mel asked, sounding disappointed. "I want to get back to my girls."

"You will, but the first priority now is fuel, and the pump with the special M3 mix is at McGuire. Please keep your eye on the gauge and otherwise, keep your fingers crossed that we make it over the Atlantic."

# II:
# EXTRICATION

# CHAPTER 12

January 11, 2045
Wednesday, Early Evening (EST)
East Coast of North America
**Sixteen days after the event**

Kid was waiting for the general to ask Mel again. It didn't take long.

"How is the fuel level?"

"Low but holding. I think we will make it," Mel said with greater confidence then when she responded 15 minutes prior. After a moment, she turned toward the back seats. "I can't believe that Heidi actually used to be your friend."

"I can't either," Sara responded.

"I tried to warn you, subtly, to keep some distance from her," the general interjected.

"Warn me?" Sara leaned forward. "Why?"

He exhaled. "Although she seemed to have stabilized and was living a pretty normal life, Heidi lost it once, big time, when she was in her mid-teens."

Kid was still steaming about not landing, but his ears perked up. "How do you know so much about her background? I never knew about her losing it, and I don't think Brian did either."

"Because he used his military clearance to access her records," Sara answered accusingly. "Like he did with almost every person I ever hung around with."

The general did not even attempt to deny it. "Guilty. And

because I was technically not allowed to do that, I never would have said anything, at least not directly, unless I saw some imminent danger."

"She's gone now, so can you tell us what happened with her?" Mel jumped in.

The general pursed his lips. "Well, she grew up a complete daddy's girl until she was 15 years old and her father ran off with a new woman. Heidi felt completely abandoned, and her mother gave her no love or support. Then her father and his new family decided to go on a vacation to Mexico without her. They had the gall to be cheerily packing and singing songs right in front of her. Heidi lost it and tried to kill them all, including her father."

Mel blurted out, "What? How?"

"She removed all of the lug nuts from the car her father was driving to the airport, except for one that she left hanging by a thread. Of course, the tire came off and caused a tragic car accident. Heidi's step-mother was killed. Her father and step-sister survived, but the step-sister was seriously disfigured. Heidi was found guilty of voluntary manslaughter, but because she was a minor at the time, she was just institutionalized for a year."

Kid knew his mouth was hanging open. A word the general had used to describe Heidi's past resonated in his mind. *Abandoned*. He recalled Heidi mentioning that when he was with her in Vermont, but he had not asked for clarification. He could not believe she was capable of murder, and he shivered upon realizing how close he had gotten to her. *Had he known the risk…*

"That is really messed up," Mel said.

"From what you are saying, Dad, Heidi's instability seemed to stem from her feeling abandoned by her father," Sara observed. "But I know Karen Stone also felt abandoned by her father, and she isn't unstable at all. How is it two people with similar traumas can be affected so differently?"

Her father turned. "I think it all comes down to having consistent stabilizing forces in your life, especially when you've had traumas like that."

"I agree with that," Kid said. "I think the same was true with the Sherman brothers, Sid and Scott. Heidi had said they felt abandoned by society and the system, and I guess they never had consistent stabilizing forces in their life either." He saw that Sara was deep in thought, so he asked, "What are you thinking about?"

"Oh, I was thinking of Karen, and who she had in her life. Her mother was not a bad woman and loved her daughter, but Alice Stone was always working. When she wasn't, she was usually drunk and angry. So who was the stabilizing force in Karen's life?"

Kid met General Hyland's eyes and they both smirked.

"That's simple," the general said, beating him to the punch. "The answer, at least for the last five years of her life, is…you, Sara."

The general then reminded Mel, "Keep in mind, we need to swing wide of the central New Jersey coast. We can't risk being detected or spotted from the ships."

"I was going to come in from the north."

"Let's resume lights-out mode," the general said and flicked the switches.

The inside of the craft was enveloped in darkness with the only exception being the faintly glowing gauges necessary to fly the craft.

A few moments later, Kid caught something out the window. Pressing his face to the glass, he was spellbound, "Do you see this? Mel, make sure you don't run into anything."

She slowed down.

"He's right Mel, take it up a bit," the general agreed.

"I will, and it is time to swing south anyway," she noted.

Waving Sara over, Kid had her sit on his lap so she could see out the window. He put his arm around her waist and held her tightly. "Now that is a sight," she muttered.

The others in the M3 tried to also get a view. Several gasps erupted. It was Estelle who said what Kid was thinking. "That is just…spooky."

Below them, in the dim glow of the last quarter moon, was a completely blacked-out New York City. Flying over lower Manhattan, they did not see a single light. The skyscrapers were darkened outlines, standing like eerie tombstones for well over eight million corpses. The city that never slept was now forever asleep and was a mass grave. Kid felt Sara shiver as she stared out the window. Many sights were unnerving these days, but the pall cast over the largest city in America and one of the largest in the world resonated on a whole new level. It served to drive home a reality that sunk in more every day and with every dramatic sight. Kid fought his olfactory senses as they offered samples of the rotting smell that would emanate from New York City when the weather warmed. He shook his head and breathed out his mouth to keep his queasiness at bay.

Goosing the throttles as she swung past Sandy Hook, New Jersey, Mel was upon the airfield at McGuire Air Force Base in seconds. After several minutes of scoping out the airfield and the buildings, ensuring that no new vehicles were present, the general said, "Mel, get lower, but don't land it."

Once she was within 20 feet of the ground, the general turned on the spotlight and aimed it down.

"There's our truck," Kid said as he looked down at the SUV they had driven to McGuire before securing an M3.

Moving the light back and forth, the general focused on a couple of the dead bodies on the ground. Kid cringed when the general focused the beam on a body that appeared to be charred. "What happened to him?" the general asked.

"He was behind a thruster when we took off," Kid answered.

"That's a tough way to go. Well, everything appears as we left it. Take it down," General Hyland said. "Kid, enlist the help of a few people from back there. We need to hide the truck down there as well as the five dead bodies before they send a group from the ships out here and figure out that we're still alive. While you're doing that, I will go with Mel and get us refueled."

"I am on it," Kid said. He turned and asked Tony and Emilio Severino to help.

They climbed down the ladder and stacked all five of the cold, rigid corpses in the back of their SUV, which was still parked in what Kid believed was the taxi lane, although he couldn't tell because it was covered by snow. Once the bodies were loaded, Kid turned on the vehicle and parked it in front of the two vans that were parked in front of the terminal.

The refueled M3 flew back and landed. While the general lowered the ladder, Mel called out, "Come on, let's get home. My girls are probably driving everyone crazy."

The takeoff was smooth. They reached the Lakehurst Naval Air Station in seconds. Coming in low to Hangar One while still in lights-out mode, they landed behind the large bay doors.

Kid hopped out and zippered his coat as high as it would go to combat the freezing air. The temperature was probably 20 degrees colder than southern Italy, and he still needed to adjust. He motioned for Mel to wait and keep the aircraft running. "Let me make sure everything is alright first," he said and then ran around the side of hangar.

Kid came back out with Jess and motioned for Mel to shut it down. They helped the group from Italy out of the craft, and they all headed for the door on the side of the building.

"What is this place? It looks familiar," Adele asked.

"Welcome to Hangar One at Lakehurst," Jess said as he lit a kerosene lantern and led them inside.

Adele was shining her flashlight in every direction. When she aimed up, she muttered, "Where is the ceiling?"

"Good luck spotting anything up there," Jess responded. "The ceiling is a couple hundred feet high."

"Lord," Estelle started in a high-pitched voice, "what did they keep in here, hot air balloons?"

"Close. They kept dirigibles," General Hyland answered.

A portly older woman from Italy named Theresa Marconi said in imperfect English, "The scum of society? Why would they need such a big space?"

"No. *Dirigibles.*" The general chuckled. "Big airships, filled with hydrogen or helium? Like the Hindenburg?"

Theresa nodded. "Oh, you mean blimps. I see."

"How long is this space?" Adele pointed her light toward the opposite side of the hangar.

"More than 950 feet," Jess said. "But get this, the Hindenburg was so long that it barely fit inside here."

Kid turned to him. "That's interesting, but how do you know that?"

"There's a small museum in the corridor over there. There's a ton of information about the hangar and its history."

"You must be really bored if you've now taken to museums," Kid noted. In all of the years they had been friends, he could not recall one time where Jess visited a museum of any kind.

Jess laughed and waved everyone over to another door. "The rest of the gang is this way."

"They are still awake?" Kid hesitated and checked his watch. "Oh, that's right. Italy is six hours ahead. It's only 7:30 P.M. here."

"Yep. Anyway, we're holed up in a bunch of old classrooms and the main office of the school that was out here. But, we do have food and heat."

With the enticement of those last words, the group immediately lined up behind Jess.

"Food and heat already? How so?" General Hyland asked.

"I ran over to RPH this morning and grabbed our food supplies and propane heaters. We had to go over there to get your mother and Maria's medications anyway. But don't worry, I covered my tracks coming back here."

"I am sure you did," Kid said, fully confident in his best friend.

Speaking to the general, Jess added, "Oh, and I also grabbed your laptop computer while we were there."

"I was about to ask that, Jess. That is a relief. That computer has a lot of important files and resources on it. It needs to stay with us."

"Was RPH completely eerie?" Kid asked.

"Actually, when we pulled up Clarence said the building felt dead. And when we went in, we made the mistake of opening the door to the basement. It was so flooded that the water was almost up to the top of the stairs. And when I shined a light, a bloated body was floating in the stairwell."

Jess grimaced and shook his head. "Anyway, welcome to our latest humble abode." He opened the door and started walking up the corridor that used to be a school.

In the first room Katy and Karly were already in bed, sleeping peacefully. Mel gingerly sat on the edge of the large air mattress, but the bed rocked. Both girls woke up to see their mother fighting back tears. "Mom!" Karly Spatz said as she rubbed her eyes.

Kid watched from the door as her sister Katy sat bolt upright and screamed, "Where have you been?"

Mel crawled in between the girls and put her arms around both. The girls were chatting at the same time, telling her everything that had happened that day.

Sara stepped into the doorway next to Kid and smiled. "Hi, girls. Are y'all happy to see your mom?"

"Yes," Katy said.

"Who is...y'all?" Karly asked.

"She means us," Katy answered. Turning to Sara, she whispered, "She doesn't speak southern yet."

"We do have our own language." Sara chuckled. She then winked at Mel and said, "See, I told you that you would make it back."

Mel smiled. "I believed you. It just feels like I've been away from them for a week, but do you realize we were barely gone one day?"

"I know, but it was one a long one. We're going to get some food. Are you hungry?" Sara asked.

Immediately, the girls started chatting about wanting more chocolate chip cookies. Mel shushed the girls. "She didn't mean you two! Did you already have cookies today?"

Both girls quietly murmured, "Yes."

"That's what I thought. Anyway, it's too late. You need to go back to bed." After the girls begged their mother to stay, Mel said, "I'll pass on the food, Sara. I'm too tired to care about eating anyway. Listen girls, I'll stay in here if you two promise to go right to sleep." The girls agreed readily, but before the door was even closed the girls had already resumed their chatter.

In the hall, Karen ran up and embraced Kid and Sara. "Food is almost ready," she announced.

"Thanks. It can't be ready soon enough," Kid said and noticed a number of bald spots on Karen's scalp. His focus was interrupted by someone tousling his hair.

He turned and found himself face to face with Maria. She hugged him and said, "Look at you. What happened over there? Were you run over by a train, or what?"

"Let's just say that everywhere we go, we seem to find tunnels and battles. We'll fill you in," Kid said.

"Alright, Mr. Bed-Head. This is how you usually look by Sunday morning when we go camping."

"Oh, and your hair was any better by that point of the weekend?" Kid patted Maria's cheek.

"No, but that's why they invented ponytails." She pointed to the one currently holding her dark hair.

"Ah, the ponytail. So by Sunday morning you not only smelled like the back end of a horse, you looked like one too," he quipped. "The complete package."

Maria smiled. "Good one. Keep it up and you'll find yourself with one more battle today."

Kid put his arm around her shoulder. As they walked, he tugged her ponytail. "Did you ever wonder…"

"Don't even start," she warned.

"Alright, I won't." He started laughing. "I wouldn't want to beat a dead…"

A sharp elbow found his solar plexus before he could even finish the sentence.

After all introductions were made, Kid and Jess brought in more of the air mattresses, cots, and sleeping bags from the main hangar, where the group had started stockpiling supplies. Evelyn, Karen, and Maria prepared food for the group on the two camping stoves they had set up in the hallway.

Everyone turned in early that night, notably the Italy survivors whose internal clocks were still set six hours ahead to Central European Time. Romeo, formerly Utopia Project member 801, was predictably asleep at 9:00 P.M. sharp.

Kid wrapped his arms around Sara as they bedded down. Both were exhausted and ready to crash. While falling asleep, Kid's last words of the eventful day were more of a plea. "Tomorrow, can we please have a day of peace? Just…one...day…"

# CHAPTER 13

id awoke early the next morning, and it annoyed the hell out of him. The prior day had taken everything out of him, and then some, yet he could not fall back to sleep no matter how hard he tried. Getting quietly out of bed, he made a cup of coffee and took a walk. He stepped into the vast, open portion of the hangar which felt empty but was not as several clearly retired planes were sleeping peacefully inside. The only modern craft was a white U.S. Navy blimp that was not tiny, but in Hangar One it looked like a matchbox car would look inside a normal sized garage. He imagined the massive Hindenburg dirigible parked inside the hangar. It certainly would not have appeared empty then. Walking out the back door, he breathed in the cold morning air. The ground had a layer of snow and for the moment, the world was serene and peaceful.

He thought of all of his brushes with death over the past few weeks. By now he should be on a first name basis with the Grim Reaper, who had graciously spared him on multiple occasions. One of these times, the Reaper would tell him he had reached his third strike, or more accurately, his ninth life, and that his time was up. Prior to the destruction, Kid's life had been so remarkably simple. He could never have imagined having the strength to do the things he had done in the past few weeks to survive what he had survived, or to take the lives of others. Only in those gladiator moments does one realize what he is made of and how he will respond. He knew now, and it made him feel strong in ways he had never felt before. He wanted to believe his core had not changed and that he was still a compassionate and principle-oriented person. Still, he could not deny that he had grown and was a new man. The horrible event notwithstanding, and though his vision had not changed, the physical world somehow looked different. For a few moments Kid simply absorbed the world around him. He took in the snowy ground, the wisp of wind, the clouds in the brightening sky, and the massive hangar behind him. After a moment, he turned to go inside to get another cup of coffee.

To Kid's envy, the rest of the group slept until mid to late morning. Then everyone assembled for a midday brunch in the large open room that Jess said once housed military simulator equipment. The survivors referred to it simply as the meeting room and had outfitted the space with several large folding tables and folding chairs. General Hyland and Kid sat at the head table which was positioned like a dais. Even without formal recognition, they were treated like the leaders of the group of survivors. Everyone not only seemed comfortable with that but looked to Kid and General Hyland to be the leaders.

Kid still was not sure how he wound up in that role. General Hyland was used to being near the top of the chain of command. Kid was not, at least not in any formal position. A couple of times in the past Jess would say, "Ask Kid. He's the head of our group." In those moments, he always felt awkward. He never thought of himself as the head of anything, but when he did, he feared letting people down. Back then he also never had to ask people to put their lives on the line. That was a heavy burden, one with which General Hyland had much more experience and much more training to handle.

While eating dry cereal, General Hyland appeared to be counting. He turned to Kid and said, "Only 30 people in our group. A handful are senior citizens, and five are young children."

"Not exactly a formidable rebellion," Kid noted.

"No, but it is all we have. There are no other areas of the world left unscathed," retorted the general.

"At least they don't know we are still alive," Kid said as he spooned dry, stale, cornflakes into his mouth.

General Hyland did not seem to find any comfort in that. "They might not know for certain, but when their teams don't return from Italy, they will begin to suspect."

• • •

On Utopia Project Ship Number One, Elder-3 stood on the bridge with Elder-10. They both stared over the ocean until Elder-3 finally blurted out, "Why have our teams not returned from Italy yet? They have been gone for too long."

Shrugging his shoulders, all Elder-10 could offer was, "Maybe they are still clearing the area."

"The area in Italy that they had to cover was not that large. They should have been back by last night at the latest," countered Elder-3.

"Something unexpected must be holding them up," Elder-10 finally admitted.

"Yes, something is afoot," Elder-3 said as he gazed at the sky. "Something…is afoot."

• • •

Inside Hangar One, General Hyland said, "We need to keep an eye on the Utopia Project and their base camp. Besides wanting to monitor their progress, I want to know when they start running missions over to the mainland, and where, so we can be on higher-alert."

"We need to spy on them, but from a safe distance," Kid responded. "And it is going to be hard to see Surf City on Long Beach

Island from a distance unless we are really, really high up. The place is too developed."

"Well, you lived over on the coast. Where do you recommend?" the general asked.

"Let me think about it." Kid was drawing a blank at the moment.

"If you need top-end surveillance equipment, you can get it at Fort Dix," Dr. McDermott said while adjusting his octagonal glasses. "I am sure you know this Eric, but they have all kinds of high-tech devices there."

"Yes, I am aware, but how do you know that?" the general asked.

Chris jumped in and said, "While you were gone yesterday, the doctor and I took a ride over there to find a special medication for Karen. We were able to pick the security cards out of a few puddles that used to be higher-ranking officers and use them to get in. The security system and emergency lights were still operating."

"If I had known you were going over there, I would have given you my security card," General Hyland noted. "And as far as power at the Joint Base, the auxiliary power runs from renewable energy sources, like the fields of solar panels over there. The lights, security systems, and even the temperature-sensitive areas will probably stay on for years until the solar panels or inverters fail."

Dr. McDermott turned to the general. "We had access to everything, and I mean *everything*, including stockpiles of biological and chemical weapons. I nearly knocked into some when we were searching."

"There is definitely a substantial cache of biological and chemical weapons over there." The general paused and seemed to be contemplating. "Anyway, today is a day to rest and recover, but we should head over to Dix tomorrow and get more weapons, and also some surveillance equipment."

"Y'all went there yesterday to find special medication? For what?" Sara turned to Karen. "Are you alright? I did notice that you are missing patches of hair."

"Well…" Karen started.

"You're scaring me. What is going on?" said Sarah hesitantly.

"Mrs. Hyland noticed my skin and scalp condition and had Dr. McDermott check me out. He said I am…sick."

"Sick? But why would you need special medication?"

Kid had a terrible feeling in his gut. He knew where this was going, and he took Karen's hand.

She exhaled and appeared to be holding back tears. "He said I have radiation poisoning."

Sara grabbed Karen's other hand. "How?"

Dr. McDermott answered, "The beams from the sky had concentrated radiation, and although Karen was not hit directly, a beam ran literally right next to her. It cut her house in…"

Kid cringed, but to his relief, the doctor caught himself.

"…the beams went right through her house."

"Did you find medication for her?" Sara sounded concerned.

"We found Neupogen in the medical and chemical stores at Fort Dix," the doctor said. "It treats radiation poisoning and specifically targets the white blood cell count. Karen has to get a needle every day until her blood counts are where they should be. The radiation just needs to work itself out of her system, and in the meantime, she has to steer clear of infections and colds."

Karen added, "Doc said my hair will fall out before it grows again. My mother would have been happy. She hated my purple highlights." She tried to laugh but got choked up.

Sara hugged her. "Remember, like we told you before, you are one tough girl. I know you will be fine."

Karen tried to smile. "Thanks. I won't go down without a fight."

Kid smiled and patted her hand, desperately hoping that Karen wasn't too contaminated to be saved.

Friday morning, after eating breakfast, Kid was waiting to leave for Fort Dix with Sara, her father, Chris, and 801.

While he waited, Kid listened as Jess, Maria, the McDermotts, and the Moores worked out a plan for the rest of the day in terms of cleaning, gathering supplies, rearranging, preparing food, and of course, keeping the coffee flowing.

Five of the survivors were excluded from any chores, including Estelle Severino and Theresa Marconi who both had age and medical issues. Wendy Levy was still nursing a sprained wrist and a dislocated ankle.

Evelyn Hyland, despite her protests, was also not given any assigned chores. After Kid's harrowing trip to secure her rare formulary from the Merck plant in New Jersey, she had resumed her regular medication regimen. However, she was still weak. She was allowed to help with the meals where she could, but she was only tasked with resting and regaining her strength.

The fifth survivor not assigned any chores was Karen. She was also told to just rest, especially since her strength was being sapped by the Neupogen being injected into her system. She looked frustrated and put her hands on her head as she turned to Dr. McDermott.

"Why can't I help?" Karen held out her hand and paused when she saw a wad of hair stuck between her fingers. Kid was stunned and worried. Fortunately, Karen surrendered and argued no more.

As Kid and the group went to leave, they stepped into the cavernous hangar. Mel was there watching her daughters Katy and Karly as they played with the three children from Italy. Given the size of the hangar, the kids had plenty of running room. Kid and the group waved and headed out.

Later that afternoon, Kid's group returned from Fort Dix. They entered the meeting room in Hangar One where many of the other survivors were conversing. General Hyland took a seat and detailed the haul from the Army base, including the plethora of guns, ammunition, and grenades, as well as high-tech surveillance equipment. They had also brought back every missile they could find for the M3. Although the craft could only be armed with four at a time, they now had a stockpile of 20 missiles.

Kid was rummaging through a cardboard box he had placed on a table. Taking out a device that was no larger than a cigar, he said to Sara, "I can't believe the range of this little scope." Looking through the high-powered lens, he added, "With no obstructions, we would be able to clearly see them, both the base camp and the ships, from 30 miles away. And even at that distance, we should be able to read the numbers on their uniforms."

Sara asked, "See them…from where?"

Putting the scope down, Kid was flustered. "I don't know. I need to figure that out. We need to keep an eye on the Utopia Project, not only for our own safety, but so we can study them and the areas they are occupying in Surf City. Remember, our inevitable goal is put an end to that project and awaken the humanity in their members. We will have to go on the offensive at some point, so we'd better start planning."

Sara nodded in agreement and then turned to General Hyland. "Dad, you mentioned before that you thought their group might become weakened and come undone if some key elders were eliminated, right?"

"Yes. It might be our only hope. We just need to identify which ones we think are key elders." He turned on his laptop computer. "Let me pull up the list."

Adele noted. "We need to determine which ones will fight us to the death."

"Their death," the general clarified.

"Yes, their death," she confirmed. A few minutes later, the general turned his eyes from his laptop screen. "It looks like around…50?"

Adele turned toward him. Her expression made one thing clear. She was not buying it.

# CHAPTER 14

January 13, 2045
Friday, Afternoon
Forked River, NJ
**Eighteen days after the event**

The general seemed surprised by Adele's reaction and asked, "You think more than 50 would need to be taken out?"

She nodded her head without hesitation. "Since we have the list of elders, we can go name by name."

"Taken out? You mean…killed?" Estelle repeated quietly. She folded her hands together, as if in prayer.

Kid thought most of the survivors from Italy looked like deer in headlights. They had not been hardened to the nearly perpetual battling that he and the others had endured over the weeks since the destruction.

Thirty-two year old Italy survivor Annette Vicarro ran her hand through her curly brown hair. She was a slender woman with large, brown eyes and long, upturned lashes. Her skin was naturally dark enough to pass for a suntan. She seemed overwhelmed by all that had happened and the talk of taking out people was probably not helping any. She wrapped her arms around her 10-year-old daughter Gia and held her tight.

Next to her, 30-year-old Debbie Severino, wife of Emilio, also sat quietly. Her twin eight-year-old boys, Al and Sal, were not so quiet. They seemed restless and in need of a way to release their pent up energy. Seeing Debbie struggling, Mel came over and offered to take the twins so they could run around the hangar. Debbie took the offer without hesitation.

The first of the Italy survivors to break out of the collective trance was 38-year old Tony Severino. He seemed to have grasped the situation and was ready to join in and act. He stood up, revealing his full height of five feet, eleven inches, and ran his hands through his black hair. "If there are only 20 to 30 who we need to take out, why can't we pick them off with snipers? I happen to be an expert marksman," Tony said as he rubbed the black, scraggly stubble growing on his chin.

His mother Estelle looked at him with concern marking her facial features.

Kid recalled a conversation he had had with Estelle. She said that Tony's interest in guns had always made her uncomfortable and that she encouraged him to focus on his job as a fisherman on a commercial boat. She never had such worries when it came to her younger son, Emilio. He was happily married to Debbie, was a successful chemical engineer in Naples, and in his spare time Emilio played piano. She said that both of her children enjoyed their hobbies immensely. Kid was amused when Estelle added that she preferred the hobby where a hammer launched a note and not a bullet.

General Hyland turned to Adele. She nodded her head, as if confirming that Tony was legitimate in his self-praise. The general noted, "Tony, a marksman may come in handy at some point, but I am sure after we took out a few elders, they would take additional precautions, and we would never get a shot at the rest."

"Honestly, I should also mention that I have never aimed at people before," Tony said.

Maria quipped, "Well now. That's a relief." Sara laughed aloud.

The general and Adele went over the list of elders. Of the 220 elders, a handful had already perished, including the two most senior and powerful elders, Elder-1 and Elder-2. But the general pointed out that Elder-3 was now in charge and was probably the most violent and sadistic of the top elders. The general and Adele then identified the elders they thought needed to be taken out in order to have any hope of taking command over the remaining elders and the 20,000 members.

Counting the names on his list the general exhaled. "I guess my estimate was pretty rough. I count 81 that would have to be eliminated. Much more than I realized."

"102," Adele countered after checking her list.

*Not good*, Kid thought.

They began discussing the elders Adele had identified that General Hyland had not. Kid and the rest of the group sat watching and listening to the debate. Seeming exasperated, Adele actually added a couple more elders to her list as they continued to review.

Finally, Karen asked a question that made them pause. "With how this is going, wouldn't it be easier to identify the ones you trust without a doubt, rather than the ones you don't?"

"Good question," Kid said.

The general and Adele both fell silent and sat back in their chairs.

"She has a point," General Hyland finally affirmed.

Within moments, they had agreed on a list of only 12 elders they would both unequivocally trust. They had known all 12 for many years and had spent much time inside and outside the Utopia Project with them. The core beliefs of these elders were not truly aligned with the project, and they knew them to be good people at heart. It would also help that several of them had skills that would be essential in the rebirth of an efficiently-functioning society.

"So now we are talking about saving just 12 good ones and taking out the rest?" Chris confirmed.

His son nodded. "I hate to do it; I really do. There are so many with expertise in important areas, but it seems to be the only way. Even saving 12 is going to be an immense challenge."

"We need to catch them when all of the elders are congregating," Chris said. "Do they ever do that?"

The general pondered. "The only time the elders congregate together is when they have group meetings and when they sleep since there are dedicated elder hallways."

"Entire hallways? That would mean we would have to go room by room, which isn't practical," Chris commented.

"How often do they have group meetings?" Kid asked.

"There are very limited scenarios where they would have a group meeting for *all* elders," Adele answered. "The few times they have, the meeting was held in the member dining room on ship number one. It is the only space large enough to accommodate all couple hundred of them."

"Would every elder be at the meeting, even the ones already stationed on the mainland?" Kid asked.

Adele and General Hyland both seemed unsure and pondered for a moment. Finally, the general offered, "I'm not sure of the protocol, but I don't think they would leave anyone out."

Adele added, "I agree, especially since the elders on the mainland could jump in a boat and return to the ships pretty quickly."

The general pulled a booklet from his laptop bag. "I doubt this specific scenario is covered, but I have the Standard Operating Procedure manual for the project, which addresses the protocols for emergency meetings."

"Can we give it a look?" Sara asked.

"Be my guest," he said as he handed it over. "But we need some lanterns. It is getting dark."

Kid realized he was right. The gray enveloping the room was deepening.

After turning on a battery-powered lantern, Sara and Kid sat together at a table with the manual and started going through page by page.

Kid pointed to a section. "Listen. Here is something about emergency meetings. There's a bunch of minutiae about notification, agendas, location -- which it says should be in the main dining room of ship number one unless otherwise posted -- but then it gives some examples of when such a meeting shall be called, including, and I quote, 'for an imminent but not immediate, threat'."

Karen looked confused. "What does that mean?"

General Hyland tried to clarify. "If, for example, the ships were under attack from another country's navy, the leading elder would respond immediately to defend the ships. It would be considered an immediate threat and there would be no time to call a meeting. But if they were warned 12 or 24 hours in advance that an attack was coming, they would call a meeting with all elders to establish a game plan. That would be considered an imminent but not immediate threat. Actually, they called such meetings a few times in the week before the event."

"So in terms of getting the elders all in one place at one time, what can we do to force an emergency meeting?" Kid contemplated.

Adele was the first to speak. "That's a tough one. I can't think of anything we could do to force such a meeting. With an attack from a group like ours, the lead elder would just dictate the response. Even if we broke out heavier artillery, I suspect the lead elder would consider it an immediate threat and would respond without having a meeting."

"What if we announced in advance that we were going to attack?" Karen asked.

The general pondered and then said, "Besides giving up any element of surprise we *might* currently have, I find it hard to believe they would call an emergency meeting for anything our small group did to threaten them, especially with Elder-3 in charge. He would treat us the same as a band of rogue pirates and handle it himself. I guess the most complete description would be that we need to create an imminent but not immediate threat from a formidable enemy."

Adele stood up and stretched her arms. "I think everyone could use a break. Plus, we are probably all starving about now."

Jess exhaled and also got to his feet. "I could use a break. I was mostly just a spectator and my head is still about to explode."

Romeo looked closely at Jess's skull.

Putting a hand on Romeo's shoulder, Jess said, "Figure of speech. My head is not going to literally explode."

Straight-faced, Romeo said, "But earlier, after you made a noise, you said that your ass exploded."

Everyone bust out laughing.

Jess smiled as his face turned red. He patted Romeo's shoulder. "Remind me to go over with you something we call…discretion."

Saturday morning Kid woke up with his arm around Sara and his face buried in her brunette hair. He raised his head, causing the over-sized cot they were sleeping on to creak. Peering around the old school classroom, the sharp squeak had not disturbed any of their room-mates. Jess and Maria, Karen, and 801 were still sleeping peacefully.

Kid gently lowered his head back down to his pillow and thought of the two tasks at hand that they still needed to accomplish. First, they needed to case out the ships and Long Beach Island and get a lay of the land and a status update. But where could they find such a vantage point without getting too close? Second, they needed to figure out how they could force an emergency meeting of all elders. Like the Standard Operating Procedures manual said, there had to be an imminent but not immediate threat from a formidable enemy. He tried to think through and solve these problems, to no avail. Maybe his brain was not alert enough yet. Solution? They had quality Colum-bian coffee beans, a bean grinder, and a percolator. That would be his play. Despite getting out of bed slowly, the cot still creaked loudly.

Early afternoon, after refilling the propane heaters, Jess showed Kid around the museum in the hangar. It was not much of a museum. Rather, it was more like a memorabilia collection in a messy, cluttered and dusty room. Still, the pictures of Hangar One and the dirigibles of the day were fascinating and caught Kid's attention.

Jess pondered aloud, "With this hangar being 200 feet tall, I wonder if it was the tallest structure in Ocean County in 1921?"

"Maybe at the time, but there are now definitely taller buildings and…" he paused, "structures. That's it!" He dashed out of the room. Seeking out Sara, Kid said, "I know where we can get eyes on the ships and the base camp, but from a safe distance. And this will help." He held up the powerful scope he had secured from Fort Dix. "Come on. Dress warm, but don't wear anything bright, or anything shiny or reflective. Just tell your father we are casing out a few places to see if we can get a view of the ships."

"Alright. But where are we going?" she asked.

"I'll tell you on the way. If I tell you now, I doubt you will want to come with me."

# CHAPTER 15

K id and Sara drove for 30 minutes until they reached a fenced and gated facility in Forked River. After using the back end of the windowless cargo van they were driving to ram the chain link fence until it tore away from its posts, they climbed through the hole they had made. They ran over to the guardhouse and were pleased to find that the auxiliary power was still on. They were able to open the gate with the simple press of a button. Running back to the van, they proceeded to drive up the long entrance road.

After they stopped, Kid got out and looked up at a tall, squared-off building. The imposing structure was formerly the reactor building of the Oyster Creek Nuclear Generating Station. Until decommissioning started in 2018, Oyster Creek was a commercially viable plant, and for many years was the oldest operating nuclear plant in the United States. He knew that spent, but highly radioactive, material was encapsulated on site, where it was supposed to decay naturally over a period of many years.

"Bring the blanket," he said and then closed the vehicle door.

With her breath visible in the cold air as she walked around the front of the van, Sara said, "You've got to be kidding. Look at how high that building is!"

"We are not going on top of that," Kid responded.

"Well now that's a relief." She smirked.

"It isn't tall enough. We are going to the top of the off-gas stack next to it."

She spotted the stack, and the smile evaporated from her face.

He added, "Which is why I didn't tell you in advance where we were going."

They made their way to the north side of the off-gas stack. Using bolt cutters he had the foresight to bring along, Kid snapped the chain locking the enclosure around the base of the ladder. He took the blanket Sara was holding and threw it over his shoulder, since he knew they would need it where they were going.

"The ladder looks like it heads straight into the clouds," she said as she gazed above her head. "Are you sure we should be that high during the day? Do you think they can see us up there?"

"I don't think so," he said and pointed up. "The ladder is enclosed by a metal cage for its entire run up to the top." He knew the cage would keep them out of sight, but just as importantly, it would provide them with some level of safety and security, at least psychologically.

After making sure they were both not wearing anything bright or reflective, he started climbing the rungs.

"This must be twice as tall as that building!" she concluded as she started to follow Kid, one rung at a time.

"At least. But there is an enclosed landing surrounding the top, so you will feel secure when we get up there."

"Are you sure this is safe? Hasn't this plant been shut down for a long time?"

"Over 25 years," he answered.

"Then why are these structures even still standing?"

"Good question. I know the decommissioning process has been caught up in litigation for years. I wouldn't worry. This stack is as sturdy as the day it was built."

"Oh great. And when was that?" she huffed as she climbed right behind him.

"I think the plant opened around 1969." The pace of his breathing was ever-increasing.

"That's more than 75 years ago!" she exclaimed.

Now higher than the massive former reactor building, Kid stopped climbing and took a quick breather. The wind was becoming more and more frigid the higher they ascended. He realized they were only halfway to the top. He peered down and made sure Sara was still right with him. Kid made the mistake of pondering when the ladder and enclosure were last serviced or inspected. He would not dare ask that question aloud, especially since he noticed rust and decay in many spots. Looking closer, a couple of bolts affixing the ladder to the stack were not only deteriorating. They were popping out.

He resumed climbing. Despite the sturdy block construction of the structure itself, Kid still felt like it had a slight sway as he approached the top. He wondered if it might be his imagination, or an attack of vertigo. The higher he went, the more vulnerable he felt. Fortunately, not far above him was the platform surrounding the top of the stack. He did not know what it was ever used for, but the landing circled the top of the structure and had a waist-high metal safety enclosure around it. Kid was breathing heavily when he finally reached the platform at the top.

"Whoa," Sara huffed between breaths as he helped her up. "Now that is a climb."

Kid held her hand as they walked around the platform to the east side, where they took a seat. As their breathing returned to a normal pace, Sara shivered. Kid took the blanket from over his shoulder and laid it across her body. Every wind gust was like a frigid slap, so they huddled close together.

"I cannot believe how high up we are right now," she noted. "What an adrenaline rush. It is disorienting, and I am not afraid of heights."

"I counted the steps up." Kid realized that he habitually counted his steps when he was nervous and confronted with an unfamiliar or dangerous place, like he did when they were walking through the tunnels behind RPH. "This thing is easily taller than a 30-story building," he concluded.

Kid then made the mistake of leaning forward on his knees and gazing down from the edge of the platform. As his weight shifted, he grabbed the bar of the enclosure. The metal deck underneath him bowed and creaked. The sudden noise froze him, as did the frightening view of the ground below. The reactor building did not even appear that massive from such heights. He realized just how precariously they were perched, like a high-diver standing on a tiny platform waiting to jump into a tiny pool. Easing back, he put his head against the blocks of the stack and resolved to not move any more than he needed.

"Let me radio my dad so he doesn't worry about us," Sara said.

"Alright, but don't tell him exactly where we are. He might worry if he knows we are at a nuclear plant. Just say we are checking out some tall structures in Forked River."

"Got it," Sara said and spoke with her father briefly over the walkie-talkie.

Kid then turned his focus on the view in front of him and a little to the south. The three Utopia Project ships were clear to see, and he knew exactly where Surf City was on Long Beach Island. Kid chuckled and then felt a wave of sadness. Sara looked at him expectantly, so he pointed and clarified, "Seeing those ships reminded me of Drex's words. He referred to them as an unholy ark trinity, launched by Satan himself."

"Drex was right," she agreed.

He pulled the tiny but powerful scope and a small, collapsible tripod from inside his deep coat pocket. "The sun is behind us and is blocked by the stack. We shouldn't have to worry about reflecting any light that they could see."

"Yeah, let's not make that mistake again," Sara said, referring to

RPH. "You really can see all the way to the ships with that?"

"I'll tell you in a minute, but this is a 30-mile scope with a daylight mode, and we are not even close to being that far away. And get this, it's a video camera too, battery-powered, so you can record what you are viewing."

He extended the tripod legs and mounted the scope on the tripod. It took a few minutes for Kid to lock in on a particular elder on one of the ships, given the fine tuning that had to be done to view a target so far away. His hand, which had never been perfectly steady, twitched ever so slightly, and he lost his target. He put his knee down on the metal decking. The slight jolt shifted the view even more. "This thing is sensitive," he muttered. "I can't even breathe on it."

With some practice, he was able to adjust the view to follow specific points. He first focused on some boats hanging from davits on the middle Utopia Project ship. He realized that the nylon davit lines, the ones he and Jess had cut before rescuing the girls, were obviously now fixed. He then honed in a group of members on the deck of the same ship. As he predicted, he could read their uniform numbers. He tried to record some video and capture images at varying distances so he could show General Hyland everything going on. He thought the functionality of the video recording function was odd until he actually used it. To start and stop the video recording, the viewer simply blinked his or her viewing eye three times in quick succession. This allowed the person to record without even touching the scope, which was critical given that the view shifted from the slightest touch.

Kid then focused on a couple of small boats on the ocean which were transporting members and supplies to the mainland. The boats came to shore and were pulled aground so the members could get out without stepping in water. On the beach he spotted a group of members who appeared to be constructing their own version of a boardwalk, heading down toward the waterline. This was confirmed as the members who exited the boats marched on the sand and headed up the wood plank walkway.

Finally, he turned his sights to Surf City. Even at his current height, the view was partially obstructed by dense clusters of buildings and houses.

"How many members do you see on the island?" Sara asked.

"Maybe a couple hundred? They seem to be using the old Surf City Hotel as their headquarters. But I don't even know if that building could house a couple hundred people. Take a look," he said and gently moved over.

Sara slowly put her eye close to the scope and took in the sight of the Surf City Hotel.

"Maybe some of them go back to the ships for the night?" she suggested.

"Maybe. That or they will go back because the ghosts are getting to them," Kid noted.

"Ghosts?" she asked and turned to him.

"Yeah. The Surf City Hotel is pretty infamous, locally. The building stands on the ruins of an old hotel called the Mansion of Health. In the mid-1800's a ship called Powhattan crashed in a storm, killing all aboard. Fifty bodies washed ashore off of Long Beach Island, and the Mansion of Health manager took the money belts and cash from the corpses. He got busted when the empty money belts, which he had buried, resurfaced after another storm shortly after. But by then, the hotel was supposedly haunted by the ghosts of the dead who were robbed."

"I see. Remind me not to book a room there," Sara quipped and moved away so Kid could look again.

While trying to get a better view of the Surf City Hotel, Kid caught a glimpse of some activity on the western side of the island. Zooming out a bit and refocusing, he realized that a boat was motoring across Barnegat Bay and heading south. The craft parked at a pier in Surf City and a few large pieces of equipment were off-loaded and placed on a flatbed trailer. A vehicle towed the trailer away and drove to the Surf City Hotel.

"Interesting. Some equipment is being taken ashore at a dock on the western side of the island," Kid said as he lowered the scope from his eye. "They must be driving through the inlet and then coming south in the bay."

"Why would they be doing that?"

"Not sure. I guess they need to off-load bigger pieces of equipment at a pier, rather than trying to lug them up the beach, which would be difficult, if not impossible."

While Sara took another turn with the scope, Kid sat back and took in the larger view. Crossing his arms, he realized he was chilled to the bone. When she was done and satisfied they had seen enough, Kid put the scope and small tripod away inside his coat. "You ready to get down?" he asked.

"Sure, if I could move my arms and legs. I think they are frozen. Maybe we should go around to the other side of the stack for a few minutes, the side with the sun, and thaw out some."

"It is already starting to set, but maybe seeing any sun will give us the illusion, or delusion, of being warm. Come on."

They got up and walked around the top, staying close to the tower and avoiding looking over the edge. Facing west, they again took a seat. Sara made sure her coat was fully zipped. "Definitely a delusion."

Kid shook the blanket to lay it over them. They huddled closely together, trying to keep the sub-freezing temperatures at bay.

With his discomfort diminishing, Kid was able to fully behold a sight he could not describe in words. The sun was beginning its descent. The puffy cumulus clouds seemed aglow. He found himself in a timeless moment of absolute calm, which he wanted to hold onto as long as he could. Lowering his eyes, in front of them were thousands of acres of snowy pine forests, with all of the vegetation clinging to the last touch of the sun's rays before succumbing to the icy darkness. Some pines seemed to be reaching for the light while others had accepted their fate and settled in to endure another night.

For 15 minutes Kid and Sara held each other tightly in silence at what seemed like the top of the world. Neither one moved. The sunset was too majestic, they were fairly warm for the moment, and the climb down was daunting. It was a perfect recipe for malaise and inaction.

As Kid stared at the pink, cotton-like underbelly of a cluster of clouds, a chill suddenly ran through him. Having grown up just a couple of miles from the nuclear power plant, he knew the fears people harbored of meltdowns -- even with the spent radioactive material being encapsulated. Seeing the glowing clouds, he wondered if a meltdown or release of radioactive waste would have turned the clouds the same pink color.

A nudge from Sara broke his reverie. "We have quite the vantage point up here."

"We do," he agreed. "And you were right about the adrenaline rush with being up this high."

"I know," she answered. "Where else can you get this kind of view of the sky? No picture could ever capture the depth perception or the largeness of a scene like this."

With dusk closing in Kid said, "We need to get down while we can still see where we are going. I didn't think to bring a flashlight because I didn't expect us to be up here past daylight."

"And I was finally warming up, a little," Sara said as she threw the blanket off. Her body almost immediately began to shake from the frigid breeze.

Kid kissed her surprisingly warm lips, and they both got up.

Looking down, Sara commented, "I almost forgot we were at a nuclear power plant. If there was a meltdown while we were up here, we would be screwed!"

"The plant is in the decommissioning phase," he said as they walked around the landing to the ladder. "No nuclear reactions are going on. So I wouldn't worry about a meltdown."

"Oh. So we have nothing to worry about."

"Well, that's not entirely true either. They have a bunch of radio-active material encapsulated on site."

"Great," she muttered.

"It needs to be constantly monitored to make sure there are no breaches, or releases of deadly toxins into the ground, or air, or even water. That's why the plant is still open with staff working here, and why the nuclear warning sirens are still operational and tested every so often…"

As he went to descend the ladder, he stole one last glance at the glowing clouds. Despite the cold breeze and the perilous drop below his feet, something was resonating in the back of his mind. He stopped and tried to capture it before it faded with the radiance enveloping the clouds. It was at that inopportune moment that Kid had an epiphany. *An imminent but not immediate threat from a formidable enemy.* He knew they had to get back to Hangar One as soon as possible.

"What's the matter?" She noticed that he had stopped and was staring into space.

"I think I've got it. Come on. I'll tell you after we get down from here."

Once he reached the ground, Kid ran back to the van. He grabbed a flashlight and a crowbar, which he then used to access the former reactor building. Stepping inside the control room, he winced. The smell was unmistakable and hit him before his defenses kicked in and reminded him not to breathe out his nose. He cursed himself for not knowing better by now. He was able to warn Sara to hold her nose before she entered. The building was running on auxiliary power so the room had dim emergency lighting. He just did not know for how long. He could see enough to spot the remains of a person, likely an onsite monitor, partially spread across a chair but mostly on the floor. The grotesque pile of bones and melted human tissue seemed to embody all of the nuclear plant meltdown fears that local residents lived with every day. Nobody discussed such anxieties as if the words alone might trigger a meltdown.

Now breathing only out his mouth, Kid walked into an adjacent room and found Emergency Management Plans sitting on a shelf.

Following a diagram in the plan, he cased out the many banks of switches on the walls. He found the bank for which he was looking. He grabbed a couple of rubber bands and wrapped them around the relevant switches to make them easier to locate again. Taking the plan documents, he wanted to get out of the room before he inadvertently caught another whiff of the foul air. They left, and he was relieved to close the door behind them.

Kid and Sara decided to keep the van head lights off to ensure they could not be spotted, which made for the painstakingly slow drive through the darkness back to Hangar One.

She turned to him. "So, tell me about this epiphany you had at the top of the stack back there."

# CHAPTER 16

Entering the side door of Hangar One, Kid turned on a flashlight and illuminated the path back to the meeting room. Most of the survivors were congregating within. Kid was thankful to be hit by a wave of warm air as Sara and he entered the room. But it was a quick reminder that they needed more fuel for the heaters and probably did not have enough to last through the night.

"Hey Jess. Ready to run out with me and get more propane?" he asked his friend, who was sitting just inside the door.

"You're back!" Jess fist-bumped Kid. "Already done. Clarence and I grabbed more while you were gone."

Kid breathed easier. It was one less challenge for the night. It again struck him that the main focus each day was ensuring they had the basic necessities to get from that day to the next. He was still adjusting to living in survival mode, and he took nothing for granted like he did in the world before the destruction. Just having heat, food in his stomach, water to drink, and shelter from the elements were great accomplishments.

At a table, General Hyland, Adele, Karen, Chris, and Tony were having a discussion. The group stopped the chatter upon seeing Kid and Sara.

The general beckoned for them to come over. "Where did you go?" he asked.

"Oyster Creek…nuclear power plant," Kid answered.

The general cocked an eyebrow. "What were you guys doing there?"

"At first, using the tall off-gas stack to get a view of Long Beach Island and the ships," he responded. Pulling the scope out of his pocket, he added, "This is also a video recorder, and we got some shots. We just need to connect it to a computer."

"There is a nuclear plant close by?" Chris asked.

"Yes," Kid said. "It is no longer on line, but the spent radioactive material is being stored at the site and will be there a long, long time."

The general looked at Sara. "What did you see from atop this stack? How many members and elders were already stationed on the mainland?'

"We estimate a couple hundred members and a handful of elders. They seem to be holed up in and around the Surf City Hotel," his daughter responded. "But listen, you need to hear Kid's idea. If it makes sense, we may have solved an important piece of the puzzle."

"Hold on," Kid started. "My idea hinges on the answer to two important questions." He looked at the general. "First, did the leaders of the project know about the Oyster Creek nuclear plant?"

The general nodded assuredly. "They were well aware."

"And did they know there was radioactive material being stored on site?"

"Yes, but it was considered a non-factor. The radioactive material is encapsulated."

Bending over, Kid exhaled loudly and muttered, "Then the plan has a chance." When he stood upright, he met Sara's eyes and winked at her. She nodded and winked back. She clearly understood how critical these two questions were to his plan.

Holding up the Standard Operating Procedures manual for the Utopia Project, Kid announced, "I think we know a way to trigger an emergency meeting of the elders, assuming they follow the protocols."

The general looked skeptical and started reiterating the criteria that had to be met for an emergency meeting to be called.

"Please, Dad," Sara cut in. "Hear us out."

"Alright." The general sat back and said, "Let's have it."

Kid laid out his idea in detail.

General Hyland summarized what he had just heard. "So you think that by turning on the entire network of nuclear warning sirens, it will trigger an emergency meeting of the elders?"

He nodded.

"What do you think?" Sara asked as she looked at her father.

At first General Hyland did not respond. Finally, he leaned forward and said simply, "It's brilliant."

Adele added, "I agree completely. I never would have thought of that, but I think it will work. Even though the plant is no longer on line, if we turn on the nuclear warning sirens as Kid proposes, it would likely be considered an imminent but not immediate threat."

"And wouldn't toxic radioactive waste be considered a formidable enemy?" Kid asked.

The general nodded, "I would think so. They didn't come this far to lose the society to a radiation leak. They would probably send a team out immediately to see if there is a radiation leak, but concurrently, they would have to call an emergency meeting of all elders right away to develop a plan to depart if they are in danger." He paused. "You lived close by, Kid. I assume you've heard these sirens before, since these nuclear plants are required to conduct routine tests of their warning systems?"

"More times than I can count."

"But they haven't," the general said and pointed, as if the ships were just outside the hangar.

Kid just assumed it would be obvious that the sirens were for the plant, but he only knew that because he grew up close to the facility. The general had a point.

"They need to connect those dots," General Hyland concluded. "It should be common sense, as soon as the alarms sound, I hope they turn their sights to the nuclear plant."

"That shouldn't be hard. Just start waving a big flag on top of that ridiculously tall stack that Kid made me climb," Sara quipped.

Kid smirked but then opened his eyes wide. "That's actually a good idea. We could put a bright red light at the top of the off-gas stack and turn it on when we activate the sirens. Their eyes will turn right to the plant."

"I think this plan just might work" Adele said. "Great thinking Kid."

General Hyland nodded in agreement. "Yes. Now we just need to figure out how we can take them all out when they do meet, all but the 12 we want survive. That will not be easy."

Adele rubbed her face and yawned. "I think we have exhausted our mental capacity enough for one day."

"You're right." The general relented and stood up. "Let's call it a night."

The meeting ended, but Kid and Sara stayed and talked for a little while longer. He was not the least bit tired and did not know if that was because his mind was racing from all the planning they were doing, or if the adrenaline still lingered from climbing the off-gas stack at the nuclear power plant. Finally, he said to Sara, "Go wash down?"

"Absolutely," she responded. She did not seem tired either.

They walked in darkness to a separate building with a shower room. The sizeable tiled space had six shower heads sticking out of the wall, but there was no running water. It did have a drain, though. The general believed that the showers had been inoperable since long before the destruction. A two-burner camping stove was set up along one wall in the room, next to a 55-gallon barrel filled with water. For bathing, water could be heated up on the stove in two large pots.

The door to the shower room was unlocked so Kid and Sara walked in and froze. The room was not empty. "Guys! Seriously?" Kid felt like he was scolding mischievous children. By now, he knew he should not be surprised but was still caught off guard.

By the light of a lantern, they could see Maria on all fours. Jess was on his knees behind her, and they were both naked.

Sara covered her eyes, grabbed Kid's hand, and they quickly backed out of the room.

Maria's voice cracked, and she sounded winded. "Sorry. Occupied."

"We can see that!" Sara said as she closed the door.

Kid started laughing as they took a short walk. "Can't they just lock the door for a change?"

"That would make sense," Sara said. "Makes you wonder if they do it on purpose. Maybe the risk gives them a thrill. And..." she stopped. "Wait a minute."

"What is it?"

"I'll bet they took them already."

"Took what?" He was confused.

"The Viameen pills! Remember I told you about those sensitivity enhancers they handed out on the ship during sexual activity periods and how my hand was shaking so much that I accidentally grabbed five? And then put four in my pocket? I kept them."

"Yes, I remember." He knew where this was going and turned to her. "You didn't."

Looking sheepish, she turned her eyes down. "Well, I gave Maria two of the pills and told her to save them for a special occasion. I'll bet they already took them, which is why they're all sexed up in there."

They both turned as Jess stepped out of the shower building, looking a little embarrassed. Maria did not. She just smiled and said, "We left the lantern on for you."

"You guys are lucky it was only us," Kid said. "What if one of the senior citizens had opened the door?"

"Are you kidding, they're already in bed. They all washed down earlier today. You know us. We always wait to be the last ones to bathe on purpose. You two are messing up our routine!" Maria started laughing. Grabbing Sara's arm, she tried to whisper, but Kid heard every word. "Oh my God. I cannot believe how well those pills work."

Sara pinched her brow and said, "Maria, those were supposed to be for a special occasion." She was trying to admonish her, but they both had smiles on their faces.

"Oh this was a special occasion. Problem is, they work so well that I'm really just getting started," Maria said and ran after Jess.

Kid could only laugh. "Those pills work too well."

Sara stepped closer and ran her hand down his chest. With her lips an inch away from his, her next words sounded seductive. "Want to see for yourself?" She opened her palm and held out two small Viameen pills.

He really did not need any pill, but he could see the mischief in Sara's eyes. He shrugged his shoulders.

She handed him a pill and prepared to pop one in her mouth. "I jump if you jump," she said, quoting a line from an old movie.

"Ah, *Titanic*. That didn't work out too well for the guy in the end."

She laughed and popped the pill in her mouth. He did the same, and they both took a swig from his water bottle. They stood and looked around for a few minutes. Kid started to feel flush almost immediately. He thought of kissing Sara's neck and swore he could actually taste her skin. He shook his head and opened the door.

They entered the shower room. Sara turned to close and lock the door while Kid went to the camping stove. He grabbed the two large pots, dunked them into the 55-gallon water barrel to fill them, and put them on the ground. He dropped to his knees, turned on the stove burners, and centered the pots over the flames. When he turned around, Sara was already naked. He was shocked that she could disrobe so fast, but his breath caught in his throat as a wave of sexual arousal coursed through him.

With Kid still on his knees, Sara aggressively grabbed his hair and held his head against her bare midsection. He wrapped his arms around her waist. She tilted his head back, bent down, and kissed him hard. "I'm not sure what's come over me. I've been on an adrenaline rush ever since we climbed that stack at the nuclear plant."

"Me too." Kid tightened his arms around her waist and stood up. Lifting her in the air, he took a few steps and pressed her against the wall. The tiles were cold, and she yelped and arched her back away from the wall.

In the dim lantern light, they stared, eye to eye.

"So you want to battle, huh?" Her voice was gruff as she unbuttoned his pants.

After he pushed his pants down to his ankles, his hand was free so he grabbed the hair behind her neck. "Let's go."

For a second they engaged in a battle with both of them wrestling, then twisting handfuls of hair. Sara tried to use her legs to push away from the wall, but he kept her pinned. She bucked and her forehead smacked into his lower lip, making it bleed.

Letting go of his hair, Sara said, "Oh, baby, I am sorry." She gently kissed his lip until hers turned a brighter shade of red.

"Don't try to soften me up." He said while still holding her hair. As he looked at her bright red lips, he made his point with a single thrust of his waist.

Her eyelids fluttered and she looked up. "I definitely do not want you … softened up." She stopped pushing off the wall, grabbed his hair again and locked her legs behind his lower back. With a perfect entry angle, she drew her legs in tight and forced his waist all the way forward.

While engaged, Sara huffed in his ear, "By the way, I only pretended to lock the door." Before Kid could react, she almost ripped the hair from the back of his head and tightened her legs around him. She continued to arch her back and then release, rolling her hips in a circular pattern. Although worried that the door could open any minute, he couldn't stop.

When their intimate, albeit aggressive, encounter was over, they gently bathed each other.

"Do you feel alright?" she asked as she put her clothes on. "The pill didn't bother you?"

"Not at all. I feel really relaxed, for a change."

It was time to leave so Kid took Sara's hand, walked to the door, and reached for the handle. He pulled, but the door wouldn't budge.

Sara stopped him and held up the lantern. "Hold on. You have to unlock the door first," she said and twisted the deadbolt's thumb-turn.

He turned and gave her a look of mock disapproval. "Wait, you said you didn't lock it…"

"I lied, and you not only bought it, but I think it excited you."

He was, for a change, at a loss for words.

She kissed him gently on the cheek and winked. "I guess we know who won that battle."

# CHAPTER 17

January 19, 2045
Thursday, Morning
Hangar One, Lakehurst, New Jersey
**Twenty-four days after the event**

Kid took a moment to reflect on the prior few days. The best way he could describe it was that the group operated with a sense of purpose, but not a sense of urgency. They were busy all of the time with the many daily tasks, chores, and even repairs and minor renovations. But they had yet to solve the last critical piece of their planned offensive. It was an offensive that he thought could not come soon enough. Kid had solved the first two dilemmas days ago. Number one, he had found them a suitable surveillance post with the off-gas stack at the nuclear power plant. They now climbed to that post every day to get a status update on the base camp progress and the ships. Number two, he had figured out a way to force an emergency meeting of the elders. The last critical piece had him, and everyone else, stumped. They needed to figure out a way to isolate the 12 trusted elders and eliminate the rest when they did force an emergency meeting.

Kid was standing outside with Mel, watching the children playing in the snow and trying to roll a snowman. He commented that 13-year-old Megan McDermott seemed to prefer the life of a carefree child. Mel watched her and muttered, "Can you blame her? Who would want to grow up in a world like this?"

Walking back inside, Kid decided to get in some exercise. He stepped into the former classroom they converted to a makeshift fitness center after finding some old gym equipment. Tony and Dr. McDermott were exercising in one area while across the room. Sara was using her hands and feet to work a 50-pound heavy bag. Her agility, speed, and strength were on full display, enough so that Tony and Dr. McDermott stopped and stared. After a spinning back kick, Sara took a breather.

Dr. McDermott was on a stair climbing machine and asked, "Sara, you've obviously had some training?"

Through heavy but measured breaths, Sara said, "Yeah, my Dad made sure I was trained in self-defense when I was young, and then I chose to keep up with it."

"Remind me not to mess with her," Tony commented as he resumed his sit-ups.

"Good call," Kid added as he started jumping rope.

General Hyland remained at the table after the breakfast dishes were cleared. He grabbed a blank notepad and put it in front of him. While thinking, he tapped the point of a pencil on the open page. He still could not solve the issue of isolating the 12 trusted elders if an emergency meeting was called. *There has to be a viable way!*

Adele said, "Eric, you told me you took out all of the satellites when you were on that Mallard Island, but how did you do it exactly?"

The general paused and then clarified, "I programmed the satellites to fire on each other in sequence. I destroyed all but the last satellite since it couldn't fire upon itself."

She sat up straight and looked somewhat concerned. "Wait. There's still one left?"

"It is still up there, but I made it overheat to the point of melting down. The weapon system is fried. Useless now."

Adele nodded. "What about video capability, since it is a separate system?"

The general paused. He had not been as concerned with that at the time. His primary concern had been the weapon system. "With overheating the satellite, it should also be out of commission. The Utopia Project leaders do not have the codes to access the satellite system anyway. Only I have them."

"That they would overcome in time. They had some technology whizzes in the group there," Adele observed.

The discussion generated a curiously in the general. "It would be easy enough to verify that the last satellite is dead. Can you hand me that laptop, please?"

While grabbing the bag from next to her, she pointed to a bulky item in the side pouch. "What is in there?"

"That's the wireless antenna. I used it to link up with the satellites." Unzipping the side pocket, he pulled it out and called over, "Jess, can you put this outside on the ground? Make sure nobody is near it. The powerful waves coming off of that thing are not good for anyone's health."

"Sure. Let me find an area where the kids aren't running around."

Upon Jess returning to the room and giving a thumbs-up, the general linked his computer with the wireless antenna. He logged in and spent a few minutes navigating. 'Oh no, no," he muttered. He jumped to his feet so suddenly that his chair fell on its back. Stepping into the hallway, he yelled, "Get everyone inside, now! Now!"

Kid froze when he heard the general's raised voice. *Something's wrong.* Snapping out of it, he grabbed Sara's hand and tore out of the fitness room. Running to the door to the outside, they waved everyone in.

When they made it to the meeting room inside the hangar, everyone else was already there. Adele was trying to calm the Italy survivors.

Sara asked her father, "What is happening?" She was breathing heavily from the sprint, after having just worked the heavy bag.

"We have a problem, a big problem," the general uttered.

"What kind of…problem?" several voices sounded in unison.

The general exhaled. "The 48th satellite. I had tried to overheat it so that it would melt down entirely, but the video capability survived. The auto recharge, which is solar based, has the satellite all charged up again."

"So they already reconstructed the missing codes?" Adele asked.

"I'm surprised, but yes. I could see from the logs and system status that they got the satellite online just yesterday afternoon, so they are able to link up and use the video." He paused and sighed. "Thankfully, the weaponry is destroyed, or we would have even bigger problems."

Adele only looked partially relieved. "And we are fortunate they just got it operational now, but doesn't the video have infrared capability?"

"Usually it would, but it was tied into the weapon system, so it is not currently functional," General Hyland clarified. "That is a programming issue though and is fixable. Not easily, but it can be done."

Kid and Sara looked at each other and both seemed to be contemplating the repercussions.

The general set his chair upright and sat on the edge of the seat. "And, they beefed up the security to make all access read-only, probably for anyone other than Elder-3. So I could not alter or delete files, or change settings. I got in far enough to see that they had video access. I didn't even have the authority in the system to see the video feed myself, and I can't do anything about it."

"By you logging in, does that mean they know you are still alive?" Kid's mind was racing.

"Doubt it. I was logged in as Elder-53, since I know his credentials, and I was only in the system for a minute with read-only access. That would not be flagged."

"Wait, does this mean we have to stay out of sight all the time?" Sara asked.

He nodded. "There is no telling when we will be in sight as the satellite circles the globe, so the answer is yes."

"With only having one satellite, I'm sure they widened the video field as much as possible," Adele added. "But if they get the infrared operational again, even hiding will not save us. They will be alerted that there are live human beings when our area is scanned as the satellite passes over."

"I hate to say it," General Hyland started, sounding somber, "but it is probably a matter of *when* they get the infrared operational, not if."

"That is a big problem," Kid reiterated. "We can't live this way."

Mel chimed in, "Now we can't even go somewhere far away to live out the rest of our lives in peace, like I had thought about doing at one time. It isn't even an option anymore."

Glancing around the room, Kid realized that a few of the Italy survivors must have been contemplating the idea of doing just that because they hung their heads and appeared deflated.

The general jumped to his feet as if trying to shake off the shock.

"Listen, at least we did not find out the hard way that they now have video access. And if they had recreated the computer codes to link up with the satellites and add a security layer before I initiated the destruction of the other 47 satellites the other day, I never would have succeeded, and they would have all 48 satellites at their disposal, weapons, video and all."

Closing the laptop, the general stated with assurance, "We need to accelerate our plans for an offensive. We are already out of time, and we didn't even know it until this moment."

"What if they have already spotted us?" Sara asked.

"I don't think they have," the general answered.

She looked concerned. "How do you know?"

"Because they would have attacked already."

After getting past the stunned silence, Kid said, "Jess, we need to find a tarp or something to cover the M3 outside." He turned to the general. "And don't worry, we will make sure it is really fastened down this time," he added, referring to the tarp that blew off of the M3 on the Island of Capri.

General Hyland nodded his head. "The M3 would be a dead

giveaway. Please, try to move quickly."

Taking off in a sprint, Kid and Jess left the room. The hangar had tarps and covers of all shapes, sizes, and colors. They headed outside with a white covering which would blend in with the snow on the ground. The M3 was covered and on their way back in, the guys reluctantly knocked over and pulverized the snowman the kids had built.

Now that everyone was safely inside, the general called for an emergency meeting. Unlike how the day started, there was now a palpable sense of urgency. Kid listened as Chris got right to the point. "Alright, we got as far as using the nuclear plant threat to force an emergency meeting, so that all of the elders will be together in the member dining room of ship number one, and we have been working on how to do that for days now, but then what? We have to get this figured out."

General Hyland abruptly stood up. "I'll be back. I need a few moments alone to think through a few things. I can no longer just wait for my thoughts to coalesce."

Nobody said a word as General Hyland stepped out. As the silence dissipated, the volume of the chatter in the room started escalating. Kid and Chris Hyland discussed the open piece of the plan to go on the offensive: how to separate out the 12 trustworthy elders as identified by General Hyland and Adele and take out the other elders assembled in the dining room. Every option put on the table was cut to ribbons, although not in any rude or hostile manner. Kid knew they had to critique every option from every angle to make sure they were thinking of everything. Having not found an approach that they thought would work, the group was sitting in silence when the sound of firm, purposeful footsteps cut the air.

General Hyland walked in and stated, "I know how we can get aboard the ships, and how we can separate out the 12 elders we want to save."

After hearing the general's detailed plan, the group, already warmed up and ready to analyze, peppered General Hyland with questions. They ran every aspect of his plan through the mill. He had answers to almost every question and concern. For those few 'what if's' where he had no solution, he said, "Even the most perfect plan is never 100 percent foolproof. But what I have laid out has a high probability of success. My greatest concern is trying to coordinate all of the moving pieces. This offensive requires a nearly perfect synchronization of tasks and for nobody to get caught or held up in doing their part. If any part of the plan comes undone, the entire plan could come undone."

Kid, after looking at the plan from a technical perspective, finally could not escape seeing it from an emotional perspective. He did not like the level of involvement, and direct danger, that Sara would face with her father's plan. She would basically be leading the charge. Evelyn was not pleased with the plan for the same reason. General Hyland responded by saying, "Do you think I like it any more than any of you? Unfortunately, I do not have any other viable ideas."

As a show of strength and confidence, Sara grabbed Kid's hand. "I'm the only one who can do this, Kid, so I have to. I'm ready. And many of us will be putting our lives on the line with this plan."

Resigned to the fact, Kid uttered, "I know. And you know I don't question your ability to do anything…"

"Smart man," Maria commented.

"…but I hate the fact that you would be on the front line," Kid finished.

Chris commented, "Eric, if your plan works, the final hurdle isn't as high of a hurdle. There are many more options in taking out the elders in the member dining room if the 12 elders you want to save are not in there."

Jess asked, "How many entrances and exits does this dining room have where they will be meeting?"

Adele jumped in. "Three. The main entrance, which is a set of double doors, and then there are two separate exit doors out the back of the kitchen."

"And the doors are the automatic sliding kind, like the bedrooms?" Jess followed up.

The general nodded. "Yes, almost all of the doors inside the ships are automatic sliders."

"Once the elders are inside for the emergency meeting, we need to be able to lock all doors closed so nobody can leave, and then take them all out." Kid made eye contact with Jess. Neither one said a word, but Kid could tell his friend was thinking the same thing he was.

"We know how to make the doors stick…" Jess started.

"Pennying," Kid chimed in.

"What is pennying?" Chris asked. Kid and Jess proceeded to explain the process whereby coins are shoved into the frames for the sliding doors, thereby preventing them from opening. After hearing the explanation, Chris said, "Great idea, but I am thinking that we can find a better wedge to accomplish the same thing without having to carry a pocketful of change."

Adele, after hearing the general's plan, contended that even if they could take out the elders, the conditioned members were still a big threat. She and General Hyland were now the enemy, and the regular members may not take orders from them any longer, or worse, may try to kill them. In the end, she summed it up by saying, "Listen, you all handle the elders, and I will handle the regular members. I worked with these members for years, so I will come up with a plan to address them."

Over the next hour, the group divided up the necessary tasks to be done. They had much to do over the next few days before commencing with the planned attack. Much of the preparation work had to be done inside the hangar or in the dark of night to avoid detection.

With the meeting winding down, Kid sat back and rubbed his cheeks with his hands. He knew his eyes were bleary. Despite all of the thorough planning, he realized the odds were still very bleak. He would never verbalize such feelings, and to the contrary he outwardly remained focused on the possibility of success. Dwelling on the odds would do little to keep him or the others motivated. The plan was so complicated with so many moving parts. He met General Hyland's eye, and somehow knew that Sara's father was feeling the same way.

The general finally adjourned the meeting. For a moment nobody moved, and the room was eerily silent. Maybe others knew the odds as well. What Kid felt looming in the pervasive silence at the end of the meeting was what they all knew hung in the balance. It was not just the fate of any one of them individually. It was the fate of humanity itself.

# CHAPTER 18

January 19, 2045
Thursday, Afternoon
Hangar One, Lakehurst, New Jersey
***Twenty-four days after the event***

For the rest of the day on Thursday, General Hyland and the group anxiously prepared for the planned attack, but they could not risk moving about outside during the day and being spotted by the lone remaining satellite. Daylight hours were fortunately shorter in January, but to avoid detection after sundown, they had to drive without the benefit of headlights. Unfortunately, they didn't have any moonlight to help either, so they had to drive at an agonizingly slow speed.

That night General Hyland and his father drove in darkness to Fort Dix to grab specification sheets and manuals for the biological weapons kept on the base. The general knew where to find the key to the safe where such important documents were stored. After securing what he needed, he loaded the documents into an empty copy paper box. He would spend the daylight hours the next day, Friday, determining which biological agent would best suit their purposes for the planned attack.

Before leaving the base, as part of the general's plan, they needed to secure regular member uniforms. They proceeded to take the uniforms from the dead soldiers that had been stacked in a bathroom, except for the one that was burned and scorched. Given the random bullet holes and blood stains tarnishing the ones they took, when they got back to Hangar One they would have some washing and mending to do.

While driving back, General Eric Hyland slowed down and stopped the vehicle as he approached the ghostly outline of an overpass that went over the road. He seemed hesitant to go under it.

"What is it, Son?"

"A moment of déjà vu. I remember an overpass just like this one, but somewhere in New York State."

"I'm sure you've gone under hundreds of overpasses," Chris noted. "What's so special about the one in New York?"

Putting the vehicle in park, Eric sat back and exhaled. "During my freshman year at West Point, I borrowed a friend's car and was on my way back to the academy, driving on the New York Thruway..."

"So you were using your Plebe leave pass for the semester?" his father smirked.

The general smiled at his father's reference to the name given to all freshmen at West Point -- a name equating them to the poor Plebian commoners in ancient Rome. "Yes, and I had to get back to campus, but the traffic had stopped moving. So I turned off the car like everyone else and was staring at the outline of an overpass just like this one. And then something happened that changed my life."

"What happened?"

"A group of sport motorcycles approached on the other side of the road and the lead bike lost it. The driver was thrown in the air and hit the concrete overpass. Her head just...exploded, and her smoking bike slid by me on the other side of the road."

"Her?" Chris asked. "How did you know the biker was female, especially if, and not to be grim, her head exploded?"

"Because the guy on the bike behind her pulled off the road and while walking in circles on the highway, he was screaming, 'She was my only sister!' Then a car swerved around the corpse, and the heartless son of a bitch behind the wheel started beeping and waving his hand at the distraught brother, telling him to get the hell out of the road."

"You've got to be kidding," his father uttered.

"I wish I was." With the recollection Eric again shook his head. "Who would do something like that? It was a moment so cold and so inhuman. And if that wasn't bad enough, other people started yelling and laying on their horns. The whole incident severely damaged my faith in humanity."

With a faraway look in his eyes, the general said, "I felt for the brother, losing his only sister."

Chris turned his eyes down. "I could see how that would strike a chord."

The silence lingered until Eric continued. "Anyway, after that, I had decided that I was going to quit West Point and find a career where I could make a difference in saving the human race, a race that obviously needed to be saved. So when I got back, I told the officers I was quitting."

His father looked stunned. "You never told me this."

"I know. I was afraid to. But my superiors convinced me that the military had the resources and influence to help the human race, and that they were working on many pilot projects with just such a focus. One of them was what would become the Child Condition-ing Program. They convinced me that they would blend my technical expertise with projects targeted toward helping humanity, so I stayed."

"That was a powerful moment for you," Chris noted.

"It was. And had that biker incident never happened," the general said conclusively, "I never would have turned my focus to projects I thought would help or save the human race, like the Utopia Project, and we wouldn't be sitting here right now."

He started the car back up and glanced pensively at the overpass as he drove under it.

• • •

Thursday night, Kid, Jess, Emilio, and Dylan drove on Route 37 East and then picked up the Garden State Parkway south to Forked River. A couple of times Kid had to swerve to avoid vehicles strewn about the unplowed roads, which he was used to. Every previously busy road had cars strewn about. The unsuspecting drivers were going about their lives when the destruction occurred.

They first stopped at the Oyster Creek Nuclear Generating Station in Forked River. While Emilio and Dylan were instructed to secure all of the air freshener spray bottles they could find in the building, Kid and Jess used shovels and took on the gruesome task of scraping up the remains of the melted body on the floor of the control room. Kid found it merciful that the mound was mostly rigid, having dried out and settled over time. The gore filled three heavy-duty plastic bags, which were taken, along with a soiled chair, to a dumpster outside.

After dosing the control room repeatedly with bleach and air freshener while leaving the doors open so the space could air out, Kid brought the group in and pointed to the switches he had wrapped with rubber bands. Outside, in the cold but otherwise fresh air, he took Emilio and Dylan to the off-gas stack and showed them the ladder that he and Sara had climbed.

When Kid's short tour of Oyster Creek was over, the group drove a little further south and stopped at a house on the lagoon system in the town of Waretown. Under Jess's direction they worked with hardly any light to retrofit a sailboat belonging to one of his former co-workers. They had to make a run to the local hardware store and get some supplies, including black paint. By the time they had finished working on the sailboat, dawn was almost upon them.

January 20, 2045
Friday, Late Afternoon
Hangar One, Lakehurst, New Jersey
***Twenty-five days after the event***

Late Friday afternoon, as soon as the sun set, General Hyland, Chris, Kid, Sara, and Dr. McDermott headed to Fort Dix within the Joint Base for another mission-critical purpose.

"What time did you finally wake up today, Kid?" the general asked as he drove. "You guys didn't get back to the hangar until dawn this morning."

"Some time after midday. Late enough that I had spaghetti for breakfast. But since Estelle makes her own sauce, or gravy as she calls it, I could eat spaghetti for breakfast every day."

"I hear that," the general commented as he pulled into the base and shut the vehicle down. "Alright, follow me, but please, do not touch anything."

After accessing a highly secure area, General Hyland donned a hazmat suit and air mask before entering the area where biological weapons and gases were stored. Having done his research the day before, he knew exactly what he was looking for. Casing out the inventory using a battery powered lantern, he found the canisters of P55. Even though he was wearing a sealed hazmat suit, he still hesitated to touch it. It was a gas so lethal that one whiff of it resulted in immediate death.

General Hyland carefully picked up the canister with two hands and laid it on a table. The tube was surprisingly small, and the general thought it resembled a relay baton from a track meet. On the side of the canister was a tiny digital screen with an even smaller power button. He put a book on each side of the cylindrical tube to keep it from rolling off the table, and he turned around. Having read the manual for the remote detonation process, he scanned the shelves just inside the door and was able to locate the handheld digital detonators.

For the next several minutes, he worked to pair a handheld detonator with the canister and created a simple password to initiate a 30-second countdown to detonation. Upon deployment, he programmed the canister to launch to a height of seven feet before it started spinning at a high rate of speed, casting its deadly gas far in every direction. Given the coverage area, an entire dining room filled with elders could easily be killed with just one canister, but that left no margin for error or canister failure. Given that, General Hyland gently carried over a second canister and also paired it with the handheld detonator.

While the others waited patiently outside the secure weapons area, the general finished his task by locating a small, fully-sealed and indestructible box about the size of a shoe-box. He carefully placed the two canisters of P55 and the handheld detonator inside. Leaving the secure area and stepping out of his hazmat suit, the general held the box tightly. For the entire ride back to Lakehurst, the box never left his hands. Even once inside Hangar One, he held it on his lap.

Despite everyone beginning to wind down, the general and Kid encouraged everyone to force themselves to stay up late that night, until at least 2:00 A.M., and then sleep late Saturday. With the plan to unfold late Saturday night and into Sunday morning, they were hoping everyone's sleep schedule would be slightly shifted so that they would be alert and rested for the offensive.

With all preparations complete, Kid checked his watch. 10:00 P.M. He was tired but knew it was too early to go to bed. "Everything is done, and since we are staying up until 2:00 A.M., we have time to kill."

"What to do," Sara pondered as she sat on the tabletop. "I am too anxious to just sit here. How about taking a walk?"

Thinking for a second, he said, "Sure. And I know where we can go. The spot where we went to reconnect last April after I kept begging you."

She smirked and put her hand on his shoulder. "You really didn't have to beg me. I was so ready to meet you again. I just didn't want to show it."

"Oh, now the truth comes out. I did all of that begging and groveling for nothing?" He leaned back against her closed knees.

"I wouldn't say that. I rather enjoyed it." She laughed while wrapping her arms around his neck. She opened her knees while pulling his body closer and said a little more seriously, "Actually, it made me realize that you cared for me as much as I cared for you."

At that, he leaned up and kissed her cheek.

Maria, sitting on the table next to them, said, "Alright, Mr. and Mrs. Make-me-want-to-gag, where is this special reconnection spot?"

"The Lakehurst Diner, just up the road," Kid answered.

"Are you looking to be alone, or can Jess and I go with you?" she asked. "I need to watch my blood sugar, but if I am not going to sleep for a while. I definitely need to eat something."

Kid's and Sara's eyes met, and they both shrugged. "Feel free to come along," Sara offered.

"Although it is night, remember not to do anything that could expose you to the satellite still in the sky out there," the general reminded.

# CHAPTER 19

January 20, 2045
Friday, Evening
Lakehurst, New Jersey
**Twenty-five days after the event**

Walking on the snow-covered South Hope Chapel Road, the group passed a small, Norman-Gothic chapel. Made of gray stone, it stood in the trees off the road. Staring, Maria said, "Is it me, or does that creepy church give you the feeling that if you walked over to it, you would actually step back in time?"

"I wouldn't say it is creepy, but it definitely has a strange, medieval vibe," Jess said.

"It is old, but certainly not medieval," Kid said. "It was dedicated in 1932."

"Oh, well excuse us." Maria bumped into Kid and gave him a light elbow to the midsection. She turned to Sara. "Mr. Know-it-all over here."

Maria and Sara started laughing until Kid, having picked up a stick, was able to crack both of their rear ends at the same time. The snap was loud, and the stick broke in half. Both girls screamed.

Reflexively, Maria turned and smacked Jess, who had nothing to do with it. She kept walking and laughing until Jess pelted her in the back with a snowball. Turning around, her eyes narrowed. "Oh, now your ass is mine. Sara, they are declaring war on us."

"What? How did I..." Sara started but was hit in the chest by an errant snowball throw from Jess. He waved apologetically. She smiled but through clenched teeth muttered to Maria, "Game on." They both reached down and quickly packed snowballs.

Kid was still chuckling at the errant snowball hitting his girlfriend when he was pegged in the forehead. Sara burst out laughing and brushed the snow off of her gloved hands. "Is something...funny?"

"Not anymore." He turned to Jess and both nodded as they reached down into the snow. Within seconds, they were heaving volley after volley of snowballs until Sara and Maria ran over by the chapel and took cover behind a couple of pine trees.

After taking hit upon hit, Sara screamed, "Charge!" Maria and she ran at Kid and Jess. While playfully wrestling, the girls succeeded with what clearly their new plan -- to stuff snow down the guys' pants.

Now tired, all four of them were bent over laughing and panting at the same time.

"We're acting like children. I guess we needed that," Kid noted.

"I didn't need snow down my pants," Jess responded.

"Poor Jess. His balls are bluer than ever," Maria said laughing.

"We need to be careful not to tire ourselves out too much." Kid started walking through the five inches of powder covering the asphalt. "We have the longest, toughest night of our lives coming up tomorrow."

As Kid reached for the handle at the door of the Lakehurst Diner, he stopped.

"What are you waiting for?" Maria asked.

"If there is anything we should have learned by now, it's to make sure we're prepared for the sight and smell of death. This diner would have been open when the destruction came."

"True. But I have to eat something, so I'll just hold my nose and head for the kitchen," Maria said. She grabbed Jess's flashlight and opened the door. The rest of the group followed her in.

Kid also turned on his flashlight upon entering. Shining the beam of light straight ahead in clear view were the remains of two patrons spread over and under two of seats along the counter.

"Answers that," Jess noted. "Let's grab some food and head down the road to that church to eat there."

"Good idea. While Maria and you case out the kitchen, Sara and I need to go sit for just a minute for nostalgia's sake."

Kid took Sara's hand and started walking toward the booth in the back where they had reconnected in April of the year before. "Jess, remember the food back there has been sitting for more than two weeks," Sara called out.

"Got it." Jess pushed open the swinging doors to the kitchen, following Maria.

Going to the last booth in the back, Kid and Sara sat across from each other. He stood the flashlight so the light shined straight up at the ceiling. They held hands across the table, and as his vision adjusted to the dim lighting, he found Sara's eyes. They stared at each other, and he felt the usual warmth of their connection.

"So much has happened since we were here last April," Sara started. "To think at that time the only thing I had to worry about was how our meeting would go. I so much didn't want things to go awry."

"I was nervous, first and foremost, that you would even show. I figured you'd stand me up again like you did at the bench up in Vermont," he quipped and started laughing.

Sara squeezed his hands and opened her eyes wide, "What? I…"

Before she could get the words out, Kid leaned over the table and kissed her on the cheek.

"I…" she tried, but he quickly kissed her cheek again.

Finally she just started laughing too. She kissed his cheek and pushed him back in his seat. "I…" she started and raised a finger, playfully warning him, "…couldn't wait to get here and see you again. Couldn't you tell that from the moment we made eye contact?"

"Yes. I almost melted." They both turned their heads and noticed the remains of two bodies in the booth across from them. "Bad choice of words."

Pinching her nose, Sara stated, "Geez. This is a far cry from the last time we were in here, when I was absorbing the smell of the beautiful rose you gave me. Kiss me, and let's get out of here." He leaned over the table and gently kissed her lips. She squeezed his hands and stood up.

Walking to the front, Maria and Jess were in the kitchen loading a box with food and bottles of soda. "Jackpot. We found an apple pie, still partially frozen," Maria said excitedly. "Jess, throw a bunch of silverware and napkins in the box."

While leaving, Kid made the mistake of shining his flashlight at the space behind the counter. There he saw a mound of human remains and recognized the standard uniform of the waitresses who worked there. He recalled the nice woman who had waited, or nearly waited, on Sara and him the prior April. He was hoping it wasn't her body he was seeing until Sara pointed to the black mound of hair at the edge of the puddle. Although it had partially unraveled, it was clearly the bun of the same waitress. When Kid turned to Sara, she looked sad, and her eyes welled.

"Time to go." Kid stood next to the case of desserts and noticed that they no longer seemed fresh. The piece of German chocolate cake appeared petrified and hard as a rock. Clicking off his flashlight, he held the door open so the others could exit.

Walking up the road, Jess was still holding the box as they approached the entrance to the Cathedral of the Air chapel.

"Why is the door in the back?" Jess asked.

"Good question," Kid responded as he realized Jess was right. It was odd that the rear of the chapel faced the road, as if turning its back to the world. "I guess they needed the entrance to face west, based on where the altar is."

Pointing to a metal plate fixed to the wall next to the door, Kid said, "This is how I knew when the chapel was dedicated." The plaque, which had a green tint from many years in the elements, was inscribed with an American Legion dedication dated 1932. "I read this when I came here for a wedding once."

With the chill in the air, Kid was glad the door was not locked. Walking in, he shined his light and stopped. "But how did I miss these," he muttered. On the wall were two large plaques dedicated to other dirigibles that shared a fate similar to the Hindenburg: the U.S.S Akron and the U.S.S. Shenandoah. He recalled General Hyland mentioning that there were more casualties with the crash of the U.S.S. Akron than the more famous Hindenburg. Looking at the length of the roster of the dead, he was clearly right.

"You could have been more of a know-it-all," Maria quipped as she walked around him.

Stepping inside the nave, Kid glanced up at the top of the vaulted, dark-wood ceiling. Grabbing two decorative candlesticks, Kid put them on the top step leading up to the altar. After lighting them, he was able to turn off his flashlight. The group sat in the front row of pews, with Kid and Sara on one side of the aisle and Jess and Maria on the other.

Everyone dug in and ate as much cold food as their stomachs would allow. Maria grunted with relief as she scoffed down a piece of apple pie. Kid was eating pepperoni, cheese, and crackers.

"It pisses me off," Jess grumbled.

Kid asked, "What is that?"

"I finally could afford to put a deposit down on an NFL virtual seat package and this happens." Kid smirked as he wasn't expecting such a response. But he knew that for years Jess had wanted to secure a virtual seat season pass for the New York Giants football team. Although it was much less money than the cost of an actual seat at the game, it was still not a cheap endeavor. But by purchasing a virtual seat, Jess could put on a headset and watch the game from the 50-yard-line while sitting on his couch.

"Is this a Catholic Church?" Maria's eyes wandered.

"It is non-denominational," Kid noted. "That's the only other thing I remember from the wedding I attended here, besides the stained glass windows."

"Stained glass windows?" Sara glanced around. "What was so memorable about them?"

"When we finish our food, I'll show you."

After eating, Kid grabbed another candle and lit it. Sara and he walked up to the altar. Above the cross was piece of stained glass inside a circle. The decorative glass had five points that were rounded and resembled the petals of a flower. Walking around the perimeter of the church, he held the candle higher to illuminate the decorative, custom-made stained glass panels.

"You weren't kidding," Sara whispered in awe. "They are incredible. Most of the artwork is related to flight."

"When I was here for that wedding, they said that the scenes depicted man's quest to reach the heavens," Kid noted. "Hence the name of this place, Cathedral of the Air." Like a tour guide, Kid walked around and pointed. "Let's see. Pegasus the winged horse. Icarus. Dirigibles. And as I'm sure you know -- the Wright brothers' first flight."

"Wing-warping," she muttered.

"What?" he asked.

"Oh, that's the first thing I remember when I hear the Wright brothers. It was from a science class in high school."

"Science? You mean history?"

"No, it was science. Physics actually. We had a section on aeronautics. Our teacher had his own version of a wind tunnel, and we had to experiment with flight designs like the Wright brothers to determine the impact of wing-warping." Kid was looking at her expectantly, so she continued.

"That is when you twist and flex the wings of an aircraft to adjust to the wind, which allows you to maintain a course, or turn, especially in the face of heavy winds. One of the Wright brothers supposedly thought of it while twisting both ends of an empty box in opposite directions."

Kid absorbed what Sara was saying and tried to understand the concept. He had never really thought of it before, but he understood how flexing the wings could alter a flight trajectory.

"I wish we did cool experiments like wing-warping in my class when I was in high school. All I remember doing was making a tornado in a soda bottle," he said.

In the back of the chapel, Kid and Sara sat in a pew. He was a bit overwhelmed at the moment. He was sure it was because of the burden he was carrying in his subconscious about the life or death mission planned for the next night. He couldn't explain it, but Kid felt compelled to bow his head and pray. He prayed first for safety and second for success. He tried to sway the Lord by reminding him that if they lost the battle, God would die, if that was even possible, with humanity. So if there was ever a time for God to intervene, it was now.

Kid turned his head and went to say something to Sara. He realized she too had her head bowed in prayer. He was not surprised. He knew that they were very much philosophically aligned when it came to religion. They both devotedly believed in God but had a hard time aligning with any particular church or sect.

When Sara raised her head, Kid grabbed her hand and stood up. They walked to the front of the chapel. They took a seat in the first pew next to Jess and Maria. The group sat in silence staring at the cross hanging over the altar. Inside the Gothic chapel, they all seemed to be caught up in the same thoughts. Finally, it was Maria who put it on the table. "Tomorrow night is all or nothing, isn't it?"

Kid nodded his head slowly. "Yes. We're throwing everything we have to try and save humanity."

"Let's be straight," Jess said. "Tomorrow night into Sunday morning, we will live and succeed, or we will die and fail."

"So tonight may be our last night on this planet," Maria concluded in a somber voice.

Sara exhaled heavily. "It may be. We are taking our one and only shot at this. We have to."

"Look around at this disgusting world we now have," Kid added. "We can't live in this, not without some kind of hope that we can make this world a better place going forward. That is why we choose to fight rather than go hide somewhere and just wait to be caught. What kind of life would that be?"

"A dead end," Sara answered.

"I have to admit, I am scared shitless about tomorrow night," Maria said.

She turned to Kid and Jess and seemed to be expecting some consolation. Instead, Kid shook his head in agreement. "So am I, Maria. So am I."

"Me too," Sara agreed. "How can't we be?"

Everyone sat staring at the cross behind the altar. Finally, Kid dropped to his knees. "God bless us all."

They all bowed and repeated Kid's words before stepping out the door. Making the short walk back to Hangar One, they were all ready for what could be the last sleep from which they would ever awake.

# CHAPTER 20

January 21, 2045
Saturday, Evening
Hangar One, Lakehurst, New Jersey
**Twenty-six days after the event**

Saturday, everyone slept as late as possible and tried to rest throughout the day.

Come 10:00 P.M. that evening, Kid and seven others from his group, including Sara, General Hyland, Adele, Jess, Maria, Tony, and Dr. McDermott were ready to embark and get in position for the offensive. They were considered the mission's first team, and all were wearing insulated thermal underwear, as well as hats and gloves.

The mission's second team included Emilio and Dylan, who were going to follow behind in an SUV and get in position for their part of the operation. Despite her weakened state, Karen insisted on accompanying the second team to provide moral support.

It was a difficult good-bye for many, knowing that some or all of those leaving may never return. Estelle held her son Tony's hands and kissed the back of each before putting them against her cheek. She also kissed her son Emilio and reminded him that even though his part of the offensive was less dangerous than Tony's, it was every bit as important.

Sara was face to face with her grandmother. "Can you move in that uniform?" Evelyn asked. "It looks tight."

Wiggling her shoulders, arms and waist, Sara said, "It is small, but it has some stretch. It could be worse. At least mine belonged to a female. See hers?" She pointed over at Maria, who was also wearing one of the Utopia Project uniforms from a dead soldier at the McGuire airfield. Evelyn glanced over. "From the four uniforms we had to choose from, the only one that came close to fitting her was from a male member, and," Sara lowered her voice to a whisper, "the male uniforms do not leave much room for breasts."

"I see," she whispered back.

"Maria calls it her mammogram simulation suit."

"She looks uncomfortable," Evelyn said as Maria reflexively tugged on the front of her uniform, as if doing so would create more room for her full bosom.

"And we still have to slip the cylinders of P55 inside the front of our uniforms. So we may both be flat-chested by the time we are done." She hugged her grandmother.

Kid hugged Mel and her girls before saying, "Be at the ready."

Mel put her hand on his shoulder. "The M3 is fueled, armed, uncovered, and ready to roll. Good luck. It is going to be a long night, but I've already seen enough to know that if anyone can pull it off, you guys can."

After walking out of Hangar One, Kid got his group into a vehicle and headed south down the Garden State Parkway. Emilio followed close behind at the wheel of an SUV. The moonlight was faint at best, so Kid could only sustain a maximum speed of 30 miles per hour. He slowed as they turned off the Forked River exit and came to a complete stop when he finally reached the entrance to the Oyster Creek Nuclear Generating Station.

Kid, Sara, and Dr. McDermott jumped out into the cold air to bid the smaller group farewell.

Turning to Emilio and Dylan, Kid asked, "Do you guys remember where everything is inside the plant from the tour the other night?"

Sitting in the front seats, both nodded and said in unison, "Yes."

"And you have the strobe light?"

"It is in the back," Emilio answered with his Italian accent.

For his peace of mind, Kid walked behind the vehicle and opened the hatch. He reached in, flipped a switch and a pulsing red light hit him right in the face. He quickly shut it off and closed the back door.

He walked to the driver side window. "Time?" He proceeded to make sure their watches were all synchronized.

"Walkie-talkies. Set to channel nine?" After they confirmed, Kid patted the one on his hip and said, "Remember, you have different walkie-talkies than we do. Yours only communicate with each other and the group back at the hangar, including Mel. The first team can't have you accidentally beeping in at an inopportune moment."

Both again nodded.

"Finally, weapons?" Kid asked.

Emilio said, "I don't have a weapon." He looked at Dylan and then back at Karen. Both of them shook their heads.

"Maybe I could give you one of ours…" Kid started.

Dr. McDermott interjected and said, "They were not provided with any because the second team had no need for weapons. They are just supposed to turn on the sirens and the light and get back to the hangar. Not to mention, Dylan has never fired one."

The doctor seemed uncomfortable with his son handling a gun, so Kid nodded and let it go. And it was true that the second team should not need weapons, but in Kid's mind, everyone should be armed at all times.

"Good luck," Kid said and offered his hand. While shaking, Emilio used his other hand to catch a lens as it fell out of his eyeglass frame.

"You need to fix that," Kid said.

"I know." Emilio took off his glasses. "I need to glue it back in or something."

"Here." Dr. McDermott reached into his pocket and pulled out a handful of small superglue tubes. "I keep these in case I need to seal an open wound, or bind something, in a crisis. Take one. I have plenty. That can be your weapon," he quipped.

Peering in the back seat, Kid said, "Karen, you're in charge. Keep these guys awake and ready."

She looked nervous but smiled. "Who is going to keep me awake?"

"The boys and I here thought of that and prepared for a long night. Joe will keep you awake," Kid responded.

"Joe?"

"Dylan may have the operation's most critical supply." He pointed. Dylan held up a thermos full of coffee.

"You do think of everything. Wait." Karen opened the back door. She stepped out and gave Sara and Kid each a quick hug. Lowering her voice, she added with a serious tone, "Make sure you make it back. I don't know what I would do without you guys."

Kid stood at the open driver side window. After depositing a few beads of superglue, Emilio had reinserted the lens into the frame and was holding it in place. "That should do it," he commented.

Nodding his head, Kid said a few final words to the group in the vehicle. "Remember, the strobe light and sirens need to work in tandem and start simultaneously for this to work. I know you know this, but your part of this plan is critical. You are the ones who set the entire plan in motion, and if that doesn't happen, it is doomed from the start."

Karen's eyes opened wide. "We won't let that happen," she stated firmly. As Dylan went to hand her the thermos, she added, "Thanks, but I don't need any Joe. I could not be any more alert than I am now." Emilio adjusted his glasses and drove through the open gate into the plant.

Kid put his vehicle in drive and headed south. Motoring in the dark of night to the municipality of Waretown, they parked next to a lagoon bulkhead. There, Kid, Sara, General Hyland, Adele, Jess, Maria, Tony and, Dr. McDermott boarded a small boat with a sail Jess had painted black a few nights prior. Jess took the helm and after pushing off, he navigated out of the lagoon and started across Barnegat Bay. The sailing was difficult over the choppy water, but they were silent and invisible. Jess's knowledge of tacking was the only thing that allowed them to make it across the bay at all. As they approached the western side of Long Beach Island and the northern end of Surf City, he pulled down the sail and paddled them toward a small sandy beach. As expected, ice rimmed the shore and extended out several feet. When they could not get any closer, Kid went to jump out.

"Wait!" Jess whispered. From the bottom of the boat, he grabbed a pair of thigh-high fishing waders. "Put these on, and when you get to shore, take them off and throw them back to me."

"I'm glad you think of these things," Kid whispered as he slipped the waders over his sneakers and climbed on the ice. After two steps, the ice started breaking, but his feet remained dry. Upon reaching the sand, he took off the waders and tossed them back to Jess. After Jess came ashore, he and Kid together were able to pull the boat onto the small, sandy beach.

Over the next couple of hours, Kid and General Hyland's group moved quietly to set up before the designated time just before the sun came up over the Atlantic Ocean. They first checked for the presence of a night watchman at or around the Surf City Hotel. Casing out the hotel from several angles, there did not appear to be anyone standing to post. The only sound was the collective hum of several generators that had been set up outside the hotel.

They moved toward the ocean at the end of the block behind the hotel and noted that four transport boats rested side-by-side on the sand. The boats were all between 20 and 25 feet long and were a third of the way up the beach, which Kid assumed was to keep them at a safe distance from the ebb and flow of the tide. As Kid approached in the darkness, he could see that all four boats rested on a series of rollers affixed between rows of 2x4 rails that ran southeast down to the beach. The bow of one of the four boats had a cable attached that ran out to sea. It appeared to be a pulley system to launch the boats, but Kid was not exactly sure how it worked. Jess started following the cable and disappeared into the darkness.

Nearby, Sara inspected a stockpile of wood. Various lengths of 2x4s, 2x6s and large pieces of plywood were arranged in neat stacks on the sand.

Kid followed a boardwalk up the beach until he reached a crest. There, the makeshift boardwalk met a real one, and the short path continued in between head-high sand dunes and connected to North 8th street. It was apparent that the Utopia Project members used 8th Street as their primary pathway from the Surf City Hotel to their boats on the beach. As Kid walked on the boardwalk, he crouched down and noticed that the uniform lengths of 2x6s were fastened together with twine.

He was ready to enact a part of the plan he had thought of while viewing the construction of the boardwalk from the off-gas stack at Oyster Creek. Now he just needed some shovels, which he expected to be able to secure without issue.

He was about to go searching when Jess approached. "See those rocks just up the beach?"

"I can't see that far from here," Kid answered. "I can barely see you."

"About 100 feet south of here, there is a rock jetty that extends pretty far out to sea. The cable runs through a couple of huge eye bolts drilled into rocks near the end of it. I think the boats are launched by pulling the cable on the jetty while sliding them down to the waterline using rollers and 2x4 rails. It's simple, but I'll bet it works," Jess said.

"I knew you would figure it out," Kid noted. "Tell everyone to bring it in and follow me. We have to get some shovels and get to work."

The group cased out some sheds behind nearby houses and found the tools they needed. In the dark of night, they took turns digging in teams of two. Kid was breathing heavily from the physical labor, but the work was done quickly with an hour to spare.

The relentless sub-freezing wind was taking its toll, and the group needed to thaw out, so Kid and General Hyland led them to a house on the ocean a few blocks away from the Surf City Hotel. They congregated inside a dramatic and well-appointed living room. Kid moved aside a puffy throw pillow and sat on a plush, flower patterned couch. There was no heat in the house, but just getting out of the constant wind made them all feel warmer. *The air at the ocean is never still.* Kid thought again. The first thing everyone did was empty the beach sand from their shoes onto the floor. He then put his feet up on the dark cherry coffee table. The homeowner, if still alive, would probably not be too pleased, Kid thought.

Although the attack plan had been reviewed many times, Kid and the general thought it best to review one more time. At 3:20 A.M., before stepping out of the luxurious beach house and back into the frigid wind, the general gave the order.

"Everyone prepare to move into positions. Are all walkie-talkies set to channel one?"

After everyone confirmed, he turned and offered his hand to Kid. After shaking hands, the general surprised him with an embrace. "Good luck, Kid."

"Same to you."

For the next few minutes, everyone in the group embraced each other as if they were at an airport and were all boarding separate one-way flights into oblivion. With all of the good-byes in the past few hours, it only emphasized what Kid already knew; the offensive to be launched that morning was a winner-take-all endeavor. They were putting everything on the line for their one chance to alter the rebirth of mankind. This good-bye had a certain finality that hit home with everyone.

They would succeed, or die trying.

It was an age-old quote that he had heard many times in his life, mostly in war documentaries and in stories about life-or-death rescues, but it never fully resonated until now. He finally understood the gut wrench, the swimming brain, the peaks and valleys of emotions, and even the inner conflict nobody sees. He felt the desperation in his silent plea to somehow be saved and not have to go through with it.

He battled overwhelming fear, and with his hands and muscles shaking, he summoned more and more resolve to combat those fears and steady himself. And then came the moment of realization. Nobody was coming to save them, and there was no turning back. A strange calm fell over him, an acceptance of fate, regardless of the outcome.

After embracing Adele, General Hyland turned to his only daughter. "I wish I had a better plan, one where you were not in harm's way at all." His voice was coarse and strained.

"We are all in harm's way, but I believe in this plan. I love you Dad. Don't worry, we can talk more about it after we succeed."

"I love you too, hon," he whispered back.

Next Sara turned to Kid. Her hair, which Adele had freshly trimmed to again meet Utopia Project standards, was stuck to the salty wetness on her face. Kid brushed it off and kissed her cheek.

Jess and Maria came over and shared a group hug. They did not know if they would see each other ever again. But nobody was considering backing down for a second. They were not going to let fear rise above their resolve. Kid could feel it, and it made him love this group ever more. Even now they fed off of each other, and it not only solidified the bond they shared, but it strengthened their collective and individual resolve.

Looking at the three of them, Kid said simply, "The sun will rise today regardless of what happens. But we have a chance to alter what it shines upon, both today and for the future."

"And to save the part of us that is still captivated and inspired by a rising sun at all," Sara added.

"Amen to that." The general interjected, sounding reverent. And then, like flicking a switch, he appeared emotionless as he called for their attention. With authority he said, "Everyone knows where to go and what to do. Let's move out."

# CHAPTER 21

January 22, 2045
Sunday, Before Dawn
Hangar One, Lakehurst, New Jersey
**Twenty-seven days after the event**

ehind Hangar One Melanie Spatz was wrapped in a blanket, resting in the cockpit of the waiting M3. The tarp had been pulled off, and the fuel tank was full. She needed to be ready to lift off with a second's notice. She also had two walkie-talkies turned to full volume sitting on the console next to her. One of them was for the mission's first team and was set to channel one. The other was for the second team going to the nuclear plant, and it was set to channel nine. Although she had no specific assignment in any of the missions, Mel suspected that she may be needed at some point, which kept her from falling asleep.

In the passenger seat was Chris Hyland, also awake and covered by a blanket. Behind them sat Romeo, who was sleeping soundly. Mel knew that once 6:00 A.M. came around, like clockwork, he would be awake and at the ready. She really thought Romeo should have been involved in one of the main missions. Everyone fully trusted him. But given his one relapse at the house on Mallard Island, General Hyland was not 100 percent comfortable with him participating in any such missions. Even if the odds of a relapse were minuscule, it was a chance the general was not willing to take.

Evelyn sighed as she sat on the edge of her cot in the main meeting room of Hangar One. She covered her mouth and waved apologetically to the many eyes that turned her way in the dim light. The room was occupied by all survivors who were not part of a mission down south or were not waiting in the M3 outside the hangar. Even the kids were sleeping in the main meeting room in a fort they made using three folding tables with blankets draped over the sides. Hidden underneath in sleeping bags were Katy and Karly Spatz, Gia Vicarro, Al, and Sal Severino, and even 13-year-old Megan McDermott.

In the same room, but a little distance away from the fort, the remaining adults had arranged their cots around two propane space heaters. On a table in between the heaters stood a wide candle and two walkie-talkies. One unit was tuned to channel one and the other to channel nine, and they both were left on at a lower volume.

Only two of the survivors had been able to fall asleep that night. Theresa Marconi was snoring steadily, and Wendy Levy was in a soundless slumber. Everyone else was too worried about someone, or something, to really sleep. They had conversed in low whispers throughout the night, sharing their fears and trying to comfort each other.

Evelyn was worried sick about Sara, Eric, Kid, and Karen. She knew she would be a nervous wreck until it was all over.

To keep her mind occupied, her eyes traveled around the room. She tried her best to recall the fears that weighed on the other individuals in the room.

Estelle Severino was also sitting on her cot with her hands clasped in prayer. Before they had retired to their beds, which functioned primarily as seats for most of the group that night, Estelle has asked them all to join her in praying for not just her two boys, Tony and Emilio, but for all of the brave souls who had embarked on either of the missions.

Evelyn's eyes moved over and settled on Pamela McDermott. The woman was lying down, but her eyes were wide open. Pam had expressed great concern for her son Dylan and worried that she had sheltered him too much throughout his life. When it came to her talented husband, Dr. Craig McDermott, her primary concern was that he was simply clumsy at times.

Next was Annette Vicarro, who did not like the odds that the missions would succeed. As a distraction from such larger issues, Annette obsessively checked on her daughter, Gia, who was sleeping in the fort. Annette was convinced that Gia was going to wake up in the middle of the night screaming because the child did not know where she was.

Evelyn's eyes then turned to Marissa and Clarence Moore. They were propped up in a large double-sized cot. Marissa was whispering away to him. The Moore's had both expressed their great fears for safety of those participating in the missions, but Marissa had paced for several minutes and would not say a word. She finally pulled Evelyn aside, out of earshot of Pamela McDermott, and said she was feeling extremely anxious because if Dr. McDermott did not survive, Marissa would then be the lead medical professional for the group. "I am not sure I could handle it myself," she had uttered.

Finally, Evelyn turned to the battery-powered clock on the wall. Despite having over-sized hands and Roman numerals, she was barely able to discern the time. Standing up, she moved closer to get an accurate read as she counted down the minutes until the plan was scheduled to commence.

• • •

On the beach in Surf City, Kid checked his watch. 3:55 A.M. Everyone was in place, and despite the constant whistle of the wind, he could hear his heart beating like a drum. "Any second now," he whispered to Tony, crouched next to him behind the bunker of sand.

After observing only silence, Kid again checked his watch. 4:00 A.M. A wave of nervousness cut through the cold air and passed through him. "Come on," he whispered as he waited.

． ． ．

At the Oyster Creek Nuclear Generating Station, Karen checked her watch as she stood at the base of the ladder leading to the top of the off-gas stack. The time was 4:00 A.M. She held a walkie-talkie in her hand and was waiting to tell Emilio in the main control room to flick the switches. She thought of Kid's words. He had said that the plan is doomed from the start if her group did not do their part, and they were already behind schedule.

Staring at the top of the stack, she waited for the strobe light to come to life. That would be her cue, but it was not coming. She tried to follow the ladder with her eyes, but to do so, she had to change her angle to capture some of the waning light from the narrow sliver that was the moon. Dylan had started up quite some time ago with the bowling ball-sized strobe light in a backpack. He should have long since been at the top. She knew something had to be wrong.

About three-quarters up the side of the stack, she spotted a form clinging to the ladder. Her breath caught in her throat. "No! No!" she said, her voice conveying the panic she felt inside.

Dylan was frozen in place.

． ． ．

At Hangar One everyone was now fully awake, including Theresa and Wendy. Most of the people were sitting on their cots, but Evelyn was pacing back and forth. Looking at her watch, she whispered, "4:05. They are behind."

Debbie Severino also stood up. "The call should have already gone to Emilio to flick the switches," she noted, sounding a bit distressed.

"Maybe they are just not ready yet," Pamela McDermott offered.

"That is probably the case," Evelyn responded and tried to smile. She said it but was having a hard time believing it. When it came to schedules and staying on time, she did not know anyone who was more of a stickler about it than her son, Eric. In her heart, she feared that something had already gone wrong with the plan. But she would not say a word. The group was already anxious enough. And in truth, so was she.

• • •

Despite feeling weak and depleted from radiation sickness and the medication with which she was being injected, Karen hurried to climb the ladder of the off-gas stack at the Oyster Creek Nuclear Generating Station. After 50 rungs, she needed to stop and catch her breath. Calling to the inert form on the ladder above, she received no response so she continued her ascent.

When Karen finally reached Dylan, she noticed he was hugging the ladder so tightly that he seemed to have melded with it. Too exhausted to even yell, she pulled at his pant leg. He nearly jumped off the rung in fright, having not heard her approaching. She huffed and puffed and was having a hard time even holding onto the ladder. Her knees and lungs were both knocking. Karen checked her watch and inhaled sharply seeing it was 4:13 A.M. "Go!" she tried to shout, and her volume barely exceeded a whisper.

Still, Dylan heard her. "I can't," he said, sounding distressed. "I was never afraid of heights until now. I can't move!"

"We are blowing the mission." She willed her weak and damaged body to make a final desperate push and take control before it was too late.

"I can't do it," he repeated.

She summoned her resolve, and her voice was firm. "Dylan, we don't have time for me to become your damn counselor. They are counting on us. So either you go, or hand me the strobe light and move!"

Starting to protest again, Dylan did not get one syllable out before Karen found the bottom of her diaphragm and screamed, "Move!" She started to push his legs out of the way so she could climb. His left foot was knocked off of the ladder rung that was sustaining him.

He yelled, "Don't!" and scrambled up the ladder, seeming more afraid of Karen now than of the perilous heights.

At the top of the off-gas stack, Dylan fell in a heap on the metal platform. She came up behind him and pulled the strobe light out of his backpack. Crawling around the perimeter until she was facing due east, she tried to flip the unit on. Dylan recovered enough to point out the power button. A neon-red blinking light pierced the dark of night. Karen grabbed her walkie-talkie, depressed the call button and yelled, "Emilio, now!"

In the control room of the former reactor building far below, Emilio flipped the rubber banded switches and ran to the door. He could hear the closest siren begin to wail. If Kid was right after having studied the Emergency Management Plan documents, the closest few sirens were hard wired from the plant, and the auxiliary power would bring them to life. Then by wireless connections and battery backups, the remaining sirens should be activated and create a deafening ensemble.

• • •

At Hangar One Debbie Severino inhaled and covered her mouth as the walkie-talkie came to life. Karen was radioing down to Emilio.

Pamela McDermott got to her feet. "I thought Dylan was supposed to radio Emilio?"

Evelyn was still pacing. "Your son is probably right there with Karen. But that is just step one," she said. "I doubt we will be able to hear the sirens from here, but they should be on now."

Outside the hangar, Mel heard Karen over the walkie-talkie on channel nine. She sat up straight and turned on the M3. After making sure the craft was in lights-out mode, she lifted off. With the thrusters perpendicular to the ground, she raised the craft straight up in the air. Once high enough, she spotted the pulsing red blip in the distance and knew it was the strobe light. She pointed it out to Chris, who nodded and confirmed, "That's the signal." They spoke in quiet voices as to not wake Romeo, who was sound asleep in the seat behind them.

A wave of adrenaline coursed through Mel and sharpened her focus. As she lowered the craft to the ground and shut it down, she whispered, "So it begins."

• • •

Restlessness made Kid stand up from behind his bunker of sand on the beach. General Hyland, positioned behind his own sand mound across the way, also popped his head up. Although his vision was adjusted to the darkness, Kid could only see the white of another pair of eyes, but he would know the general's steely gaze anywhere.

"What is taking them?" the general asked quietly but with concern. "We are running out of time!" he added, as if dawn was about to pounce at any moment.

Kid went to answer. His face froze with his mouth agape. Through the cut in the sand dunes marking the North 8th Street beach and across the bay to the west, a bright blinking red light pierced the dark sky. He raised his hand and pointed.

A moment later, at 4:20 A.M., the noise came. At first the sound was barely discernible, like a growl emanating from the depths of an animal's gut. But the sound continued to rise in volume, and every time Kid thought it was at maximum, it increased another notch. The tone and roar of the nuclear warning sirens made the hair on the back of his neck stand up. With the battery backups finally being called into action, dozens of sirens came to life and wailed in unison. Having lived a few miles from the plant, Kid had heard many nuclear siren tests in his life, but they paled in comparison to the real deal. For a second he mused that the noise was loud enough to wake the dead. But given the hundreds of thousands of corpses within range of the sirens, he found his own thought tasteless.

Crouching back down behind his sand bunker, Kid's heart raced faster than he thought was humanly sustainable. The sirens were deafening, which he assumed was by design. There was no turning back now. If he was a fighter, this was the bell to start the fight. "This better work."

His bunker faced northwest, but he turned to gaze upon the ocean as the lights of all three Utopia Project ships came to life, including the flood lights covering the decks. The multiple points of illumination from the three vessels merged into one eerie visage, making the ships look like a ghost flotilla.

Within a minute, Kid had gone from a world of silence, darkness, and stillness to a scene of utter chaos. Nuclear warning sirens blared, a red strobe light flashed on top of the nuclear plant's off-gas stack, the ships were lit up at sea, and bright spotlights were sweeping the water in all directions.

# CHAPTER 22

On Utopia Project Ship Number One, Elder-3 was with a group of high-ranking elders on the bridge. They had been abruptly awoken in the dark of night by the wail of sirens. It took them little time to ascertain that the sirens were part of the nuclear warning system, especially after spotting the emergency signal blinking brightly on the plant's off-gas stack. Elder-3 was frustrated by this unanticipated disturbance.

Elder-10 concluded, "This must be a malfunction of the emergency warning system. The records indicate that the plant was already in the decommissioning phase and has been offline for many years."

"Does that mean that there is no radiation danger?" Elder-3 asked.

None of the elders would commit, and there were no Utopia Project contingency plans regarding a nuclear power plant in the decommissioning phase.

Elder-3 looked out the window at the blinking light on top of the off-gas stack. Although all windows on the bridge were closed, it annoyed him that the elders had to speak at higher than conversational volume due to the steady wail of the sirens. He said, "Get Elder-27 and Elder-68 here right away. They are both engineers with expertise in the nuclear field."

Within moments Elder-27 and Elder-68 were standing front and center.

For a long moment Elder-3 was silent. The others on the bridge were watching him expectantly, but he needed to zero in on the true risk they were facing, if any. Finally, he turned to the two engineers. "If Oyster Creek Nuclear Plant has been compromised, is it possible that we might be in danger from radiation?"

"That plant was in the decommissioning phase. We doubt it," Elder-68, a lanky American, said almost dismissively.

Elder-27, a stocky, stone-faced Russian, nodded in agreement.

"We will repeat the question. Is it possible that we might be in danger from radiation, or not?" Elder-3 asked impatiently.

"Possible or probable?" Elder-68 countered.

Elder-3 turned abruptly toward him and was about to shout when Elder-27 opened his mouth. "Possible, Sir, yes. They were storing spent material on site. If the encasement has been damaged or broken, it is possible."

Composing himself, the lead elder said, "Go on."

"If containment has been breached, and if the wind is blowing from the west, it would be of concern given how close we are to the plant. It may not be an immediate danger, but having our group dusted with radiation could cause problems now, or even down the road."

"Which direction is the wind blowing?"

Elder-110 checked some controls on the bridge. "From the south, Sir."

"Good." Elder-3 was relieved. "It does not appear to be an imminent threat then, which is good because much progress has already been made in setting up the base camp, and..."

Elder-10 cut in, "Excuse me, Sir, the wind is shifting. It is now coming from the southwest."

"Check again!" Elder-3 snapped as he stared out the window.

"Same, Sir."

Struggling to find the right words, Elder-8, who knew only his native Japanese language until three short years ago when he replaced the terminally ill Japanese representative on the Board of Elders, commented mechanically, "We cannot ignore the possible threat. Our protocols demand that we must plan for a departure until…"

"We are aware of our protocols," Elder-3 cut in. He exhaled and resigned himself to dealing with the necessary action to be taken. "We must prepare for an orderly departure until we determine if this is a credible threat."

Elder-10 seemed frustrated as well. "Sir, while we prepare for departure, we would recommend that Elder-27 and Elder-68 go immediately to the nuclear plant to ascertain if this is just a false alarm."

Elder-27's stone-face finally softened. He did not look comfortable with the suggestion.

Before he could speak, Elder-3 answered.

"We do have a supply of hazmat suits, which we suspected we would need at some point. We also have Geiger counters to detect the presence of radiation. We do not want any more delays than we have already experienced, but we cannot afford to risk radiation poisoning."

He turned to Elder-27 and Elder-68. "You two secure what you need and depart right away. We already have several service vehicles available in Surf City. Take one, head to the nuclear power plant and report back immediately via walkie-talkie."

Both elders hesitated and then nodded.

Elder-3 continued, "We will continue to prepare to evacuate until we hear from you as to your findings. Dismissed and move out! And shut down the damn sirens and flashing lights. They are giving everyone a headache."

He turned to Elder-10. "Call an emergency meeting of all elders, except those two of course," he said and pointed to Elder-27 and Elder-68 as they headed out the door. "Bring all members back from the mainland, starting with the three elders stationed there. We need all elders assembled in the member dining room on Ship Number One as soon as possible. We must brief them and prepare to evacuate."

•  •  •

It seemed like forever that the group lay in wait, bombarded by the cacophony of sirens. Across from Kid and Tony, Jess and General Hyland had a firm grip on the other end of a long 2x4. Only a couple of inches of the board were holding up a sheet of plywood over a large, deep hole in the sand. Kid knew that they had to time their action precisely. They also had to hope that the elders from the base camp would be at the front of the line. General Hyland was quite certain the elders would be leading the group down to the beach and would be in the first boat launched.

Kid heard voices very close by; too close by. He had not considered that the wail of the sirens might drown out the sound of the approaching enemy group. He could hear the footsteps of a large group marching in unison but also in haste. The clap of their boot soles changed pitch, and he knew they had reached their makeshift boardwalk. Kid's bunker was no more than five feet away when they passed his position. A hollow, muffled echo sounded as the soldiers marched on the piece of plywood. Their footsteps slowed and then stopped.

The gig was up. "Now!" Kid shouted.

Kid, Tony, Jess, and the general pushed the 2x4 forward and out from under the edge of the piece of plywood. The trapdoor dropped into the pit along with the first several members of the Utopia Project. The hole, painstakingly dug out, measured six feet wide by 15 feet long, and nearly eight-feet deep. They knew that once someone fell in, it would be just about impossible to get out without assistance. And if anyone tried to climb the unstable sand walls, especially in haste, they would likely bury themselves alive.

While Jess shined a flashlight into the hole, General Hyland leaned in and started firing at the elders. His technologically advanced weapon was fired below ground level so that the bright bolts would not be visible to the ships at sea.

At the same time Kid turned to see Dr. Adele Carmelo run up to the crest of the North 8th Street beach entrance. There she encountered a group of members who had obviously seen the action and were charging. She held up a firm hand and shouted, "Hold!"

The members stopped in place but did not stand down. They looked ready to spring.

Kid drew his weapon and was ready to fire.

Speaking loudly in an authoritative voice, Adele added, "Cancel all enemy response orders. There is no longer an enemy."

She stood still, waiting for a reaction.

Finally, the members stood down and relaxed. She lowered her hand and breathed a sigh of relief.

Kid ran back and shined a light into the pit. Two of the three trapped elders were frozen after being shot. Two of the regular members had become collateral damage and were also standing as rigid as stone statues. The third elder had pulled out his own technologically advanced firearm and was trying to take aim at the general. With instinct kicking in, Kid jumped in the hole on top of the elder. He fought to keep a hold of the elder's wrist as he did not want to suffer the wrath of another Medusa firearm shot. They struggled and bumped into the side of the pit. The sand wall started collapsing, and grains cascaded down like an avalanche.

"I can't risk a shot with you there, Kid! Move back!" the general yelled.

Not believing he had any choice, Kid pulled out his pistol, put it against the elder's back and went to pull the trigger. He struggled with his free hand to keep the elder from turning his wrist and firing over the shoulder. With the alarms blaring for a few seconds, winding down, and then wailing again, Kid was trying to time a loud gunshot to match the sirens' crescendo. But he also knew the timing would not mean much if he was shot while stalling. As the volume of the sirens escalated again, the elder went to push backward and turn around. Kid could not wait. He had to fire and did. The elder slumped forward as the bullet tore through his heart from behind. By a split second the loud concussive blast preempted the siren's dramatic crescendo.

• • •

On Utopia Project Ship Number One Elder-3 was on the deck while Elder-27 and Elder-68 were about to be lowered to the water to investigate the status of the nuclear power plant. Before the davit was activated, he held up a hand, demanding silence. "Did you hear that?" he turned to Elder-10.

"What, Sir? All we can hear are sirens."

"It sounded like a gunshot far in the distance," Elder-3 commented as he stared toward Surf City. He paused and then a hint of suspicion coursed through his voice, "Grab Medusa firearms for Elder-27 and Elder-68. They need to be armed."

After providing weapons to the departing elders, members activated the davit. Their boat lowered to the churning sea below.

• • •

"Need a hand here," Kid said from the sand pit

The general peered at him. "While you are down there strip off the uniforms of the three elders and hand them up. Remember, we need them."

Kid obliged and tossed the uniforms up before Jess pulled him out.

"How many of the members are still alive down there?" the general asked.

Lying down, Kid shined his flashlight into the hole. "Three."

"While we change into the elder uniforms, help them out of there. Then we need to get all of the members down to the waterline and ready the boats for departure," the general directed. "It is time to move onto the next phase of the operation, and we need to move quickly. We are already behind schedule."

General Hyland took the uniform of the dead elder closest in size to him. He then sized up and handed the other two uniforms to his father and Adele. The one given to Adele had the bullet hole and large blood stain on the back from Kid's shot. They changed and were ready to jump into the first boat to be launched.

When they walked down the beach, Adele addressed the large group of members. First, she asked them about their current orders.

An older member in front indicated, "We have been ordered back to Ship Number One."

"Who was put in charge of getting the members back to the ships?"

The same male member, who Kid figured was around 18 years of age, stepped forward. "We were."

Adele addressed him. "Your specific orders?"

"To fill each boat until all members have returned, and then we are to jump in the last boat to be launched," member number 103 answered.

"Good. Proceed as ordered. When we leave, this man will be in charge." She motioned for Dr. McDermott to step forward. "Obey his orders."

Pointing, Adele said, "Now, proceed with launching the first boat only!"

Jess took a group of ten members to the rock jetty. Their job was to pull the cable that ran through the eye bolts and was clipped to the bow of the boat.

Kid peeled off the rain tarp from the boat and threw it in the bottom. He then assembled a group of five members, got behind the stern, and yelled, "Push!" To his friend he called out, "Jess, go!"

With Kid's group pushing and Jess's pulling, the boat slid on rollers down the 2x4 rails and splashed into the shallow surf.

General Hyland directed his small team of survivors to get in the boat, including Jess, who had run down from the jetty. He then filled the boat with several regular Utopia Project members. Turning to Dr. McDermott, the general said, "Let us get a little head start, and then they can proceed with launching the three remaining boats." The doctor waved in acknowledgment.

Kid was the last to jump in. He gave a thumbs up to Dr. McDermott, standing on the beach. "Stay safe, Doc. You'll be back to camp in no time."

The doctor was only staying ashore until the rest of the regular Utopia Project members were gone. Once the beach was clear, he was to return to Hangar One.

"I hope you guys will be too," Dr. McDermott said and then directed a group of members to push the stern while the members on the rock jetty were ordered to resume pulling the cable.

As soon as the boat was afloat at sea, Jess lowered the outboard engine and throttled up while Kid disconnected the tow cable from the bow. The craft rose and fell over the incoming waves as they headed toward Ship Number One. "Shit! Not again," he snapped.

"What's the matter?" Kid asked.

Jess pointed. "Another boat is heading our way."

# III:
# LIBERATION

# CHAPTER 23

January 22, 2045
Sunday, Before Dawn
Surf City, New Jersey
**Twenty-seven days after the event**

"I got the wheel, Jess." General Hyland pointed to the floor. "You, Kid, and Tony need to hide anyway."

The general looked up at the approaching boat He counted two elders aboard, one of whom he recognized. The craft was going to pass pretty close by so the general tried to veer further away. He hid his face by bending his elbow and putting his forearm over his nose, as if shielding from the ocean spray. The boat with the other two elders began to slow down as if they wanted to communicate. The general did not even look their way. He just waved a hand and plowed forward.

"There were two elders in that boat. Kid, radio the doctor on the beach and warn him!" he said with urgency.

He looked down to see Kid being tossed around in the bottom of the boat pulling out his walkie-talkie. "Doc, do you hear me? Come in!"

"Here Kid. What is that boat doing heading toward shore?" Dr. McDermott radioed back.

"That's what we are calling you about. There are two elders coming your way."

As he held the steering wheel, the general said, "Tell him to hide fast and to take them out if he can."

Kid conveyed the message. By the huffed response, the general could tell that the doctor was already running. "If they called for an emergency meeting of all elders, why would some be coming ashore?" Dr. McDermott asked.

Glancing up at the general, Kid waited for an answer. General Hyland could only shrug his shoulders in frustration. He feared that either the emergency meeting did not include all elders, which could seriously hinder their attack strategy, if not destroy it completely.

"We don't know," Kid radioed.

"Maybe they are being sent ashore to shut down the sirens?" Adele offered.

Turning and peering back, the general said, "Possibly, but if he can take them out we won't have to worry about what they are doing there. Tell him they have already reached the beach."

Kid pressed the button of his walkie-talkie. "Listen doc, they have already reached land. We don't know what they are doing there, but try to take them out."

"I'm at the street now, but I see them," Dr. McDermott responded. "I am heading to the Surf City Hotel. Powering down."

"Wait!" the general yelled and pulled his own walkie-talkie from his hip. "Doc, whatever you do, do not radio back. We will be on the ships in a few minutes, and it will give us away!"

After a tense pause, Dr. McDermott closed by saying, "Roger that. Out."

General Hyland was relieved that the doctor had received his message. He said to Adele, "I fear for the doctor. We tried to do some weapons training, but he is a poor shot. I was hoping he would never have to use a weapon, and I didn't think he would have to for his part of the plan."

"It is in his hands now. We need to be 100 percent focused on our part of the plan," she answered. The general nodded in agreement.

A few moments later, as they approached the ships, the general said, "There are teams of members waiting for us at the davits. When I give the word, Dad, Adele, look down so they can't see our faces from the deck."

• • •

Dr. McDermott reached the Surf City Hotel and opened the door to the restaurant on the first floor. Running inside, he hid under a table near the back and pulled out his weapon. He heard a creak as the front door opened. He tried to tune into the elders' conversation, but they were on the other side of the room. Unable to make out a word, the doctor quietly crawled between tables until he was close enough to hear them. One elder had an accent, maybe Russian, and was harder to understand. "They told us vehicle keys were hanging on the wall in here. Ah, here they are. We have it, although we wish we were not going at all."

The other elder spoke in perfect English as he stated, "Believe me, the last thing we need to do is head over to a potentially hot nuclear plant."

"No," the Russian said tersely. "Containment better not be lost at that power plant."

Dr. McDermott built his resolve, stood up, and went to fire his weapon. The two elders were already gone. At first he felt relieved. The nuclear meltdown ruse seemed to be working. But the moment of calm in his gut then turned sour. What if his son, Dylan, along with Emilio and Karen were still at the plant? Concluding he needed to take out the elders, he opened the front door. Their vehicle was already too far down the snowy road.

The doctor reached for his walkie-talkie, but then remembered he did not have the right one to contact Dylan. He only had the smaller unit being used to communicate with the rest of the first mission team -- General Hyland's group, and he could not simply change channels. To prevent accidental calls at an inopportune moment, the second mission team, including Dylan, had a completely different model walkie-talkie with different frequencies. They could only communicate with Hangar One, which was considered home base.

The sickening reality was that he had no way to communicate with his son and warn him. If Dylan was still at the plant, he probably would not see the elders coming until it was too late. And nobody in the second mission group was armed.

While grabbing keys for a vehicle to also head over to the nuclear power plant, Dr. McDermott tried to rationalize and tamp down his fears. With any luck, Dylan and the others had already left and were on their way back to Hangar One. But with the chill running down his spine, he felt anything but lucky.

As he started driving toward the Oyster Creek Nuclear Generating Station, it dawned on him that although he did not have the right walkie-talkie to reach Dylan, the group back at Hangar One did. The group there had one walkie-talkie for each of the mission teams. All the doctor had to do was radio Hangar One and tell them to contact Dylan on the other walkie-talkie. But, if General Hyland's team had reached the ship, the doctor's call could give them away and jeopardize the entire mission.

His torment and conflict manifested itself by his slapping the steering wheel hard and yelling, "They are not even armed!" Grabbing his walkie-talkie, he went to press the button and stopped. He firmly placed it on the seat next to him and grunted loudly. Glancing down at the unit, he again slapped the steering wheel, this time yelling, "I know everything is at stake, but how can I sit quietly and let my son be blindsided and killed!"

• • •

Alongside Utopia Project Ship Number One, General Hyland's boat was hoisted up by a davit. *Get ready. Just act like you never left*, the general coached himself.

As soon as the boat rested on the deck, he looked about the ship.

One elder was overseeing the tender-docking operation, but the real work was being handled by groups of regular members stationed at each davit. General Hyland jumped out of the boat and started immediately giving orders to the members on deck. To his relief they followed his commands without hesitation.

"What are the orders for the members we are bringing from the mainland?" The general asked as he stood upright in his elder uniform.

"The senior member in the boat shall drive it back to the mainland to pick up the next batch of members. The others are to report to Hallway Eleven below. We will escort them," a member answered.

"Proceed. All you shall go to Hallway Eleven, except for these two." He pointed to Sara and Maria. "We will lower the boat."

"Yes, Sir."

At that, the senior member remained in the boat while the rest of the members disembarked. While gathering the group to be taken below, no mind was paid to Adele or Chris, who were dressed as elders and did not arouse any suspicion.

While the members marched away, the general helped Adele out. Sara pulled the tarp from over Kid, Jess, and Tony on the boat-bottom.

Adele snapped, "Eric! Foe." She turned around so her face would not be seen and added, "Heading this way." She motioned for Sara and Maria to get down.

One of the regular members on the deck stood with a stack of towels for the ocean-splashed new arrivals, so General Hyland took his weapon out of its holster and draped a towel over it. He saw the enemy elder coming his way, and it was not one of the twelve that needed to be saved. The general took another towel and put it over his head. He stole glances as the elder walked over. He was waiting for the elder to be so close that he could stick a weapon in his gut from point blank range and not be seen doing it.

Suddenly, the walkie-talkie on the general's hip came to life and blared, "Eric, I hope you're not on the ship yet because I need to reach

Pam. It's an emergency. Pam, its Craig, pick up!" Dr. McDermott said with urgency in his voice.

The approaching elder stopped in his tracks upon hearing the words and pulled out his weapon.

With the muzzle of the general's weapon sticking out from under the towel, he fired without hesitation. The enemy elder was hit as he was depressing his own trigger, and although he stood frozen, his weapon launched bolt after bolt at General Hyland's feet. The general shuffled back, but then the enemy elder started falling sideways and errant shots flew in every direction. Adele leaped inside the small boat with the rest of the group. General Hyland took refuge behind a davit arm, which barely provided cover. The only one hit by a bolt was the Utopia Project member with the stack of towels, which cushioned his face as his rigid body fell forward.

"Craig, what's wrong?" radioed back Pamela McDermott.

The fallen elder came to rest on the deck with his finger rigidly on the trigger, and his shots continued in a volley, hitting the side of the small boat hiding Adele and the others. "Stay down!" the general yelled. The gun stopped firing when life left the dying elder and the smart gun no longer registered a signature.

The temporary calm was interrupted by Dr. McDermott's voice over the walkie-talkie. "Eric, I'll be quick, and I'm sorry. Pam, I don't have the walkie-talkie to reach Dylan, but you do. Call him and tell him to get away from that plant. Two elders are driving over there right now!"

At that point, General Hyland cased out the ship and ensured that no other elders witnessed what had just unfolded. He only saw small groups of members standing some distance away at the other three davits, seemingly oblivious to, or even ignorant of, the confrontation that had just occurred. The members were focused on their assigned tasks as the next three boats from the mainland were approaching the ship.

Pamela McDermott responded from Hangar One. "Oh God. I think he is still at the top of the stack. I will call him right now, and we will stay off of the line from here on out."

"Clear," the general called as he helped Adele out of the boat. Kid, Sara, Jess, and Tony followed.

"Eric, if you didn't already have your weapon in your hand, he had you nailed," Adele said.

"I know. I can't believe Doc called in. The group at the nuclear power plant must be in trouble."

"And they are not armed." Kid sounded flustered.

The general pulled his walkie-talkie from its holster. "Listen, Doc and Pam, I hope you were able to alert Dylan, but you need to stay off of the radio from here on out. Our mission was not compromised, but if you radio again, it will be. So shut it down, and we pray that Dylan, Emilio, and Karen are safe. Out!"

Turning to Adele, he muttered, "I should have had us all turn off our walkie-talkies until Sara and Maria were in position."

"Too late now," she responded. "But I don't think you have to worry about any more interruptions."

"I sure as hell hope not." He turned to Sara and Maria. "Based on where we are, do you remember from the ship plans how to get to the back door of the kitchen?"

They both nodded.

"Good. Remember, there should already be other members in there preparing and serving refreshments to the elders for their meeting," the general reminded. "Just blend in. Be emotionless, and don't make eye contact with any elders. Good luck."

"You girls got this," Adele said confidently and winked with one of her bright green eyes.

She winked back at Adele and also at her father. He nodded and put his palm on his chest. Sara pursed her lips. He realized she took his gesture to be an emotional one, but now was not the time. "Secure?" He tapped his chest.

Touching her own chest, where the tubular canisters of P55 poison gas were hidden, she huffed, "Yes, Dad."

Maria also checked the canisters hidden under her uniform. The girls then made sure that they each had a small handheld walkie-talkie in one pant leg pocket and a couple of small metal wedges, which looked like miniature railroad spikes, in the other.

As Sara went to leave, she turned to Kid. The general saw them make eye contact, and he felt the powerful connection between them. Neither one said a word, and neither one needed to. The girls then left and walked calmly, but stiffly, across the deck.

Spotting a storage room, General Hyland said, "Adele. Please open that door. Guys, I need a hand." Kid helped General Hyland carry the dead elder to the storage room, while Jess and Tony did the same with the member that was lying face first in the stack of towels.

"All of you stay in here," the general said as he ushered Adele into the storage room. "Be right back."

"Where are you going?" she asked.

He pointed to the lone member still in the small boat. "I have to round up a couple of members to launch him and send the boat back ashore. The elder up here I shot would have been directing the members, and with him gone there is nobody to do that." He closed the door to the storage room, leaving the group, and the dead bodies, inside.

A few moments later, the general stepped into the storage room.

As soon as he closed the door, Adele turned on a flashlight. The beam settled on the open but dead eyes of the elder who had been shot on the deck.

"Done," the general said. "Hand out the gas masks."

Jess wiggled his shoulders and took off his backpack. "Won't the members on deck alert somebody as to what just happened out there?" he asked.

"No," Adele answered. "They don't work that way. They could care less. They will simply follow their current orders."

"They really are mindless zombies," Jess said as he pulled out the gas masks from his backpack.

"That's exactly why I left the project," she noted ruefully.

After everyone took a gas mask, the general reminded them all of the next step in the plan. "As soon as the canisters are in place and the girls are out of the dining room, Sara will call. We will need to move fast. Remember, before we can detonate, we need to stick wedges in the dining hall doors to trap them all inside."

Everyone acknowledged. The waiting became more intense with every passing second.

# CHAPTER 24

January 22, 2045
Sunday, Morning
Forked River, New Jersey
***Twenty-seven days after the event***

At the top of the off-gas stack, the walkie-talkies came to life. Karen assumed it was Emilio calling up again to ask when they were coming down. This time it was Pamela McDermott calling from Hangar One, and it sounded urgent. "Dylan, where are you?"

"I'm here, Mom. Still at the top of the stack."

"Listen to me. Your father just called us on the other walkie-talkie and said that two enemy elders are on their way over there! You have to get away from that plant!"

"I can't get down yet. Still too afraid. I'll just wait it out up here."

"No! You have to get down from there!"

Raising her walkie-talkie, Karen said, "I'm still up here with Dylan and will help him."

Karen grabbed Dylan's arm. "We are getting down, now!" Despite the freezing and relentless wind for the past couple of hours, they had both been sitting on the metal platform with their backs against the off-gas stack. She was trying to coach him so that they get down from the tall stack, but his fear had not diminished. With the phone call from Dylan's mother, they had no choice but to get down and leave the plant.

Again raising her walkie-talkie, Karen snapped, "Emilio, did you get all of that?" He did not respond.

Peering down from the top of the stack, she gasped as she saw Emilio standing on the ground. She tried to radio him again to no avail. After their last radio communication, he said he was going to come over and climb the stack to help get Dylan down. Either he had left his walkie-talkie in the control room, or he had turned it off. Either way, Emilio was deaf down there. She realized that meant he did not hear the frantic call from Dylan's mother about the elders coming their way.

Leaning over the metal platform, Karen waved her arms. Emilio seemed to see her at the top and waved back. She realized that even if she was screaming, he would never hear her. She looked up and gasped as she spotted vehicle headlights coming north on Route 9, approaching the plant entrance. They were running out of time. She waved her hands wildly to warn Emilio while pointing at the headlights turning into the plant entrance.

On the ground, Emilio was staring at the top of the off-gas stack. He then ran back to the control room in the reactor building.

Elder-27 and Elder-68 parked in front of the former reactor building. Elder-68 opened the window and held out a Geiger counter. "No radiation. This must be a false alarm. Unless we get a hot reading, we are not putting on those suffocating hazmat suits. Let's get to the control room and shut down the sirens and lights." Elder-27 followed him as he walked toward the reactor building with the Geiger counter in his hand. The needle did not move, even as they entered the building.

Emilio picked up the walkie-talkie he had inadvertently left behind on the countertop in the control room and pressed the button. "Karen, what are you guys doing up there?"

Karen's response sounded frantic. "Emilio, hide! Quick. Two elders are coming inside the building right now!"

"Got it. Signing off!" With only seconds to spare, Emilio crawled under a table and turned off his walkie-talkie.

He watched as one of these elders walked in and examined the banks of switches. In short order, he found the ones that turned off the blaring sirens. As the noise died away, the elder mumbled, "Finally. What a headache. Now how do we shut off the flashing red light at the top of the off-gas stack?" He continued flipping switches. "Elder-68, is the light still blinking?"

The other elder stepped outside and yelled, "Yes!"

"We have flipped every switch in here. We are at a loss."

Sounding annoyed, the other elder said, "Forget it, we will climb to the top of the stack and manually shut down that annoying light before it gives someone a seizure."

Emilio's breath stopped for a second. Karen and Dylan were at the top of the stack, unarmed, and with an elder climbing up, they would be trapped and defenseless.

• • •

*I don't know how we are going to pull this off,* Sara thought.

On Utopia Project Ship Number One, Sara and Maria entered the back door of the kitchen and found a sizable group already at work. Members were preparing light refreshments to be served to the elders who were all assembling in the dining room for the emergent meeting. Trays with coffee carafes were being carried out to the dining area while platters of fruits and pastries were placed on push carts to be wheeled out. Knowing the orderly manner in which they operated, Sara got in line to carry out a tray of carafes. Her face remained expressionless despite the rapid beating of her heart and the wetness of her palms.

Following the plan, Maria went to the sink to help the members' clean dishes. Although dressed for the part, she had been quick to remind the general and Kid that she was not the actress Sara was.

Given that, Maria was not supposed to go into the dining area where the elders were until absolutely necessary.

Now her turn, Sara was handed a tray within carafes, cups, and condiments. She noted that the automatic sliding door was set to stay open since people were continually coming and going. She walked into the dining area and spotted the male member who had taken the tray in front of her. That server was heading toward the back of the room so Sara went the same direction. She had to catch surreptitious glances, but the layout was easy to confirm. There appeared to be 16 rows of seats facing a single table which was clearly the dais for the Board of Elders.

While distributing carafes along the length of a table, Sara could see that the elders were seated in number order, as her father said they would be. The elders were either already sitting or were close to their seats. They were conversing in low, serious voices. Servers were strolling about purposefully. Sara passed Elder-158, Elder-157 and when reading the uniform number of the next elder, she nearly made eye contact as Elder-156 reached for the carafe she was putting on the table. *Don't play the role, be the role*, she coached herself; clinging to the adage from when she acted in school plays. Despite the fear that was making her stomach do flip-flops, she reminded herself that she looked no different than any of the other girls her age in the Utopia Project society. She was invisible so long as she acted like everyone else.

She was searching for two elders in particular. Given their identifying numbers, both would be in the front half of the room. These were the two elders that her father said would rally the rest of the elders on the list. But it was just a matter of time before the Board of Elders called the meeting to order, and then it would be too late. She saved one coffee carafe and walked mechanically toward the front. She turned at a row where she hoped to find at least one of her two targets. Halfway up the row, another elder snapped, "Wait!"

Her heart skipped a beat, but she knew better than to make eye contact.

"Place that coffee here," the female elder instructed. Sara nodded, complied, and continued walking up the row. She had no more coffee carafes and was taking a huge risk by not heading back to the kitchen. She finally stopped in front of an older American man who was staring straight ahead, and seemed weary. He already had a coffee carafe next to him, so Sara grabbed a sugar packet off of her tray and held it out. He waved her off. "We do not need sugar."

"Sir, we were told to give you this," she whispered and reached out with the sugar packet, all the while fighting the tremble in her hand.

The elder raised his head. Although she was taking a huge chance, Sara made eye contact with Elder-53, General Barnes. He had been a close comrade with her father, and she had met him several times throughout the years. Her father believed the elder would recognize her and take the note. She prayed that was the case.

He peered up at Sara suspiciously, but there was also some level of recognition. For a second, she felt a surge of panic. What if her father and Adele had been wrong, and he could not be trusted? What if he had developed an absolute loyalty and allegiance to the project? If so, she was dead where she stood, and she knew it. But it was a chance they had to take.

At first he stared at her fingers and then after making eye contact again, he reached for the packet. She put it in his open hand with a folded note, written by her father, that she had been palming since walking into the dining room.

Heading back to the kitchen, Sara looked back as Elder-53 abruptly stood. A spike of fear surged through her. He walked out of his row and headed toward the dais in the front of the room. Was he turning her in? To her great relief he walked past the dais and headed for the door to the hallway.

She heard Elder-53 say, "Restroom," to the elder guarding the doorway. As Elder-53 stepped into the hallway, Elder-10 raised his clipboard and made a notation.

Back inside the kitchen, Sara stood at the window and observed the dining area. After only being gone for a minute, Elder-53 walked back into the room. He strode around and whispered in the ears of other elders. Sara felt a wave of optimism. Elder-53 must have read the note as he appeared to be rounding up the other trustworthy elders, and one by one, they were leaving the room.

Maria was standing next to her and snap whispered, "It's working!"

Sara gave a quick nod and took in a deep breath. It was time to move onto the most dangerous, and critical, phase of the plan. The entire mission had led to the very moment. She nudged Maria and said, "More…offerings…are needed. Grab a full push cart and follow me. Eyes down."

Several push carts loaded with fruit and pastries were ready to be moved into the dining room. The girls each grabbed a cart and wheeled them out the door. Sara whispered to Maria, "See how they've started lining up these carts in the back of the room? Take the back left corner. I'll take the right. Stick your canister under the food but don't let them see you do it."

Sara wheeled the tray into the back right corner, and with her back to the room, she unzipped the top of her uniform. She pulled out her canister of the lethal P55 and slid the cylinder into a stack of bananas. Satisfied with her work, she turned to leave and an elder was standing right behind her. She almost made eye contact but swung back around to better arrange the food on the tray.

"We will take one of those," he said as he reached for a banana.

A gavel was slammed loudly. "We must call this meeting to order. Everyone take your seat. Restrooms may be used *after* the meeting has concluded," Elder-3 announced with a stern tone. "Close all doors."

Sara watched as Elder-10 pressed a button and the double doors from the hallway to the dining room slid closed. She turned to see the elder next to her looking toward the dais, but his hand was outstretched behind him. She almost gasped. His fingers were only a few inches from the metal canister, which looked like a silver baton nestled underneath the yellow bananas. Sara snagged a banana and smacked it into his waiting palm. The elder took it and went quickly to his seat. She left the cart in the back of the room and started walking toward the kitchen.

"Done?" she asked as she strode next to Maria.

"Almost got busted, but yes," Maria responded. "You?"

"Same," she answered and stopped at the door to the kitchen as Elder-3 pounded the gavel again. He stood. "Are all elders present and accounted for?"

Elder-10 checked his clipboard. "No, Sir, we still have eleven elders in the restrooms. Four are in the Women's Room, and seven are in the Men's Room."

"Have the three elders from the mainland reported in?"

"No, Sir. They have not reported in, nor has the elder who was on the foredeck awaiting their arrival," Elder-10 said.

"How is that possible? We were informed quite some time ago that their boat was approaching." A look of what might have been suspicion, coupled with frustration, came to Elder-3's face. He seemed to sense that something was afoot.

"Elder-10, go to the north side foredeck and see what is holding up the elders from the mainland. Then, Elder-21," he called and pointed. A rigid elder rose at his seat. Elder-3 sounded agitated as he pointed toward the hallway. "Go round up the elders in the restrooms and tell them to move it, quickly. This meeting must get started!"

Sara walked slowly and milled around so she could hear what was going on. Finally, she had no choice but to head into the kitchen with the last remaining members. Suddenly, Elder-21 ran back into the dining room and said something quietly to the lead elder. Sara turned one final time. A wave of panic spiked through her as she watched Elder-3 rise abruptly from his seat at the dais and follow Elder-21 into the hallway.

The door to the kitchen slid closed, and Sara stared through the square of glass in the top half. She saw Elder-53 talking to what had to be the last elder on the list, given how many had already left the room. Suddenly Elder-160 jumped back a step and pointed accusingly at him. Sara didn't need to hear any words to know what was going on. "Oh, no. No," she uttered as her panic intensified.

Sara turned to Maria. "He's calling out Elder-53! He's going to blow the whole plan. Come on!" Grabbing Maria's hand, they ran for the walk-in freezer. Inside the large, cold box, Sara turned on her walkie-talkie and pressed the call button. "Dad!" She only had to wait for a second.

"Sara, where are you?" General Hyland asked with an urgency in his voice.

"In a freezer in the kitchen."

"Did you place the canisters yet?" he asked.

"Yes! One in each back corner of the dining room," Sara answered, continuing the rapid-fire back and forth.

"And you are out of the dining room?"

"Yes, but listen, everything is going haywire. Elder-160 isn't going along with it! I think he's calling out Elder-53."

"They are the last two. The other ten elders from the list are already with us on deck."

"And Dad, Elder-3 and another elder ran out of the dining room. I don't know where they went!"

"Stay on the line, Sara!" She then heard him snap to the other mission team members with him, "The gig is up! We need to wedge the doors right now. Masks on and follow me!"

Her father then started huffing out words and she could tell he was running. "Sara, we need to detonate...right now. Shimmy the two doors to the kitchen...and get away from there. Remember, one whiff... of that poison gas...will kill you. Go, now. You'll have 30 seconds."

"Wait! What about Elder-53?" Sara asked. "He's trapped in there!"

"There is nothing...we can do for him. We have to detonate now. Shimmy the doors...and get out of there. Got it?"

"Yes!" Sara radioed back.

"30 seconds, starting...now!"

The countdown had begun.

# CHAPTER 25

At Hangar One, Evelyn and the others were listening to the communications over the walkie-talkie set used by the first mission team. Upon hearing the frantic back and forth between Sara and Eric, Evelyn had to sit down on the edge of her cot while holding a cup of water in her hand. Between the first mission team and the second mission team, she was wondering if it would have been better to not tune in at all. The anxiety that came with two play-by-plays was becoming too much.

Estelle put her fingers together and prayed.

The moment was upon them. The fuse had been lit and with it a 30-second countdown. They all sat still in the hangar entombed by a collective sphere of anxiety. Everyone knew what was in the balance.

Pamela finally posed the question that all of them had likely thought of many times over. "What if this fails?"

The question lingered for a second.

"What can we do," Pamela added, "other than hide and wait for the end to come?"

"I think Gia and I will go back to Italy and live out the rest of our days there," Annette Vicarro said but then hesitated a second. "Although she is developing relationships with the other children here."

Marissa grabbed her husband's hand. "Clarence and I would probably go back to our house in Vermont so we could die in the bed we shared for almost 30 years."

"What about you, Mrs. Hyland?" Pamela asked. "What will you do if this mission fails?"

"Oh, I don't know. I'd rather not think of that. Let's think positive and hope we never have to make such decisions."

In Evelyn's palm was her pill -- the one she needed to take every day to sustain her life. Her lips parted, she raised her hand to pop it in, and then she stopped. Closing her mouth, she lowered her hand and held the pill in a closed fist. If she lost her loved ones today, she would never take her life-saving medication again.

· · ·

Sara grabbed Maria's arm. "We've only got 30 seconds!" As they burst from the freezer, Sara pointed. "Wedge the door on the right, and I'll get the one on the left."

Without explanation or concern for what the members might see, the girls both shoved spikes between the doors and the door frames as they had practiced multiple times on the mainland. After sticking the metal spike in the frame and giving the back end a few solid whacks with her palm, Sara was sure the door was stuck closed. She then turned and prepared to defend the entryway at all costs. There were no elders in the kitchen, and the members back there watched but did not move to confront her. More than anything, they just seemed curious.

After signing off with Sara, General Hyland clipped his walkie-talkie to his belt as he ran up the hall. He was leading Kid, Jess, and Tony, but the dining room was dead ahead, so he pointed and waved them forward. They were all donning their gas masks, and he needed to do the same. He slowed enough to put the gas mask on his face and made sure it was secure and sealed. As Jess reached the main cafeteria double doors, he slid on his knees and jammed a few metal spikes between the door and the door frame. The general was sure it was much quicker and more efficient to use the little metal spikes to wedge the doors than it would have been to use stacks of coins like Kid and Jess had done when they were on the ships.

Kid and Tony were finishing the second set of doors when two elders came out of the restroom up the hall. One was Elder-3, who immediately pulled out his Medusa firearm.

The general and his group were all stranded in the middle of the hallway with nowhere to hide. He yelled, "Down!" and opened fire. His shots missed the mark, but they forced Elder-3 and Elder-21 to duck back into the restroom, which bought enough time for his team to pile into a nearby mechanical room.

The general slipped into the room with them. "Watch for them leaving the restroom," he said as he pulled out the detonator for the P55 canisters.

In the kitchen of Ship Number One, Sara knew 30 seconds had long since passed. She stood up, turned, and gasped upon seeing Elder-53's face in the window. She heard a motorized whine as he tried unsuccessfully to open the sliding door. The wedge was working. Elder-53 knocked and motioned for her to open the door. He seemed to know something bad was about to happen.

Sara made eye contact with Elder-53 and her heart sank. Here was the man who had rounded up 10 of the 12 elders to be saved, a debt that could never be repaid, not even by the simple opening of a door? No, it could not end that way for him. She made a snap decision. She would open it for just a second, long enough to pull him into the kitchen. She bent down and tried to remove the spike wedging the door closed, but it would not budge.

She was about to drop to her knees and use both hands when suddenly, the two canisters in the dining room came alive and started spinning in the air as they rose from the fruit trays. They rotated like fast moving fan blades as they flew around the room and fired streams of the yellow-colored poison gas in every direction. "No, no," she uttered, knowing she was too late.

"To the back of the kitchen!" Maria yelled as she grabbed Sara and pulled her none too soon as a canister bounced hard against the section of glass which encompassed most of the top half of the door. The tempered pane did not shatter, but cracks extended until the window resembled the web of a large, deadly spider.

Sara stopped and turned. Through the cracked window she could see the dining room was in absolute chaos. The two canisters were bouncing off of the walls and flying over the rows of tables. The room was filling with a yellow haze. Elders slumped onto tabletops and crashed to the floor from just one breath of the noxious vapor. A few elders made a dash toward the double doors to the hallway, but the wedges held fast, and the elders collapsed in a heap.

Elder-53's face appeared. He started slapping both hands against the already-weakened window.

"Oh, shit," Maria uttered as she grabbed Sara's arm. "That glass is going to give. Let's get out of here!"

As Elder-53 grabbed for his throat with one hand, the fingers of his other hand clawed at the window and he slid to the floor.

Coming to her senses, Sara followed Maria out the back door. She had barely stepped into the hallway when the cracked piece of glass caved in and noxious vapors were cast into the kitchen. She paused for a split-second, long enough to see members start to fall as a yellow fog infiltrated the room.

The girls tore off and did not look back.

"Where to now?" Maria asked.

Sprinting up the hall, Sara said, "To the rendezvous point on the deck."

• • •

Karen and Dylan saw the enemy coming up the ladder. They had nowhere to hide. All they could do was step quietly on the old metal platform and slip around to the side of the stack opposite the ladder. They waited for what seemed like an eternity.

Finally, Karen peeked around the corner and saw a tall, lanky elder holding the strobe light, trying to turn it off. A stiff wind blew the bandanna from her head. She reached for it, but was too late as it wrapped around the railing right next to the elder. She ducked back, afraid she had blown their cover.

Her fears were confirmed a second later when an eerie voice emanated from the other side of the stack. "Do we have company up here?" The metal platform creaked as his voice came closer. "Come out of the darkness little girl."

As Dr. McDermott approached the nuclear power plant, he peered at the silhouette of the off-gas stack, which looked as tall as a skyscraper. To his horror, a body appeared to plummet from the top, holding something that was leaving a red visual trail during the descent. The doctor punched the gas pedal and turned into the entrance, scraping a concrete jersey barrier on the way in. The vehicle slid to a stop with the headlights illuminating a crumpled form on the ground at the base of the off-gas stack. He fought back the bile in his throat and was nearly overcome by fear and dread as he got out of the car.

Approaching the clearly dead body lying prone on the ground, the doctor dropped to his knees. He reached down and turned over the shattered carcass. Staring skyward, he put his hands over his face.

At the top of the off-gas stack, Dylan asked, "Did I redeem myself?"

Karen was still in disbelief. "And then some. When you charged, you hit him so fast and hard that he still had the strobe light in his hands when he flew over the rail," she added.

"He wasn't expecting it," Dylan concluded. "You did a great job of distracting him."

Grabbing her bandanna, which was wrapped around the railing on the east side of the platform, Karen said, "He never would have known we were up here if I didn't peek around the corner. Sorry about that Dylan."

"Don't be sorry. If it wasn't for my sudden fear of heights, we never would have been trapped up here in the first place."

"It is time to confront that head on and get down from this damned thing before the cold or something else gets us," She said, tying the bandanna over her skull. She glanced down at the vehicle that had pulled up near the base of the off-gas stack. In the glow of the vehicle headlights, she saw a person kneeling next to the fallen elder. "Doc?" she muttered, relieved just for a split second.

She gasped. "Emilio is hiding, but your father doesn't know there's a hostile elder in the control room!"

"Dad!" Dylan yelled down from the rail. With the height and the swirling wind, the sound didn't reach the ground.

"We have to get down there." Despite appearing fatigued, Karen grabbed the ladder and prepared to descend.

"I need to warn him." Dylan also grabbed the ladder. "Can you move to one side?" he ordered more than asked.

Karen moved over and Dylan rapidly descended the rungs. His fear for his father seemed to have trumped his acrophobia.

Dr. McDermott took his hands from his face and coached himself to breathe slowly and deeply. He didn't have to be a cardiologist to know that his heart was beating at an alarming rate. He cleared the panic-visions lingering in his brain and turned his thoughts to his son. The body on the ground was that of Utopia Project Elder-68, but where was Dylan? The doctor got to his feet, still awash in glow of the vehicle headlights as he walked toward the base of the off-gas stack. Up above, he saw the silhouette of two people climbing down the ladder. As soon as Dylan neared the bottom, his father recognized him. "Dylan!"

"Dad! Watch out! One of those soldiers is still down there."

Pulling out the pistol he was carrying, Dr. McDermott crouched and scanned the area. When his son reached the ground, the doctor hugged him hard. Dylan whispered, "Emilio was hiding in the control room in the main building. We don't know where the soldier is now."

Looking around high and low, the doctor pointed at the ladder. "If Emilio is in the control room, then that could only be…"

"Karen."

"What! She is in no physical condition to be climbing a several hundred foot ladder!"

"She's stubborn Dad."

"You stand guard and watch for the soldier," he said and handed his gun to his son. "I am going to make sure she can make it down." The doctor began climbing the rungs.

Having descended two-thirds of the way, Karen stopped to catch her breath. She was hugging the ladder and panting. Dr. McDermott was concerned as he reached her. She waved him off and continued down. The doctor watched her every step as he descended just below her. He was ready to catch her if he had to.

After she reached the ground, he helped her over to his vehicle and sat her down in the back seat. She seemed exhausted. "Lay down and stay out of sight. I'll be back," he said as he gently closed the door.

He turned to his son and took the gun from his hand. "Come on. Let's find Emilio. Stay behind me."

Dylan followed his father to the front of the main building. Opening the door, they tip-toed through the lobby and up the hall. The doctor peeked into the control room. The elder was examining the many banks of controls lining the wall.

The doctor waved his son back, and then he jumped into the room and opened fire. Despite firing from close range, not a single bullet hit the mark.

The elder crouched and spun around while reaching for his weapon.

# CHAPTER 26

Dr. McDermott stood frozen as the elder reached for his weapon. The doctor was sure he was dead where he stood, but the elder's firearm seemed to be stuck in its holster. The elder looked down at his side and used both hands to try and free it. While he struggled, Emilio jumped out from under a table and yelled, "Doc Fire! Hurry!"

Dr. McDermott snapped out of it and squeezed off two shots as he ran toward the elder. One hit the mark, but it was all that was needed as the bullet caught the elder in the neck. The enemy collapsed to the ground in a heap, like a rag doll, and the doctor suspected the shot had perfectly severed the cervical spine.

Dylan bolted over. "That was close, Dad."

Bending over with his hands on his knees, the doctor was breathing heavily, more from the adrenaline rush than the physical exertion. "I got lucky. He couldn't free his weapon."

"It wasn't luck." Emilio reached into his pocket and held up a small tube of superglue. "This came in very handy, and not just for fixing my glasses."

Dr. McDermott stared at the tube. "How so?"

Emilio continued, "When that elder came into the control room, after he shut down the sirens, he sat in a chair waiting for the other elder to come back. He rolled backward against the counter I was hiding under. His gun and holster were right in front of me, so I squeezed a bunch of drops and superglued his gun to its holster."

"Smart," the doctor acknowledged. "That saved my life because, obviously, I am not a good shot."

"It worked out."

The doctor put his hand on Emilio's shoulder. "Yes, it worked out, and I'm glad it did." Shaking his head, he added, "I could not imagine poor Estelle's heartbreak if she lost her son."

"At least this one is safe."

With the look on Emilio's face, the doctor wished he could take his words back. Although Emilio was unharmed, there was no word on the status of Estelle's other son, Tony.

• • •

In the mechanical room by the main cafeteria doors of Ship Number One, the general pulled out his Medusa firearm. "Let's go, while they are stuck in the restroom," he said loudly, since the gas mask would stifle his voice.

He opened the door and led Kid, Jess, and Tony up the hall. While passing the double sliding doors to the dining room, he turned as a figure shot through the haze with a hand covering his mouth and nose. Suddenly the glass pane covering the top portion of one of the doors shattered as an elder tried to escape the poisonous vapors. His body hung halfway through the window as his hand made a final grasp.

Startled by the breaking glass and the desperate lunge, Tony stumbled as he backed away. Unfortunately, the fingers of the dying elder snagged Tony's gas mask and pulled it half off. As Tony tried to adjust the mask over his now exposed mouth, he collapsed to the ground.

"Tony!" Jess yelled through his gas mask as he scrambled toward their Italian comrade.

"I'm sorry Jess, he was dead before he hit the ground. There is nothing we can do for him," the general said. "Keep moving. We can't let them escape! We have to finish this!" he snapped as he continued up the hall.

Elder-3, while taking shelter in the restroom, held his walkie-talkie to his ear. An elder in the dining room was updating him. "There are canisters flying around the room! They..." he began to choke. The only sound that followed was a strained, deep, demonic-sounding attempt to breathe.

"We knew something wasn't right," Elder-3 said to Elder-21 next to him. "We are under attack! But by whom? All of the survivors were supposed to have been eliminated!" he said and ran out of the restroom with his Medusa firearm in his hand.

Elder-3 saw an armed group coming up the hall, all donning gas masks. Knowing he was outnumbered in terms of troops and weapons, he grabbed Elder-21's arm. "Follow me!" he barked, and they bolted around the first corner up the hall.

As they were rounding a corner in the hallway, Sara was saying to Maria, "I don't think any elder in that dining room could have survived the attack" when they ran straight into two elders.

Instinctively, Sara's self-defense training kicked in, and she clothes-lined the one with the     uniform number indicating, Elder-21, slamming his back against the floor.

She turned to see the other elder throw an elbow at Maria. Her friend tried to avoid it, but the elbow caught Maria in the chest, and her feet flew out from under her. She crashed hard to the ground and grunted harshly, "Asshole!"

That elder turned toward Sara, and she gasped when she saw that it was Elder-3. He started to raise his weapon, but she kicked him in the groin and screamed, "Run!"

Grabbing Maria under the arm, she helped her around the corner.

Sara was hopeful when she saw her father and Kid running toward them, but both started pointing at their gas masks and waving her back. "Poison cloud that way!" her father yelled and pointed back, his voice muffled by the mask.

Sara had nowhere to go. Forward was a cloud of lethal vapor. Behind were two hostile elders.

"Duck! Get down!" her father bellowed, so she pulled Maria to the floor.

The two elders rounded the corner. General Hyland fired his Medusa firearm. Kid fired his 38-caliber pistol. Miraculously, the elders were able to retreat to the hall from which they had come without taking any hits. The general and Kid ran forward with their weapons raised. After passing the girls on the floor, they pulled off their gas masks.

"Stay here!" Kid said to Sara and Maria. "The air on the hall that way is toxic."

Looking up, Sara noted the yellow haze filling the hallway. And then like a ghost, Jess emerged through the fog and joined them.

The general was crouched before the turn to an adjoining hallway. Raising his hand to put them all on high alert, he led with his weapon and stepped around the corner. Instead of firing, the general lowered his hand. "Where did they go?"

Pulling off his gas mask, Jess pointed behind him. "I don't know where we are going, but we have to keep moving."

Sara thought the same thing. They needed to get as far away as they could.

Glancing around, the general said, "Jess, put your mask back on and go back to the group of elders waiting on the deck on the other side of the ship. Make sure they know not to come in. Tell them to stay outside and far away from this cloud."

"Got it." Jess secured his gas mask.

"Wait!" The general inspected the placement of Jess's mask to make sure it was completely sealed. "Alright, Jess, go." Turning to the others, he said, "The rest of you follow me."

Getting to her feet, Sara grabbed Maria's arm, and they followed the general.

With the peril they faced between poison gas and enemy weapon-fire, Elder-3 and Elder-21 had made for Utopia Project Ship Number Two. As soon as they were aboard, they had released the rope bridge and let it fall to the water below, isolating themselves from the middle ship and cutting off their pursuers.

Now hidden behind the deck rail of Ship Number Two, Elder-3 held his weapon in front of him, trained on Ship Number One, and specifically the door to the deck.

When someone finally came out, Elder-3 lowered his weapon for a second. "You!" He was stunned that it was General Hyland, who was supposed to have drowned with the rest of the remaining survivors in the flooded tunnels under the old building with the lake behind it. "Die you traitor," Elder-3 mumbled and pulled the trigger.

The general stood outside a door to the deck on the starboard side, facing Ship Number Two. "Where did the rope bridge go?" he mumbled and then sensed a shot before it was even fired. He hit the ground as the bolt from either Elder-3 or Elder-21 hit the door frame next to him. "Back!" he yelled and crawled inside while pulling the door closed. "This way." He sprinted up the hall and opened another door. The group followed as he began ascending a circular staircase.

Reaching the ship's bridge, Kid walked to the outdoor balcony.

"Keep low, Kid, in case they start firing from the other ship," the general said as he followed him out. Sara and Maria joined them, and they all crouched behind the balcony wall.

"This is a problem," the general added. "When they escaped over to Ship Number Two, they released the rope bridge so we can't follow them."

"At least they're off of this ship," Sara said.

"Yes, but we are now isolated from a whole ship's worth of our members, 6,000 to 7,000 of them. We need to save them."

The general met Sara's eyes, and both froze upon hearing the deep, muffled rumble of an engine.

"I know that sound," he muttered. Leaning over the balcony, General Hyland felt distraught upon seeing smoke wafting behind Ship Number Two. "They've started the propeller engines. They are going to try to take the ship and run!"

"They are still anchored," Kid noted. "And to raise the bow anchor, don't they need the crane since the windlass alone can't handle the weight?"

"Yes," the general confirmed. "But it only takes one person to operate the crane."

"Unless there is no crane." Pulling out his walkie-talkie, Kid said, "Mel! Are you there? We need you!"

Elder-3 and Elder-21 had then gone up to the ship's bridge. From there they were able to check all systems and start the engines that turned the propellers. Elder-21 was then sent down to use the crane on the deck to hoist the bow anchor from the seafloor. Elder-3 was tapping his foot, gazing out a window on the bridge, waiting for Elder-21 to reach the deck below.

Suddenly, two of the windows on the bridge exploded. Elder-3 covered his face as the blast slammed him back into the wall. When he moved his hands and opened his eyes, he saw a swelling fireball rising from the deck. He stumbled up to the frame that once held a large window. The wind whipped his hair as he took in the devastation.

Elder-21 burst into the room, almost knocking the door off its hinges. "We fell halfway down the stairs from that explosion. What was…"

Both braced as a loud creak sounded, and they watched as the boom of the crane buckled and slammed hard to the deck. Elder-3 felt his fury rising ever more.

"Bullseye!" Mel said as she watched out the window of the M3.

"Perfect shot!" the general radioed. "Do you see any elders on the deck of that ship?"

"No, your father, Romeo, and I are looking, but we don't see anybody. Why did we take out a crane?" she asked.

"Without the crane they can't raise their bow anchor and try to escape."

"Who can't escape?"

"Do you have the hang of landing enough to put it down on the deck of the middle ship?" he asked, ignoring her question.

"I believe so. I just about have the landing part down pat."

"We will fill you in after you land. I want the M3 here in case we need it in a hurry, but hopefully your job is done for the day," the general added.

"Sounds good. On my way." She put down the walkie-talkie, banked hard, and muttered, "Sounds *great*, but somehow I doubt it."


"Now we cannot raise the anchor," Elder-21 said resignedly on the bridge of Utopia Project Ship Number Two.

Elder-3's fingers curled and tightened into balled fists. His plan to take the ship and escape was thwarted. A moment later, his fists unclenched. He smiled as he turned to Elder-21.

"Sir?" his fellow elder started. "We do not understand. Why…"

Holding up a hand, Elder-3 said, "We know how to take care of the bow anchor and get our escape plan back on track."

# CHAPTER 27

January 22, 2045
Sunday, Morning
New Jersey coast, Utopia Project Ship Number One
**Twenty-seven days after the event**

General Hyland watched as Mel landed the M3 very smoothly on the deck of the ship. While waiting for them to disembark, he took a moment to assess the battlefield. The crane on Ship Number Two was destroyed, so that ship was not going anywhere without the ability to raise the bow anchor.

All of the elders in the dining room on Ship Number One were dead, and the P55 poison cloud was dissipating. Donning gas masks, a couple of elders had opened the doors at each end of the hallway to bring in fresh air, but until they were sure the fog had lifted, the area was to be avoided at all costs. The hallways and even the deck in the vicinity of the dining room were also off-limits. Fortunately, the members on all three ships were still in a lockdown. Upon waking that morning, they had been ordered to remain in place in their rooms until the elder's emergency meeting was over. That lockdown order would remain in effect until there was 100 percent certainty that the air was clear.

Along the deck rail, facing Ship Number Two, ten members with Medusa firearms stood to post. They were instructed to keep a vigilant watch for Elder-3 and Elder-21 on Ship Number Two and to fire on sight.

Standing on the forward deck, Kid, Jess, and General Hyland discussed what to do next. They were joined by two of the surviving elders, Elder-113, a female British Army officer named Marjorie Dawson and Elder-96, a male African-American Marine Lieutenant named Jimmy Hertzog. They concluded that they needed to reconnect the rope bridge to Ship Number Two so that they could mount an attack and finish the battle. The question was how.

It was Jess who offered the solution. "I can climb the anchor links and slip into their ship through the hawse pipe."

The general was impressed. "Isn't that how you got into the ship the first time to rescue the girls?"

"Exactly. Once I am inside, I know my way around. I'll run up to the deck, throw over a line, and someone can tie it to the other end of the bridge. Then I can reel it in and reattach it," he finished.

Feeling encouraged, the general said, "It may work. The bridge is not hard to connect, but..." he paused, concerned about a potential weakness in the plan, "...it is heavy. It will be tough for just one person to reel it in."

"I can do it," Jess concluded.

Kid nodded in agreement. "If anyone can do it alone, it's Jess."

"Alright." The general turned toward the group of elders. "We need line with lengths long enough to reach from the deck to the waterline."

"Got it. We know where to find line," Elder-96, Jimmy Hertzog, said in his deep, baritone voice and took off.

Having disembarked from the M3, Mel, Chris, and Romeo ran up and joined the group.

The general waved to them and then turned to Jess to continue planning. "You need to take someone with you to stay at the waterline and tie the line to the other end of the bridge."

Although he had just landed, Romeo took a step forward. The former Utopia Project member 801 offered, "We will help."

"Thanks, but I was going to ask Kid," Jess started and hesitated.

"As a former scout, he can tie a good knot."

"We know how to tie many knots," Romeo countered.

Kid just shrugged and did not seem the slightest bit insulted, so Jess let it go. "Alright, Romeo, you're it. Grab a couple of oars so we can row over. We don't want to turn on the engine and give ourselves away."

A few moments later, Elder-96 ran on the deck with a long length of line coiled over each shoulder. He handed one to Jess and the other to Romeo.

The general said with a sense of urgency, "We have what we need, so let's move." Turning to the others, he pointed to his Medusa firearm. "We need to cover Jess in case they attack him before he gets the bridge attached. And once he gets it attached, we need to cross and defend it."

The elders all leaned on the deck rail and trained their weapons on Ship Number Two as the tender with Jess and Romeo was lowered to the waterline.

The general also leaned on the rail, but he was looking down. As soon as the boat reached the water, Jess grabbed the dangling bridge and hoisted it out of the water hand over hand. When he reached the thick loop at the end that was used to fasten the bridge, he held it tight and waved Romeo on. Digging in with the oars, Romeo rowed like a machine. Within moments they reached the anchor chain at Ship Number Two. Jess fed the loop around an anchor link and handed it to Romeo. The line around the link was keeping their boat from floating away. The general could not hear Jess but knew he was instructing Romeo to hold on tight.

Climbing onto the first link above the waterline, Jess wadded up a section of line and threw it over the second anchor chain link over his head. He grabbed the dangling end, tied it to the top of the link on which he was standing, and climbed while pulling himself up.

Adele ran to General Hyland's side and whispered so only he could hear, "I checked the system. He is on that ship!"

236

The general exhaled and looked up at the sky. "Just our luck."

Elder-43, a portly but energetic male Russian military officer, was standing on the other side of the general. "Who is in command of Ship Number Three?"

"Good question. I don't think anybody is." The general stepped back and moved his eyes between Elder-43, Ivan Andreyov, and Adele. "Can you two go over and take command of Ship Number Three for the time being?"

Both nodded, and as they went to head for the rope bridge to the next ship, Adele stopped and whispered to the general, "Eric, the… members on Ship Number Two need to be saved."

"I know," he whispered back as he met her green, worried eyes.

Kid stood between Sara and a very jumpy Maria as a long moment passed. *Come on, just like the first time*, Kid thought as he watched Jess climb. He was thinking of when they infiltrated the ships to rescue the girls. Jess had climbed the links with relative ease.

The scream of a loud metallic freight train made Kid jump, and his heart rose into his throat. He watched Jess jump for his life as the anchor chain fell out from under him and the links were swallowed by the sea. The bitter end of the chain whipped away from the ship and came down like the tail of a serpent. The last few links cut the boat in half and Romeo disappeared.

"No!" Maria screamed as she leaned over the rail.

"Lower me down! Quick!" Kid yelled as he ran to the next davit with a boat. Without hesitation, General Hyland ran over.

As Elder-96 joined them and said, "Since they could not raise the anchor, they just released the bitter end and dropped it instead."

"That is a problem. That means they are no longer stuck in place," the general concluded as he engaged the davit. "I hope the guys are alright, but Romeo didn't even have a split second to get out of the way." As the boat was being lowered, the general called down, "Watch out for Ship Number Two drifting since it is no longer anchored!"

Kid waved his hand. As soon as he reached the water, he released the davit lines and turned on the boat motor. He was no longer concerned with stealth as he sped over to Ship Number Two. He spotted Jess treading water and waving his arms. Kid pulled up and had to help his fatigued friend into the boat.

"Are you alright?" Kid asked. "That anchor chain dropped right out from under you."

"Yeah, I was able to jump far enough away." Jess waved up to Maria on deck, letting her know he was alright.

"Barely," Kid said.

"I know. Now I'm just freezing to death." He shivered.

Both glanced up at the deck of the ship next to them as Maria yelled while waving her hands frantically. "What about Romeo?"

Jess seemed to be jolted and stood up. "Where is he? Romeo?" he called out.

Shaking his head, Kid said, "The anchor chain... it came right down on him. Look, it cut the boat in half." Floating toward shore along slightly different trajectories were the two splintered and shortened halves of the tender.

"Son of a bitch!" Jess yelled. "Pull closer. See if we can find him."

Kid drove through the flotsam, but having seen the moment of impact, he knew Romeo was crushed by the mammoth anchor chain. They cased out the surface of the water, scanning the rolling waves and the choppy, turbulent surface. They saw no sign of a body.

"Romeo, 801, is gone," Kid concluded. On some emotional level it helped, although only minimally, to think of Romeo as a number at that moment. During the heat of battle, when running on adrenaline, such emotional hits could be kept at arm's length. But Kid had learned that it always closes in once the fight is over. He knew he would be devastated when it sunk in.

It was then that Jess noted, "That would have been you, Kid, if Romeo didn't volunteer."

A chill went down Kid's spine. His friend was right.

Kid motored over the Ship Number One and affixed the davit lines. The boat was raised to the deck. Maria was waiting there and embraced Jess tightly.

At the deck rail of Ship Number One, Kid joined General Hyland, who was conferencing with the remaining elders. The general stated, "With that ship no longer anchored, Elder-3 might be able to escape with a ship full of members. We can't let that happen."

Right on cue, they were startled by the sound of the windlass raising the anchor at the stern of Ship Number Two. Then behind the stern, the ocean water began to bubble and froth as the propeller blades turned with increasing speed. Ship Number Two started reversing back out to sea.

"They are making a run for it!" the general yelled.

Elder-96 asked, "Shall we raise anchor and prepare to give chase?"

"Yes and fast. They already have a head start."

The general radioed Adele on Ship Number Three and apprised her of the status. He concluded by advising her to remain anchored on the coast, but to be ready to send reinforcements if needed.

Kid turned to the general. "Do you think we can catch them?"

The general shook his head. "Our ship is no faster than theirs. Unless they make a mistake or slow down, we will not gain any ground."

"How much fuel do they have? Will they run out?"

"Not for a long time, Kid. Although it is, or was, against maritime law, all three of our ships carried vast quantities of extra fuel."

After a pause, the general shook his head and appeared aggravated. "Had the attack today been 100 percent successful, the confrontation would be over. Now we are at risk of losing a ship filled with thousands of members and letting two enemy elders escape," he lamented.

"Then let's stop that ship and end this," Kid stated.

"We must," the general agreed. "The question is how without endangering the lives of all of the members aboard?"

Standing along the deck rail, they watched as Ship Number Two backed up into deeper water.

Kid snapped his head around. "Wait! Mel is here with the M3. Why don't we have her blast a hole in the ship to stop it, or at least slow it down?"

"The missiles on the M3 would have no impact on the thick, strong hull of that ship. It would be a distraction but would not slow it down at all."

Momentarily deflated, Kid pondered until another thought hit him. "What if we fired a missile at the propellers and damaged them? That would slow them down, if not stop them."

"That would require a really precise shot. It would be nearly impossible," the general said.

"But what if I could make that shot?"

They watched as Ship Number Two finished turning around and started heading out to sea.

The general seemed to be at a loss in terms of options. "I guess it *could* work." He pulled out his walkie-talkie. "Mel, where are you?"

Her response was immediate. "On deck next to the M3. Why is one of the ships moving?"

"They are trying to escape with a ship full of members. The battle is not over yet," he said. "How many missiles do you have locked and loaded?"

"Three, after taking out the crane. What are we aiming at?"

"The propellers in the back of their ship."

"How am I supposed to make a shot like that? And with a moving target?"

Also raising his walkie-talkie, Kid said, "That's where I come in. I'll be right there." He went to leave, but Elder-96 stepped up and said to General Hyland, "Engines on and systems are a go. Elder-88 is ready to raise the stern anchor, and we will raise the bow anchor."

As Kid grabbed Sara's hand and took off, he heard the general snap, "Do it!"

• • •

At Hangar One Pamela McDermott's eyes were still red from bawling after nearly losing her husband and son at the nuclear power plant. Her relief was short-lived, as they were now heading over to the beach to assist in the main battle any way they could.

Estelle had grabbed Pamela's hands. "Your boys are brave. Whatever happens is in the Lord's hands now, and is His will."

"Your boys are brave too, Ms. Severino." She kissed the old woman's hand.

Behind them, the children were running in and out of the room playing tag, oblivious to crises at hand.

With only snippets of communication coming from the walkie-talkies, the adults were trying to piece together what was going, as well as trying to ascertain who had the upper hand in the ongoing battle. They dared not try to call them over the walkie-talkie lest they cause a distraction at a critical moment in the fight.

Clarence looked at Evelyn. "It sounds like the first part of the attack worked, but not perfectly. Some elders survived and are taking one of the ships and making a run for it. They are trying to stop them."

"Well, you heard Eric," Evelyn responded. "The battle is not over yet."

Marissa chimed in. "But based on the communications, we know that your husband, Eric, Sara, and Kid are still alive." She tried to take Evelyn's hand, which was clenched in a fist. "What are you holding?"

Opening her palm, Evelyn revealed her life-saving medication.

"Mrs. Hyland! You need to take that!"

With a pained smile, Evelyn closed her fist. "No, I don't think I am ready quite yet."

# CHAPTER 28

Kid and Sara reached the M3 and jumped aboard. As soon as Mel was in the air, Kid used the monitor between the front seats to set his sights on the rear of the fleeing ship number two. Hitting the ship itself would have been akin to throwing a pebble at the side of a barn. He had to hit the propellers but they were not only below the waterline, they were a moving target. He would have to adjust for the ship's speed as well as the anticipated depth of the propellers. Within seconds, Mel was hovering behind ship number two as it motored out to sea.

Kid unbuckled his seat belt and stood up. Putting his face against the window, he stared down. "Back off a bit, Mel. I need a better angle." With the craft dropping back, he estimated where he would have to fire to hit the spinning propeller blades. If the missile went low, it would travel harmlessly into the sea. As he plopped back down into his chair, he immediately adjusted the settings on the monitor next to him. "Ready Mel? Hold steady. Here we go." He went to hit the button to fire a missile.

"Wait! Look on deck!"

Kid spotted it right away. The elder he assumed was Elder-3 was on the deck and had a missile launcher on his shoulder- the same kind of tube they had seen before on Mallard Island during a previous battle. The elder crouched down on one knee.

"Kid…"

Hitting the button and firing, Kid watched as the missile shot out of the tube like bottle rocket and dove toward the back of the ship. "Go! Get out of here Mel!"

Mel jammed the throttle, turned the engines almost perpendicular, and the craft headed for the clouds as the missile hit the water 10 feet behind the ship.

Turning back Kid spotted an eruption at the back of the vessel, as if a tiny volcano had awoken just under the surface. A hunk of metal flew out of the water like a clay slung by a trap.

"Did y'all see that?" Sara leaned between the two front seats.

Mel squinted her eyes. "What was it?"

"A piece of the ship flew straight up in the air."

"Let's hope it was a propeller blade," Kid said.

Leveling off, Mel was holding a hand over her head. Her fingers were touching a plastic encasement with a large red button underneath. "Any sign of a missile heading our way?"

"No, we must be out of range. I don't think those shoulder launched missiles are meant for long distance targets," Kid answered.

Relaxing a notch, Mel lowered her hand and held the steering control tightly.

"What was the red button you were ready to hit?" Sara asked.

"Cabin-eject." Pointing, Mel clarified, "The red button ejects the two front seats *and* the row of seats you are sitting on, all as one. I wasn't about to leave anyone behind."

"The entire cabin ejects?" Kid peered at the switch.

"The manual says it does."

He hesitated for a second, and then turned to peer out the window. Seeing ship number two below, Kid commented, "From this altitude the ship looks like a toy floating on the water."

Mel added, "It's still moving, but it is clearly veering south and seems to be slowing. You must have knocked out the propeller on the right side."

"I think it worked," Kid agreed. "We should be able to catch them now."

Pointing out the front window, Mel started, "Is that…"

Sara leaned forward. "The cruise ship we passed when we headed over to Italy!"

"But it is closer to the coast now. It must be drifting west." Kid watched out the window. He turned to Sara. "Anyway, let's go back to the ship and talk to your father about what we're going to do when we catch them."

At that, Mel made a sharp turn and dove toward ship number one.

Watching out the window of the M3, Kid saw that the aircraft was turning hard and diving, but it still amazed him that with the equalization technology in the craft, he was unaware that they were even moving. There was no G-force pressure, no stomach drop. Nothing. It was uncanny.

On the deck of ship number one, Kid and Sara met with General Hyland and the others. The general said, "Good call on going after their propellers. They are only a couple of miles ahead and the gap is closing."

Another elder pointed. "Further in the distance, what is that other vessel?"

Kid saw it, and knew exactly what it was. "That's a cruise ship we passed when we went to Italy. It is just drifting aimlessly off of the coast."

"Is it my imagination, or is ship number two heading straight for it?" Sara asked.

They watched for several minutes, trying to speculate as to what the enemy elder was up to. Elder-3 passed the drifting cruise ship, circled around and tried to pull aside. Ship number two was a much taller vessel and its gunwale passed over top of the cruise ship's deck rail and cut one of the three towering water slides in half. Even at such a distance, metallic scratching sounds, like steel fingernails across a chalkboard, emanated as the ships' hulls rubbed together, making Kid cringe. It then appeared that mooring lines were being thrown so the vessels could be tied together. With the main deck of ship number two hovering over the deck of the cruise ship, they could simply step from one ship to the other.

Several minutes later, ship number one approached the cruise ship and General Hyland called for a full stop. "Don't get too close. We don't know what Elder-3 is up to. I am sure he is planning something, like a trap, ambush or even a straight up assault. He will not go out quietly, and without a last stand," he said. "But we have the numbers. We will be tactical and cautious, but we need to take them."

"I can smell the death from that cruise ship all the way over here," Jess said.

"I thought I smelled something," Maria noted. "That is disgusting."

"Can you imagine the carnage? There are probably more than 5,000 dead bodies on that thing."

"Like the ship in the Rime of the Ancient Mariner times about…25," Sara commented absently.

Right on cue, Kid watched as a bird with an imposing wingspan flew past and landed on the bow of the cruise ship, but it wasn't an albatross. Rather it was a turkey vulture with the prospect of an unlimited carrion feast.

General Hyland, Kid and Chris conferred and decided their best shot was to tie up to the cruise ship on the opposite side from Utopia Project Ship Number Two. This way, if they somehow lost the battle, the survivors still left on ship number one could untie and push away from the cruise ship before being completely overtaken. And they didn't have to worry about being caught at sea since ship number two was down a propeller. And by approaching on the opposite side of the cruise ship, they thought they had a better chance of tying off and disembarking without being attacked as they suspected they would be if they tried to directly board ship number two.

Adele and Elder-43 were contacted as they captained ship number three. They were ordered to load a tender and send out all of their Medusa firearms. The general explained that each ship had an equal number of firearms, which meant that Elder-3 had 100 of them at his disposal on ship number two. By adding the firearms from ship number three, the general's group would have a two to one advantage in terms of weapons.

After the tender from ship number three arrived, the additional Medusa firearms were taken aboard. As the weapons were handed out, each receiving member's fingerprints were programmed to fire their assigned weapon. The orders given to them were clear- shoot anyone armed or hostile standing in the way of Elder-3. General Hyland voiced his position that he did not want any members killed, but if some had to be sacrificed to defeat Elder-3, then that was a price they had to pay. Kid agreed that they needed to put everything they had into this battle, and end it once and for all.

They approached the cruise ship and everyone was ordered to take cover. They had to also watch for missiles since Kid and Sara had warned them about Elder-3 having a missile launcher. The last thing Kid noticed before taking cover were the big, dramatic letters on the side of the cruise ship that said, 'Neptune.' He realized the grim irony that just a few days ago, he had stood face to face with a statue of Neptune in the hidden rooms under the Island of Capri in Italy.

Kid ducked behind the gunwale amidships and winced as the smell of rotting flesh entered his nostrils. They were getting close to the Neptune cruise ship now. He reminded himself to breathe only out his nose, and yelled for everyone else to do the same. The expression of disgust on many people's faces made it clear that he had advised them a few seconds too late.

December 26, 2044
Monday, 10:45 PM
Atlantic Ocean
**_Moments before the event_**


Nancy Sims was ready to go home. She had enjoyed her time on the Neptune cruise ship, but it was time to get back to the real world. Her sister clearly did not feel the same way.

Margie Sims-Mancini held up her red plastic cup, filled with vodka and cranberry, and said, "Cheers, Sis!"

Nancy, standing next to her in the shallow end of the pool on the cruise ship, barely lifted her cup of water. "Whoopee."

"Oh, come on, Nancy. Don't be such a stick in the mud. It's our last night. We need to take advantage. Tomorrow night we will be back in Bayonne," Margie said. "And we better live it up now. Since we are heading north in the Atlantic, it is only going to get colder and colder."

"I'm already cold. I wish we were back in St. Thomas." Nancy stood in a red, flower-patterned bikini with the pool water up to her waist. The commotion on the lido deck was giving her a headache. The pools were too crowded and the bass-driven music was too loud. It was a party atmosphere and everyone seemed to be making to most of the last night on the cruise; everyone, except Nancy. In her mind, the vacation was already over.

"Then sit down and let yourself sink lower in the water. It's a heated pool," Marge offered.

As Nancy sunk down to her neckline, she added, "And I don't think I will touch another drop of alcohol for the rest of my life. It doesn't work for me. Remember, I'm the work out girl."

"I told you we would get the most out of the unlimited drink package! What are you complaining about? You are the one who should be living it up. Not only are you 3 years younger than me, you are single." Marge stood in the waist-deep water and guzzled half of her cup of vodka and cranberry while she danced to the tune blasting on the deck, the same tune that was played time and again, night after night.

"Marge, you're only 38 years old. There isn't much of difference once you hit your thirties."

"There is after you've had three kids like I have," she said, slightly slurring her words as she patted her stomach. Her solid teal one piece bathing suit did not hide the little pouch at her midsection. "And then have to take care of them and a 300 pound husband every day. My moments to be free, and cut loose, are few and far between, so I have to take advantage. Who knows when the next one will come?"

Nodding, Nancy took a sip of her water. Her sister was still attractive, but it was true that her demanding family life had aged her prematurely.

"And you?" Marge continued. "You only have to worry about taking care of you. And you've had more guys hit on you during this cruise than I've had hit on me in my entire life. What I would give to be in your shoes, even for one night. Live it up for once. The next decent guy who makes you an offer, take him up on it. Because if you don't, maybe I will." She smiled, but didn't laugh. She then downed the rest of her drink and threw her cup on the pool's decorative concrete apron.

Right on cue, a hairy chested but fit patron, also holding a red cup, bumped up against Nancy in the pool. The hair on his head was as dark as his prominent patch of chest hair. He played it off as if it was an accident, saying, "Oh sorry. Didn't see you there. Are you having a good time?"

Rolling her eyes, and ready to fend off yet another solicitation, she turned to her sister. "Marge?" She saw only a backside as her sister climbed the steps out of the pool. "Hey! Don't leave me! Where are you going?"

Blowing her sister a kiss, Marge pointed at a tall slide and then high-fived a couple of partygoers.

"The slides are closed because of the party in the pool."

Marge yelled, "I know!" She danced and her long hair swayed back and forth as she approached the steps at the base of the slide.

Nancy exhaled and for just a brief second wondered if she should listen to her sister about living it up for once.

"Nancy!" she heard her sister shout. "Up here!"

"Get down from there!" Nancy stood up in the pool and shivered as the cooler air blew against the wet skin of her chest and midsection. Reflexively, she crossed her arms and hugged herself.

"That is a bad idea." She turned to see the words came from the mouth of the dark-haired man, who was right beside her. She found herself staring at his hairy chest, imagining her hands running through it.

"What is?" she asked.

He smiled and pointed up. "The slide is closed and the water is off. She is not going to have a fun ride. A friend of yours?"

"No, that's my crazy older sister."

"Here goes nothing," Marge yelled from high above, her voice sounding like it was coming through a tin can.

"Can't wait to see the expression on her face. Let's watch this," the dark-haired man quipped and put his arm around Nancy's shoulder. She didn't flinch.

While following her sister's descent, she could see Marge's eyes were wide open and she was screaming, but Nancy couldn't tell if it was in delight, or in agony.

A cruise ship employee on the deck below started yelling that the slide was closed.

With the water shut off, Marge would slide down a few feet and come to a stop on the dry surface of the slide, and then push off again. Nancy suspected that Marge wouldn't do this again. But that was the way her sister always was. She was the daredevil and would try anything once.

To Nancy's horror, a red beam came out of nowhere and zapped her sister on the slide. At first, she thought it was a bolt of lightning but it stayed in place for a full second. When it disappeared, she let out a blood curdling scream as her sister's body was reduced to a mound of bloody gore on the slide, like it had simply melted.

By this time, red beams were touching down all over the deck. Horrified and panicked screams cut through the blaring music. She turned to the dark-haired man, but he was making a break for the steps out of the pool. A red beam found him and drilled him below the surface of the water. The water turned red and Nancy saw something disgusting float to the surface. She gagged as it appeared to be a clump of dark, hairy flesh. Turning around, she watched red beams strike down other patrons in the pool and on the deck. The gore was sickening.

She looked up in time to see her sister's bloody skull start rolling down the slide. Nancy felt sick upon seeing a few strands of long hair still attached and whipping about as her sister's head bounced toward the pool below. But then mercifully, Nancy's world went red and then black.

# CHAPTER 29

January 22, 2045
Sunday, Late Morning
Coastal New Jersey
***Twenty-seven days after the event***


K id tried not to grunt as Utopia Project Ship Number One collided with the cruise ship. It seemed like a gentle bump, but sent his shoulder hard into the gunwale. He looked up to see the taller deck of the Utopia Project ship cut into a slide on the Neptune and its frame bent, but the structure did not topple.

"Team Zero! Tie off, bow and stern!" General Hyland yelled. At that, two mooring lines were thrown over the side, and members slid down to the deck of the Neptune. They moved in haste to tie the lines and hold the ships together.

A deep, loud screech cut through the air. It sounded like the hull of the Neptune was getting crushed between the two larger Utopia Project vessels. The deafening creak lasted for a couple of seconds, and wound down with a series of loud, echoing pops.

Getting to his feet, the general said, "Teams One though Eight, at the ready! All leaders, make sure your walkie-talkies are set to channel one."

Four teams of 25 members, one led by General Hyland, would focus on ship number two, and make sure no enemy members, or no more enemy members, came aboard the Neptune. Meanwhile, the other four teams of 25 members had the gruesome task of searching the interior of the cruise ship. The overall mission was simple, find Elder-3 and Elder-21.

"All teams, let's move!" Leading Team One, General Hyland waved his group on as he ran forward. Kid watched as the general jumped the rail and landed on an upper deck of the Neptune a few feet below.

Kid, Chris, Jess, Maria and a few of the remaining elders took up positions along the gunwale as it hovered over and above the deck of the Neptune. They had firearms in their hands and were prepared to provide cover or added firepower. They were also watching the now-quiet Neptune for any snipers.

Given the several thousand corpses rotting and decaying on the vessel, Kid struggled not to breathe out of his nose. The first thing he saw was a mound of sludge halfway down the water slide. Obviously patrons were still using the slide when the destruction came, and Mother Nature had not been courteous enough since then to wash away the gore. Looking down, the deck was even more gruesome, as it was covered with piles of melted corpses, many in large groups. There must have been a big party on the Neptune the night of the destruction. Peering over the rail, he saw a large pool below, with several plastic red cups floating on the surface. The water was murky, and shown a lighter shade of red. Given the number of floating cups, he presumed that the skeletons and remains of several dozen patrons were lurking in that watery grave.

*Eyes open*, General Hyland coached himself. *It is too quiet.*

His group moved along an upper deck on the Neptune, passing several sun chairs occupied by melted corpses. With the garments visible in the puddles, it was clear that the occupants were fully clothed and not sunbathing when the beams hit. They descended the stairs but as soon as they reached the main deck, a group of enemy members stood up behind a long bar and unleashed a volley of shots their way. The general hit the ground and his 25 members followed, although a few of them were too late. Bolts hit a couple of members at the back of the group, and they fell over frozen.

The general knew he couldn't disable the enemy members by yelling, '*Ion*' because it would have disabled his own members too, so he barked, "Fire!" and sent a volley of shots toward the bar where the five enemy members were positioned. The general's first shot hit one in the chest and took him out, but the other enemy members did not duck back behind the bar and kept firing. He realized it was a suicide assignment. The general lost a few more of his members as the shots continued to come their way. "Keep firing!" he repeated. He was able to take out one more enemy member with a bolt to the face, but was nearly cut down himself. General Hyland's members fired relentlessly until they took out the remaining three members behind the bar.

Turning and glancing behind, the general had lost eight members. It was a bad trade-off. Without hesitation, he ran behind the bar and grabbed the enemy weapons. He then instructed his team to secure the weapons of their own fallen members. Having collected 13 weapons, he had a member run them back to ship number one. The 13 Medusa firearms could be reprogrammed and used again in the fight.

"Unbelievable. Members killing members," General Hyland mumbled as he scanned the deck of the Neptune. He realized that more ambushes would likely be set up and right now his group was out in the open. He waved his hand and ran for the other side of the Neptune's main deck, which was overshadowed and encroached upon by the massive upper deck of runaway ship number two. The four teams assigned to search the cruise ship were making their way carefully toward the doors to the inside of the ship. Like the general's team, they had been attacked by a small suicide squad, but they were also fighting against random enemy members who were hidden all over the deck.

From somewhere on the Neptune, a voice screamed loudly, "Now!"

All at once, chaos erupted and the scene exploded into a firestorm of Medusa bolts coming from every direction. Nearly 50 enemy members burst from doors fore and aft on the Neptune and fired relentlessly. Smoke bombs ignited all along the deck rail of ship number two, creating a growing curtain of fog. Through the smoke screen, a hail of Medusa fire was unleashed in every direction, including down at the deck where General Hyland's group stood in the open.

"Take cover!" the general yelled and led his team in a hasty retreat behind the same long bar that the enemy had used to attack them.

With bolts also coming their way, Kid's group ducked down below the gunwale. Lifting his head, he peered straight across at the deck of the other Utopia Project ship. *Where the hell are those shots coming from?* The higher deck rails of ship number one and ship number two, with the cruise ship sandwiched in between them, looked like two theater balconies facing each other. But the balcony of the other ship had weapon fire from seemingly dozens of members bursting through the cover of a smoke screen. They were like ghosts in the fog, but with deadly weapons.

Kid's walkie-talkie blared, and he jumped. "Kid! Weapon fire is coming at us from the deck rail of ship number two. We are hiding behind a bar, but we are still taking hits! We need assistance."

"We are on it," Kid responded. He pointed with his weapon and yelled, "Take out the enemy behind the deck rail over there! They are picking us off like fish in a barrel!"

"I can't see anyone through the smoke over there, Kid!" Jess said as he fired.

"Don't waste bullets firing blindly!" retired army general Chris Hyland interjected and then turned to the elders. "All of you with Medusa firearms, aim for just above the deck rail over there. Fire into the fog and sweep back and forth. Coordinate fire and fill in all of the gaps."

Without hesitation, the elders said simply, "Yes, Sir," and started firing. Their hailstorm of bolts slowed down the fire coming through the smokescreen, but they had no way of knowing if anyone was actually hit.

While firing down toward enemy members swarming the deck of the Neptune, Kid heard his walkie-talkie again come to life.

"Kid, come in!"

It was Dr. Carmelo's voice and she sounded alarmed. She probably just wanted to know what was going on, so he continued sharpening his aim at one of the enemy members who was firing without pause. Kid pulled the trigger of his 38-caliber pistol and the member crumpled after taking a shot in the chest. Before Kid could train his sights on another enemy, Adele's voice came through so loud and desperate that he froze. "Kid! Pick up! They are trying to escape in a boat, heading out to sea!"

Looking out to sea, from his vantage point, all Kid could see was smoke. As he went to put the walkie-talkie to his lips, General Hyland, who was tuned into the same radio channel, blurted out, "Kid, if there is a boat, you have to get it! Do you read me?"

"I read you. But should I be leaving mid-battle?"

"We are at a stalemate here anyway, so yes, go."

"On my way," Kid radioed.

As Kid went to run, Sara followed, staying at his side. Mel was at the ready, buckled into the pilot seat of the M3. She had the craft fired up before Kid and Sara even jumped aboard.

"Mel…" Kid started.

"I heard." She held up her walkie-talkie and then dropped it into on her lap. "Let's get that boat before they escape." She sounded eager to give chase as she raised the M3 off the deck of ship number one in a vertical ascension.

Once high enough in the air, Kid saw it. A boat was traveling east away from the ships. He realized that the enemy was using the position of the ships, the smoke and the distraction of the chaotic all-out battle to their advantage. And were it not for Adele keeping a close watch from ship number three, the small escaping tender may have been a mere speck in the distance by the time the battle ended and the smoke cleared.

Within seconds, Mel was behind the fleeing craft and mumbled, "Where do you think you're going?" She turned to Kid and noted, "They could've taken a faster boat."

The members aboard, 15 by Kid's count, turned and looked back at the M3 coming behind them, but the one elder standing at the bow remained facing forward.

Sara picked up the walkie-talkie. "Dad, are you there?"

"Go ahead."

"Are you alright?" she asked.

"Still in a stalemate, but it is one they can't win. We have taken out all of the enemies on the deck of the cruise ship. We still need to finish off the group on the deck rail of ship number two but I am safe at the moment. Did you catch the boat yet?"

"We are right behind it. An elder is standing at the bow."

"It is probably Elder-3. Use the machine gun and try to take him out."

Taking the walkie-talkie, Kid said, "But a missile would blow them all to hell and back."

The general repeated, "Use the machine gun, so we can spare as many members as we can."

Chris chimed in over the walkie-talkie, sounding suspicious. "Hold on. Elder-3 knew that we had an M3, right?"

Kid answered, "Yes. He saw us and was getting ready to launch a missile before. Why?"

"Look," Mel said to Kid. "They've stopped and the elder is holding something up." The elder had turned toward the hovering M3 and he was holding a white piece of paper in front of his face with both hands.

Squinting his eyes, Kid tried to read it. "He's trying to communicate something to us. Be cautious but get a little closer, Mel."

"He wants us to read it. He is pointing at it," she concluded as she lowered the craft.

Kid unfastened his seat belt and got closer to the window. He peered closely and read the sign. "We surrender?"

A voice blurted through the walkie-talkie, as Chris asked, "If Elder-3 knew we had an M3, he would also know that he couldn't outrun it in a small boat. Would he be that stupid?"

Sara grabbed Kid's arm and he followed her eyes as she glanced back at the flotilla. Something in her grandfather's voice seemed to alarm her.

Kid turned back around and looked down at the sign the elder was holding. For just a second, the paper blew out of one of the elder's hands and revealed his face before he quickly reestablished his two-handed grip. Mel must have also caught a glimpse because she said exactly what Kid was thinking, "He's awfully young to be an elder."

Sara suddenly gasped, and screamed, "Hold on tight!"

To Kid's dismay, she flipped open the plastic cover and hit the red cabin-eject button.

# CHAPTER 30

In a split second Kid was thrust down into his seat. He saw nothing but blue sky. He was heading for the sun, and what struck him was the feeling. When moving in the M3 with the equalization technology he had never felt anything. But now his stomach had been punched and the air was being sucked out of his lungs as he continued his ascent. He was no longer in the calm and womb-like capsule of the M3. *Why did she eject us?*

He heard Sara yell, "Kid! Belt..." and then she was cut off by a loud explosion below. *That's why.* He could not move his head to look, but assumed the M3 had been hit by a missile.

He tried to yell back to Sara but could not get a single word out because his lungs were being crushed. Plastered to his seat, he felt like he was wearing a suit made of lead. *Why did Sara scream 'belt'?* He struggled to turn his eyes down and realized he was not wearing his seat belt. As the afterburners started to fizzle out and the ascent of the ejected cabin slowed, it hit him. "Oh no." He tried to move his arm but it seemed to weigh a hundred pounds. All of a sudden, his arm felt lighter, and he easily grabbed his seat belt. Their ascent stopped, and for a second they hovered in the air.

"Hold on!" Sara screamed, her voice sounding strained.

Kid tried to fasten his seat belt, but he was too late as the cabin began a rapid descent. He was barely able to grab the belt with both hands when his body flew out of the seat. Holding on for his life, his feet were pointed at the sky as the cabin plummeted faster. His grip on the belt was the only thing keeping him from flying away, but the force was immense, and he could not hold on much longer.

Then he heard a loud pop.

The drag lessened by a notch so Kid started reeling himself in.

"Brace yourself!" Sara yelled. "Protect your head!"

His eyes opened wide, and he heard an even louder snap as a parachute deployed above their heads and filled with air. The cabin stopped short, and his body came crashing down. He cradled his head with his arms as his upper body landed hard on the seat. The wind further knocked out of him, but before he could take a desperately needed breath, the fully-opened parachute was swept up by a strong wind current. Kid thought his chest was imploding as the cabin jerked hard and again rose at breakneck speed. The last thing he remembered before he blacked out was seeing the seat belt in front of his face on the seat as if taunting him.

"Kid! Wake up. Kid?" Sara called out as she shook him. For a moment, he did not know where he was. Lifting his head, he rubbed the back of his kinked neck and looked at Mel next to him. Past her, he saw the expanse of the Atlantic Ocean.

"How long was I out?"

Shrugging her shoulders, Mel answered, "Maybe a minute?"

"That's it? Felt like I was out for hours." Kid shook his head to clear the cobwebs.

Sara unbuckled herself and gently massaged Kid's neck and shoulders as he sat up in his seat. "You hit pretty hard." She stood behind him. "But we're lucky you're still in the cabin. You almost flew out. Sorry I couldn't warn you sooner, but I only saw the missile at the very last second."

Kid tilted his head from side to side and stretched his neck muscles. "Lucky you saw it at all." A gust of wind tousled his hair and whipped the large parachute above them so hard that the floating cabin turned 180 degrees and was now facing the flotilla.

Sara's hands froze on Kid's shoulders. "What is going on there?"

Alongside the enemy-commandeered Utopia Project Ship Number Two, the blue tarp covering a boat at the waterline was now flapping in the wind. A second later it came free and blew away, floating across the sky like a massive magic carpet.

Mel stood and was peering toward the flotilla when she blurted out, "No! Look in that boat with the blue tarp! Is that guy holding a missile launcher?

Snapping to, Kid also stood up. "That must be where the missile that hit the M3 came from. Wait, they are aiming our way again! They are trying to finish us off!" Kid said as he searched around the floating cabin. He could feel that they were descending. Looking down, he saw that they were still several hundred feet from the surface of the water. Even if they landed, the cabin was large, making it an easy target. They would be sitting ducks for a missile strike. Glancing at the parachute above, Kid noted it was affixed to the square cabin at each of the four corners. An idea hit him.

"We have to cut the cabin free before they blast it! Quick, grab onto a line at a corner where the parachute is attached. Hold on tight, and as soon as I cut the line, try to wrap it around your hands and feet to hold your weight!" Pulling out his knife, Kid directed the girls to opposite corners. Sara grabbed the line firmly as he walked over. "Ready?"

She nodded. "As much as I will ever be."

He sawed the line with his knife until it broke free. As the corner of the cabin dropped, Sara went whipping up into the air. She looked like an expert bull-rider, holding the line as it snapped and bucked. The parachute started collapsing since it was no longer uniformly anchored at four corners.

Running over to Mel, Kid yelled, "Hold on!" He cut her line

causing her to also fly up into the air.

In the boat in the water alongside Ship Number Two, Elder-3 held a loaded missile launcher on his shoulder and was looking through the sight. He lifted his head for a second when the cabin started falling faster. He tried to aim again as it dropped toward the sea.

Kid knew the worst was yet to come. He wrapped a seat belt around his wrist and held it tightly as he reached out with his other hand to cut the line holding the third corner of the cabin. As soon as the third line snapped, the parachute completely collapsed. The two girls were holding their lines tightly but were being whipped around. Held now by only one line, the dangling cabin plummeted even faster.

The only thing preventing Kid from falling into the sea was his firm grip on the seat belt, but he needed to climb and cut the cabin completely free. He used the belt to pull himself up and climb over the seats. Even in that moment, it struck him that Jess would make such a climb look easy. Reaching with a trembling hand, he grabbed the final line still attached to the parachute. With all of the strength he could muster, he pulled himself up a foot at a time. Once his entire body was above the cabin, he bent down and tried to saw the line below his feet.

He stood upright and stiffened as a scream approached him. Mel was being blown around like a wind chime in a hurricane. Swinging at a high rate of speed, she came within inches of slamming into him. As soon as she passed, he continued cutting the line below his feet. He had to hurry. The cabin was falling faster and faster toward the hungry ocean below.

With the cabin less than 100 feet from the waterline and descending at an increasing rate of speed, Elder-3 again took aim with the missile launcher. He started a countdown for his last missile. "Three, two…"

Kid was launched into the air as he finally sawed through the rope. The line broke free. The cabin plunged into the ocean below, and after a shallow dive, it leveled off and floated on the surface. While he was looking down, a missile flew under Kid's feet and continued for several hundred feet before harmlessly diving into the ocean.

"Damn you!" Elder-3 yelled and threw the missile launcher into the ocean. He immediately reached for his Medusa firearm and ordered the members with him to do the same. Glancing back at the four occupants in the boat with him, the elder noted bitterly, "We should have taken the time to secure a larger force."

Holding on for his life, Kid was hurled skyward. With him gripping a parachute line, and the girls each holding one, the canopy above filled with air and snapped open again. The fourth line was slapping around violently and snapped Kid's cheek like the crack of a bull-whip. He wrapped his line around his feet and wrist to better stabilize himself. As the parachute stabilized, he noticed that the girls had also wrapped the line around their feet and arms to support themselves. He was thankful they had followed his instructions. He knew that if they did not find a way to relieve the pressure on their hands, there was no way they would have been able to keep holding on. Giving each of them a thumbs up, they both waved back to assure him they were alright. But then Sara started pointing vigorously.

Turning his head, he saw that the strong wind was blowing them back toward the flotilla and the small enemy boat that was firing missiles. Kid had to somehow steer the parachute away from danger. At that moment, he thought of something from their recent visit to the Cathedral of the Air chapel in Lakehurst. It was not only worth a try, but it was the only thing he could even think of trying. Turning his head, he gauged the wind's direction. He struggled to swing his feet and reach Mel to his east. His momentum pushed himself closer to her and yelled, "Grab my waist band!" She grabbed it with her one free hand and struggled to keep hold.

"What are you doing?" she called out.

Right then, a continuous volley of bolts from Medusa firearms started tracing through the sky. The shots were not hitting the target, but they were getting closer.

"We're heading right for them!" Sara yelled as a shot flew under her, close enough that she lifted her feet.

"Keep holding me!" Kid yelled as he reached above Mel's head and grabbed her line. Once his full weight was on it he yelled, "Alright, I got it. You can let go." He was able to hold his line and Mel's together with his hands despite the natural force that tried to rip them apart. He pulled himself up hand over hand until his feet were over her head. Under the weight of two people, the southwest corner of the parachute edged down toward the sea. It compromised the relatively level and smooth descent they had been making with a person at each of three corners. As he had hoped, with two-thirds of the weight on one line, the shape and form of the parachute canopy was altered, causing them to veer southward away from the flotilla.

"We're turning, Kid!" Sara called out, as she floated much higher in the sky than he and Mel. "And just in time!"

He pointed up. "Canopy-warping!"

"What?"

"Canopy-warping. Like the Wright brothers did, but with a parachute instead of wings," Kid yelled, referencing a prior discussion at the Cathedral of the Air.

She gave him a quick thumbs-up but had to grab the line with both hands as the wind whipped her around.

Kid peered down and knew it was too much to hope for that they could reach land. He just knew that when they hit the water, someone needed to get them before hypothermia did.

Watching the parachute drifting further away, Elder-3 freed the blue tarp and throttled up. His 26-foot Sea Ray, with a 350-horsepower outboard engine, roared as he buried the throttle and almost immediately went up on plane. He turned in the direction of the runaway parachute.

As soon as Elder-3's boat cleared the front of ship number two, he jerked the wheel to avoid colliding with another boat.

# CHAPTER 31

January 22, 2045
Sunday, Midday
Coastal New Jersey
***Twenty-seven days after the event***

While still aboard the Neptune, General Hyland had heard a distant explosion, but he could see nothing with the deck of Ship Number Two looming over the cruise ship. At first he figured Kid had blown up the escaping enemy boat, until Adele had radioed him in a panic. She broke the news that it was the M3 that had exploded. His heart and breathing had stopped until she said, "But the entire cabin was jettisoned right before missile impact! I am trying to locate Sara and Kid!"

With the enemy mostly neutralized on the Neptune, the general had climbed back onto the deck of Ship Number One. The smokescreen had largely dissipated so he picked up a pair of binoculars, ran up to the bridge, and scanned the sky. He was overwhelmed with relief upon spotting what appeared to be Sara, Kid, and Mel. The binoculars remained glued to his face as the cabin made a quick descent, and Kid was holding on for dear life. Several minutes later, he spotted Sara clinging to a parachute line while Kid was cutting the cabin free. *Why would he do that? The cabin is what will keep them out of the frigid water,* he reasoned. *Kid would not do such a thing without a reason.* His conclusion was confirmed a minute later when he saw a missile just miss its target as the cabin fell to the sea.

Lifting the walkie-talkie, he asked, "Adele, where are those missiles coming from?"

"I can't tell! I don't see anyone on the decks with a launcher."

"I am going after them!" The general ran down to the deck and made for the nearest boat.

He rounded up his father, Jess, and seven members with Medusa firearms to come with him. They lowered the boat to the water.

Gunning it, the general drove around the bow of Ship Number One and nearly slammed into another boat as it passed mere inches in front of him. The enemy was on the move, and he was not about to let them take out the survivors clinging to the parachute lines, especially not his daughter.

With the boats facing off for a second, General Hyland was able to assess the enemy team they were up against. Only five members were aboard the enemy craft. Elder-3 was at the throttle. For some reason he was dressed in the uniform of a regular member. It was then that the general realized the ruse. The first enemy boat to make a run for it was a decoy, led by a member dressed as Elder-3. Meanwhile, it seems that the real Elder-3 had waited in a boat at the waterline, ready with a missile to take out the M3 as it pursued the decoy.

Glancing back to his own 24-foot center console boat, the general had a team of ten people. He liked his odds in a head to head battle, but before the general could even reach for his weapon, Elder-3 stood up and yelled, "It's Hyland! Kill him!" as he fired his weapon. The four other enemy members with him also opened fire.

"Return fire!" the general yelled as he ducked and pulled out his own Medusa firearm.

One of the members in the general's boat was hit and fell over, but the others returned fire. Between Jess and the general, three of the enemy members were cut down immediately. As soon as the fourth enemy member was killed in short order, Elder-3 seemed to realize that the battle was over. He ducked and pushed the throttle forward. His bow rose toward the sky as his boat roared away.

The general dropped into the driver seat and gave chase. The members on board launched a volley of bolts and bullets, but both boats were skipping and jumping through the field of whitecaps so aiming a weapon was nearly impossible.

"We will never catch them!" Jess yelled.

"Why not?"

"They have a 350 horsepower engine. Ours is only a 225, and we have more people in the boat to weigh it down."

General Hyland stared ahead and realized that the gap between his boat and Elder-3's was quickly growing. He checked the throttle. It was buried. He did not know where Elder-3 was heading, but the parachute no longer seemed to be his target. Casing out the ocean in front of both boats as they headed south, the general could see the large casino buildings of Atlantic City far in the distance.

"Plus look!" Jess yelled. "Sara and Kid are about to land in the ocean. Someone needs to get them quick. They won't last long in water that cold."

"We'll get them. Hold on tight." General Hyland turned the wheel and headed north to secure his daughter. Glancing over his shoulder, he made sure Elder-3 was still maintaining a course toward Atlantic City.

A few minutes after the parachute hit the water, General Hyland pulled up as Kid, Sara, and Mel were all swimming hard for the shore. They still had several hundred feet to go when Jess and the general hauled them aboard. Inside the craft, the three wet passengers held each other in a tight group hug. "Hold on. One more quick stop," the general said.

"Please hurry, Dad. We're freezing," Sara said through chattering teeth.

He nodded as he buried the throttle and made for the decoy boat that Elder-3 had sent ahead.

The general drove back past the flotilla and retrieved the 16 members, including the Elder-3 impostor, from the decoy boat. The davit lifted the bloated craft to the deck above. Upon climbing out, the general inquired about the status of the battle on the Neptune. He learned that the enemy had been defeated on all fronts. It was then that he had a realization. "Elder-3 escaped, but what of Elder-21?"

The other elders on the deck all looked at each other in surprise. "He wasn't with Elder-3 out there?" one asked.

"No. Which can only mean one thing. He is still on one of these ships. Let's search."

Three teams of ten members were established to search the Neptune. They were provided with surgical masks, which General Hyland knew would not spare them from the thick stench within the vessel.

Kid, Sara, and Mel were taken below on Ship Number One to get dry uniforms. Then all three returned to the deck wearing gray one-piece jumpers. General Hyland had seen Sara in a uniform, but he was unable to suppress a smirk upon seeing Kid.

"What?" Kid looked down. "Not my style? Doesn't work for me?"

Chiming in, Mel said, "Who cares about style so long as it is dry and warm."

"I need to find some normal clothes,' Kid mumbled.

Elder-113, Marjorie Dawson, walked up to the general and pulled her surgical mask down. With her British accent she said, "Sir, we have found Elder-21."

"Did you take him out?"

"No, he tossed his weapon to us and stayed in his seat."

"Seat? Where is he?"

"Ah, Sir, we think you should come see for yourself."

He nodded, and she handed him an unopened surgical mask.

Jumping down to the deck of the Neptune, the general matched Elder-113's brisk stride. Pushing through a set of double doors, they stepped over puddles of melted bodies on the stairs and descended to the floor below. Approaching the door of a restaurant, the general muttered, "A Brazilian steakhouse." He then had a recollection. "Elder-21 was Brazilian."

"Yes," the other elder said as she grabbed the door handle. "Prepare yourself. It is gruesome."

The general responded, "Given what we've seen on the rest of the ship, how much more disgusting could it be?"

Elder-113 paused, raised her eyebrows, and then opened the door.

Walking in, the first thing the general noticed was that the Brazilian steakhouse must have been bustling when the destruction came since there were melted bodies at nearly every table. Tall three-prong skewers laid on tables, separate serving trays and even the floor; many with once-savory chunks of meat still affixed. It was then that he spotted Elder-21 sitting in a chair. His back was to the door, and he was staring at a wall decorated with artwork and pictures. The display was labeled, 'The 5 Major Regions of Brazil.' Right in the middle, with a line connected to the Southeast Region, was a picture of Christ the Redeemer perched atop the granite Corcovado Mountain in Rio de Janeiro. Given the elder's Brazilian heritage, the collage must have been a reminder of Elder-21's homeland. That did not seem particularly odd, but Elder-21 was sitting squarely on a rotting mound of melted flesh.

The general winced and walked around the table, all the while avoiding the piles of gore on the floor. When he saw what Elder-21 was doing, he raised his hand to cover his eyes, but the sight registered before he could turn away. The elder was holding a radius and ulna like it was a corn on the cob, and he was actually biting off scraps of muscle and tendon. Although not typically squeamish, the general felt queasy and grabbed a chair. He wondered if the clearly deranged elder had chosen to stay behind or was left behind by Elder-3.

Elder-21 continued staring at the wall, until he finally blurted out, "What have we done?"

General Hyland said nothing.

Jumping to his feet, Elder-21 screamed, "Look at what we've done! This is our new world?" He used his hand and motioned toward the plethora of melted bodies.

As bizarre as it seemed, the general understood what the elder meant on some level. Nothing could have prepared the project elders and members for the carnage they would confront after the destruction. It was not the death, which was bad enough, but the magnitude. It seemed that rotting corpses blanketed the entire world and lay in wait around every corner and behind every door.

The distraught elder walked over to a table and stuck both hands into one of the mounds of gore on a chair. He grabbed remains and rubbed the viscous mess up and down his arms as a deep chuckle emanated from his throat. "Death. Everywhere is death. We are swimming in it." He grabbed a skewer that was lying on the table and stuck it into the pile. He speared rancid intestines and held them up. It looked like he had snagged a shriveled, ribbed snake. Biting into the entrails, he tore a piece free and while chewing, said, "It is everywhere, choking us, so we might as well speed the process along, right?"

Feeling nauseous and horrified, the general pulled down his mask. "Do you know where Elder-3 was heading?"

"No idea. He knew we couldn't win this battle so he wanted to escape and regroup. If you didn't eliminate him, he will be back."

"Why did you not stay with him?"

"For what? So we could escape and live in a world of…" he again swept his hand toward the melted bodies, "…this? There is no escape, other than death." Elder-21 whipped the intestines off of the long metal skewer and held it high above his head, like Poseidon raising his mighty trident.

General Hyland jumped to his feet and pulled out his weapon. "Put it down!"

Elder-21 screamed, "All that's left is death!" He dropped to his knees, turned the skewer upside down and positioned the sharp points against his midsection.

"Don't do it," the general warned.

Bending over, Elder-21 repeated, "All that's left is death," and with the points of the skewer placed just under his rib cage, he let his full weight fall to the ground. The three prongs tore through his body and erupted out his back. He fell sideways on the ground. A look of peace came to his face as death took him.

Shaking his head in disgust, General Hyland shuffled slowly out of the room. As he went to close the door, he almost peered in one last time. "Don't look again," he muttered as he walked away. "You'll see it enough in your nightmares."

Adele, who had taken a tender over from Ship Number Three, embraced the general firmly when he returned to the deck of Ship Number One. He quickly separated when he realized Sara was watching. "Did we see where Elder-3 went?" he called out.

Elder-96 stated, "We tracked him until he was far down the coast. We lost sight of him when his boat neared the high rises down there."

"He turned into the Absecon Inlet toward Atlantic City," Kid chimed in.

The general pondered for a second. "We took out the members he had with him so he is now alone, but as long as he is still alive, we are at risk. Wait, the video was still working for the one remaining satellite." Turning to Jimmy Hertzog, formerly Elder-96, he asked, "Can you go check the satellite status? We could use it to have eyes on the Atlantic City area for at least the parts of the day when the satellite is on this side of the world."

"Yes, Sir."

The general grabbed his arm. "Jimmy, this is all over now. Call me Eric."

# CHAPTER 32

January 22, 2045
Sunday, Afternoon
Coastal New Jersey
*Twenty-seven days after the event*

aving defeated the enemy, General Hyland, Kid, and the remaining leaders of the survivor group assembled on the deck of Ship Number One. The game plan was simple, untie from the stinking cruise ship of death and head back to shore, off of Surf City.

On Ship Number Three, which was not part of the flotilla, the members were allowed to resume their daily schedules after having been in lockdown all morning. The general and few former elders boarded Ship Number Two, and after they ensured that all of Elder-3's hostility orders were canceled, the members were also allowed to resume their daily schedules. On Ship Number One the members were to remain in lockdown until it was certain that all of the lethal P55 gas had fully dissipated.

Finally, when the general thought it was safe, he sent a member down to the main dining room of the ship. Moments later, the member returned. Seeing him, the general breathed a sigh of relief. Although he knew it was cruel, the member had been the proverbial canary being sent into a mine. The general expected all of the P55 gas to have long since evaporated, but he needed to be sure. He then assigned a team of members to go down to the dining room and bring all of the dead elder bodies up to the deck. Another team was assigned to clean and sterilize the dining room and kitchen so that they could finally prepare something to eat.

After untying both Utopia Project ships from the Neptune and getting away from the stench, the members on those ships were finally able to eat lunch. The members were all ravenous, having missed a morning meal for the first time ever in their lives. General Hyland ordered that the Wastewater Plant and Desalination Plant workers be the first to eat, so that they could proceed with their important work shifts.

While the two ships traveled slowly back to the shoreline, Jimmy Hertzog, formerly Elder-96, came over to speak to General Hyland on the deck. "Sir, Eric, we tried accessing the remaining satellite. We, I, had to enlist the help of Elder-92, Akira, and the news is not good. The satellite appears to have disappeared. After being unable to communicate with it or even locate it, we checked the logs. It appears that before Elder-3 made his escape he turned on the thrusters and sent the satellite toward earth. Which means…"

"It has crashed and burned. Of course, Jimmy," the general finished. "I should have thought of that when trying to destroy the last satellite myself. But now we have no satellite video to help us locate Elder-3, and we can't stop until we find him and take him out."

"We all know how he is," Jimmy added. "He will not quit and will do everything in his power to try and destroy us."

Kid interjected, "If we still had an M3, we could have been there in seconds to hunt him down. Where can we get another one?"

"The closest base that would likely have one is the Dover Air Force Base in Delaware. It should be the first order of business, but that is for tomorrow morning. It has been a grueling enough day for us all."

As soon as the ships reached shore, they were anchored at the bow and stern. Ship Number Two no longer had a bow anchor, so it had to be tied to the other two ships. All vessels were again joined together by rope bridges.

The members aboard the ships seamlessly resumed their daily routines, except for participating in conditioning sessions which were replaced by an additional physical activity period.

General Hyland and Kid called for a meeting of all surviving members and elders on the deck of Ship Number One. The group was comprised of the ten elders that had been spared, plus Sara, Jess, Maria, Mel, Adele, and Chris. For the first time since the battle, with the ships again anchored, the group was able to take a moment to breathe. All seemed exhausted as they stood in silence. They seemed to be steeling themselves for the next round of orders and tasks to be done.

The general said, "Listen, I know we are all battle-weary and are probably functioning on adrenaline alone, so for tonight here is what is left to be done: eat and rest."

Most of the survivors seemed relieved. Many audible exhales sounded.

Jess called out, "Look ashore! There are people waving."

General Hyland grabbed a pair of binoculars. "It's Dr. McDermott! He has his son Dylan with him, and Emilio, and…Karen."

"We have to break the news to Emilio, and his mother, that we lost Tony," Kid reminded them.

"I know," the general said somberly. "I wish we didn't lose anyone. But given what we were up against today, we are lucky to have only lost Tony and Romeo, and a number of regular members during the battle." After a momentary pause he added, "We should get everyone we left at Hangar One and bring them aboard. They are probably waiting on pins and needles to know what happened out here."

Kid volunteered, "I'll go ashore, pick up Emilio and head to Hangar One. I'd rather break the news about Tony to him and Estelle at the same time." He turned to Sara.

"I'll go with you," she said without hesitation.

"Are you sure?" the general asked. "The news you're bringing will be heartbreaking, especially to Estelle."

Kid and Sara paused for a second, and then both nodded. "Someone has to do it," he muttered.

"Can I go with them?" Mel asked. "I'm sure my girls have tormented them all enough."

"Of course," the general answered. "I will radio the group at Hangar One and let them know you are coming."

"Then we'd better get moving," Kid noted as he turned and looked at the deck. His eyes stopped on the stacks of dead elders who perished from the P55 in the dining hall. "Wait, where is Tony's body?"

"On a table in the medical ward," the general answered.

"Good. He needs to have a proper and honorable burial."

"And he will." The general put his hand Kid's shoulder. "After you leave, I will have a group of members load these…" he pointed to the stacks of elders on the deck, "…into another boat and dispose of them on the mainland."

He then turned around to the group and advised, "Listen up. Get two boats ready to go ashore. Kid, Sara, and Mel are taking one and will need it to bring aboard everyone from Hangar One. But we need someone to take another boat and bring back Dr. McDermott's group from the beach. We need the doctor here to tend to some injuries."

"What happened to just eating and resting?" Jess quipped.

The general turned to Maria. "Did he just volunteer?"

"Sure sounded like it to me."

• • •

At Hangar One the group had grown increasingly anxious. They were all staring at the walkie-talkie set to channel one.

"The last we heard, someone was firing missiles," Wendy said.

"That was some time ago. And then…nothing," Evelyn added. Her hand was still in a fist.

"Why don't we just try to call them?" Wendy asked.

"If we do not hear from them very soon, we will do just that,"

Evelyn responded.

"Why wait?"

"Because it could jeopardize the mission, depending on what is happening at the moment. We have to stay patient." Evelyn picked up the walkie-talkie and stepped into the cavernous hangar. She noticed that her hand was trembling, and she could barely walk. Her condition was deteriorating, and she knew she did not have much longer. A second later, she jumped upon hearing an ominous double beep and looked down at the walkie-talkie in her hand.

Evelyn walked back into the main room. Everyone stopped and turned to her. Evelyn said, "As soon as I stepped into the hangar, they radioed."

Everyone not already standing jumped up. Those already standing took a few steps in her direction.

Marissa had her hands in the air. "What did they say?"

"I will tell you, but first, can you hand me a bottle of water?"

Marissa grabbed the water and ran over with it.

Unraveling her trembling fist, Evelyn finally popped her life-saving medication into her mouth.

• • •

Kid motored toward shore, mist splashing in his face. His adrenaline level was coming down from the battle high, and he suddenly felt exhausted. He looked at Sara and could tell she was also coming down and was not nearly as tense as she had been.

She said to him over the whine of the engine, "Given what went down today, it is totally trivial, but you know what I just realized? With how my father and Adele hugged on the deck, I think there is something there."

"They are probably just happy to be alive."

"Well, that plays into it, I'm sure. But there was something deeper. I felt it."

"So you think they are more than just project colleagues?"

"Adele has been my non-blood aunt for as long as I can remember. So they have been more than project colleagues for a long time. But not at the level I saw back there."

"Alright. So what if they are more than that?" he asked.

"Why wouldn't he just tell me? Especially something as important as that."

"Why don't you just ask him?"

"We always had an open and honest relationship. We communicated about everything, the good, the bad, and the ugly. I didn't think I had to."

Not knowing how to answer, Kid turned his head and looked behind. Trailing in another boat were Jess and Mel.

At the beach Dr. McDermott, Dylan, Emilio, and Karen were initially stunned to learn that the battle was won on the ships. As the realization sunk in, Dr. McDermott started laughing and smacked Kid on the back. "I am in shock! I didn't think we had a chance!" he stated.

Uncomfortable in a Utopia Project uniform, Kid changed into normal clothes he found in the Surf City Hotel. Sara and Mel were perfectly happy to stay in their uniforms, claiming they were warm and comfortable. Kid asked Emilio to come back with them to the hangar. The younger Severino brother agreed, fortunately without asking any questions. After waving to Jess, Dr. McDermott, Dylan, and Karen, Kid proceeded to secure one of the vehicles outside the hotel. He jumped in with Sara, Mel, and Emilio and motored on the snowy roads toward Hangar One.

Katy and Karly Spatz ran outside the hangar to greet Kid's vehicle as he pulled up. Mel hugged and kissed her daughters. Sara was laughing as Katy and Karly came over and hugged her too. Kid had to ask, "What am I, chopped liver?" before the girls came over and embraced him. His words registered, and Karly pulled back while saying, "Liver? Bleh!"

Inside, Sara was greeted most warmly by her grandmother. Evelyn exhaled loudly with relief upon learning that her husband and son had also survived.

Kid and Sara together broke the news of Tony's death to Estelle and Emilio Severino. The old woman had to sit while she bawled. Emilio hugged his mother. Her friend Theresa Marconi waddled over and hugged them both tightly while saying, "I know it hurts, Estelle, but your boy, he died bravely."

Finally, Estelle wiped her eyes and whispered, "It is the Lord's will."

With a convoy of two packed vehicles, the group from Hangar One headed down to Long Beach Island. Kid's vehicle, which included Estelle and Emilio, was quiet and somber. Conversely, when he looked in the rear view mirror, he could tell that Mel's vehicle was just the opposite. Mel had a smile on her face, and the kids were all laughing and jumping about.

As dusk was falling, the group from Hangar One was loaded into a boat and taken out to Ship Number One. It was decided that they would all sleep on the ship that night, in the now-vacant elder bedrooms, and have the luxury of food, heat, and a warm, normal bed.

# CHAPTER 33

On deck the group stood in a circle around a gurney as Estelle Severino said goodbye to Tony. Kid watched with a lump in his throat as she put her head on her son's motionless chest for a long time and wept. Finally, she requested that he be given a burial at sea. Her son had spent his entire life on the water in Italy as a fisherman, so it would be only fitting. At the same time, Maria asked if she could go with them and bring a uniform number 801, so it could be put out to sea to honor Romeo.

Tony's body and a fresh uniform number 801 were loaded into a tender. Estelle, Emilio, and their family friend Theresa Marconi got in, as did Maria, Jess, Kid, and Sara. They drove the boat far out on the ocean after darkness had fallen, offered prayers and gave Tony's body and Romeo's uniform to the sea. On the ride back, Kid felt mentally numb.

Later that evening, after ensuring that the rank and file members were back into their routines, General Hyland, Kid, and the survivor group were all sitting in the elder dining room. Kid was holding Sara's hand, and they were leaning against each other. He was so thankful they had survived and was still shocked that they had. He felt overwhelmed by their triumph, enough to overcome the usual surge of anxiety when he was about to speak to a group.

"Alright listen everyone," Kid started as he stood, and the room quieted. "I know we have to talk about what to do next, but before we do, I wanted to take a minute to say thanks to everyone for your part in what we accomplished today. Were it not for Mr. Hyland's planning, and everyone putting it all on the line, we never would have succeeded."

Standing up next, General Hyland said, "Thanks Kid, but it was a team effort, and your help with the plan was invaluable." Turning to the rest of the group, he continued, "This was our one chance to take control of the membership. Despite how outnumbered we were, we did it. So much had to go right today, including Sara and Maria getting behind the enemy lines to plant the P55. Even after the main battle, were it not for Kid and Mel's quick action in taking out a propeller, Ship Number Two would have escaped with thousands of the members. You all did your part and then some. Think about what was at stake here today."

Everyone took a moment to pause and reflect.

Kid knew all too well, having thought about it thousands of times.

The general continued, "The survival of humanity itself." He paused. "Had we failed, besides us being killed, the Utopia Project's society would have been the new world. Against odds that were far worse than we probably realize, *we* now have control of all 20,000 of the project's members. Going forward they will live, not as automatons, but as human beings. I am sure we will have many discussions about the future direction of the new world, but the important thing is that the direction is ours to set."

Karen then chimed in saying, "I think we should forever just refer to today as…the liberation, as in the liberation of humanity."

The group applauded.

Kid thought the phrase was perfect and knew right away it would stick.

"Love it." Sara smiled.

Kid nodded in agreement and added, "Hundreds of years from now, the leaders of society will still look back upon…the liberation and its significance. We need to write down everything that happened today and leading up to today. On this date, January 22, 2045, a new world was born."

That night Kid and Sara bedded down, and after a kiss goodnight, he wrapped his arms around her and slept like a baby for nearly ten hours. It was the best night's sleep he had had since before the destruction.

The morning after the liberation, General Hyland met with all of the former elders at 5:00 A.M. on the bridge of Utopia Project Ship Number One. He was joined by Adele, Kid, and Sara. In an hour, the usual 6:00 A.M. wake up tone would ring. Their members would get up to start their routines. So he really wanted to discuss a short-term game plan. He knew that much needed to be done for a 20,000 member community to function every day.

It was decided that for now, the former members would maintain their daily schedules, including meals, hygiene, and work schedules. But all conditioning activities were to cease indefinitely. That included the '*Ion*' word conditioning, as well as the conditioning regimens for the young offspring. The rotating of members to change their room and roommates every week would also be stopped.

Activity periods would remain, but the focus turned to one in particular. Some, including the general, Kid, and Sara, wanted to eliminate the sexual activity periods right away and replace them with additional physical activity periods. Dr. Adele Carmelo did not disagree philosophically, but she objected. She explained that sexual activities needed to be phased out and should not be taken away cold turkey. The former Utopia Project members were used to satisfying their sexual desires on a regular basis and quite frequently. In fact, in the project it was encouraged. So taking away that outlet so suddenly would likely cause distress and discomfort, if not downright destabilization of the members. In the end the group agreed that the sexual activity periods would remain, but the members would no longer have them on a weekly basis. Effective immediately, they would have such periods on a bi-weekly basis and that schedule would remain for a couple of months. They would then transition to having one period every month, and eventually it would be eliminated entirely. The general's final comment was, "We need to cover the windows for that activity room and make sure my mother, Estelle, and Theresa do not look in there. They would be at risk of having heart attacks on the spot."

The morning was frigid, prompting a discussion about the location of the base camp. A few of the former elders wondered if it might be better to raise anchor and head further south, where the temperature was more moderate, or settle closer to a wildlife tract whereby animals still roamed and could be a source of food. In weighing the pros and cons, the leaders also saw the value in having a self-contained island with only one bridge to the mainland. This allowed them to have better oversight with the members until they became acclimated to the new world in which they would be living with the new freedoms they had. Much effort had already gone into setting up the current base camp, and they were only a day or two away from having power in all of Surf City from solar arrays. There was no vote, but they all agreed that the base camp would stay where it was for now with the caveat that in one year they would reevaluate the base location.

Before the early morning meeting concluded, the general reminded them all, "The other top priority is to hunt down and eliminate Elder-3. So long as he is alive, we are at risk. We need to secure another M3."

"You said the closest base that might have one is Dover Air Force Base in Delaware?" Kid inquired.

"Yes."

"That's only a couple of hours away. I will drive Mel down there so she can fly it back. Let me go wake her up."

A small group comprised of Kid, Sara, and Mel took the road trip south. When they arrived at Dover Air Force Base in Delaware, they were pleased to find several M3 transports. After one was fully fueled up, Mel flew the entire group back from the base to the Utopia Project ships. The trip down by car took two hours. The trip back by M3 took a couple of minutes. Kid instructed her to fly around Atlantic City on the way back, hoping to spot Elder-3. She expertly weaved between the tall casino buildings as they searched the ground below.

"Head toward the marina section," Kid instructed.

Mel peered out the window. "Where is that?"

"Sorry. I forget you didn't grow up around here. It's over that way." He pointed. "A few of the most popular and long-standing casinos were over in that area. The Absecon Inlet runs right alongside it." They flew over the beach lining the Absecon Inlet.

Kid said, "Hold up! Can you take it lower, Mel, but not too low?"

"What is it?" Sara asked.

Peering down, Kid was focused on an object. "The boat that Elder-3 took off in. It's right down there. See it grounded on the beach?"

"I see it," Mel acknowledged.

"We don't know where he is now, but at least we know where he disembarked," Kid concluded. "Everyone look around and see if you can spot anything."

"With all of these high rises, he could be anywhere," Sara muttered.

After seeing no signs of the last surviving enemy elder, they flew back and landed on the deck of Ship Number One.

Just before midday a heavily armed team was assembled to thoroughly search the Atlantic City area and find Elder-3. The general and Kid had both wanted to go, but given their unofficial roles as leaders, the other survivors insisted that they stay back. The team was being led by United States Army Major Jimmy Hertzog and Jess Kellen, who knew the local area better than anyone.

*Talk about trying to find a needle in a haystack*, Jess thought as they flew to the boat Elder-3 had grounded along the Absecon Inlet. While Mel was flying low and inconspicuous, Jess noticed the first impediment to their ability to track Elder-3. A few days prior freezing rain had fallen, turning all of the snow on the ground into a slushy uneven mess. It would be nearly impossible to spot footprints.

Mel parked on a small stretch of beach and dropped off Jess, Jimmy Hertzog, and five regular members. The plan was for her to come back to get them in two hours but to stay in contact via walkie-talkie in case of an emergency. After everyone was out, Mel lifted off to head back to the ships.

Since he knew Atlantic City, Jess led the search team. They started at the abandoned boat which was left on the beach just before Brigantine Boulevard. From there they had to make some guesses as to where Elder-3 may have gone since they did not have any tracks to follow. They assumed that with the countless places to hide, and given the significant stock of food to be found in Atlantic City, Elder-3 could be comfortably hiding close by. The high-rise casinos, some over 50 stories tall, would also give the enemy elder some great vantage points to keep an eye out. Jess then verbalized the obvious. "If he is staying up high, he likely saw us coming."

They kept their weapons raised and watched high and low as they moved toward the closest casino. Entering, they all paused at the sight of the lavish gambling house. Mounds of rotting flesh covered the plush chairs at the blackjack tables. Playing cards and stacks of chips laid in wait on the fuzzy surface of the tables, untouched since the moment of the destruction nearly a month prior.

Jess walked over to a blackjack table and was careful not to step in any muck. He saw the dealer had two cards. The card facing up was a ten, so Jess flipped the one facing down. "Ace! Blackjack. Of course. Never bet against the house." He looked at the players' cards. "And you all would have been wiped out." He noticed that one player had gone all in on the hand and would have lost hundreds of dollars in one fell swoop. "Saved you from that agony, not that it would have mattered in the end."

The craps tables were ringed by melted bodies. In one area, Jess noticed that a skull had come to rest on a table ledge, overlooking the craps board as if waiting for the next roll, hoping to avoid the dreaded seven. The surviving intruders held their breath and ran around searching, but they quickly realized that each casino would have hundreds and hundreds of rooms to search. At that, they decided to search the main floors of each building and just search for obvious signs that Elder-3 might be there. After two hours, and searching several casinos and other buildings in the marina section, the group headed back to the pickup point. Mel arrived right on time and brought them back to the ship.

While he and Jimmy debriefed with General Hyland and Kid, Jess stated his conclusion. "Finding Elder-3 in Atlantic City is going to be like finding a needle in a cluster of haystacks."

"There has to be a better way," the general said. "Until we figure it out, we need to post a few members at each of the main roads out of Atlantic City. If they see Elder-3, they should report in, insert ear plugs, and then run."

"Insert ear plugs and run?" Jess asked.

"Yes, so Elder-3 can't try and override their orders and take them into his fold."

The general turned and said, "Jess, can you and Jimmy coordinate this? I am sure you know where we need them posted. And Jimmy, they will need winter gear, walkie-talkies, and we will need to rotate members a few times a day."

Jess nodded. Jimmy did as well while saying, "Maybe Elder-3 died, or offed himself like Elder-21."

The general looked askance at him and muttered, "If we could only be so lucky."

# CHAPTER 34

January 31, 2045
Tuesday, Morning
Coastal New Jersey
***Thirty-six days after the event***

In the ensuing days after the liberation, the survivor group worked tirelessly to stabilize and establish a new society. Despite the overwhelming number of tasks to be done, there was a palpable mixture of hope and excitement in the air. General Hyland and Kid were pleased to learn that the power from the solar panel farms on the mainland just over the Route 72 bridge had already been rerouted directly to Surf City prior to the liberation. But with only a couple days of work remaining to establish the final connections, the survivors were fortunate that former Elder-92, Japanese electrical engineer Akira Matsuda, was one of the ten who was chosen to survive. It just so happened that he was the key elder engineer responsible for the electric power initiative. The power supply to Surf City was now almost 100 percent restored, and they could operate electrical appliances, lights, equipment, heaters, and maybe most importantly, local utilities. They had also been able to route electricity to the three Utopia Project ships to ensure that all generators remained fully charged.

Food was plentiful for now, but they needed a plan for the long term. A team had been assigned to evaluate where on the mainland a large garden could be planted as soon as winter started to break. Kid and the group from New Jersey expressed, and the others were surprised to learn, that despite New Jersey's reputation for being a polluted asphalt jungle, it was named the Garden State for a reason. Many staples and crops grew well in New Jersey, and Kid assured everyone that once they ate Jersey tomatoes or corn, they would understand.

Adele's charge was to develop a regimen to extricate and remove the vast majority of the deeply-rooted conditioning already ingrained in the members. This would change their behavior, so she needed to ensure their society was prepared for the possible conflicts and unruliness that could follow. Having nearly 20,000 citizens discovering their humanity and acting out all at once would be simply unmanageable, so the deconditioning program was to be rolled out in phases. Before starting the first phase, Adele had asked everyone to stop calling them 'members,' and thereafter refer to them as 'citizens.'

The first phase of the plan was currently underway. It involved deconditioning a group of a couple thousand citizens so that they would no longer follow the regimented lives to which they were accustomed. If everything went as expected, a month later the next group of a couple thousand would be deconditioned. At that pace, it would only take ten months to address all of their citizens.

Some of the older citizens who were already deconditioned in phase one started to gravitate toward each other and develop relationships almost immediately. A few had already evolved into romances. With no longer rotated their quarters, they could see the same individual for more than one week at a time.

Soon after, other emotions born of human nature started to appear, such as jealousy. Adele had said simply, you cannot have emotions such as love, without jealousy being part of the package. That was why, as a part of the deconditioning process, the citizens learned about coping skills. Emotions and feelings, even irrational ones, should not be pushed aside, buried, or ignored. They should be acknowledged, so the response to those emotions could be addressed and handled. The managing of emotional responses and resultant actions was an ongoing process, one whereby all adults had to do their part as life coaches.

One of the more simple, yet daunting, tasks had been giving each person an individual name after undergoing Dr. Carmelo's deconditioning process. That chore was assumed by the seniors from Italy, Estelle and Theresa, who both took the job quiet seriously. In one circumstance, they spent fifteen minutes debating whether a young man looked more like a 'Mark,' or a 'Neil,' or a 'Tom.' They had lists of names from which to choose, which included Italian names, and many other nationalities as well. Adele had remarked that the Italy contingent needed to use a good variety of names, "Lest the society's roster sound like the family from the old Godfather movies."

As part of the plan, current citizens were given a first and last name, and those names were entered in the computer system by former Elder-107, David Lightbody, an expert in technology and databases. When Theresa met him and saw his skeleton-thin physique, she whispered to Estelle, "His name suits him." David was responsible for entering names into the database and linking them with the thermographic profile for each individual. Citizens who had given birth to offspring, or children, for the project would be sharing the same last name as those children, which would combat incestuous inbreeding and genetic calamities down the road. Previously, avoidance of inbreeding was to be addressed just by using the thermographic profiles of their members to ensure that related members did not cross paths in sexual activity periods.

The phasing out of sexual activity periods was still on schedule. Each citizen now had such activities on a bi-weekly rather than a weekly basis. There were no negative reactions or consequences with any of the citizens to date. To the relief of everyone, Evelyn, Estelle, and Theresa were still completely unaware of the existence of such activities.

Given that the number of sexual activity periods was being reduced with a plan for a full phase-out, the group realized that pregnancy and birth rates would slow significantly. The former elders were still adjusting their mindset because they were used to an environment on the ships that encouraged and pushed for as many pregnancies as possible as quickly as possible. With all of what needed to be done to establish the new society, a slowdown in pregnancies was welcomed most by Dr. McDermott, who now had to also serve as the chief obstetrician.

Needing a break, General Hyland, Adele, Kid, and Sara decided to get away for a few hours. The general and Kid had walkie-talkies in case they were needed back at camp, but that sunny afternoon they decided to take a short ride north on Long Beach Island and head toward the Barnegat Lighthouse. There was a stop Kid wanted to make along the way, so he pulled over before reaching the inlet.

Sara looked around. "Why are we stopping?"

"That's the Haddock House." He pointed.

She smirked. "I sense a haunted house story coming."

"Inside the house, above the doorway, it says, 'the sun never sets on this door'."

"Someone obviously missed the mark there," the general noted from the back seat. "The door faces west, so the sun sets on it every day."

"That's right, but it wasn't always that way," Kid continued. "The doorway had that saying since it was built in the late 1800's, but it used to face east until the house was knocked off of its foundation in a storm in the early 1900's. When they moved the house to a new location, they turned it around so that the sun always set on that door, and the house has been cursed ever since. Within a few years, the owner and his wife were dead, and the hauntings began."

"What kind of hauntings?" Adele asked.

"See the top of the house? Let's just say that many, many people who have stayed there swear it is still occupied. They say they hear voices and feel odd vibrations up there."

"Isn't that a…" Adele started.

"Widow's walk," Kid finished.

He turned to see her bright green eyes staring at the top of the house. She suddenly had a visible chill. "Can we go?"

General Hyland grabbed her hand. "You're freezing. What's wrong?"

"That widow's walk is creeping me out. For a second it felt like it was, almost, beckoning me." Sara had a more spasmodic chill. Trying to shake it off, she forced a chuckle and said, "Maybe Kid is just a good storyteller."

Sara squeezed Kid's hand. "Let's leave."

Driving a little further up the road and reaching the Barnegat Inlet, Kid pulled up to the towering structure that locals referred to as, 'Old Barney.' They all got out of the car, and while walking over to it, Sara announced the key points from a sign they passed along the way.

"Barnegat Lighthouse. Built in the 1850's. 172 feet above sea level."

Kid used a crowbar to open the door, and they took their time climbing the circular staircase inside. Once at the top, they marveled at the view as the sun was making its descent for the evening.

Sara turned to Adele. "Are you feeling better?"

"Much. Other than being winded from climbing. The staircase feels like you're walking in a circle that never ends!"

Kid smirked.

Sara turned to him. "What is it?"

"That just reminded me of poor old Drex, and his 'Circle Analogy'."

"I really miss that guy." Sara sounded sad.

While looking through a narrow window slot, the general said, "I don't remember hearing this one."

Kid started, "I don't think we told anyone. Drex equated the legal system to circles on the roads, or 'roundabouts,' as some people called them. You know, where roads cross and rather than having an intersection with stop signs or traffic lights, the road is a circle?"

"I know exactly. I hated driving around them," the general noted.

"Drex pointed out that on paper, a circle was an optimal traffic solution. The premise was simple. No traffic flow would be forced to stop since all vehicles would merge together and keep moving. I finally asked, if they are so optimal, then why have most circles been removed?"

"That's what I would have asked," the general said.

"When I did, Drex yelled, 'Exactly!'" Kid recalled. "He said that they failed because a circle on paper is predicated on human behavior being rational, predictable, and consistent. People driving were not rational, predictable, or consistent. Some were too aggressive. Some were too meek. Some were too ignorant, erratic, whatever."

"What is the parallel between circles and the legal system?"

"Because in Drex's view, the legal system was also in many ways predicated on the fallacy that people are rational, predictable, and consistent, including juries, attorneys, and even judges," Kid added as he wrapped his arms around Sara and stared out at the vast ocean.

"He is completely right," Adele agreed. "Human behavior can very much be a wild card."

The general exhaled. "Laws and rules are another area we will have to tackle in the future, and I wish Drex was still here so we could defer to his wisdom. Fortunately, it is an area that is not an immediate concern, since everyone is pretty much…conforming at this point."

"But," Kid started, "the real challenge is establishing laws and rules that ensure we still function well as a society when people are *not* conforming."

General Hyland thought for a second, and then nodded in agreement.

After climbing down the circular staircase, the group got in the car and started driving toward Surf City. On the way back, Kid stopped at the surgery center on Long Beach Boulevard that was being used as their medical facility. They greeted Dr. McDermott who had been busy establishing a full medical team, including having Marissa leading the nurse practice.

"Come check this out," the doctor said and walked them back to the surgery rooms.

The general looked around. "Where did you get the new equipment?"

"That hospital a few miles west on Route 72. They had just installed several new, modern pieces. We are borrowing them."

Noticing several citizens walking around in blue scrubs, Sara asked the doctor how their training was coming along. Given that only a few survivors had knowledge and experience in the field of medicine, it was critical to train more, in case something were to happen to Dr. McDermott or Marissa.

"Training them? I am starting to wonder if they should be training me!" The doctor explained that he was pleasantly surprised to find out that many of his team, who were formerly Type A workers in the Utopia Project, had already undergone basic training in the medical and biomedical fields. He was amazed at the knowledge and proficiency they already possessed. During training sessions he led, he said that they had dissected corpses, and they were not at all squeamish when using scalpels or probing instruments. Dr. McDermott concluded by saying, "The medical team we are building here is more advanced in a week than I expected them to be in six months."

February 1, 2045
Wednesday, Morning
Coastal New Jersey
*Thirty-seven days after the event*

The next day, ten days after the liberation, the survivor group and former elders furthered the process of establishing their own leadership structure. After having discussed it many times, they knew that they inevitably wanted to establish a fully-functioning democracy, but that would be months and years in the making. In the short-term, only a president and vice president would be elected.

Kid looked around at the assembled group on the deck of Ship

Number One. They represented the adults and former elders who they all agreed could currently vote, although the plan was to extend that privilege to all people over 18 years old after the deconditioning process was complete. Dr. McDermott was the election facilitator since he made it clear that he had no inclination, or time, to run for any leadership positions. For the time being, the voting process was quite direct and unsophisticated. Nominations were sought, and votes were tallied by counting raised hands. A person could only vote for one candidate for each position, and the simple majority ruled.

When nominations for president were solicited, Kid was ready and waiting. He raised his hand right away and nominated General Hyland. The general won unanimously.

For the position of vice president, before Dr. McDermott even finished calling for nominations, Evelyn had her hand in the air. Her husband Chris was whispering to her. Kid assumed she was going to nominate her husband, which he thought would be a good move. Chris Hyland was a natural leader. But his eyes opened wide when Evelyn said, "I nominate…Kid Carlson."

Before Kid could even react, the nominations were closed, and he was unanimously elected vice president. He stood there stunned as the group applauded his nomination. He was not accustomed to being designated as a leader, at least not officially.

With the leadership roles now filled, the general requested that all of the other adult survivors, unless they objected to serving, be part of an advisory committee to the president and vice president. Everyone agreed.

The general then added, "We will need everyone's input in developing a more comprehensive governance structure. We will need a good system of checks and balances, and one that will stand the test of time."

"Fortunately, I think all of us are pretty much on the same page at this point," Jimmy Hertzog commented.

The general hesitated. "That is true, and it makes it easier for us to function well. But like Kid said yesterday when we were talking about laws and rules, the real challenge is establishing a governance structure that ensures we still function well as a society when everyone is *not* on the same page."

Dr. McDermott noted, "We need to figure this all out before kids start being born into this new society."

A debate ensued that centered on how to handle and care for the new citizens born into the world. Some of the former elders, including General Hyland, thought that all newborn citizens could benefit from having a basic, minimal level of conditioning to ensure conformance with the laws and rules of the new society. They believed this could be done at an early age, all the while new citizens would grow up relatively free, and be able to make individual choices.

Kid, Sara, and Adele stood firmly against this.

"I don't ever want to hear the word 'conditioning' again," Adele said in the most serious of tones.

After a passionate discussion, it was Sara who offered an alternative. "Children, starting at an early age and at different stages of development, could receive targeted and meaningful life-training regarding their roles in society and the rules of society. The foundation of all lessons would be a respect for others, life, community and, of course, God." Most of the group nodded their heads in agreement.

"What is the difference between training and conditioning? Aren't we just doing the same thing and calling it something else?" former elder Jimmy Hertzog asked.

Sara was quick to answer, "Not at all."

"What's the difference?" Jimmy challenged.

"Conscious choice," she answered. "With conditioning, your response or reaction is automatic and involuntary. With training, you are guided, informed, and even prepared, but your response is voluntary. Your response and your actions are by your own choice."

Jimmy shrugged. "Who will do this training?"

"First and foremost, the parents. Children need to be raised by their parents, not some impersonal, innocuous, rotating maternity worker," Sara said with conviction. "And the supplemental life-trainings could be handled by different experts and counselors, and life coaches."

Everyone turned to General Hyland in his role as president to make the final decision.

Kid saw the irony in the comment made just moments ago about the challenge in functioning well when everyone was *not* on the same page. It did not take long.

The general said, "First, we will no longer use conditioning or anything called conditioning." He wasn't looking at Sara, otherwise he would have seen the corner of her lips turn up for a split second. Kid caught it.

"And second," the general continued, "since we will not utilize any conditioning, we must implement some life-training programs to help families. But before doing so, we will form a small group of maybe five people to meet and develop these programs, which will then be reviewed and finalized by the advisory committee."

Everyone seemed satisfied with the general's decision and thanked him for considering all points and input in reaching a compromise.

As the day came to a close, General Hyland and Kid were standing on the bridge of Ship Number One. Both were leaning on the rail, staring at the lights on the mainland in Surf City. Above them the stars were out, and the night was clear.

"You know, Kid, it is a good time to be in these leadership roles."

"Why do you say that?"

"We still have a long way to go, but I feel so optimistic about the future, and you and I are going to lead our society into that future."

"Well, when you think about it," Kid started, "good progress has already been made in establishing the new society, and we have only been at it for ten days."

The general was staring up at the sky. "We are working toward stability now, and the members all need to be deconditioned, but then what? We need to be looking to the future. We need guiding principles, so we don't lose our way."

Kid shrugged. "Maybe like when I was in the scouts: duty to God, country, others, and self. Something like that."

"Something like that," the general agreed. "It's a start. But there are no other countries, and family has to be in there somewhere. So maybe a duty to God, society, including others and family, and then self. For now, we just need to make sure we continue making progress, and keep stabilizing more and more every day," he said as he clapped Kid on the shoulder.

Nodding, Kid said, "Keep moving forward." His own words made him pause. He stared straight ahead and would not look behind, fearing that he might see some life-altering revelations lurking right behind them.

# IV:
# CONFLUENCE

# CHAPTER 35

February 3, 2045
Friday, Late Afternoon
Coastal New Jersey
**_Thirty-nine days after the event_**

Twelve days after the liberation, Sara and Kid were having an early dinner with her father and Adele in the Surf City Hotel. The facility was crowded, given that a group of nearly 400 had already been transitioned to live on the mainland. After eating, her father asked Sara for a moment of privacy, and they stepped outside. She had a suspicion as to why. After climbing some stairs, they stepped onto an outdoor balcony that faced the ocean and Utopia Project Ships.

"Sara, please sit down…" the general said as he pointed to a chair. As she slowly sat, he started, "There is something I need to talk to you about."

"Let me guess. You want to discuss your true relationship with Adele?"

Guilt shone in his eyes. "How did you know?"

"I could feel it, ever since we picked her up in Italy. I just knew."

Shaking his head and looking down he muttered, "I'm sorry. I should have told you years ago."

"Years?" she blurted out. "What do you mean years?"

The general heaved a heavy breath and continued. "You know that she was called 'Aunt Adele' because she was a friend and is not related in any way. We have been dating for some time, and I don't know why, but I was worried about telling you. I didn't know how you would react."

"Something as important as you dating someone and for years, and you don't tell me? How many years have y'all been together?"

Turning away while apparently calculating in his head, her father said, "Keep in mind, we started dating but did not have a normal relationship. There were big gaps of time where…"

"Dad, how many years?"

"More than 15," he finally admitted. He seemed surprised himself that it was that long.

"So this started when I was just a little girl, probably before I even went to kindergarten?" Her frustration was growing as she huffed, "I thought we had an open and honest relationship! You were the one who harped about communication all the time. Was that a one way street? I told *you* everything. Everything! No matter how you might react."

"You are right. And I told you almost everything. I guess I was worried that you might think I was trying to replace your mother."

"Come on Dad, I didn't expect you to spend the rest of your life alone. I would have understood, had you just talked to me about it. Did you think I wouldn't be able to handle it?" She crossed her arms, hugging herself.

"I am not sure what I was thinking. Maybe it was me who couldn't handle it," he said.

"Listen, you were a great dad, but to be honest, I am feeling kind of…betrayed right now." She stood up and turned to leave.

"Please hon, don't say that." He grabbed her hand. "If I didn't share something, even if the reasons don't seem as rational now, there were reasons."

Sara felt overwhelmed and needed to think. She pulled her hand away and said, "I need some time alone to process this all. I'm going back to the ship." She walked down the steps.

"When you are less angry, we need to talk some more. I wasn't done…" he called after her from the balcony.

She did not look back. He may not have been done, but she was.


After getting Kid and taking a tender back to the ships, Sara told him that she needed an hour alone to think. One minute her mind was exploding with thoughts, and the next it was blank.

More than an hour later, Sara was sitting alone on the bridge of Ship Number One. The space was dark, save for the bubble of light emanating from a candle on the table next to her. She was staring at the nighttime sky and was lost in thought. With power now being supplied to Surf City, she could see the lights of multiple buildings, including the hotel where she had left her father.

"Knock, knock."

She turned to the figure standing in the doorway. "Hey, Kid. Sorry, I know I've been here longer than an hour."

"Are you alright?" He seemed hesitant to walk in the door.

"Grab a seat." She patted a folding chair next to her. As he sat, she answered, "I'm alright. I'm just not ready to leave yet." She grabbed his hand and intertwined her fingers. She didn't want him to worry.

They were facing a bank of windows and the twinkling points of light dotting the coast. For a long, silent moment, they absorbed the view. Sara finally spoke and started a conversation that would last for nearly an hour. She looked at him admiringly. She didn't know how he did it, but Kid had succeeded in validating her feelings of hurt, yet she felt much calmer. She had even agreed that she would say her peace to her father and would eventually forgive him. That was not going to be easy.

As they stood up to leave, General Hyland and Adele entered the bridge. The general was holding a coffee carafe, and Adele was holding a tray with cups. Sara stopped but said nothing.

"They told me I might find you up here," her father said. "Please, don't leave. Give me just a minute. I come bearing freshly brewed coffee."

She turned to Kid, and his lips were pursed as he awaited her response. She sat down on a folding chair so he sat next to her. Grabbing two chairs, the general and Adele took seats opposite them. "Coffee?" the general offered.

"No thanks," Sara said without hesitation.

"Sure." Kid took a cup.

"Listen, Sara, I want to apologize with all of my heart. I should have told you long ago about us," he motioned toward Adele. "I was wrong."

Sitting with her arms folded, Sara did not react.

"And you are entirely right that it was me who preached about communication. I am a damned hypocrite. You have every right to be angry with me. And in fairness to Adele, she has been advising me to tell you for years."

Softening just a little bit, Sara noted, "You should have listened to her."

"I know I should have." The general sipped his black coffee. "But all I can do is say I am sorry and beg your forgiveness."

Staring out the window over her father's shoulder, Sara didn't say a word. While awaiting some response, he started tapping his finger on his coffee cup, and his face looked strained.

She turned her eyes and glared at her father, and then turned to Adele. Both of them seemed to shrink a bit. At that moment, Kid grabbed her hand. Sara met his eyes and remembered their long conversation from just moments before. Finally, Sara sighed. "Listen Dad, I will accept your apology but don't expect me to just get over this like it never happened."

"Understood."

"And Adele, don't think I hold anything against you because I don't."

"Thank you, Sara. I was worried how you would feel about me now." Seeming a little emotionally frayed, Adele motioned toward the serving tray on the floor. "Are you sure you won't take that cup of coffee?"

Hesitating, Sara finally gave in. "Alright."

Kid sipped his coffee and asked, "Did you two meet while working on this project?" He sounded like he was making small talk with a couple they had just met at a party.

"We started *dating* while we were both working on the project," General Hyland replied.

Sara was confused. "Wait, Adele, you only worked for the project for 15 years, but Dad, you said you've been together for *more* than 15 years. When did y'all actually meet?"

The general and Adele looked at each other and then down. Exhaling, the general clarified, "We met the day you were born."

Sara was stunned. "What? How?"

Adele said, "Back then I was on staff at Fort Gordon in Georgia as a psychologist. I worked in a highly confidential military project called the CCP…"

"The Child Conditioning Program," Sara cut in. "That awful project."

"Yes. And I was the psychologist assigned to your mother."

"You knew my mother, Amanda?" She leaned forward and stared intently.

Adele hesitated. With a smile that seemed forced, or even nervous, she said, "Not real well, but yes. She was a wonderful woman. Her passing was such a tragedy."

Sara was sensing that there was more to the story, and for some reason, Adele's usually bright green eyes seemed a bit clouded. "Why did you hesitate when I said her my mother's name?"

With her face flushing, Adele put her coffee cup down. "Sorry about that. It's just that all of the women involved in the CCP were given fake names and identities to protect them. That is how I knew your mother, not by her real name."

The general started stirring in his seat and put his hand on Adele's leg.

"The women involved in the CCP? Wait…" Sara started.

General Hyland jumped in without hesitation. "Before you even ask Sara, your mother was in the hospital and already had been given an alias before the project was canceled."

"I was going to say, Dad, you told me I was born *after* the CCP project was canceled."

"Yes," her father replied.

"And that I slept in the same bassinet that the CCP's Baby Doe had slept in."

"That is also true."

Adele seemed taken aback and then quickly bent over and nervously smoothed her pant leg.

Sara perfectly recalled her father's representation of the events surrounding her birth. But why did Adele, who was there for it all, look... surprised?

"So what was my mother's alias? What was her name?" Sara asked.

"How could we remember that? That was so many years ago," the general sounded dismissive, and it was irksome.

With her eyes fixed on Adele, Sara pressed, "You said you knew my mother by a fake name, but you don't remember it either?"

"No. I'm sorry. I really can't recall." Adele turned toward the general and then gathered the coffee cups, some of them still half full, and put them back on the serving tray.

"If I thought about it hard enough it might come back to me, but it is not important now," her father added as he reached across and patted his daughter's knee. Standing up, the general said, "What is important is that you know about Adele and me so we no longer need to hide our relationship. Do you want me to leave the coffee carafe here?"

"Yes, please," Kid jumped in.

At that, General Hyland kissed Sara on the head and walked out with Adele following close behind.

"Well, at least you know the truth," Kid said once they were alone.

She stared at the lights of Surf City out the window. "About that, yes."

"About that?" He put his arm around her. "So now you think there are secrets hidden everywhere?"

She pinched him under the arm.

"Hey!" he said as he jumped.

"It's natural to think that way after there's been such a violation of trust," she countered.

"That's true." He slowly put his arm back around her on guard for another pinch.

Falling into him and putting her head on his shoulder, she said, "I don't know. Logically, you are probably right, and I don't want to seem paranoid, but my gut tells me there's more."

February 4, 2045
Saturday, Morning
Coastal New Jersey
**_Forty days after the event_**

Unable to fall back to sleep on Saturday morning, Adele sat up in bed. As soon Eric moved, she pounced. "Good morning."

"Good morning to you too," he mumbled. "Why are you up so early?"

"I'm sorry, Eric. I didn't sleep well last night…again."

"Again?"

"Yes. I haven't slept well in days."

Sitting up next to her, Eric Hyland ran his hands through his hair. "What's on your mind?"

"Is it me, or are some of the former elders treating me funny? I can see it in their eyes. They look at me with almost…disdain. It is really bothering me."

"I noticed the same thing. I actually talked to Jimmy Hertzog about it yesterday. He has no issue, but he reminded me that for the entire week before the destruction, all we heard from the Board of

Elders was how much of a traitor you were for deserting your post, smuggling out your memo, and sending it to Lily Black."

"The elders thought I sent my memo to…her?"

"Yes. We heard it over and over from them in that final week before the destruction."

Adele knew that it didn't look good that she had left the project abruptly, and then immediately after, the press all of a sudden had a copy of her confidential memo.

"Do you believe that?" she asked.

She inhaled sharply when Eric hesitated in his response. She felt shock and dismay.

"No, no." He grabbed her hand. "No, I don't." He was trying to backtrack, but he had been caught off guard. His hesitation showed that he was not completely sure. It was one thing that the other elders believed that she had sent her memo directly to Lily Black and the press, but Eric? The thought was making her stomach feel sour. Did this mean he would forever be unsure? And that he would forever wonder? She took her hand back and folded her arms across her midsection upon realizing that her stomach would also forever feel sour.

Eric seemed conflicted as he added, "At least not all of it. But…"

She inhaled and was about express her displeasure. But he grabbed her hand and sat up straighter.

"Hold on, hold on. Let me explain. When I first caught up to you in Italy and asked if you knew how your memo got off the ships and got to the press, in truth, you only gave me half an answer and kind of choked on your words. You said you didn't know how the memo got to the press, but you avoided the part about smuggling it off the ship."

She had resolved that she would never discuss the God-forsaken confidential memo ever again. It was impossible to reveal anything without implicating herself. Without any proof to the contrary, it would be assumed she was guilty of *everything* she was accused of doing. She had nobody to blame but herself for being in this predicament.

"You're not the only one to hold a secret," she muttered.

He gazed at her and appeared half agitated by her words and half curious.

"I took my memo off of the ships when I left the project. I smuggled it out in a bloody tampon on a day when Elder-152 was working the security checkpoint because I knew he was squeamish. And then I disguised myself as an old woman and mailed it from a post office in Palermo, Sicily."

"So you did mail it to Lily Black?" He looked disappointed.

"No! God, no. I mailed it to the White House. And I knew their screening protocols. My memo should have remained completely confidential!"

Having done her homework before mailing it, she knew her envelope would be opened and inspected by a front-line screener in the White House. Inside they would find a confidential and incriminating Utopia Project internal memo she had authored, which memorialized the atrocities going on aboard the ships. Given its content, the communication would move immediately up the chain. After investigating and confirming the memo's authenticity, the United States president and the chairman of the joint chiefs would never allow such atrocities to continue. With the implications for the United States government, Adele had suspected the memo would be the impetus for the Utopia Project to be significantly changed, even stopped altogether.

"So yes, I am guilty of sending it out, but to the president of the United States, not a sleazy Washington, D.C. reporter."

"How did it get into that reporter's hands?" he asked.

"I don't know! I wish I did. Listen, I know you and the other elders have every right to be upset with me for smuggling the memo off the ships and mailing it anywhere. But I just wanted the president to look into the Utopia Project and scale it back. That's all. The absolute worst I ever thought could happen was that they would shut it down." Turning to him, she grabbed his arm. "Be honest with me Eric. If I could somehow prove that I sent it to the White House and not Lily Black, would that make a difference in how you feel about me and what I did? Or how the other former elders feel about me?"

He did not hesitate for a second. "A huge difference. I believe you, Adele, but yes, it would make a difference with the former elders who don't know you the way I do. They would all agree that by the White House protocols, if you mailed it there, it never should have seen the light of day. It would prove that you never intended for it to become a public document."

"You may say you believe me, but there will always be a little part of you that is unsure. So you know what this means? I need to find proof that my memo was sent to the White House and that Lily Black somehow stole it or got unauthorized access to it. How am I supposed to find that kind of proof at this point?"

Off the cuff, he suggested, "If we could find the envelope you sent it in, it would have the White House address on there right?"

"Yes!" She jumped to her feet. "Maybe it was still in Lily Black's possession. If I can find her office, maybe I can find that envelope?"

"Where would you even begin?"

"She worked for the Washington Post, and their headquarters was that huge building in D.C. I know exactly where it is. I just don't know where her office is."

"Let's go. I'll call Mel." He started to get up.

Holding out a hand, her voice and her bright green eyes were firm. "Eric, please, stay here and tend to things. Honestly, this is my cross to bear, my own personal mission. I need to do it alone."

Thirty minutes later, Mel was airborne in the M3. Adele guided her for the few minute trip down to Washington, D.C. She pointed. "Put it down on the grass in front of that huge building."

"I wonder why there were a bunch of police cars parked in front," Mel pondered aloud as she adjusted the thrusters.

"Good question. You would think it was a murder scene."

Running into the building, Adele said, "This is the headquarters of the Washington Post. We need to find the directory and see where

Lily Black's office is."

"Lily Black? The famous reporter? What are we looking for in her office?"

"Absolution."

Ten minutes later, they stood in front of a door on the ninth floor. Turning the knob, Adele peeked inside. She shined a flashlight as she walked in. The first thing she noticed was that the office had floor to ceiling glass windows. She gasped when she swept the beam of the flashlight and stopped on one particular window pane. Walking closer, she uttered, "What the hell..." as her light revealed a woman's bracelet stuck to the glass. Stepping forward, she could see the etched words, 'Lilith' on the illuminated portion of the shiny black piece of jewelry. Moving the beam slowly, she was shocked to see flesh and blood smeared all the way down the glass where it melded with a pile of flesh, bones, and innards on the ground. The pieces of clothing she could see sticking out of the mess appeared to have belonged to a female.

"Hold your..." she started.

Unfortunately, a whiff of the disgusting smell had already entered Mel's nostrils and triggered a gag reflex. She stepped out the door for several minutes. Re-entering, while holding her nose, Mel asked, "What the hell happened in here?"

Adele was shining a flashlight on Lily's desk. The beam revealed a handgun resting on top of a newspaper. Moving the light toward the floor, she froze as she spotted a second mound of flesh behind the desk. "I don't know, but it appears Lily Black was armed and had company when the end came."

"I still don't know what we are looking for," Mel said. "It is disgusting in here so we should do what we need to do and get out."

"An envelope. We are searching for an envelope addressed to the White House."

For fifteen minutes, Adele and Mel checked every document in the office. They checked every counter top, opened every drawer, checked every file folder, and even emptied the garbage can. Dejected, Adele dropped her rear-end heavily into Lily's desk chair. She blurted out, "This is going to be impossible. It's like trying to find a needle in a haystack, without even knowing which haystack to start with." She raised her hands and covered her face.

"Sorry, Adele." Mel moved the gun and picked up the newspaper from the desk. "It looks like Lily here was in a bit of trouble." After perusing an article, she flipped the newspaper around and started reading the back. The front page headline was now facing Adele.

Inhaling so sharply that she inadvertently caught a whiff of the potent, foul air, Adele gasped, "Hold it!"

Mel froze with the newspaper in her hand.

Adele got up slowly and stepped forward. Her eyes were glued to the front page headline and lead story. "Son of a bitch..." she uttered.

# CHAPTER 36

December 26, 2044
Monday, 10:45 PM
Washington, D.C.
***Close to zero hour***

Sitting in her ninth-floor office of the Washington Post, reporter Lily Black groaned as she leaned back in her chair. With such a disturbing headline to run tomorrow morning, she had to look away from the advance newspaper copy on her desk. She could not believe her own paper would publish a story so incriminating to her. No, she *could* believe it. Her industry thrived on readership and hits, regardless of who is targeted, how the information is obtained, or what the implications may be. She knew that better than anyone. Caressing the obsidian bracelet her father had given her many years ago, she spun it around her tiny wrist. The word etched into the bracelet, 'Lilith', disappeared in a blur. She turned her chair around and looked out the window at the lights of Washington, D.C.

Running her fingers through her long auburn-dyed hair, she reflected on her recent roller coaster ride of highs and lows. A month ago she had been feeling down about her legacy after being an investigative reporter for thirty years. None of her articles had made the front page of the Washington Post for a few years now. She had some successes in the past and had broken some stories that got traction around the country. But she never had a story that captivated the entire world. She needed a story that would cement her legacy forever.

She came close only once.

After the Civil Crisis of 2025, a story that her newspaper did *not* break, she had spent time staking out the Eisenhower Army Medical Center in Georgia in hopes of finding the elusive Baby Doe of the CCP. That would have been the story of a lifetime! But every promising lead became a dead end. To her great surprise, she failed. The final straw came when she tried in desperation to strong-arm a green-eyed doctor for information, and their confrontation nearly escalated into a full-on fist fight. She continued to write about Baby Doe every year, but as time passed, her hope of finding the child and breaking the story to the world, grew dimmer and dimmer.

Despite feeling down, a little more than two weeks ago she dragged herself to an event at the White House and met a quiet staffer named Adam Leaf. As far as appearance, he was fortyish, slightly overweight and balding, but with his White House position, she saw only one thing -- opportunity. She was desperate for a new pipeline to siphon some scoop from inside the Capitol. All of the staffers she used to know had moved on.

Although she was fifty-five-years-old, Lily had done everything in her power, including plastic surgery, to maintain her sex appeal. When she met Adam Leaf, she could tell right away that he was attracted to her. His nostrils flared as he took in her perfume while staring at her breasts, which were intentionally exposed by the low neckline of the dress she was wearing. He tried to speak and only stammered. She smiled. *I've got his attention.* While talking, they discovered they both frequented the same out of the way bar, and she enticed him to meet her there the next night.

At a small table in a dark corner of the bar, they had a drink and talked openly. She was able to disarm most people, and it was effortless with him. He described his confidential position as a mail and correspondence screener at the White House. Realizing that he might be the first to see the next newsworthy item, she needed to more than befriend him. She needed to ensnare him. They both turned as the newscaster on the main screen in the bar announced that a prominent politician was found guilty of acts such as 'coercing oral sex.' Adam made the mistake of joking that his wife might file the same claim. His significant other obviously hated giving him oral sex. It was the opening Lily was waiting for, and she had found her ace. She would play it when the time was right.

"That's a shame. I couldn't imagine anyone ever needing to be coerced to have sex with you, oral or otherwise." She could not resist tempting him.

Adam Leaf's eyes opened wide, appearing desperately hopeful. Seizing the moment, she flicked out her tongue like a serpent and proceeded to lick her lips. He started squirming in his seat. She had him.

That first night, they took separate paths but met back at her place. She lived alone and had no children, nor had she ever wanted any. They would have cramped her lifestyle too much. Besides her quest to publish the next big story, her life had been consumed by the rush and thrill of tempting men, which was why her fourth husband had moved out a few years ago.

When Adam came to the door, she pulled him inside. She had crossed some lines before in trying to get inside information, but she needed to take it to a new level. Her life was passing her by, and she didn't know if any more golden opportunities might ever come her way. Engaging the deadbolt, she turned to face Adam.

He was trying to play it cool, but his eyes showed his overwhelming anticipation. He said, "Listen, we need to set some ground rules. You are a famous reporter, but you know my position in the White House, and you know that I can't share any information with you."

"That is not what I want from you," she lied.

"Then what do you want from me?"

"This," she whispered seductively as she unbuttoned his pants.

For the next week they met regularly and were intimate, but she gently rebuffed his requests that she perform oral sex. He was becoming desperate in his desire for it, so it was time to play the ace she had been holding. She told him that her performance of such an act required her fully letting her guard down, and she would if he did the same -- by sharing some top-secret, newsworthy information with her. She swore she would never divulge her source. He contemplated for a moment. Then tightened right back up and declined.

She needed to take the temptation up another notch.

A little more than a week ago, she dropped to her knees in front of him. She slowly traced the circumference of her lips with her tongue and maintained eye contact while pulling his pants down. He was quivering in anticipation and was right where she wanted him. She stopped and said she was starting to feel a bit used and asked if he really cared for her and valued her. He gave her some phony bullshit about his strong feelings of love and respect, but she told him she could not let her guard down unless he did. He needed to provide some forbidden, confidential document that was not available to the public, to prove how much he really did care. "Do you promise you will bring me something tomorrow?" she whispered.

He contemplated as she knelt in front of him. Seizing the moment, she moved her face forward and let out a strategically-placed, hot, lustful breath. His legs began to tremble, and he squeaked out, "Yes."

Rising to her feet, she kissed him and whispered in his ear, "You are in for one hell of a treat tomorrow."

The next day, December 19, 2044, is a date she would never forget.

Adam walked into her place that night and immediately tried to stick his hand down her pants. Grabbing his wrist, she said, "Where is the information you were going to bring?"

"Well, I was thinking. Maybe..." he started.

She got in his face and yelled, "Maybe what?" She grabbed the doorknob. "Maybe you stop dragging me along and get the fuck out? You're nothing but a user..."

"Wait!" he yelled and ran over to the computer bag he had tossed on the counter. Handing her an envelope, he said, "The mail is all backed up, but I opened this today."

"What is it?"

"It's a memo about a secret, inhumane project off of the coast of Greenland being funded by our government."

"Is it legit?" she asked.

"Seems to be."

Taking the envelope from him, she softened as she opened it. "Sounds like a juicy story. Even if it is a fake, it will take a few days for it to be refuted."

"Remember, you can never reveal your source, no matter what."

"I know," she said as she unfolded the piece of paper.

"And shred that envelope," he added as he fully disrobed.

"Don't worry. I will." She read the confidential memo about the Utopia Project and knew in an instant it was a story that would spread like wildfire. All of the articles and newscasts would refer back to the reporter who broke the story -- her. The excitement was making her seriously aroused. Putting the paper on the table beside her, she sat on a plush chair and beckoned Adam to approach.

He came over and stood right in front of her. She hesitated for a second, but then conceded, "All right. You did good, Adam." In less than a minute he collapsed to the ground. She grabbed him by the hair and lifted his head. "Get up, now. Tonight, is also my night."

Breaking out of her recollection, Lily exhaled as her mind went back to the newspaper on her desk. It was an advance copy of the next day's edition, and Adam Leaf's pending indictment and his bombshell accusation was the headline story. That very day the authorities had come for him, but Adam went on the run because he says he wanted the world to know the truth before he was silenced. Given the article before her, Lily knew he had run straight to the Washington Post headquarters. In the exclusive article, he admitted to removing the confidential memo from the White House and giving it to Lily, but he claimed that was only because she seduced him. She knew she would have to refute his accusations. More than anything, she just wanted this side drama to go away and not derail her momentum.

For the last week, her Utopia Project stories were front page news every day and were being quoted by the largest online and print publications in the world. And given the protests flaring up in multiple countries, it would stay front page news for some time. The eyes of the world were on the story that she, Lily Black, broke. She had finally created the legacy she sought for her entire career. She would not let it be ruined by anyone.

She turned from the window and froze. Standing between her and her desk was Adam. At first she felt only shock. How did she not hear him come in? How did he get in the building? She remembered that the story on her desk was a Washington Post exclusive. That explained how he got in the building. After coming in for an interview earlier that day, he probably never left.

Like falling into freezing water, once her initial shock subsided, fear took over. She swallowed hard, knowing she had reason to be afraid. After she broke the Utopia Project story a week ago, she was descended upon by the authorities. They confiscated the original memo and the original envelope addressed to the president of the United States, which Adele never shredded, and never intended to. The envelope helped prove the memo's authenticity. But she was not expecting to be shaken down, at least not so quickly, so she never hid the originals. Being a good reporter, she would not reveal her source. She knew the information would be traced back to Adam. She felt like she had betrayed him by keeping the envelope when he had asked her to shred it. It led the authorities' right back to the White House and inevitably to him. He had already served his purpose, and she already had her story of a lifetime. She never expected to see him again, but he was now standing in front of her, and she was alone.

The fear that was squeezing Lily's throat became a choke hold when she noticed that Adam had a pistol in his hand. Although dreading what she would find, she gazed up into his eyes. He looked defeated and despondent. But there was something more there, like flickers of rage that gave his eyes a nervous tick. "Adam, please hear me out…" she started.

"Shut it! There is nothing to say. You betrayed me!" He whipped her across the head with the long, solid barrel of his pistol.

Although it was more of a glancing blow, her scalp felt like it was aflame.

"Thanks to you my life is over!" he bellowed. "I've lost everything. My wife. My family. My job. My future. I am now a wanted man, and they will get me, any minute now."

She screamed as he grabbed her hair and pulled her off the chair and onto her knees. Holding the pistol against her lips, he said, "Put your hands behind your back and open that mouth that destroyed by life."

"Mmm," she uttered as she shook her head with her lips pressed firmly together.

He whipped her again, but this time across the face. She touched the skin above her eyebrow, and when she pulled her hand down, it was smeared with blood.

"Hands behind your back," he snarled as he stuck the barrel against her lips. "Open, now! Before I get in the hard way by pulling the trigger and blowing a hole in your face."

With no options, and since she gave herself only a two percent chance of survival, she stopped fighting. Parting her lips, she licked the barrel and tasted metal as he stuck it in her mouth. She pretended to enjoy and be turned on by the demented act of sucking the gun barrel. Maybe he would become aroused and distracted, giving her an opportunity to steal his weapon. He started thrusting the barrel in and out of her mouth, painfully jabbing the back of her throat.

"That's right, enjoy this act because it will be your last."

As he rammed the pistol, she moaned and started rolling her head in a circular motion. The pitch of her shrieks increased with her pain presenting as pleasure.

"Here comes the climax, you evil temptress…" He put his finger on the trigger.

Going wild, she used one hand to shove the pistol faster into her mouth. He did not pull her hand away. He was too busy unzipping his pants.

With one last desperate idea, born of the words he had threatened her with, she turned her head to the side and jammed the barrel inside her cheek. She bent his wrist and squeezed his finger on the trigger. A bullet exploded through her right cheek, creating a gaping hole. But her aim was dead on as the shot hit Adam in the chest. His eyes went wide as he brought his hands to his breastplate and collapsed on the floor behind her desk.

She screamed in horror and threw the pistol on her desk before covering the side of her face with her hand. Stepping around Adam's dead body and grabbing the phone on her desk, she called 911. She was having a hard time talking between the shock, the adrenaline, and the hole in her face. After conveying that she stopped an attempted murder, killed her attacker, and needed emergent medical care, she hung up the phone. She dropped heavily into her chair and pulled open her bottom desk drawer. Grabbing a mirror, she held it up and inspected the hole in her cheek, which had frayed edges and was bleeding in multiple streams. She was compelled to stick her fingers through the opening and poke her visible teeth. The wound was ugly, and pain was setting in as the shock wore off, but it was a small price to pay to save her life. She could fix the hole in her cheek with another plastic surgery.

Grabbing a wad of tissue and holding it to her face, Lily sat for a few minutes. Hearing sirens approaching, she got up and stared out the window. A line of flashing lights was parading into the driveway of her building. She turned and looked down at Adam Leaf's lifeless body. She realized that with her injury, nobody would second guess her claim of self-defense. A strained smile came to her face when she also realized that a dead Adam could not counter when she refuted all of his claims in the article on her desk. Hers would be the last word.

Despite the searing pain in her cheek, she actually began to laugh, and it became uncontrollable. She leaned against the window with her bare arms and put her uninjured cheek against the cool glass. "Lily Black can never die. Nor can my legacy!" she yelled between bursts of laughter.

She was laughing hard with her eyes closed when she felt something course through her, like a wave. She felt violently sick and opened her eyes. The world had turned a blinding red color. She yelled in pain and tried to pull away from the window, but the skin of her arms and cheek seemed to have melded with the glass. She froze for a second. Maybe she was in shock from the near-death experience and was seeing and feeling things.

But then she tried to speak and only gurgled, "What the…"

Her body started sliding down the glass toward the ground, leaving her flesh behind. The last thing she saw as the world went black was her precious obsidian bracelet stuck to the window, and the word, 'Lilith.'

# CHAPTER 37

February 4, 2045
Saturday, Midday
Washington, D.C.
**Forty days after the event**

As soon as Adele left Washington, D.C. and got back to the ships, she asked Eric Hyland to gather up all of the former elders.

"Did you find the envelope in Washington, D.C.?" he asked.

She shook her head. "No. I found something better."

The group of former elders gathered in the elder dining room. They all took a seat and she stood facing them. The first thing she did was admit that she had smuggled her own memo off the ship, put on a disguise, and mailed it from a post office in Palermo, Sicily.

"The board members were right," said former elder, Thomas Kinnon.

"With that part, yes, but," Adele continued, "I did not send the memo to that sleazy Washington, D.C. reporter, Lily Black. I sent it to the White House, to the president, where it should have remained confidential and never should have been released."

"Then how did it get out?" Thomas sounded skeptical.

"We were told that you knew Lily Black and that she was an old friend of yours," said former elder, Marjorie Dawson.

"Not even close. I met her once, at the Eisenhower Medical Center in Georgia 20 years ago. She got in my face when I was driving out of the facility, and we had words. That's it."

Sitting on the edge of a tabletop, she continued, "Listen, some of you, no matter what I tell you, may still believe I sent my memo to Lily Black, or you might always have a little nagging doubt. If I could prove to you all, beyond a shadow of a doubt, that my memo was mailed to the White House, would you consider forgiving me at least in terms of my intentions? If I had mailed it to the White House, you know it never should have been released. And if it was never released, it never would have led to the destruction of the world."

Jimmy Hertzog spoke up first. "I can only speak for myself, but I would say, yes."

All nine of the other former elders also answered in the affirmative. Adele turned to Eric and looked at him expectantly.

He seemed surprised. "You really need me to answer that?"

"I do. In some ways, maybe more than anyone," she said.

"I never truly questioned your intentions, but the answer for me would be an unequivocal yes."

Walking over to the doorway and taking the rolled up newspaper that Mel was holding, Adele gazed upon the group. "I wish I had never sent the memo in the first place, but after seeing this, I was finally able to forgive myself. I hope you all can now see your way clear to forgiving me too." She handed the rolled up newspaper to Eric.

Starting to unroll it, he pointed at the date. December 27, 2044. "This is the newspaper that would have come out the day after the destruction." He held up the newspaper for the group to see. The headline read in bold letters: 'The Devil Made Me Do It'. Underneath, in smaller letters it said: 'Post Exclusive: White House staffer Adam Leaf to be indicted for providing confidential Utopia Project memo to reporter Lily Black, claims she seduced him.'

After they all absorbed the words, it was Jimmy Hertzog who broke the silence. "We should have known better. Adele, I would say you are very much forgiven." The others all nodded in agreement.

Eric also nodded, most fervently, as he added, "And then some."

Adele pursed her lips and walked out of the room. She didn't want them to see the tears that accompanied the vindication she had finally found and so desperately needed.

• • •

In the past day, Kid had become more and more concerned about Sara. She seemed downcast and lost in her thoughts. It just was not like her. But her father's revelation on Friday night about his long-time relationship with Adele had knocked Sara off center. Her foundation seemed rattled. The recent strong reminders of her mother probably did not help her state of mind either as they rubbed an emotional sore that he realized would never fully heal.

On Sunday, the day their society had dedicated as a day of rest, Sara seemed restless from the moment she opened her eyes. "Kid, let's go talk to Adele. I want to ask her more about my mother since she said she knew her. Plus, honestly, I am trying to figure out why she was acting weird when we were talking about it. There's something she isn't telling me, and I want to know what," she added conclusively as she put on a long, black coat. She grabbed his hand, and they walked out the door.

Kid did not know if it was a good idea for her to ask such questions, but Sara seemed determined. He was not about to get in her way of seeking to fill some of the void in her soul left by the loss of her mother. They knocked on Adele's door, and a young child opened it instantly as if he had been standing right behind it.

"Devin! No!" Adele snapped. She reacted harshly by grabbing the boy's wrist and pulling him away.

"Ouch!" the boy yelled.

They were both momentarily stunned by Adele's behavior.

Adele saw them and looked caught off guard. "Sara! Wait right there. Just give me a minute." She continued to pull the boy away, and tried to close the door.

Someone inside the room said quietly, "Shh."

"But, Dad…" the child pleaded.

Instinctively, Sara cast a sharp, loud inhale, and then stuck her foot in the door to prevent it from closing. "Dad?" she whispered.

Adele stared up at her with bright green eyes that could not hide her shock.

The child pulled his wrist free, which made Adele turn for a second, long enough for Sara to stick her head in the narrow door opening. Pushing the door open, she yelled with a harsh voice, "Dad?"

Kid was shocked to see who was sitting on the bed

General Hyland stood up and appeared not only guilty, but seriously distraught. His face had turned a sickly shade of red.

"Dad?" she yelled again, sounding incredulous. She then started to grit her teeth, something Kid had never seen her do before.

"Sara, I had told you that we needed to talk some more and that I wasn't done. You know now that Adele and I have been together for some time. But what I needed to tell you was that nine years ago we had a child that we gave to the project."

"Are you kidding me?" Sara doubled over and put her hands on her knees. Tears began running down her face.

Her father reached for her, but she took a step back. She was beyond upset, and her words came out hauntingly hollow. "You also failed to tell me I have a brother?"

Right then and there, Kid knew it was going to be a long road for the general in terms of reconciling with Sara. She was so hurt, and it was so hard to watch, that Kid felt tears welling in his own eyes.

"He wasn't supposed to be a brother in the traditional sense, or even a son for that matter," the general said. "I never even thought of him in that way until now. He was just another member of the Utopia Project. Another number."

With a thick, hoarse voice, she said, "He has a name. Devin. He is a human being with your genes. He is my blood." She turned and headed for the door. As she crossed the threshold, she stopped. "First, you don't tell me that you're working in the Utopia Project and with a freakin' clone of me. Then you finally tell me you've been dating Adele for over fifteen years, and now this? You did betray me. Not just once or twice, but how many times, Dad?" At that she stormed away.

Kid left to go after her. He too was stunned. He thought Sara and her father had the best of communication and were always open and honest with each other. He was sure the general had his reasons for harboring information, but such big life events should have been shared with his daughter. In truth, she had every right to feel betrayed.

Catching up to Sara, Kid tried to talk to her. She was rigid and had closed up entirely, like a form of self-mummification. The two most recent back-to-back revelations that her father had been dating 'Aunt' Adele Carmelo for many years and that Sara actually had a brother were a nasty one-two punch. She was reeling.

"Sara, I am so sorry," said Kid.

"It is not your fault, Kid. Given what we've been through, I can't believe I am saying it, but my whole world was just rocked! Again!"

"I know. It is a lot to take in."

"Has my whole life been a lie? Or even a half-truth? What am I going to find out next?"

Knowing in his gut that he should remain silent, Kid still made the mistake of saying, "Don't think that. I am sure your Dad had his reasons for doing what he did."

She stopped in her tracks. Her glare froze him. He could see she was fighting back tears.

"Don't tell me what I'm supposed to think right now," snapped Sara.

"You're right." He raised his hands in immediate surrender and cursed himself for opening his mouth.

"Do you have any idea how deep he hurt me?" She sniffled as tears started running down her cheeks.

She turned forward and kept walking. Climbing up the steps to the deck, Sara yelled, "Wait!"

Kid stepped on deck and saw her running toward a boat being lowered at a davit on the port side. He ran up behind her.

"I need to go ashore, right away," she said to the young man working the equipment. The davit was stopped, and the boat was raised back up.

Kid was about to ask Sara where she was going when General Hyland came running onto the deck. He made straight for her.

"Sara!" he called out. "Wait. I feel awful. I am sorry. Can we talk about this? I have never seen you this way."

"I want to be alone right now."

"But listen…"

"Dad," she was beginning to grit her teeth again. Even Kid felt himself shrinking. "I don't want to talk about it right now, and I am not going to talk about it right now."

"At least tell us where you are going," Kid chimed in. He felt sick at her taking flight this way in this state of mind.

As Sara lifted the bottom of her long, black coat and went to climb into the waiting tender, she said, "Home. I want to go home for a night." Turning to her father, her smile only accentuated the sarcasm in her voice, "Assuming it really is my home. Or was that a lie too?"

The general went to respond, but unlike Kid, he wisely bit his lip. "Who is going with you?"

"I want to be alone. And don't try to reach me." She climbed into the waiting tender.

"You know the rule," her father stated firmly. "Nobody is left alone."

"I don't need…"

"Sara." The general raised his voice and sounded authoritative. "I know you are angry, but I will not let you leave without someone being with you, especially if you are staying overnight."

"I'll go with her," Karen said as she walked over. She was wearing a red and black checkered bandanna to cover her scalp, which was nearly bald from the radiation sickness. "We can have a girls' night."

Sara did not seem to want anyone going with her, but she finally conceded. "Alright, come on Karen."

*Maybe a girls' night is what she needs right now,* Kid rationalized. Sara certainly wanted to get away from her father, but she was probably not too happy with Kid at the moment either, not since he opened his big mouth a few minutes ago.

"Should you really be going?" Kid asked as he helped Karen climb into the waiting tender. "You don't seem to be at full strength."

Waving her hand, Karen huffed, "I am fine. I could use the change of scenery myself."

"What about your shots?" Kid asked. To combat her radiation poisoning, she still received daily shots of Neupogen from Dr. McDermott.

"I just got one a few minutes ago. So I am good until tomorrow." Karen struggled to get into the boat until Sara reached over and also helped her.

"Please be careful. By the looks of the sky and the temperature, I think we have some snow coming our way," the general advised. Checking his watch, he added, "And no matter what, be back by noon tomorrow, especially since Karen will need her shot."

"Bye guys," Kid said. Karen waved her hand. Sara looked at him for just a second and nodded as the boat was lowered.

Kid and the general watched as the tender reached the waterline below. Sara did not even glance back up at the deck.

• • •

After going back to his room for a moment, Kid sat in silence until he muttered, "Just when I thought everything might settle down." He was worried sick about Sara. She was angry, but more than that, she was hurt. Her father had been her stability and the constant in her world, and the recent revelations had undermined that and made her question her entire life. With her emotions so raw, Kid should have watched what he said. *Why can't you just shut your trap for a change,* he reprimanded himself while scratching his cheek.

Annoyed with himself and the itch on his face that would not subside, he went to find something to yank out an aggravated ingrown hair. He shared the bathroom with Sara, and assumed she had a pair of tweezers somewhere. While searching through her designated bathroom drawers, he pulled out a stick. He didn't know what it was at first. The strip inside the small window had two parallel pink lines. *Is this what I think it is?* He couldn't read the tiny print so he ran out to the bedroom. Holding the strip close to the bulb of his end-table lamp, he read the word and dropped heavily onto the bed. "Holy shit," he repeated several times. Returning to the bathroom, he put the stick back and closed the drawer quickly. When he looked up, he met his own eyes in the mirror. He could not escape the truth. Holding himself up with both hands on the sink, he stared at his reflection. He had to hear the words to believe them so he said them aloud. "Sara… is pregnant."

# CHAPTER 38

February 5, 2045
Sunday, Early Afternoon
Coastal New Jersey
**Forty-one days after the event**

As Sara drove an SUV toward her house, she conversed with a depleted-looking Karen. After Sara shared why she was so upset with her father, Karen said, "Wow. That is a lot to take in all at once. I don't blame you for needing some time to get away and process it all."

Approaching the entrance to the Joint Base, Sara came to a stop on the snowy entrance road. The gate was only open about six inches. "There is no reason to keep the gates closed, is there?" she said as she jumped out and ran around the front of the vehicle. She tensed as she manually pushed the gate open further, all the while being careful not to strain too hard.

Jumping back in the vehicle and shivering, Sara had to turn on the wipers to remove the layer of snow that had already covered the windshield. Reaching her house, she opened the vehicle door to step out.

Karen also opened her door, and asked, "Do we really need to bring in the shotgun from the back seat?"

Sara touched the weapon on her hip. "Don't worry about it. I'm armed."

"I'm not sure what we have to protect ourselves from anyway. The only enemy we have now is food and shelter," Karen quipped.

Standing at the front door, Sara exhaled heavily. She could not simmer the disquiet in her soul.

Karen came up behind her. "Are you having second thoughts?"

"No, I was having a moment." She opened the front door. Although it was bright outside with the snowy ground reflecting the sunlight, the foyer was dark and shadowy. "Why don't you grab a seat in the living room? I'll grab you a blanket so you can warm up. Do you need a drink?" Sara asked.

"Sure." Karen sat on the couch. "Can we make some tea?"

"Hot tea sounds good. Let me get the fireplace going so we can heat up some water, and this house. It's freezing in here. Just rest. I'll take care of it." Sara grabbed logs from the large pile stacked next to the hearth. She arranged four of them in the fireplace and used a black, iron poker to push crumpled newspaper underneath. After making sure the damper was open, she put a match to the paper and fanned the flames until the logs caught. Running to the kitchen, she grabbed the teapot and went to get a few bottles of water. Staring into the pantry, her faced looked inquisitive as she grabbed a couple of bottles. "Where did all of our water go? I didn't realize we were so low," she mumbled as she filled the teapot.

Returning to the living room, Sara rearranged the logs until she created a flat surface to rest the pot on. She brought in two cups with tea bag tags hanging over the side. "While that heats up, let me get us set up to stay the night so that we don't have to worry about it later." As she walked to the coat closet just beyond the foyer, she turned the doorknob. "The first order of business is to get the zero degree sleeping bags." With the door barely cracked, and her hand about to reach inside, she stopped. "Oh wait, we moved them to the garage. Crap, the bags will be freezing cold." She closed the closet door. "I'll be back."

Sara came back and rolled out two sleeping bags in front of the fireplace. "That should work," she noted as she grabbed the poker and tended to the logs. With the room warming up, she took off her long, black coat and sat chatting with Karen until they heard a whistle. Running to the kitchen, Sara secured a pot holder and grabbed the teapot.

After pouring the water, Sara found herself unable to drink her tea. She also had a hard time sitting still. She was too upset, and felt a rage and despondency that she had never felt before. Putting her cup on the coffee table and splashing some of the liquid, she jumped to her feet. Spotting the picture of her fifth grade father-daughter dance, she lifted it off the wall and let out a scream, which came out like a guttural growl. She held the frame above her head and was about to smash it on the ground.

Karen jumped up from the couch. "No, don't!" She caught Sara's arms as they started to swing down. "Please, don't!" she begged. "I know you are upset, but please don't do something you are going to regret."

Sara was breathing as if she had just run a marathon. Her arms went limp and she lowered the picture. Taking the frame, Karen hung it back on the wall. She turned and put her arms around Sara.

"I hate him!" Sara yelled. "I can't believe how much he hurt me. How can I ever get past this?"

"You will, one day."

"How? I just don't see how." After a moment of silence, Sara said decisively, "I need to go spend some time alone in my room. I need some time to think."

"Are you sure you'll be alright?" Karen looked concerned.

"Yes. Please, go finish your tea."

Grabbing the knob to her bedroom door, Sara's breath caught in her throat. So many things had changed, or been revealed, since the last time she was in her own room. She was upset and emotionally brutalized, and needed to sort it out. Her father had betrayed her. Really betrayed her. How could he do that? It hurt her so much, and so deeply.

Opening her door, she saw only darkness and froze mid-step. Her heavy, dense curtains had been completely drawn. She loved her curtains but they were so dense that when fully closed it felt like the middle of the night even at noon on the sunniest day. For that reason, she never pulled her curtains closed tight. Never.

Needing light, Sara remembered that she always kept a candle on her dresser top. She stepped timidly into the room and felt around until she found the candle. Pulling her top dresser drawer open, her fingertips wrapped around a long-nosed lighter as it rested in its usual place. Clicking the button, she lit the candle and pushed it back toward her mirror on her dresser. In the dim flickering light, she noticed the glint of the gold arrowhead locket around her neck and she touched it with her hand.

She noticed that some of the pictures she had wedged into the frame of her mirror were out of alignment, something she was meticulous about. Seeing a picture of her father, a flash of anger made her rip it from the mirror and crumple it. She reared back to punch her mirror. The desire to smash the glass, or something, was overwhelming. She fought the urge and grunted as she put her head in her hands.

Sara raised her head and looked at the left side where she kept her pictures of Kid. It was then that she noticed that one picture was missing, and she knew exactly which one it was. *The day at the cabin.* She stared intently at the void, wondering what happened to the picture of her and Kid laughing on the roof of Ironside cabin.

As the candle flame steadied and grew, the mirror's reflective reach extended further, revealing more and more in the darkness behind her.

• • •

At 11:30 A.M. the next morning, Kid and the general met back on the deck, which already had a layer of fresh snow. Both were clearly anxious.

Kid was also still in a state of shock from seeing the pregnancy test in the bathroom, and had hardly slept a wink. Sara would probably tell him that night. "Any word from her yet?" he asked.

"I just radioed over to headquarters on the island. She is not back yet," the general said in a low voice. "Let's give it another half hour."

As worried as he was about his Sara to begin with, knowing she was pregnant only heightened Kid's protectiveness. Uncomfortable that she was not back, he said, "Alright, but if she is not back by noon, then I think we should go get her. We can get there quickly if Mel flies us over in the M3."

The general nodded without hesitation. "Agreed."

Exactly a half an hour later, the general returned with Adele by his side. Kid, who had never left, turned to look for Mel. He spotted her sitting in a chair watching Katy and Karly playing in the snow with a group of young children. Kid walked briskly and approached her. "Mel, can you give us a ride? We need to go to Sara's house over in the Joint Base."

"Sure. Right now?"

"It will only take a couple of minutes, but we must go," General Hyland added decisively.

Mel seemed to sense their concern and got quickly to her feet. She turned to Emilio and Debbie Servino. "Can you please watch the kids for a few minutes?" She hesitated, but added, "I should be right back."

Jess and Maria walked over. They seemed to sense that something was going on. The tension emanating from Kid, the general and now Mel, was palpable.

The general turned to Adele. "Be back soon. Make sure everything stays on course here until I get back."

"Eric," she started. She then tried to lower her voice, but Kid heard every word. "I'm worried about Sara. I feel so guilty about everything that was laid on her in the past few days."

"Don't feel guilty. It was my responsibility, and I will handle it. I love you, hon," he said as he kissed her.

"Love you too, Eric. Hurry back with Sara…"

Mel took the pilot seat as Kid and the general jumped in the M3.

"We don't know what's going on, but if you're that worried about

Sara, so are we." Maria and Jess climbed aboard right behind them. "Do you mind?"

"No, but hurry and close the door," Kid answered.

Before the craft even landed in the middle of General Hyland's street within the Joint Base, Kid jumped out onto the snowy road. He stood still and scanned the area. Something just did not feel right. He should have been used to such stillness, but somehow, here and now, it felt unnatural. And then he noticed that Sara's bedroom window in the front of the Hyland house was broken, and just one pointy triangular piece was still clinging to the frame. His feet slipped as he sprinted toward the house. The fear Kid felt was growing, and his nerves only wound tighter when he noticed that the front door was ajar.

While hurrying out of the M3, the general turned to Jess, Maria and Mel. "Wait here."

Jess put his hand on his firearm. "But Kid is sensing something."

"I know, but let us check it out first." General Hyland jumped to the ground and yelled, "Kid, wait!" He tapped his Medusa firearm, reminding Kid to arm himself before entering the house.

Pulling out his 38-caliber pistol, Kid pushed the front door fully open. Listening intently, the only sound was an ominous creaking from the front door's hinge and a tap against the doorstop. The general walked up and signaled that he was going to the kitchen, and that Kid should head for the bedroom wing. Nodding, Kid stepped in and moved slowly up the hall. He was struggling to keep his breaths even as he pushed open Sara's door.

The room appeared empty as he peered from the doorway. He waited for his eyes to adjust to the dim light, and then he stepped inside. He heard a crunching sound under his foot and looked down. Seeing a vague reflection, he bent down and picked it up. Carefully holding the jagged shard, he saw it was a reflective piece of glass, so he turned around. Stepping closer to Sara's dresser, he could see an empty mirror frame, and it was no longer affixed to the dresser top, but was leaning against the wall. *How did her mirror get smashed?* he wondered.

When he turned, he found himself standing at the corner of her bed. His mouth dropped open and he froze when he saw the mural on the wall. He knew the scene all too well- the forlorn woman standing on a dock before a full moon, with a distant island in the blue ocean illuminated by beams of moonlight. But even through the hazy gray, he knew that something was wrong with the painting. "I can't see a damn thing in here," he whispered as he stepped over to the partially opened curtains. He pulled them further back to let in more light, but before turning around, he felt a cold breeze whip in through the broken window. *Why are the window and mirror both broken?* There were too many signs of a destructive rage, and it made him even more worried about Sara, and her state of mind.

With more light in the room, he turned around to look at the mural again and his concern doubled in an instant. The bizarre scene shocked him, and the hair on the back of his neck stood up. He knew Sara was angry and hurt, but maybe more than he realized. The once beautiful and mystical mural on Sara's wall had been completely defaced. Most obvious, the largest part of the wall that used to be a beautiful blue color representing the ocean was now painted all white, like snow. The hair of the woman with her back to the viewer appeared three-dimensional. Stepping closer, several strands of real hair had been glued to the wall. A bright gold chain was painted around the neck of the forlorn woman in the scene. Barely visible under her outstretched arm, Kid recognized the object that dangled from the chain. "The arrowhead locket," he whispered. Leaning back to take in the full figure of the woman in the mural, and considering the pendant and the brown hair, he had a realization. "It looks like…Sara."

He involuntarily grimaced when he noticed that the woman in the mural had a stream of dark red blood running down the inside of her leg. The blood was running into a basin between her feet, and had started to fill it. Squinting his eyes at the blotchy, thick streaks of blood, his throat became dry. He somehow knew the red smears were not paint, but were in fact real blood. A cut-out of Kid's face, which he knew was from a picture Sara kept in her mirror frame, was affixed to the wall such that his head rested sideways in the basin. Three-fourths of his face was painted with blood, as if the level had risen high enough to drown him. Painted around his neck was a chain that was tethered to the bottom of the basin so he could not raise his head. A sloppy but obvious depiction of a body from the neck down was painted on the wall, and was connected to the real picture of his head. It was meant to be Kid's body, and he was kneeling with his arms tied behind the back. "Sick," he muttered as he stared at the tortured image of himself.

Up in the sky in the mural was a picture of her father. Just like with Kid, the face was cut out from a picture Sara had in her mirror frame, and the body was painted and connected to the picture of the head. The main difference was that the general was upside down and he had something thick around his neck. He appeared to have been pulled from the top of a tower next to him that was labeled, 'World'. His painted arms extended to both sides of his body and held the control bars of a puppet master. From the bars, multiple strings were touching the paintings of Kid and Sara, as if they were marionettes. One thicker string from his control bar was wrapped around the general's neck, and was labeled with letters spaced far apart. Staring closer, Kid followed the letters, and they spelled, 'Karma.' The message seemed to be that the general brought his downfall upon himself.

Kneeling on the full-size bed and moving closer, Kid noted that the island under the moonlight now rose out of what appeared to be snow instead of water, and a simple structure stood alone on the elevated piece of land. It appeared to be a house. Prominently in the snow next to the house were two tombstones. One was a traditional slab with a rounded top. The other was in the shape of a cross, like the one Kid had made for Sara's clone. "Mr. Hyland?" Kid called out, his voice conveying the dread coursing through his veins.

General Hyland came to the door and announced, "The rest of the house empty. Sara and Karen are gone..." He froze upon seeing the mural. "What..." he said and put his hand against his forehead,

"…have I done to my daughter? This was her prized mural. I pushed her over the edge."

Kid feared the same. Was she that upset with her father, and even him? He again cursed himself for sounding like he was defending the general before Sara left the ships. As he gazed upon the wall, Kid was surprised that Sara, even if distraught, could ever produce such a sloppy mess. She was too naturally talented with a paintbrush. "Do you have a flashlight?"

Pulling a tube from his back pocket, the general handed over a small light. Twisting the top, the beam hit the wall and shone on the island. Moving closer, Kid could see the house on the island clearer. Behind the structure green trees had been painted. Moving the light over to the first tombstone, written in small letters on the cross-shaped marker were the words, 'Sara's Clone'. He held the flashlight as steady as he could, but the light trembled against the wall as he moved the beam over further. The tombstone that looked like a traditional slab with a rounded top was blank, but a small object rested on top of it. The object was round, and appeared to be a ball, but it had a straight handle sticking out. Kid could not identify what it was supposed to be, but why would there be a second tombstone next to the one for Sara's clone? A possibility came to his mind, and he physically reacted by gasping aloud and then tried to regulate his suddenly panicked breathing. *Sara is not the suicidal type. She would never…* But he had never seen her so devastated. He also did not know if hormonal changes with the pregnancy were exacerbating her emotional distress.

"What does it all mean?" The general sounded anxious.

Kid backed up on the bed and fully absorbed the entire altered mural. He uttered, "Oh my God," and quickly jumped down. "I know what this is supposed to be."

"What?"

Kid's swallowed and tried to keep his voice steady. "With the tombstone, the snow and the structure on a hill in the woods, it could only be one place. Our cabin in the woods- Ironside. But why would she paint that on the wall? She must have known we would see this. It's almost like she's directing us there."

The general seemed even more concerned. "Do you think that's where she went?"

"I don't know. But we should go and see if she's there." Kid turned to leave. He was trying to contain his fear, given Sara's apparent mental state.

The general grabbed his arm, and seemed to be in disbelief. "After everything you guys told us went down at Ironside, why would Sara go there? There is no reason in the world to go that place."

Without time to structure his words delicately, he answered, "No disrespect intended, but maybe there is. It devastated her to find out some pretty serious things that you never shared with her. Having a clone of Sara in your life on the ships, for her entire life, was one of those things. That's pretty major. Maybe she decided to go there because her clone's grave site is a pilgrimage she needed to make to come to terms with everything. And that grave, is at Ironside."

The general looked humbled.

"I'm sorry to be so blunt about it," Kid said apologetically.

"Don't be Kid. Your point is well taken and needed to be said. Let's go," the general responded and ran out the door.

Boarding the M3, Kid's voice conveyed urgency. "Get in the air, Mel. I'll direct you." He made eye contact with the general, and both nodded. All of their focus was consumed by the task at hand, and centered on the person who meant everything to them both.

# CHAPTER 39

February 6, 2045
Monday, Early Afternoon
The Pine Barrens of New Jersey
**Forty-two days after the event**

Ironside cabin was isolated and hidden deep within the vast forests of the Pine Barrens, but Kid knew exactly where to go. He directed Mel to a building on a small hill that seemed to be surrounded by a mote of snow. There was plenty of space in front of the cabin for Mel to land the M3, especially since she had become an expert in maneuvering the craft.

While the craft was descending, Kid watched out the window. Right away he spotted an SUV parked next to cabin and stated, "Someone's here."

The general was also peering out the window and said, "It must be Sara. That truck is one of ours, from the base in Surf City."

Kid did not see any activity. Besides the vehicle, the area appeared unchanged from when his group had left the cabin. After seeing the cross grave marker still sticking out of the ground, the same one depicted in the mural, he felt sharp pains in his stomach, like someone was twisting his insides.

As the M3 descended, the thrusters rotated to a vertical position and churned up a white cloud of snow. Kid jumped out as soon as the craft landed and ran through the squall to the cabin. Pushing the door open, he peered into the main room. The beds were empty and the wood stove was cold and dead. "Sara?" he called out. He listened for a sound and heard only the low whistle of the wind, which seemed to emanate from somewhere deep in the surrounding forest.

General Hyland, Jess, Maria, and Mel came into the room behind him.

The tension was thick, making it difficult for Kid to swallow. He took a few steps and approached the second room. His trembling hand reached for the hanging curtain between the rooms, and he slowly pushed it aside. Stepping in, the first thing he noticed was that the pickax they usually kept in the small third room was stuck into the wall. The pointed tip was driven into a thick cork board panel. As he moved closer, he noticed that the tip of the pickax was punched through one of the pictures on the board, and he knew without a doubt which one it was -- the photograph of Sara and him sitting on the roof of the cabin laughing. "The day at the cabin," he muttered.

He was caught off guard as the stench of death entered his nostrils. While holding his nose, he turned his head toward the bed in which Sara's clone and he had slept while at the cabin. He fell to a knee when he noticed that there was a form under the blanket, and it was the size and shape of a body. His blood turned to ice water, and a tremor ran from his head to his toes.

Stepping into the room, General Hyland groaned and also covered his face with his hand. "Don't breathe," he called out to the others following behind him. He walked over to the bed and grabbed the blanket.

"Oh please, no," Kid uttered desperately, unable to confront his greatest fear.

As soon as General Hyland pulled the blanket back, he collapsed to his knees

Everyone in the room gasped.

Kid screamed, "No!" The body was that of Sara Hyland, and his stomach clenched so tightly he could not breathe.

This time, she was clearly dead. Based on the color of her skin, it looked like the blood had stopped flowing in her body some time ago. Her gold arrowhead locket was lying on top of a black coat that covered an eerily still chest. He stared at her coat for what seemed like eternity, but her chest did not rise once to take a breath. After all they had been through, in the end, Kid had lost her anyway. It was too much for him to bear, and tears ran uncontrollably down his cheeks.

The general let out a sound that was a cross between a scream and a deep sorrowful moan. He lifted his head and stared at Sara as tears also ran down his face. "I am so sorry, honey. What have I done? What have I done?" he repeated as he leaned over his daughter's face and brushed her cheek with his hand.

Crawling up to the mattress, Kid brushed against Sara's gloved hand, which was hanging over the side of the bed. The glove slipped off and landed on the floor. When he looked at Sara's off-white, nearly gray colored hand, his stomach churned even more. She was missing three fingernails. Already. Already?

The general was brushing her cheek when his hand came to a dead halt.

Both Kid and the general were frozen in place by sudden realizations.

It was the general who finally spoke. "Kid, this isn't the real Sara."

"What?" Maria asked from behind him. "Did you say what I think you said?"

General Hyland repeated, louder, "This is not the real Sara."

Turning his eyes to the dead, nail-less fingers, Kid knew the general was right. His head dropped and rested against the mattress. He couldn't hold it up. The same dizzying emotional roller coaster with endless vertical drops and neck-snapping turns had nearly destroyed him the first time, and here he was, on it again. His heart and mind were ready to burst as outgoing waves of dread and agony collided with incoming swells of relief and hope. As he settled down, it was the feeling of dread that lingered as the obvious question came to his mind. "Wait. Who would…"

Suddenly, a voice boomed, "Freeze! Do not reach for your weapons or we start firing!" Everyone stared at the person who walked out the door from the third room.

General Hyland's eyes narrowed as he muttered, "Elder-3?"

Caught off guard and without time to grab his firearm, Kid saw that Elder-3 had a weapon in both hands. One was a Medusa firearm, and the other was a traditional handgun. The elder had a victorious smile, but his expression conveyed a bitterness and anger that could not be muted by the upturning of his lips.

"Hands in the air, and put your weapons on the ground. Then one at a time, kick them over to me," Elder-3 commanded. The group had no choice but to comply.

After all weapons were pushed over, General Hyland glared at the elder. "How the hell did you get here?"

"We were brought here right after we reached Atlantic City, with the promise that an opportunity like this would arise." He continued to smile, while gnashing his teeth. "Now all of you, on your knees! Now!"

"Brought here by whom?" the general asked, already on his knees.

"Someone who saw me escape down the coast in a boat."

"But who?"

"An old…friend," said a voice from just beyond the doorway to the third room.

Kid snapped his head up, and his breath caught in his throat.

As Elder-3 moved to the side, another person stepped out, also with a weapon in hand.

Everyone gasped again, even louder. Maria sounded distressed as she sharply inhaled. Kid uttered, "No. It can't be."

Standing in front of them, like a ghost, or a resurrection, was Heidi Leer. She had a pistol aimed at them as she stood rigid but breathing heavily. Her face was bruised and swollen, and she had a large burn scar on her right cheek. Her hair was wild, and her eyes showed a deranged anger. Her gaze settled dead on Kid, and the muscles in her face began to twitch.

"Heidi?" Maria sounded shocked. She turned to the general. "You said she bled out on top of that stone tower in Italy!"

Heidi burst into a maniacal laugh. "So you idiots did fall for me playing dead. That wasn't my blood, well," she glanced down at her crotch, as she continued.

"Some of it was. But most of it was from a bitch whose throat Elder-85 sliced with her own knife. She bled like a stuffed pig before he threw her body off the roof. No, I was barely hit, just lost a chunk of my calf, besides my face getting scorched from the missile explosion."

She gazed up and huffed as she touched her badly scarred cheek, "My step-sister would eat this up."

Looking down and refocusing her eyes, Heidi sneered, "Anyway, you should have finished me when you had the chance."

General Hyland's eyes expressed anguish and regret as he looked over at Kid. It was Kid who wanted to ensure they had finished off Heidi in Italy but was overruled by the general who made them hurry back across the Atlantic Ocean lest they run out of fuel. And now not only did she survive, but she was in a position to exact her revenge.

"Even so, how did you make it across the ocean?" the general said, his voice conveying dismay and disbelief. Kid was wondering the same.

A smile came to Heidi's chaffed lips. "I flew like an albatross over the sea…" Her lips straightened. "By boat, stupid. How else?"

"That is like a two week trip."

"Eight days. I had the pick of the litter with the fancy boats over there. Nothing was going to stop me from coming back for you. Nothing. Lucky I came after you rather than returning to the ships, or I probably would have been killed with the rest of the elders," she snickered. "Actually, once I got back here, I let you come to me. I knew you would eventually come back to the Hyland house."

Stepping further into the room, she continued, "Then after capturing Sara yesterday, I spent all night painting. Not real good at it though." Her eyes blazed into Kid's. "Not like that artistic bitch of yours."

Speaking to Elder-3 without taking her eyes from Kid's, she added, "And I told you that as soon as they saw the wall painting, they would come here. Maybe I am not such a bad artist after all. And who came to Sara's aid? Exactly as I predicted." Her tone was cocky as she peered at Elder-3. "Was I right?"

The elder nodded but seemed to be growing impatient.

Heidi turned to Kid. "I assumed that once you saw the wall, you would know it had to be me, but you seem genuinely stunned to see me. Are you?"

Kid would not answer. In truth, he was stunned. The last person he expected to see was Heidi Leer. With Sara being so distraught, he assumed she had defaced her own mural and run off to the cabin.

"I mean, come on, you had to know that was my handiwork. Who else would know about the cabin, especially the recent addition of the cross?" Heidi asked.

It was then that Kid remembered the cross tombstone in the painting. Heidi was right. Sara knew her clone was buried there, but she had never seen the grave marker or its location.

This time, when General Hyland made eye contact for just a second, Kid shared his own torment for not realizing that it was Heidi who had painted the wall.

Walking over to the bed, Heidi ripped the gold arrowhead locket from around the neck of the corpse. She tossed it over her shoulder dismissively, and it landed on the ground by the door to the third room. "You're right. This isn't the real Sara. I wasn't sure this part of the plan would work, but Kid, since you didn't bury the body deep enough, the bitch was basically on ice and was very well preserved. I had to use a ton of makeup, but I had you for a minute there, long enough to hear you both agonizing. It made the time we spent digging up the body this morning so worth it."

"Speak for yourself," Elder-3 commented. "You were not the one picking and digging. Actually, grab the pickax you stuck over there so they don't try anything with it."

Stepping over to the wall, she wiggled the pointy end of the pickax head until she freed it from the cork board. When it released, the punctured picture of Kid and Sara remained stuck on the tip.

Heidi waved the pickax at General Hyland as she walked by. "I especially loved hearing you mourn for her. How does it feel to be the one being manipulated for a change ... *Sir*?" She started laughing. "Now that is karma. The puppet master became a marionette himself." Leaning the pickax handle against the wall next to the door to the third room, she seemed to be genuinely curious. "Tell me, what gave away that it wasn't really Sara? Did I use too much makeup?" There was only silence, so she demanded, "Tell me!"

The general said, "The real Sara has two freckles up near the bridge of her nose."

"Impressive, that you would know such a minute detail."

"A good father who is close to his daughter notices a lot of things." He sounded very much condescending.

"Fuck off," Heidi snapped. "There is no such thing as a good father. They are all a bunch of selfish pricks who care only about themselves," she added as she stepped back to the door leading to the third room.

"Heidi, where is Sara?" Kid cut in, finally unable to contain his anxiety.

She turned to him and began to slow, rolling laugh, with a frightening, deep voice.

"Cut the shit," he snapped.

Her smile disappeared instantly. She stomped over to Kid and backhanded him hard across the mouth. "Who do you think you are?" she yelled, with her eyes boring into him and her hand twitching. Her tone then softened. "What's wrong? Do you miss her?" She burst into a fit of deranged laughter.

After the slap, Kid's ears were ringing so he shook his head. His cheek was on fire. Heidi had completely lost her mind, soul, and conscience. She was unstable. He knew they had to watch their words with her. That realization was reinforced just seconds later.

"I can't believe this. You used to be our friend and were part of our group! Can we talk like…" Maria started.

Heidi's face turned to rage, and she fired a bullet into Maria's arm. Jess draped himself over his girlfriend to protect her. Mel covered her head and laid flat on the floor.

Kid went to launch himself at Heidi so she stepped back and aimed at his head. "Back off, Kid, now! Now!" Elder-3 also trained his weapons on Kid.

Clenching her arm, Maria writhed in pain. "You…" she screamed, prompting Jess to quickly put his hand over her mouth.

General Hyland looked at Elder-3 and pleaded, "Stop this now, before it is too late."

"*Before* it is too late?" the elder bellowed. Walking over to General Hyland, the elder put the muzzle of his traditional handgun in the palm of his hand, and with the butt of the weapon, he reared back and smashed General Hyland's jaw. With a sickening thud as metal met bone, general's head snapped sideways. He fell first against the mattress and then slid down to the ground.

Elder-3 roared, "It's already too late! You destroyed the project and the world, our world." Kicking the general in the face, the elder screamed, "Our perfect world! My only satisfaction will be watching you die before I do." Stepping back, Elder-3 returned the grip of the pistol to his palm.

With her lips tight, Heidi growled, "For all of the people he hurt, he deserves more than that." She stepped over and reared back to also kick him. The general turned away, causing Heidi's foot to glance off the side of his head. His arms came up to cover his face as she kicked him repeatedly while yelling, "You…are…not…fucking…God!"

Kid could not take it anymore and got to a knee about to give his life to try and help the general.

Seeing him, Heidi stopped and took a few steps back, again raising her pistol. Kid stopped and froze when she asked, "So you want to know where the real Sara is?" Going to the door to the third room, she stepped inside. A moment later, Heidi came out, holding a handful of hair. She dragged a groggy and beaten body through the doorway.

On her knees with her hands tied behind her back was Sara. She was alive, but she was shivering as she was clad in only a bra and underwear. Kid noticed that she had half-circles drawn on her bare midsection with what appeared to be red magic marker, and he felt sick with fear.

"Here she is. Say hello." Heidi grabbed a handful of hair. Sara's now upturned face had multiple scratches and contusions, with dried blood coming from the corner of her mouth and running down the cleavage of her breasts. She looked spaced out and was barely conscious.

Despite her own injury, Maria screamed. Kid was about to spring. Elder-3 again aimed his weapon at him.

Heidi put the muzzle of her weapon under Sara's chin. "Sit down Kid! Don't force me to kill her. That is not my plan."

With no choice, Kid reluctantly dropped to his knees. He glared at Heidi, with a hate like he had never felt before. She was evil to a depth he could have never imagined in any person. He wanted to rip her to pieces, and when he tried to speak, his lungs had turned to stone. He could only mutter, "How could you?"

"What!" Heidi yelled viciously as she took a step closer, ready to backhand him again.

"How…could…you?" he repeated and did not flinch.

"How could…I? Are you kidding me? Look at what's been done to me! Look at what you…" getting closer to his face she added bitterly, "…*you*, did to me, Kid." When she turned back, she almost stepped on the gold arrowhead locket that was on the ground. She let out a roar as she snatched the pickax and slammed its solid, heavy head on the pendant, repeatedly pounding it into the cement floor.

Sara moaned as she watched the mangled face of her locket break off and skitter across the ground. Her eyes seemed to open a little more as she stared at the punctured picture of Kid and her on the roof of the cabin that was still stuck on the pointy tip of the pickax.

"What you *both* did to me," Heidi snarled as she tossed the pickax against the wall.

While trying to assess Sara's condition, Kid was able to make eye contact with her. She met his eyes but appeared dazed and confused. He willed her to snap out of it.

Heidi continued, "Speaking of what you both did, don't worry Kid, Sara is perfectly fine, and so is your…baby?" The same grating laugh rose from deep within her throat.

"What?" Maria asked loudly.

General Hyland moaned. Even wounded, the words registered, and he struggled to sit up.

"You heard me." With her hand over her midsection, rage flashed in Heidi's eyes. "That goddamned baby should have been growing inside me! But don't worry, Kid. You are off the hook. I got my fucking period weeks ago."

Kid fought to remain expressionless. He feared his body was swaying. It had not even dawned on him that Heidi might be pregnant from their one night together. Then again, it would be the last thing to cross his mind now since he thought she died on top of Minerva Tower. But he felt pretty irresponsible for not having considered it before. He shuddered. *What a disaster that would have been.*

Heidi's expression changed in a flash. She peered inquiringly at Kid. "I am sure you are relieved that I'm not, but you don't seem surprised that Sara is pregnant. Tell me you already knew? Damn! What a beautiful surprise that would have been. You know, we need to coordinate better with these surprises, Kid. When I expect you to be shocked you're not, and when I don't expect it, you are."

Kid tried to play it off. "Yeah, right. Sara's pregnant."

She shook her head. "Nice try. My source is *very* reliable."

He gazed at her expectantly, but knew he was beat as an evil, assured smile came to her lips. He turned away.

Heidi's tone was condescending. "Let's just say I heard it straight from the horse's mouth."

# CHAPTER 40

Elder-3 jumped to his feet upon hearing the loud beep of a wireless alarm. He turned on a computer tablet and viewed the feed from a wireless camera. He watched as a young woman strained to push the Joint Base gate open. "Someone is coming!" he yelled. "Finally. It has been weeks."

As he pulled up the camera view, Heidi ran up behind him and watched over his shoulder. She stated, "It is her. Hyland."

"Is her traitor father with her?" he asked through gritted teeth.

Staring closer at the screen, she said, "No, it looks like she only has that freaky bitch, Karen Stone, with her." After pausing for a minute, she told him her quickly devised plan. "Now hide everything and get in place. She will be here in a few minutes. And whatever you do, do not intervene in my battle with Sara Hyland. That is my score to settle."

In her bedroom, Sara stood in front of her mirror. As the candle flame steadied and grew, the mirror's reflective reach extended further, revealing more and more in the darkness behind her. She met her own eyes and wiped away the tears. "You need to pull yourself together.

If not for you, for the baby." She turned her eyes down and gently rubbed her stomach, moving her hand in a slow circle. When she lifted her eyes, she again peered into the void that used to hold the picture of her and Kid laughing on the roof of Ironside. *The day at the cabin.*

Something caught her eye so she looked closer.

Suddenly, she inhaled deeply, and the candle lighter slipped from her fingers and landed on the floor. Moving closer to the mirror, her hand rose to cover her mouth as a pair of demon eyes stared back at her from the void where the picture used to hang. She was frozen in fear. Sara blinked a couple of times. It was just not possible. Could it be an illusion? It had to be. She prayed it was and turned around. Her prayers went unanswered.

Standing in the room just outside of the partially-opened closet door was Heidi Leer. Her teeth were clenched, her eyes were crazed, and she looked like a wild animal. "Surprise..." she hissed and pulled back one of the curtains, letting in light and revealing a large burn scar on her right cheek. She was holding a Medusa firearm and while aiming at Sara, she snapped, "Loose the weapon. Throw it in the closet."

Sara was speechless. *How is Heidi still alive? What is she doing in my house? And why is she wearing my sweatshirt?* Recollections flashed through her mind and formed a strange collage. She remembered feeling sorry for Heidi given the circumstances with her falling in love with Kid and then being heartbroken. But then anger welled upon recalling how Heidi had tried to kill her and almost succeeded in killing Kid. "How..."

"Toss your gun. Now!" she yelled.

Having no choice, Sara slowly drew her pistol and threw it in the closet.

With the loud voice piercing the air, Karen got off the couch and called, "Sara? Is everything..."

Sara heard the coat closet in the foyer open, the same one she had started reaching into for a sleeping bag. She flinched as Karen let out a blood-curdling scream. The front door then opened, and she heard the uneven patter of light footsteps followed by a second heavy set of footsteps. With great alarm, Sara turned. "What the hell is going on here?"

To her surprise, Heidi threw her own pistol into the darkness of the closet. "Just me, and you. No weapons."

Sara felt a wave of sickness course through her. Now was not the time for a physical altercation.

"It seems I also get a surprise." The corners of Heidi's mouth went up as she noted, "You're pregnant, with I assume Kid's spawn?"

Sara was dismayed that Heidi had heard her talking to herself in the mirror. She wanted to deny it, but she realized it was too late because even now she instinctively folded her arms across her stomach. She had to figure out a way to save herself and her baby.

"Should've been me," Heidi snarled. "But by killing you, a piece of Kid will die too!" she screamed and rushed forward.

Caught off guard, Sara's back was slammed into her dresser, and Heidi threw a punch. The clenched fist caught Sara in the mouth and stunned her for a second. Instinctively, she reached for her lips and saw blood when she pulled her hand away. Her head was jerked as Heidi grabbed her hair with one hand and reared back to throw another punch with her other hand.

Snapping out of her shock, Sara's self-defense training kicked in. She threw a short straight elbow. She connected with Heidi's jaw and knocked her back onto the bed.

Fueled by a rage like Sara had never seen, Heidi bounced right back up and went to kick her in the stomach. With a motherly defensiveness, she covered her midsection but left her face exposed. Heidi took advantage and connected with an open-fisted backhand. Sara's cheek was on fire, and she yelled out as she threw her shoulder into Heidi's chest and again knocked her onto the bed.

As Heidi rolled off the mattress and went to stand, it was Sara's turn to employ a bull-rush. She threw a shoulder into Heidi's midsection and lifted her off the ground, slamming her into the window and shattering the glass. While pinning Heidi against the curtains, Sara threw a fierce punch to the stomach. Heidi doubled over for a second and then brought up her knee. As Sara bent over to protect her stomach, an elbow came down on the back of her head, and she was pushed away from the window.

Standing face to face and boxing, Sara knew she had the advantage, and she pressed it. Sara was landing two punches for Heidi's every one. Sara was ducking and weaving, but Heidi was unable to do the same and was taking vicious hits. Blood poured from her nose.

Finally succumbing after a shot caught her in the nose again, Heidi screamed loudly, bent down, and rushed at Sara. While standing and grappling, Heidi connected with a short but not overly potent punch that connected with Sara's midsection.

With protectiveness fueling a sudden rage, Sara hooked her arm under Heidi's, swung out her hip, and tossed her through the air into the dresser. The mirror rocked and fell forward. The sound of wood splintering was followed by the thunder of breaking glass as the top of the mirror glanced off Heidi's shoulder and slammed against the floor.

Heidi picked up a large piece of the broken mirror. She was panting heavily as she held out the sharp end. With a yell, she lunged and slashed at Sara's stomach but was stunned by a kick to the chin. In one fluid motion, Sara followed with a waist high round-house kick, connecting with her adversary's hand. The jagged piece of mirror was dislodged and cracked against the wall.

Seeming unwilling to box again, Heidi dove at Sara's midsection. As Sara bent over to again protect her yet-to-develop baby, a fist caught her behind the ear. Dropping to a knee, her ears were ringing. Heidi tried to follow her effective punch with a kick, but Sara moved to the side, caught her foot and pulled hard. Heidi's other foot flew out from under her, slamming her back against the floor.

Rolling over, Heidi started to crawl toward the closet. Sara realized that she was going for the weapons they had both thrown in there, so she grabbed her ankle and pulled her back. The girls began to wrestle and roll around the floor, but Heidi was soon overwhelmed. With her adversary's strength waning, Sara maintained a half-mount and was not letting up. In a last ditch effort, Heidi was able to connect with a short stomach punch. Sara screamed as she threw an elbow that hit Heidi's jaw. Then she wrapped her fingers around Heidi's throat. She squeezed harder and harder. And then the world went black.

*It can't end this way. I can't lose*, Heidi thought as the darkness encroached from the edges of her field of vision. Then she heard a hollow thud, and the fingers around her throat released. Sara went limp and collapsed across her chest in a heap. Elder-3 was holding his gun by the barrel and must have used the heavy grip as a club. Without even the strength to push the body off of her, Heidi could only grunt, "Get her off of me!"

Elder-3 roughly grabbed Sara's hair and the waistband of her pants and slid her body to the side.

As she sat up and caught her breath, Heidi felt flush with anger. She panted, "I told you not to intervene! This was my battle to fight! I wanted to be the one to kill her!"

"Absent our intervention, the battle was over for you," Elder-3 said flatly. "And we did not kill her. We just knocked her out," he said as he holstered a pistol with a long barrel. "Do with her what you will."

Heidi stood up, but she was still gasping so she sat on Sara's bed until her breathing steadied. She stared down at Sara's body. "I don't know. Just killing her now after you intervened would bring me no satisfaction. And look at her, she almost looks at peace. Reminds me of the expression on her clone's face when we buried her at Ironside." She sat contemplating for a moment.

"What is Ironside?" he asked.

"It is an old hunting cabin in the middle of the woods, not far from here. A place that has a special meaning for me."

"What is so special about it?"

"After burying who we thought was…" she nodded at the body, "Sara Hyland in a grave, I gave my heart away to her boyfriend, Kid Carlson. But then we found out that the girl we buried was actually her clone, and it was like the bitch came back from the dead. When she rose from the grave, she buried Kid's and my love in her place." Staring into space, the wheels in Heidi's head were turning as she whispered, "When she rose from the grave."

Elder-3 appeared a bit confused, but he did not seem to care. He motioned toward Sara's body. "What you do with her is for you to decide. It is the other Hyland we want. Her father."

"Don't worry, you will get your shot. He will come for her," she said as she lifted the broken mirror frame from the ground. She stood it up on the dresser, leaning it against the wall.

"When?" the elder asked impatiently.

"These girls were going to be spending the night here. The earliest anyone like General Hyland would come looking for them is tomorrow. So we have time…" She turned and stared at the mural on the wall, "…to kill." She used her foot to push aside the broken pieces of the mirror as she walked across the room. Reaching for the wall, she hesitated as she remembered being reprimanded once by Kid because she nearly touched Sara's precious mural. *Screw him, and her*, she thought as she not only touched it but wiped at the wall with both hands. She peered down at Sara's body and paused. Turning her head back to the painting, she started laughing.

"What is so funny?" Elder-3 asked.

Walking over, Heidi nudged Sara's stomach and rocked her body with the tip of her foot. "I had thought of what I might do for every scenario based on who showed up here, but I have to admit, I never thought of that one. So many wicked ideas come to mind." Turning back toward the mural, she said, "Since we have to wait until tomorrow for any rescuers to come for her, and given the likelihood that her rescuers will include Kid Carlson and General Hyland, I see some golden opportunities. It is all coming together. Put her in the living room for now."

As the elder lifted up Sara's body, Heidi said, "Wait! Hold her there for a second." She ran out of the room and came back with a glue stick from a kitchen drawer. She ripped hair from the back of Sara's scalp and glued it to the head of the woman in the mural on the wall. "There. Now it's three-dimensional. It makes her seem so much more real."

Walking back, Heidi used her hand to wipe at the now-drying blood running from the corner of Sara's mouth and down her chin. She ran over to the wall and tried to finger-paint with it, but it was already too viscous and lumpy. Stepping back, Heidi shook her head, clearly not satisfied with her work. She grabbed Sara's paint palette and a fresh brush from the corner of the bedroom next to the dresser. Walking over, she rested the palette under Sara's chin.

"Keep holding her."

She then backhanded Sara a couple of times hard across the mouth. "Let her head hang!" she commanded. Blood from Sara's mouth dripped with increasing speed and volume onto the palette. Heidi ran back to the wall, dipped the paintbrush, and spread the fresh red liquid on the wall. "Much better," she muttered.

Elder-3 watched her. "What are you doing?"

"I will explain my whole plan to you. It is downright vicious. You will love it. You can take her. I'm done with her for now. When she comes to, slug her again and knock her out, but don't kill her. Now leave me be. I have a lot of painting to do. So many visions in my head that I need to capture and so little time."

"Why are you wasting your time painting anything?"

"I'm not wasting my time. It is part of my new plan. When I look at Sara and think of killing her, I have to admit, it does nothing for me. I thought it would, but it doesn't. It doesn't fill that void inside me. I realized I needed a new approach. A new plan." She turned to him and clarified, "I want them to feel the emptiness of a dark and endless void inside, like I feel now." She paused as her arm rested across her midsection. "Really, I guess I have felt that way for most of my life. So after I re-paint this mural, it will lead them to a specific location, and that is where the final phase of my plan comes into play."

Elder-3 seemed perturbed. "It sounds like this plan is becoming unnecessarily complicated. Maybe we should be doing the planning. We are not used to someone else leading."

Heidi approached him without hesitation. "Listen, I know you were used to being in charge, but I am the only ally and woman you have," she said. "And you would probably be lost in Atlantic City were it not for me. You are so lucky I was on the mainland watching the battle unfold, and came down there to find you."

He seemed to relax just a bit and acknowledged, "We are allowing you to lead because you did promise me Elder-41, General Eric Hyland, and we are getting close. We can feel it." While holding Sara's limp body with one hand, he reached out with his other and did an underhand grab of Heidi's crotch.

She grabbed his wrist and pushed it back. "No time. I have to get painting. But just go with me on this. You will see the beauty in it, I promise."

Elder-3 proceeded to carry Sara's body and walk through the door.

"Just put her on the couch," Heidi said as she followed him to the foyer while gently rubbing her face and gauging her injuries.

"We need to decide what we are doing with the other girl," he said.

"What do you mean?" she asked as he laid Sara's body on the couch.

"We chased the other girl out to their vehicle and while she was reaching for a shotgun in the back seat, we slammed her head with the butt of the Colt 45. The Medusa is too light weight for such a task," he said as he patted the second weapon on his other hip. "We took the shotgun and left her body in the vehicle."

"So the bitch isn't dead?" she asked, perturbed.

"We did not know if you wanted us to kill her, so no."

Heidi grabbed the solid iron fireplace poker, stomped out the front door and opened the back door of the vehicle. With two hands, she hoisted the solid poker up to the inside roof of the vehicle and slammed it down twice in a row. Walking back inside, Heidi tossed the bloody poker onto the fireplace hearth and said apologetically, "She is now."

That night, despite being battered and bruised, Heidi would paint until the wee hours of the morning, stopping only a couple of times to admire her work. During one break, she was looking at the volumes on a living room book shelf and was pleasantly surprised to find a few medical reference books. She knew the anatomy of a female and specifically the main parts of the reproductive system and where they were, but the confirmation was welcomed. When she was done for the night, she laid in Sara's bed. With her excitement about her new plan and given the freezing air pouring in through the broken window, she hardly slept. As soon as the sun rose, she hopped out of bed, grabbed a red magic marker, and went out to the living room.

"Wake up Elder-3. We need to move. We do not know how long before they come looking for her," she said to the still form on the ground in a sleeping bag. He snapped awake, unzipped the bag and stood up.

He watched intently as Heidi finished drawing circles, capped the red magic marker, and pulled Sara's pants back up. Grabbing the long, black coat that had been laid across Sara's upper body, she worked to put it on the limp form.

While Elder-3 threw Sara over his shoulder, Heidi grabbed a makeup bag from the bathroom, a knife from the kitchen, and ran outside. After checking the fuel level in both vehicles, she choose to take Sara's SUV since the gas tank was still three-quarter's full. When she opened the back door, she spotted Karen's pale face and blood drenched bandana on the floor. *You had it coming, you freaky bitch,* she thought. *I guess you won't be giving me dirty looks anymore, will you?*

Sara's body was laid on the back seat. She appeared to be out cold, but a moment later, she moaned. Heidi, sitting behind the wheel, looked back. Elder-3 leaned over from the passenger seat and whacked Sara on the head with the butt of his Colt 45 pistol, knocking her out again.

"Easy. Not too hard. Don't kill her. We need her alive for this," Heidi said as she opened the glove box and deposited the makeup bag and a sheathed boning knife she had taken from the kitchen. She fired up the vehicle and muttered, "Just hope I remember the way out there." She put the truck in drive and started for Ironside cabin to set the trap for who would predictably be Sara's rescuers.

# CHAPTER 41

February 6, 2045
Monday, Afternoon
The Pine Barrens of New Jersey
*Forty-two days after the event*

In the middle room of Ironside cabin, Sara's arms were tied behind her back, and she was on her knees. Wearing only a bra and panties in the frigid room, her body shivered. She started wilting, and her rear end dropped to the ground.

Kid's heart did the same. He needed to help her.

Heidi kept her pistol aimed at Sara's head while saying to Kid, "How perfect. The first newborn in the new world would come from you and Sara, like you are some modern day Adam and fucking Eve." Her voice was beyond condescending.

"What are you planning to do, Heidi?" he asked bluntly. After all they had been through -- surviving a cataclysmic event, the rescue on the ships, Kid being shot and pulled back from death's door, the life or death battles everywhere from the fire tower in the Pine Barrens, to the ski slopes of Vermont, to Mallard Island, to RPH, to the Island of Capri -- this was how it was going to end? There was no way he could let it all end this way, not without a fight.

Heidi seemed to sense it. "Stay on your knees and don't do anything stupid, Kid. We have no intention of killing Sara, or you, or Jess, and Maria." She motioned toward Mel and added, "Or what's-her-name over there."

Even with Kid being on the no-kill list, he did not simmer in the slightest. Whatever Heidi had planned, it was evil and harmful. He also realized that she excluded General Hyland from the no-kill list.

Jess made eye contact with Kid and in a flash, he shared some unspoken message. Some plan or idea. Kid was at a loss, given their predicament.

"Um, Heidi," Jess started, raising his hands submissively. "Since you are, thankfully, not going to kill us, can I grab a towel from the other room for Maria's arm before she bleeds out? Please?"

"A towel from where?"

"There is a hand towel inside the compartment in the floor of the main room, just over there. Don't you remember that compartment where we kept our food? There are no weapons in there, or anything that could be used as a weapon."

Peering at Maria's bloody arm, Heidi groaned loudly, waved her hand spastically, and said to Elder-3, "I do want her to see this, so just go watch him for a second while he gets a damn towel." Turning back, she warned, "Jess, only if you hurry."

Getting to his feet, Jess took deliberate steps and kept his hands in the air. Elder-3 followed and stood in the doorway between the rooms with a pistol trained on Jess. Kid feared the elder was looking for any excuse to open fire.

Kid heard the familiar creak of the trapdoor's hinge when it was opened. "Grabbing the towel," he heard Jess say.

"Show me your hands!" Elder-3 snapped and aimed his pistol. He must've been satisfied because he impatiently waved Jess back to the other room.

Sitting next to Maria, Jess wrapped the towel around her upper forearm and tightly tied it.

When Elder-3 returned to her side, Heidi said, "Keep them covered." She then holstered her pistol and stepped back into the third room. She crouched down and grabbed something from the ground. When she came out, she was holding what appeared to be a boning knife, or a filleting knife. She waved the long, narrow blade in the air.

Kid shivered as the deepest of chills went down his spine and spread throughout his body.

"What are you doing?" Elder-3 asked. "You are wasting time. Let us finish here and go. We now have the good fortune of having an M3 at our disposal."

"Just cover them!" she snapped. "It will work out all the same. He was to be yours if he showed," she pointed at General Hyland. "And everyone else was to be mine. That was the deal, and I spent all night working on my plan. I told you that I wanted them to feel, to really feel…" she paused and a pained expression came to her face, "…the emptiness of a dark and endless void inside, like I have felt for most of my life!"

Elder-3 seemed agitated by her answer, but he covered the survivor group as directed.

"Heidi, I don't know what you're thinking about doing, but ask yourself if it will really fill that void," Kid interjected, trying to buy a few minutes. He was running out of time and had no viable options. He made eye contact with Sara and could see that she was still out of it. She needed to come to and fast.

"What the hell would you know about it?" Heidi snapped as she stepped toward Kid, pointing at him with the tip of the knife. Like flicking a switch, she softened and got close enough to be in his personal space. "Oh Kid…" She reached out gently. He pulled back a little but let her fingertips touch his cheek, which was still stinging from her backhand moments before. Her head tilted as she stared into his eyes. "I had a dream one time, where everything that went on with my scumbag father was just a nightmare and that my world was still perfect. I cried tears of joy in my sleep and finally felt at peace. And then guess what?"

He could see the torment beginning the creep into her eyes, like clouds starting to encroach upon the sun on a bright day.

"I woke up on a disgusting, fold-out couch to the sight of my whore step-mother staring at me. The void inside me burst then too and out went the peace I had felt. The space inside was back to being empty and dark, and the feeling…" she put her hand across her midsection. "I threw up all over myself."

Tears suddenly ran down her face, like a flood from a dam-break. She winced and put her hand on his cheek, petting him. "For the period of time we were together, and for the only time in my life, that void was filled, and it wasn't a dream. It was real," she said softly.

And then, as if an evil spirit had awoken in her soul, her eyes turned black. Her pupils contracted, and her lips tightened. Her hand tensed. Her nails dragged down his face, starting to dig. "And then you left me." Her voice became loud and chilling. "And when you did, the old void was still there, but even darker and deeper."

Kid pulled his head back, revealing the fingertips of her dangling hand coated with blood.

"Do you know how it feels when a void inside is finally filled, only to erupt and empty out again? Do you know that pain and emptiness?"

"All I can say, Heidi, is that I am sorry," Kid said, knowing any word could be his last.

"You are sorry," she sneered while running the knife blade across her palm and drawing blood. "You are sorry. No you're not. But you will be." She stomped over to Sara, grabbed her by the hair and pulled her into the middle of the floor.

General Hyland had recovered enough to get on one knee.

Sara was lying supine with her tied hands underneath her.

Heidi dropped to her knees and mounted her, sitting on Sara's thighs. She caressed the handle of the knife and turned to Kid. "Did you see the blank tombstone I painted on the wall, right next to the one that said, 'Sara's Clone'? And the little rattle I put on top of it? Could you tell what it was? It was kind of sloppy. But does that give you a hint?"

She pulled down the top of Sara's panties, revealing a full bullseye drawn on the skin. The middle of the bullseye centered on the area of the pelvis just above the pubic region. "Right, about, here," Heidi said as she poked the skin with the tip of the knife. "What do you think?" she asked as her eyes toggled between Kid and General Hyland.

Kid realized what she was going to do, and he felt sick to death. "Heidi, please, no…" He also got on one knee.

"We will be able to add the inscription on the tombstone soon enough. Here lies…" She took the knife with two hands and placed the tip to the bullseye on Sara's skin. Her words were coarse, her eyes red, and her words venomous, "…Sara's uterus!"

As Kid jumped to his feet, General Hyland was already on his and pushed past him to attack.

Elder-3 pulled the trigger of his traditional pistol and shot the general in the stomach two times. Kid gasped, as did everyone else. The general yelled out and fell to the floor, his arms crossed over his midsection. The elder jumped forward in a rage and put the muzzle against the back of the general's skull.

"No," Sara croaked, no louder than a whisper.

"Wait!" Heidi screamed. "Don't finish him yet. Lift his head up and turn it this way. Let his last living sight be this!"

Sara turned to Kid. After she blinked a couple of times, he saw panic growing in her eyes and could see she was becoming more responsive to her environment. "Dad," she mouthed with pursed lips.

Kid looked at the general and saw blood and life draining away quickly.

Heidi turned and again put the tip of the knife in the bullseye on Sara's skin while saying to Elder-3, "When I'm done you can execute Hyland, but with the others, do not shoot to kill. Especially not him." She motioned toward Kid. "I want them to live through this, and live with it, and relive it, for the rest of their lives."

Turning her head, she continued, "You see Kid, I told you I wasn't going to kill you. No, that would be too merciful. I have nothing left to live for, except for one thing -- vengeance. I want you and Sara to be tormented for the rest of your lives by the ever-lasting memory of me and to forever feel the same emptiness inside that I do."

"You don't need to do this. We already feel tormented that we lost you somehow," Kid said, still trying to stall for time.

"He's right, Heidi," Jess added. "It haunts us every day."

Finding the participation unusual, and even ill-timed, Kid peered over long enough for Jess to point to himself and use his eyes to signal. Kid got it.

Ignoring Jess, Heidi's eyes bored through Kid's as her voice turned hoarse and bitter. "It is not nearly enough. Not by a long shot. How about something more traumatic, like the endless void of losing a child and never being able to conceive another," Heidi stammered.

A trickle of blood ran down and over Sara's hip. Kid knew it was now or never, but how was Jess going to join in a charge while still holding Maria?

The maniacal, increasingly savage, smile returned to Heidi's face. "Don't worry, I know exactly where to aim. I even marked it out. You should be able to save Sara's life, but she will be forever…" she gripped the knife tighter and turned to Kid, "…barren!"

Out of nowhere, a red dot appeared on Elder-3's face and found the cornea and iris of his right eye. Peering over, Kid realized Jess was holding his tiny laser pointer, the one he kept in the hidden compartment in the floor. It was a novelty item that they used to spot and identify distant points of interest from the cabin's roof deck. Now Jess was trying to use it as a weapon. With the beam steady, Jess screamed, "Here!" Elder-3 turned his eyes and looked directly at the red beam. He cried out in pain and dropped his Medusa firearm. He doubled over as he raised one hand to his face, all the while still holding the traditional pistol.

In a second, Jess was up and charging. The Elder blindly fired a wild shot. Everyone ducked, including Heidi. Jess lunged and leaped through the air, catching Elder-3's chin with a flying fist. The elder's head jerked as he crumbled to the ground in a heap, knocked out cold.

Kid jumped to his feet as Jess went to reach for the weapon in the elder's limp hand.

"Stop or she dies!" Heidi screamed. She had resumed her position and was holding the knife with both hands against the bullseye. The tip was piercing skin, and blood streamed steadily down Sara's hip creating a puddle on the floor beside her. "Take one more step, and I swear, I'll just bury the knife to the hilt, so both of you, back off!"

Raising his hands in the air, Jess took several steps back from Elder-3's fallen body.

Distraught that he did not move fast enough and had lost his opportunity, Kid was moving slowly. Heidi screeched, "I said back off, Kid! Now!"

"Put the knife down!" he pleaded. "You know you can't win this against all of us."

Resuming her deranged decorum, she smiled. "I do know that. But for me, winning is not surviving; winning is vengeance." She abruptly sat up straight and started pushing the knife down with both hands.

"Heidi!" General Hyland forced out, and then to Kid's surprise, the general started singing. "I guess I'll have to go now."

Heidi froze, and then her hands started shaking.

Kid recognized the line and knew it was from an old James Taylor song. But why was he singing at a moment like this? It made no sense, but it stopped Heidi in her tracks, at least for a second.

"Yes, I guess I'll have to go now..." the general repeated melodically.

Heidi turned to Kid and pleaded with her welled up eyes.

Maybe the general was stalling her with the hope that she would change her mind, or to give someone a second to intervene. That someone was Kid, and that second was up.

Kid charged forward, like he was shot from a canon.

Heidi yelled and resumed pushing down.

The piercing knife and searing pain must have been enough to shock Sara's senses because she cried out and twisted her hips, trying to roll to her side.

With a violent collision, Kid drilled Heidi and knocked her hard off of Sara.

To Kid's dismay as they crashed to the ground, they rolled. Heidi landed right on top of him. She was still holding the knife, and while spreading her feet to maintain her mount, she tried to stick it in his throat. They were face to face as he held her hands with both of his own. It was a stalemate that lasted a full minute, but the tip of the knife was still less than a couple of inches from his throat. He kept holding her hands with all of his might, but Heidi was fueled by a desperation and rage that seemed never-ending.

Suddenly, there was a thud, and Heidi's eyes, mere inches from Kid's, flew open wide. Her body jerked, and as her breath caught in her throat, blood started pouring out of her mouth. Her strength seemed to be fleeting, so Kid ripped the knife from her hands and threw it to the side. She went limp and dropped right on top of him. Her eyes welled, and she uttered with her voice wet and strained, "Kid, don't let it end this way. Tell me you love me. Just once, tell me those three words..."

After she had tried to kill him and Sara and his baby, he was not going to soothe Heidi's evil soul as she left this planet. "The only three words I have are, hell...awaits...you," and he threw her harshly to the side.

Kid sat up and stared at Heidi's body. Her breathing stopped. Her eyes turned lifeless as they stared at the floor. She was lying face down with the pickax driven in deep between her shoulder blades. What he found most macabre was that pinned to her back by the pickax was the picture of Sara and him on the roof of the cabin.

Standing in front of Kid, Sara's eyes were focused like laser beams. Her fists were balled tightly as if still holding the handle of the pickax she had just driven down to save him. She was panting as her own blood cascaded down the inside of her left leg. As her fists unclenched, her legs started shaking, and she collapsed to the ground.

# CHAPTER 42

February 6, 2045
Monday, Afternoon
The Pine Barrens of New Jersey
**Forty-two days after the event**

"Sara!" Kid cried out as he crawled to embrace her.

While holding Sara, Kid turned and was relieved to see that Elder-3 was knocked out. Jess was gathering all of the weapons and piling them on the bed, beyond the feet of the corpse.

Kid leaned back to check Sara's wounds. She was bleeding profusely. He almost gasped but did want to reveal the panic that was growing inside of him. "Blanket, quick!" he called out.

Mel grabbed one from a bed in the main room and spread it on the floor. Kid laid Sara on her back and took off his t-shirt. Putting his coat back on and covering his naked top half, he folded the shirt. "This might hurt, and I know you're pregnant so I'll be careful." She inhaled sharply as Kid put it against the gaping, jagged wound on her midsection and applied slight but even pressure. He then folded the blanket over her body and his arm as he held the shirt in place.

"Dad?" Sara's eyes popped open wide, and she turned her head. Her father was lying on his side looking at her. His face was pale, and he was surrounded by a pool of blood.

"Sara…" he said, barely louder than a whisper.

Turning on her side, she yelped in pain. She was trying to crawl over to him. Blood was dripping steadily from her wound.

"Sara, wait. Don't move!" Kid said. "Jess, grab the other end of the blanket." They each took an end, lifted her up, and gently put her down right next to her father.

"Mel, grab another blanket for Mr. Hyland. We can use it to carry him," Kid said. "He and Sara need medical attention. We need to get them over to Doc in Surf City."

Sara grabbed her father's hand. "Dad, I'm so, so sorry. None of this would have happened if I didn't run off in a huff."

"No. I am sorry. It is all my fault," the general huffed. "None of this would have happened if I had been more upfront with you. Are you alright?"

"I will be fine." Propping herself up on one elbow, she grunted hoarsely. "I turned sideways when she stabbed me, after she had frozen for a second because of whatever song you were singing. What was that about?"

He strained to reply. "A demon from her past."

"How did you know…oh, that's right. You used your military clearance to access her records."

A wry smile came to his colorless face. "Glad I did. Listen…" he started and lost his breath.

"We need to do something about your wounds, Dad. We need to get pressure on them." She winced and gritted her teeth as she leaned over further and caressed his face. "You are so cold."

Right on cue, Jess came over with a blanket. "I'm ready, Kid. Let's move them out."

Raising his shaking hand, General Hyland said, "No, Jess. Don't move me. I still have some words to say." He struggled to catch his breath, and then turned back to his daughter. "Since the day you were born, the fate of humanity has been intertwined with your fate. Protect it at all costs."

Kid heard the words but did not understand what her father meant about Sara's fate being intertwined with the fate of humanity. The general then gasped and coughed weakly.

"Dad?" Sara squeaked out and flinched from the pain. "Please, hold on until they get us back to Surf City so Doc can fix us up. We're going together..." She began to cry.

"Kid..." the general called out, barely above a whisper.

"Yes?" Kid knelt down.

"Give me your hand." General Hyland placed Kid's hand on Sara's and held both. "Please take care of my little girl forever."

"I will. And again I promise that to you."

"Stay her guardian," he added and then turned to his daughter. "My time is short. Hear me out."

Sara nodded, forcing the tears to roll faster down her cheeks. She pulled in closer and despite her agony, she put her arm over him.

The general exhaled, and after he pulled the cross that hung around his neck out of his shirt, his hand dropped to the ground, his strength gone. He was face to face with his Sara, and whispered, "I've lived with the guilt of your mother dying. It was my fault. CCP was voluntary, and I made us participate. Hear me?"

"Barely, but yes, I hear you."

"Sara..."

Kid realized that the general's voice and his life were quickly fading. He braced.

General Hyland moved his hand and fingers just enough to touch Sara's chin. A pained smile marked his face. "There is one final truth." Suddenly, the general's eyes went wide and he expelled a wet sounding breath. It seemed like something inside him gave way, or collapsed. With one last surge, he pulled her closer and whispered in her ear. His head then came to rest on the blanket, and he stopped breathing.

Sara wailed, "Dad, no!" She hugged him tightly and sobbed uncontrollably.

Kid dropped to a knee and put one hand on Sara's shoulder. He covered his face with his other hand as he shared her unbearable pain. Tears ran in torrents down his cheeks.

Jess and Maria came over and tried their best to console.

Kid tensed and turned as Mel screamed, "Look out!"

Elder-3 bolted past her and headed out the door. He had come to and must have been waiting for just the right moment to make a break for it. "He's taking the M3!" she said as she peered out the window.

Jumping to his feet, Kid wiped his eyes and said, "Maria, help Sara. Put pressure on her wound but remember she is pregnant. I am going after him!"

From the front door, Kid saw Elder-3 climbing the ladder into their craft. "Oh no he doesn't." He broke into a sprint. If Elder-3 escaped, he would not only be on the loose, but would have an M3 at his disposal.

Elder-3 engaged the thrusters and lifted off as Kid grabbed one of the ladder rungs. He held tightly as the M3 rose quickly into the sky. Kid knew he had to let go while still near enough to the ground to survive a fall, or he needed to pull himself up into the craft. The elder tilted the M3, clearly trying to make Kid let go.

With no time to weigh his options, Kid was about to drop to the ground when he cast a final glance up into the cockpit. The elder was holding the wheel tightly but had slid half off of his seat and was bracing with his feet to keep from sliding out of the tilted aircraft. An unbuckled seat belt dropped out of the M3 and hung down. An idea came to Kid, and he made the split second decision to hang on. He scaled a few ladder rungs and grabbed the dangling seat belt. As the thrusters swung horizontal, the elder leveled off for just a second before burying the throttle. The pause was all Kid needed to pull himself up and drop into the seat next to the elder.

Elder-3 swung at Kid's face with the back of his fist. Despite taking a solid shot to the mouth, Kid continued trying to buckle himself. Every time he almost had it buckled Kid had to let go to defend his face from the punches being thrown. Finally, he just held onto both ends of his unbuckled seat belt with one hand, and reached overhead with his other. He flipped open a plastic cover. As he pressed the red button, he turned to Elder-3 and said, "I hope you brought your cape."

In mid-swing with a backhand, Elder-3 stopped to brace himself when the cabin ejected straight into the air. Kid was again sucked back in his seat as the cabin launched skyward, but this time he had both ends of his seat belt in his hands. Below them, the M3 dove and crashed into a dense group of pine trees.

As soon as Kid felt their ascension slow, he hurried to fasten his seat belt. The cabin started to fall precipitously. His belt clicked right as his body started to rise. Now buckled, he immediately reached over and grabbed the loose belt for the seat next to him.

With the cabin in free fall, Elder-3's body also rose. He seemed to realize his dilemma and searched for his seat belt. He was rising so fast that he only had one chance to grab it. He lunged for his belt, but Kid pulled it out of reach. The elder flew out of the cabin and soared through the air. With his arms flailing, he plummeted hundreds of feet toward the endless sea of pine trees. A few second later, Kid heard the cabin's parachute deploy over his head and braced as the canopy filled with air, jerking him up into the sky.

As soon as the ejected cabin stabilized and leveled off, Kid unbuckled and looked down. He was not far from Ironside, so he pulled on the parachute lines to steer as he descended. He succeeded enough so that he landed on a trail about a tenth of a mile away. The M3's cabin came to rest but was tilted as one end landed atop a cluster of scrub pines. Kid jumped out and sprinted up the trail at full-speed. When he ran into Ironside, with his only new injury being another bloody lip, the group seemed relieved.

"Sara, honey." Kid crouched to check on her. She was still holding her deceased father, but she was weakening. With the M3 down, they would need to take the vehicle parked outside.

Running to the main room, he looked for the keys to the vehicle. "Jess?" he yelled. "We need to find the keys to the…" He stopped as he heard the vehicle start up. "Thank you," he muttered.

Coming in through the cabin door, Jess said, "I had to hot-wire it. I think Elder-3 had the keys in his pocket. I saw him fly off into the woods after you ejected."

"Good, come over and help me, Jess."

Gently, Kid pulled Sara's hands from her father's body and whispered, "You need medical attention so we have to go. Lay down. We will come back for your father and make sure we give him a proper burial." Sara did not resist.

Kid and Jess grabbed the blanket she was lying on and carried her out to the vehicle. It was then that they discovered the body of Karen Stone on the floor behind the front seats. "Son of a bitch!" Kid yelled as he jumped back. Karen's bandana was soaked with blood. He was not prepared for any more physical or emotional carnage at that point.

"How did I not see that!" Jess said.

Sara sat up and saw Karen's body. She opened her mouth and looked like she was about to scream, but her eyes rolled back in her head as she passed out.

"She has a pulse!" Kid yelled as he held his fingers against Karen's cold neck. "But not a strong one. And she's just about frozen."

Despite having her arm wrapped in a bandage with a gunshot wound, Maria said, "Put Karen in the back, and I'll do CPR as long as I can. But she needs real medical help so we need to move."

While Maria performed CPR on Karen, Kid kept pressure on Sara's wound to stem the flow of blood. Jess made haste in driving out of the woods. As soon as he reached Long Beach Island, they hustled to get her to the surgery center on Long Beach Boulevard, where they were met by Dr. McDermott and his resident nurse assistant, Marissa. Upon seeing the multitude of medical crises, the doctor told Marissa to get the team assembled immediately.

Sara and Karen were placed on gurneys and hustled into the surgery center. Maria walked in with her arm wrapped in a bloody bandage.

"We'll take it from here, Kid," Dr. McDermott said. "Go clean yourself up and try to dress your wounds. You look pretty beat up yourself."

# CHAPTER 43

February 6, 2045
Monday, Late Afternoon
Surf City, New Jersey
**Forty-two days after the event**

After washing his face and hands, Kid camped out in the recovery area of the surgery center. Checking his watch, he realized that Sara had been in emergency surgery for almost two hours. He found himself pacing for long stretches of time. He was still pacing when Dr. McDermott walked in. By the facial expression and body language, Kid knew the news was bad.

"Please, sit," the doctor instructed. "I'm sorry, Kid. Sara lost the baby. It is hard to tell if from the knife wound, from stress, or from the physical abuse her body endured."

Kid's head drooped, and he stared at the floor.

"Again, I'm sorry. I did everything I could possibly do."

"Doc. I am sure you did everything you could,' Kid managed to respond.

"There is good news though," the doctor started.

Popping his head up, Kid asked, "What is it?"

"She should be able to have another child. None of her female parts was seriously damaged."

"Oh, thank God," Kid said, overcome by yet another wave of emotion. He put his face in his hands.

"She's lucky. The knife just missed her uterus," continued the doctor.

"She saved herself by twisting her body at the last second," Kid offered, reflecting on General Hyland's disrupting Heidi by singing a song that seemed to greatly affect her. He could still hear the words, 'I guess I'll have to go now.' The verse made Heidi pause, obviously just long enough. "Can I go see Sara?"

"She's obviously recovering, but she is also distraught about her father so she could probably use the support."

The door opened, and Maria walked in. Her arm had a clean bandage, and she looked pretty strong. She went to Kid and kissed him on the head. "I heard about the baby. I'm sorry. But thankfully it seems Sara will pull through."

"Thanks, Maria. How about you?" Kid asked and pointed at her arm.

The doctor jumped in. "The bullet tore up some muscle and tissue in her forearm, but she will heal. It will give you a reprieve from the elbows she likes to throw at you."

"Or not. My other arm is fine," Maria quipped.

"How about Karen?" Kid asked.

There was a silence as the doctor and Maria both lowered their heads.

Feeling a wave of sickness, Kid asked, "Is she…"

"Not dead," the doctor cut in. "But she is in a coma. She had some very serious head trauma with serious swelling of the brain. We did a ventriculostomy to drain the pressure and are administering medication and IV fluids. Plus we are also treating her radiation sickness."

"Will she come out of it?" asked Kid.

Pursing his lips, the doctor said, "I have to be honest, her prognosis is poor. These heads traumas need to be handled right away. She was in that condition for quite some time." Kid exhaled and put his face in his hands. "All we can do is pray," he mumbled.

"And we will," the doctor agreed.

The door opened again, and Sara wheeled into the recovery area on a gurney. As Kid got to his feet, Dr. McDermott said, "You can visit with her but keep her from moving or exerting for now. Her recovery will not be easy and will take some time." Taking Maria by the good arm, the doctor said, "Let's step out and give them some time alone."

Kid ran over and gently hugged Sara, and they both cried for fifteen minutes. She looked beaten to a pulp. Her lip was swollen and every visible area of her body seemed to have abrasions or bruises.

Finally she said, "Kid, I hope you don't think it is too strange, but I asked Dr. McDermott to put some of the tissue from the fetus in a vial so we can bury our baby."

"I'm glad you did." He completely understood.

"Can we bury our baby in the same cemetery in Georgia as my mother? We have to go there anyway to bury my father." Her eyes again welled up. "He had a plot there for himself, right next to Mom."

"Of course. And it won't be hard to get there because we will have another M3 soon. Mel and some others are going back to Dover Air Force Base to get another one." He kissed her forehead. "For now, just focus on resting and recovering."

February 19, 2045
Sunday, Morning
Coastal New Jersey
**_Fifty-five days after the event_**

The next couple of weeks were a time of grieving, adjustment, and recovery from injuries. Kid kept a close eye on Karen, but she remained in a coma. With every passing day his hope dwindled a bit more. All the while, Kid kept working to ensure the new society moved forward. Everyone who knew General Eric Hyland well, including his daughter, his parents, and Adele, were adamant that moving the society forward is what he would have wanted. Sara, her grandparents, and Adele spent much time consoling each other over the loss of the general.

Evelyn had collapsed upon hearing the news about her son. She was making a slow and difficult recovery. Her husband, Chris, kept reminding his wife that Eric had died saving their beloved grand-daughter, Sara. Chris grieved but seemed to find comfort when pointing out that Eric's death was one of honor and bravery.

With the passing of General Eric Hyland, a new president had to be elected. The adults and former elders stood on the deck of Ship Number One with Dr. McDermott again being the election facilitator. Melanie Spatz immediately nominated Kid Carlson for president. The group on deck, foregoing any hand raising to finish voting, just started clapping. Shaking Kid's hand, Dr. McDermott said, "I would say that the vote is unanimous."

The election for vice president was not as cut and dry. Former Elder-113, Marjorie Dawson, won a close election against former Elder-53, United States Navy officer Thomas Kinnon. After the elections were over, Kid shook hands with both Marjorie and Thomas.

When Kid went to walk away, Sara pulled him to the side. "Congratulations." She hugged him. "You'll be a great leader."

He put his arms gently around her since her healing process was still ongoing. "Thanks." He sat down for a moment on a deck box.

"What is it?"

"I'm alright. Here, sit next to me," he said as he scooted over. "I'll tell you what. I can already feel the difference in the weight and responsibility of being the president."

"But you were the vice president before, which is a position of responsibility," she noted.

"I know, but it is still a big step up. When I was VP, I always had someone above me to be the final word, especially with the tough calls."

She put her arm around him. "I know you. As a leader you will be firm but fair and will make informed decisions no matter how tough they may be. I have every confidence. Obviously, everyone else does too. In terms of being the final word, you will get used to having that, except with me, of course," she said, laughing for the first time in weeks. Immediately, she winced and put her arm across her still-healing midsection. Even through her obvious discomfort, she continued to smile.

February 20, 2045
Monday, Morning
Near Augusta, Georgia
*Fifty-six days after the event*

The next day, now two weeks after his death, a funeral was held for General Eric Hyland in a cemetery outside of Augusta, Georgia. With round trips taking barely a half an hour of flight time, Mel used the M3 to shuttle multiple loads of people down south. The temperature change was very much noticeable as the Georgia countryside hovered in the comfortable 60-degree range. Kid noticed that his nostrils were thawed out enough to actually smell the grass.

General Hyland was laid to rest at the same cemetery where his wife was buried. When his wife passed away, the general had secured a plot large enough to bury three people -- his wife Amanda, himself, and Sara.

The digging and even the headstone for General Hyland's grave was handled by Kid along with Chris Hyland, Jess, Maria, and Adele. With a learning curve and several slabs to practice with, Jess made a granite headstone that looked almost professionally carved and included the words Sara wanted on there. It had a full name, dates of birth and death, and a notation saying, 'Here lies a wonderful man; a loving father, boyfriend, and forbearer of a new world full of hope. Rest in the comfort of our never ending love and gratitude.'

Although not fully recovered, Sara made it through the ceremony. While standing with Chris and Evelyn on one side and with Kid, Adele, and her brother Devin on the other, Sara gave a brief but heartfelt eulogy before placing her father's diary on his chest.

Kid stared at the black covered book which had played such a role in the events of the past many weeks. As the coffin lid was gently closed, Kid realized it was apropos that such a book stay with its author. Sara kissed her father's casket before it was lowered into the ground with straps held by Chris, Kid, Jess, and Dr. McDermott.

After multiple trips, the M3 was loaded with the last of the funeral attendees for the return to New Jersey. Mel called out, "Kid, Sara, there is room for two more."

Walking over to the craft, Kid said, "Mel, I hate to inconvenience you, but can you leave Sara and me here for an hour or so and then pick us up?"

"Sure. Can she make it that long?"

"Actually, she is the one who asked for another whole hour. I would have settled for half of that."

"You got it, Kid. Take your time," Mel said and then within a minute, the M3 was in the air.

Kid grabbed a shovel and in between the graves of Sara's parents, he dug a one-foot by two-foot deep square hole. They had their own private ceremony to bury an opaque vial with tissue from the baby they had lost. Both cried as they kissed the vial. Then Sara gently placed it in the hole. She whispered, "Love you, baby. You will always be with us."

Grabbing the shovel, Kid filled in the tiny grave. He then walked behind General Hyland's headstone and grabbed a small, one foot tall cross he had made out of pressure treated lumber. While tapping it into the dirt and felt a moment of déjà vu.

"I didn't know what to put on it, so I left it blank. We didn't get to the point of talking about names, and it is hard to come up with one now since we don't know if our baby was going to be a boy or a girl."

Sara was sitting Indian-style, looking at the grave marker. "It's like having our own little Baby Doe. They never knew the gender of the CCP's famous baby either."

When Kid sat down next to her, she grabbed his arm. "I am so thankful that I will be able to have children in the future. I can't believe how close I was to being permanently sterilized."

"I know," Kid responded. "Doc said it was literally a matter of millimeters. When the smoke clears, and the time is right, we can try for another baby."

"Can we Kid?" She grabbed his hand and stared into his eyes. "I took the pregnancy test because I was late with my period and was battling morning sickness. But I have to say, once I accepted that I was pregnant, I became excited about it, despite the world into which we would be bringing a child. Life must go on and must continue, more so now than ever. I was already talking to our baby and singing." She fought back tears.

Kid put his arm around her. "We will try again. I promise."

With Mel set to return in twenty minutes, Sara went to her mother's grave and kneeled. Kid examined her mother's headstone, in awe of the massive carved rose that covered the top half of the slab. He found it odd that the rose was actually affixed to the tombstone and not carved out of the stone itself.

"My father was always so proud of this tombstone. He designed it himself."

"It is impressive," Kid commented and was startled by a movement over his shoulder. He turned to see Mel, very stealth-like, landing the M3 on the ground behind them. Helping Sara to her feet, Kid took her hand, and they walked over to the craft.

As she boarded the M3, Sara stopped and whispered, "Love you. I will come back to visit. I promise," as she blew kisses toward the three monuments.

# CHAPTER 44

For the remainder of the month of February and the first week of March, 2045, much progress continued to be made with the base camp and the citizens. Kid had settled into being unsettled in his role as president. His goal every day was to move their new society forward a step or even a half of a step. Some days, he felt lucky just not to go backward. He always kept in mind his conversation with General Hyland ten days after the liberation. They had discussed the need for guiding principles for the future of their society. At the time, Kid had recited the main parts of the scout oath, but the general made a few modifications and suggested a duty to God, society, including others and family, and then self. In Kid's mind, it was a great framework, so he tried to remain guided by these points.

Kid's thoughts about the future government structure went deeper and further every day. He spoke to many others about it, including Sara, Chris Hyland, and vice president, Marjorie Dawson. The day after General Eric Hyland had been elected president, Kid recalled having a deep discussion with him about the idea of creating a modified version of a democracy. Kid had pointed out that they now had a huge advantage in that there would no longer be an arms race or a need for a military, which would save them mass quantities of time and resources. They had concluded that they wanted to rebirth a society like the old America but with more checks and balances to avoid some of the pitfalls. They discussed harnessing the motivational and competitive benefits of capitalism without the downsides such as greed and corruption. Most of all, they wanted a government that worked for the benefit of the people and not the other way around.

Breathing through his nose, Kid winced. Reflexively, he put his mask over his face and inhaled deeply. Although spring had not yet arrived, there had already been brief periods of time on warmer days when the putrid stench of dead bodies wafted through the air. This had prompted Kid to establish a team to secure a significant supply of N95 respirator masks. He expected the first summer to be really brutal. Besides hoping for a steady easterly wind, he was hopeful that the air would clear after a year. The former elders all believed that would be the case, given the number of passes made by the neutron beams during the destruction.

Concerned that everyone would burn out, Kid made sure that only essential work was done on Sundays, reinforcing that it was their day of rest. The schedule worked out well as Estelle had established her own Sunday bible study group. Each week more and more of the former Utopia Project members were participating. Estelle found great satisfaction in this, as she had to explain the passages, as well as the context of the bible itself, to many people who had never even heard of it.

"It challenges my own understanding and knowledge of the bible, and I get to see it through eyes anew," Estelle had told him with a gleam in her eye.

Soon, the number of participants had grown so much that she had to break them into two study groups scheduled at different hours because they could no longer all fit in the large, member dining room on the ship. And then Sunday in the late afternoon, Estelle hosted yet another study group on the mainland. Kid and Sara had made a point of attending one study group every week. It was almost uncanny, but Kid found the bible more relevant and meaningful now than ever, with Sundays inspiring a peace and reflection inside him to which he now looked forward every week.

Over 4,000 citizens had already been moved to the mainland. The others were still on the ships, but Adele's deconditioning process was ahead of schedule. Kid and Sara could not wait to move ashore. Since most of the citizens were still on the ships, and given his position of responsibility, Kid felt obligated to remain living with the majority of their population.

Seven of the former elders were still living on the ships while three were living in Surf City. It seemed to Kid that given their involvement in the Utopia Project, many of the elders must have been either disaffected, disgruntled, devoid of close family, or even loners. *Why else would they have taken part in it and stayed through the destruction?*

Kid was relieved to find out that most of the surviving elders were of a mindset similar to General Hyland. It helped explain why they were included in the twelve chosen to survive. Like the general, they felt a sense of duty and saw merit in many of the concepts being developed in the Utopia Project. By the time they were told of the destructive plans being furthered by the Board of Elders, it was too late to leave and impossible to stop. It was clear that most of them felt trapped and helpless.

Despite the overwhelming number of tasks to be done, Kid remained committed to having meetings every few days with the former elders because he wanted to build stronger relationships and make sure they all had a sense of belonging. He felt the team really strengthening and coming together.

As of the beginning of the week, 100 percent of the power being supplied to Surf City, a portion of Ship Bottom and all three Utopia Project ships now came from the solar farms on the mainland. Overseeing their power needs was former Elder-92, Akira Matsuda, who had his master's degree in electrical engineering. He was becoming not only an expert in repairing solar panels and inverters, but he was learning how to build them himself. To ensure redundancy and transfer of knowledge, Akira was training a team of ten citizens.

Food was still abundant, but it would not be forever, not with 20,000 mouths to feed. The focus had turned to growing their own vegetables and fruits, as well as other staple crops. While working on their own agricultural initiatives, they had taken the M3 on multiple supply and non-perishable food runs around the country and the world.

For the most recent non-perishable food run, Adele recommended going to the port of Tangier in Morocco. She knew the port well and knew the specific area where canned foods from Spain and other countries were warehoused. That turned out to be nothing short of a gold mine.

On the eighth day of March, 2045, Kid and Sara were about to head ashore to check on the status of the base camp in Surf City.

Sara hugged her brother Devin goodbye. Watching the boy holding Sara so tightly, Kid was touched to see the bond that had been created between brother and sister. "You promise you'll take me next time?" he asked.

"I promise." She kissed him on the top of his head.

Walking up the hallway toward the door to the deck of Ship Number One, Kid noticed a group of former members sitting in the dining room. They all had books in hand. It was amazing enough to see them reading, but he could see that most were reading fiction. They all seemed relaxed but engaged in their books. A young man, around sixteen years old, turned his eyes away from *Lord of the Flies* and proceeded to smile and wave at Kid and Sara. While they both waved back, Kid pointed to the book and gave a thumbs up. "Love that book, Ronny. It is a classic. After you finish, tell me what you thought about it."

Ronny hesitated for a second and then said, "I will." Kid had noticed that the former members were still adjusting to using words that began with the letter 'I,' but they were overcoming it. "There are many things in here I do not understand and have to ask about, but

I can't put it down," Ronny added. "I may finish it before the end of the day."

After Sara and Kid climbed into a tender and went ashore, they noticed two school buses parked outside the Surf City Hotel. Jess and Maria ran over to meet them.

"Off to the farm?" Kid pointed to the buses. The survivors had been tilling and planting twenty acres of crops at the old Sassafras Hill Farm in nearby Barnegat. Jess and Estelle were overseeing the crop planting. What Estelle was having the hardest time with was not that the garden was so large, but that is was on flatland instead of the terraces she was used to in Italy.

"Yes," Jess answered. "We are making good progress."

"I can just taste those Jersey tomatoes now." Kid mused, licking his lips.

"I can't wait," Maria added. "Delicious and good for diabetics."

"But we'll only be at the farm until noon. Today is a special day." Jess smiled. "We are taking a field trip in the afternoon."

"Where to?"

"The minor league baseball stadium in Lakewood. I am going to teach them baseball."

Kid raised his eyebrows. "Good luck with that. Are you bringing any medical staff?"

"Two nurses in training. And yes, we have respirator masks. I imagine that on a nice day like today, with how over-crowded Lakewood was, the smell could be disgusting."

"Playing baseball wearing respirator masks? That will be..." Kid started when his walkie-talkie beeped. It was the special beep setting he had created for Dr. McDermott. He raised the unit to his lips and pressed the call button. "Go ahead Doc."

"Kid! You have to get to the medical facility right away! And bring Sara."

With the urgency in the doctor's voice, Sara raised her hand and covered her mouth.

"On our way. We are already on the mainland so we will be over there in a couple of minutes. What is going on?"

"I will tell you when you get here. Hurry."

Kid and Sara jumped into a pickup truck and drove toward the clinic on Long Beach Boulevard. When they arrived, Sara got out but stopped on the sidewalk. "I am dreading going in there."

Kid grabbed her hand, met her eyes, and they walked through the door together. Dr. McDermott was waiting just inside.

"What is it?" Kid asked.

"Come with me."

They followed him to one of the patient rooms up the hall. Kid knew where they were heading. He made eye contact with Sara, and she also knew. The doctor held the door open for them.

Stepping inside with trepidation, Kid stopped when Karen Stone, wearing a bandana, turned her head and made eye contact. "Karen?" he uttered in shock. Sara stepped in and screamed. She went to run over to the bed, but Kid grabbed her arm. "Wait." Turning to the doctor, he was trying to formulate his question in a delicate way.

Dr. McDermott headed him off. "She came out of her coma sometime after midnight, and I wanted you two to be the first to know. I did a battery of tests, and she has much fog, but she seems to have minimal to no brain damage or cognitive impairment. It is astounding. She knew who I was and recalled all of the events leading up to her coma."

They all looked over at Karen, who raised her hand and waved.

Sara seemed like she was about to burst into tears. "I want to give her a hug."

Karen held her arms open, so Sara ran over and embraced her. Sara was bawling and kissing her friend's tear-soaked cheeks. "Hi big sister," Karen said, with her voice more raspy than ever.

Kid walked over, sat on the edge of the bed, and also hugged Karen. Unexpectedly, he also started crying. "You're back," he said. "You made it, Karen."

"I thought I was a goner," she answered. "For the last month, I've been living in a dream world, waiting for the curtain to finally come down."

Dr. McDermott walked over. "She is going to need much physical therapy, but all of her vitals are good. And the swelling in the brain is gone."

"What a relief," Kid uttered.

"But, she needs to rest, and I have much to do to get her back on her feet."

"We get it, and we'll get out of the way," Sara said. "Can we visit her again tomorrow?"

"Of course."

Kid and Sara kissed Karen and went back to the pickup truck. As soon as she closed her door, Sara burst into tears. Kid held her tightly.

Karen's survival was unexpected. It brought them both an immeasurable amount of relief and happiness. It also seemed to trigger something deeper in Sara. Maybe Karen's recovery was a reminder of the traumatic events when Karen was beaten, and when General Hyland perished at the cabin.

Sara seemed to confirm this suspicion when she said she wanted to go back to her house. She had not been back to her home since the fateful day she went there with Karen. She said she wanted some of her own familiar clothes, but he knew that she needed to confront more than just her choice of wardrobe.

# CHAPTER 45

Kid and Sara drove toward Fort Dix in the Joint Base. The sun was out, and it felt like spring was in the air. The scenery along the way was peaceful, almost picturesque. Kid absorbed it all, but it seemed lost on Sara.

They went through the already-opened gate and continued on to her house. Kid parked, and for several minutes they sat in the truck. Finally, Sara exhaled loudly and got out. He followed behind as she walked up to the house and stopped. When she opened the front door, she stood in the threshold and put her hands to her face. She had tears running down her cheeks as she stepped inside. "Everything reminds me of my father," she uttered as she glanced at the pictures in the foyer and the living room.

Walking up the hall, she pushed her door fully open. As she stepped in, she dropped to a knee and put her hand over her mouth. "What did she do?" she said as she pointed at the defaced mural on her wall.

"Thankfully you have a bunch of photographs of the original mural." Kid crouched and looked her in eye. "Listen, I know it is all a shock. But remember what happened here. It was dramatic and demented."

"I know. And you told me what to expect, but it is so much worse than I imagined. I feel ill over it."

"Just be happy you are still around to be able to see it," he noted. "Speaking of feeling ill, at first we were afraid that you defaced the mural yourself being as upset as you were."

"I would never do that," she responded. "No matter how upset I was."

"We should have figured that."

After getting up, Sara walked out and made it halfway up the hallway. She stopped and stared at the door to her father's room. Kid thought she was going to proceed, but she turned and was face to face with the picture of her mother's tombstone. She froze and inhaled sharply.

"What's wrong?" He reached for her.

"I'm alright." She leaned against the wall and tried to catch her breath.

He found her reaction odd in that she knew that particular picture was there. She had showed it to Kid many times.

"Seeing my Dad's door and then the rose triggered a painful memory."

Kid was hesitant to inquire. "I am sorry. I guess being back in the house where you had so many memories…"

"No, this one didn't happen here," she noted and rested her head against the wall. "I just remembered the last thing my father said before he died. He was whispering so only I could hear." She looked at him so he just pursed his lips and nodded. She continued, "I have no problem telling you. You know I share everything with you, Kid. It's just that up until now, I had buried the memory of his last words because they were just that. And I can't remember them without the vision of his last breath and of him dying right in front of me."

Kid was not inclined to press and just put his hand on her shoulder to offer comfort and support.

After composing herself, Sara lifted the picture of her mother's tombstone off of its hook and carefully leaned it against the wall.

Reaching into the secret compartment, she gasped as she felt something inside. She pulled out a large skeleton key. "There *is* a key, just like he said," she whispered, almost reverently. "I never even knew this was in here."

"In his last words, he told you about a key?" he asked.

"That was part of it. His very last words were choppy, but he whispered to me, 'Wall pocket at our house…get key…it unlocks the truth…behind the rose made of stone'."

Her eyes turned to the picture leaning against the wall. She dropped to her knees while uttering, "…behind the rose."

A chill went down Kid's spine. This was the second reference to 'the rose,' which is what her father and she affectionately called the picture of her mother's tombstone. The first was the note the general had left for Sara in the jewelry box the night of the destruction. The note had said, 'You will find the answers behind the rose,' and that had led them to the general's diary behind this very picture.

Getting on his knees next to her, Kid grabbed the picture of the tombstone. "Behind the…" he started as he pointed at the center of the photograph, "…rose." He then stared at the key in her hand. "Maybe he left something in a secret compartment that you need that key to open?" Turning the picture over, he went to rip the heavy brown paper backing and stopped. "Do you mind?"

"No, please do," Sara said and watched expectantly.

He ripped the brown paper and looked inside. The backside of the picture was flat, smooth and slightly discolored. He inspected every inch of the frame and seemed deflated as he turned to her. "I don't see any keyhole." He held the frame still. "There are no holes anywhere."

While she tapped the tip of the large skeleton key against her palm, she peered at the picture. Suddenly, her hands stopped moving. "Call Mel."

"What? Why?"

"He didn't just say, 'behind the rose;' he said, 'behind the rose made of stone'."

It then dawned on Kid. "He meant the real one, in…"

"Georgia," Sara finished.

Kid lifted the walkie-talkie to his lips. "Mel, do you read me?"

"I am here, Kid. Are you alright?"

"Yes, but we need you to come pick us up at the Hyland house in Fort Dix. We have to get down to that cemetery in Georgia where Sara's parents are buried as soon as possible. It is important."

"On my way," Mel said.

Within moments, Mel had landed on the street in front of Sara's house. Running out, Kid and Sara boarded. While in the air, they shared the miraculous news about Karen. Mel screamed with joy, "That is the best news I think I've ever heard!" She inadvertently over-shot the graveyard outside of Augusta, Georgia, so she doubled back and touched down in a clearing.

Sara disembarked and felt the usual gamut of emotions as she approached her mother's grave. Kid followed.

The top half of the tombstone had a large decorative rose, which Sara had seen dozens of times before. In stylish script on the flower decoration were the words, 'Amanda Hyland, June 5, 1997 – January 14, 2025.' The first thing that registered with Sara, as it always did, was the date of January 14, 2025-, her birthday. Also her mother's death day. Sara crouched in front of the large rose. She had gazed upon it hundreds of times before, but this time she studied the many layers and folds.

Kid was examining every inch of the back of the tombstone when Sara said in a faraway voice, "Ah, Kid…" When he stepped around the monument, her gaze was fixed. "Look."

"Where?"

Her finger poked forward and disappeared under the fold of a rose petal. "It's hidden, but there's a hole," she said almost absently.

Kneeling next to her, Kid bent down and examined the opening. "Stick the key in."

Sara hesitated but then stuck the large key into the hole. To her amazement, it fit perfectly. Twisting her wrist, she heard a loud click.

They both stared at the tombstone, waiting for something to happen next. Nothing did so Sara whispered, "What now?"

"Pull the key out," Kid instructed.

Trying to pull the key out before turning it back to its original insertion position, the entire decorative rose pulled out ever so slightly. Sara froze.

Kid reached out and worked his fingers under the exposed gap. He pulled, and the entire decorative rose started lifting off the face of the tombstone. "Stand back." He got to his feet, and as he pulled, the rose continued to slide out.

"It's removable?" Sara watched in awe.

The rose was mounted on a solid post that had a key core at one end. Once the post was out and cleared the opening, he carried the large, stone decoration and rested it against her father's tombstone.

Sara had been watching Kid, and when she turned to face forward, she stopped breathing. She raised her hands to her face, clearly in shock.

Dropping to his knees next to her, Kid read aloud the inscription on the raw tombstone, which had been covered and hidden by the large rose.

'Here lies: Amanda Hyland, June 5, 1997 – January 4, 2025'

Leaning closer, Sara asked, "January 4? How is that possible? That's ten days before I was born."

But the next line chilled her even more. She inhaled sharply as Kid read the words.

'Known to the world as Anna Delilah'

Kid turned to her. "Anna Delilah was your…mother?"

Sara sat back on her heels. "Now that's a shock. It's the first I'm hearing it. No wonder she wouldn't tell me my mother's alias when I asked her," she muttered.

"Who?"

"Adele. Remember, she said that the women who participated in the CCP all had fake names, including my mother, even though the CCP was supposed to have ended before I was born? And she claimed to not remember my mother's alias? Now I know why."

Nodding his head, Kid read the next line on the tombstone,

'Perished while making heroic escape attempt'

"Exactly what the history books said happened with Anna Delilah," he noted. "She was trying to escape from a hospital in Georgia and fell from a window ledge."

"Yes, she fell, from a window ledge," Sara repeated with a faraway look in her eyes. "My dad had told me many times how much my mother was against that CCP project, but he never told me the truth about what happened after I was born. My mother didn't die from labor complications like I always believed. She died trying to escape that forsaken CCP project. No wonder my father felt guilty about her death."

Kid asked, "Was it really his fault?"

"He blamed himself, and what he told me in the moment before he died was that the project was voluntary, and he made my mother participate. He was always such a stickler about duty and what he thought was his duty. I'm sure that's why he felt like he *had* to participate in the CCP, despite my mother's objections."

Exhaling, she stared at the sky. "Dad, I hope where you are now you can hear me. I'm sorry you lived with that guilt and shame for all of those years. How could you have known that Mom would climb out a window and try to escape? You couldn't know. If you thought for a second that she would do something that crazy, I am sure you would've pulled out of that project in a heartbeat. I forgive you, but you need to forgive yourself. Please, forgive yourself."

For a few moments, silence hung over the cemetery. Finally, Sara said, getting choked up, "I will always love my father. He had his secrets, which he thought he had to keep, but I know that he loved me."

"He really did," Kid reiterated.

Sara was still stunned by the circumstances surrounding her birth and her mother's death. It was the final truth her father had harbored until his dying breath. History had again been changed from all she had grown up believing. The implications were significant and came to her in bursts. "Do you realize what this all means? Since I was born ten days earlier, I was actually born *before* the CCP was canceled. Maybe that is something I should have picked up on, because my father never could give me a straight answer as to how my DNA was included with the babies from that project that they used to create the first 23 members of the Utopia Project in test tubes."

"And after you were born, your mother, the famous, heroic, Anna Delilah, tried to save you and escape the CCP. It was her actions that inspired the Civil Crisis of 2025 and squashed the CCP Project."

"But it wasn't squashed. It continued under a new name."

"The Utopia Project."

"Exactly."

Kid summarized, "So your birth basically ended the CCP in 2025, a project that people feared would steal our humanity. Then fast forward. Years later you survive a cataclysmic event and help bring down the successor project, the Utopia Project, which again saves humanity. Hopefully for good this time."

She was silent as she absorbed the implications.

"Before your dad passed away, he said something about you and fate that I now fully understand."

"Which words are you referring to?" she asked.

Taking her hand, he clarified, "He said that since the very day you were born, the fate of humanity has been intertwined with your fate."

"Yes." Sara's gaze was firm, as was her resolve. "And to protect it all costs."

# EPILOGUE

March 8, 2045
Wednesday, Morning
Outside of Augusta, Georgia
**Seventy-two days after the event**


Kid and Sara sat still in the cemetery outside of Augusta, Georgia. Kid did not mind. For a change, he felt at ease. When he looked at Sara, she too looked content. She finally knew the truth, and her soul was finally at peace.

He said quietly, "Of all the billions of people on this planet, do you realize you were the chosen one?"

With such heavy implications, Sara rested her head against his shoulder and wrapped her arm around his.

He added, "And had we never met on that bench in Vermont, I would just be another one of the billions of casualties."

"That was fate too," she noted.

"But all tied to yours. Riding your coattails. Sara, you will be well-known in history, when our history is written. As a matter of fact, it is you who will be the central figure when it is written."

Sara smirked. "It seems that fame follows me. Remember, the child of Anna Delilah was as famous as she was, if not more."

"Yes, but Anna Delilah's child was the CCP's Baby Doe, who was never..." He turned to her with his mouth open.

She had a knowing look.

As the realization hit home, he knew that one of the great mysteries of their time had finally been solved. He met her eyes. His final word came out as a statement, not a question.

"Found."

# AUTHOR'S NOTES:

First and foremost, thank you for reading this book and for sharing in the Utopia Project series journey! As always, I am humbled and beyond appreciative.

Please stay connected via the utopiaproject.com website, or follow us on Instagram (utopiaprojectseries) or Facebook (Utopia Project by Billy Dering).

Finally, please consider posting a review of this third book: **Utopia Project- The Arrow of Time**. Such reviews provide invaluable feedback for the author as well as other potential readers! Thank you.

Made in the USA
Coppell, TX
15 July 2023

19231487R00229